By Force of Instinct

ABIGAIL REYNOLDS

INTERTIDAL PRESS

To Elaine

It is not often that someone comes along who is a true friend,
a perceptive and enthusiastic reader, and a good writer.
(with apologies to E. B. White)

Chapter 1

A fellow that lives in a windmill has not a more whimsical dwelling than the heart of a man that is lodged in a woman... To know this, and yet to continue to be in love is to be made wise from the dictates of reason, and yet persevere to play the fool by force of instinct.

—*William Congreve, The Way of the World*

With Mr. Darcy's letter in hand, Elizabeth wandered along the lane for two hours. How could it be that only this morning, she had been so certain of her convictions that Mr. Darcy wronged both her sister Jane and Mr. Wickham? She could hardly reconcile herself to the intelligence in the letter, proving Mr. Darcy a victim rather than a villain. At last, fatigue and a recollection of her long absence made her return home, and she entered the house with the wish of appearing as cheerful as usual.

She was immediately told that Colonel Fitzwilliam had called during her absence, and had been sitting with the ladies for over an hour awaiting her return. Her agitating reflections did not stand her in good stead for civil conversation, yet she assured herself that he was only hoping to take leave of her, since he and Mr. Darcy were to depart the following morning. She endeavoured to compose herself, and with a deep breath she entered the sitting room with a charming, if somewhat unsteady, smile.

"Miss Bennet!" cried Colonel Fitzwilliam. "I had just resolved to walk after you, and here you are!"

"My apologies that I was not here to receive you, sir," she said with a curtsey. "I fear that I lost all track of time in my rambling."

"It is hardly a matter of concern, Miss Bennet," he replied amiably. "I have been enjoying a delightful visit with Mrs. Collins and Miss Lucas; and, as it happens, I anticipate having the unexpected opportunity to take pleasure in your company in the days to come."

At Elizabeth's look of confusion, Maria Lucas said, "It appears that Colonel Fitzwilliam is not to depart tomorrow as anticipated, Lizzy! Is that not delightful news?"

"Delightful indeed," echoed Elizabeth stiffly as a worrisome implication came to her mind. She longed to ask the reason for the change of plans but feared to know it; she recalled only too clearly their discourse of the previous day when he had said they were to leave on Saturday unless Darcy put it off again. *Surely Mr. Darcy would wish to be quit of this place as soon as possible!* she thought in distress. *He cannot possibly think to renew his addresses—no, his letter said that he could not forget his feelings for me quickly enough!* She awaited with dread his further explanation.

"Well, it is quite true! An express arrived last night from my father, announcing that he and my mother will be descending upon Rosings later today, accompanied by Miss Darcy. Since it would be the height of bad manners for us to depart before they arrive," he smiled engagingly at his own wit, "here we must remain."

Elizabeth's heart sank even further at this intelligence. She tried to rally her spirits by reminding herself that Lady Catherine would certainly have no interest in the company of Mr. and Mrs. Collins with so much of her family at Rosings.

Surely he and I can manage to avoid one another for a week, and then I shall be for London myself, she thought. "So Mr. Darcy will be remaining as well," she said as steadily as she could manage.

"Yes, of course," said Colonel Fitzwilliam, "though he is in quite an ill humour about it; I believe that he was looking forward to his return to town. When he heard the news this morning, he looked quite as annoyed as I have ever seen him!"

I can only imagine! thought Elizabeth. *I doubt he could be rid of me soon enough!*

Words were insufficient for the elevation of Mr. Collins's feelings on receiving the intelligence that no lesser personages than Lord and Lady Derby themselves were to appear at Rosings. He resolved immediately to be within view of the lodges opening into Hunsford Lane for the entirety of the day, lest he miss the opportunity to make his first obeisance to the honoured guests. After relating at some length the extra effort which he would put into his Sunday sermon for the benefit of the elevated company, he hastened to Rosings to call on her Ladyship, hoping for the condescension of receiving further news of the visit from her own lips.

Charlotte attempted to engage Elizabeth in conversation, but the latter felt unequal to the circumstance and begged leave to retire to her room, owing to a headache. Concerned that her friend's ailment of the previous day seemed to have returned, Charlotte suggested sending for the apothecary, but Elizabeth demurred, saying that rest would be all she would require. "If you are still ill tomorrow, Lizzy, I shall insist!" said Charlotte.

Elizabeth was grateful to retire to the peace of her room, but her mind would not long remain still. She took out Mr. Darcy's letter once more and perused it several times, struggling to collect her thoughts. The information in his letter had been distressing enough when she thought she should never see him again, and it was all the more so for the knowledge that they would likely meet at least in passing in the coming week. *I must behave with absolute propriety and circumspection,* she resolved. *For both our sakes, no one must guess what has passed between us!* She speculated whether anyone might know already—could Mr. Darcy have confided in Colonel Fitzwilliam, or had anyone apart from Charlotte noted his interest in her?

She wondered briefly if she ought to acknowledge to him in any way that she recognized that she had misjudged and falsely accused him. He would no doubt find it gratifying, but the risk that he might believe that she was inviting a renewal of his addresses could not be justified. She would have to keep her thoughts to herself and live with the injustice of the matter.

THE FOLLOWING DAY COLONEL FITZWILLIAM put in his usual appearance at the parsonage, accompanied this time by Miss Darcy. He begged of the ladies the opportunity to introduce them; and Elizabeth, although hardly interested in becoming an intimate of anyone in the Darcy family, could not help feeling a deep curiosity as to the nature of this young woman of whom she had heard such differing descriptions. Mr. Wickham had told

7

her that Miss Darcy was very proud, but the observation of a very few minutes convinced her that she was only exceedingly shy. She found it difficult to obtain even a word from her beyond a monosyllable.

Miss Darcy was tall and on a larger scale than Elizabeth; and, though little more than sixteen, her figure was formed and her appearance womanly and graceful. She was less handsome than her brother, but there was sense and good humour in her face, and her manners were perfectly unassuming and gentle. Elizabeth, who had expected to find in her as acute and unembarrassed an observer as ever Mr. Darcy had been, was much relieved by discerning such different feelings. Had her situation been different, she thought that she might even have found pleasure in Miss Darcy's acquaintance; but, as it stood, she could not imagine any connection with the Darcy family that would not create difficulties.

She attempted to encourage interaction between Miss Darcy and Maria Lucas, since they were much of an age; but, since Maria was so in awe of Miss Darcy that she could scarcely utter a word, the encounter was somewhat less than successful. Elizabeth found herself conversing mainly with Colonel Fitzwilliam, whose easy manners covered some of the other difficulties. From time to time she succeeded in drawing Miss Darcy into the conversation for a few minutes; but, on the whole, she could not consider the occasion a success. *If only Mr. Darcy were here as well,* she thought with frustrated amusement, *we could have three silent participants instead of only two!* She wondered briefly how there could possibly be any conversation at all at the Darcy dinner table, and then recalled that both Colonel Fitzwilliam and Mr. Wickham had mentioned that Mr. Darcy could be quite lively and amiable amongst those he considered his equals. *But I will never be the one to observe such a thing,* she thought, recalling with anger his vivid recounting of his attempts to suppress his unsuitable feelings for her. She wondered if he knew where his sister was at this moment and what he thought of it.

She breathed a sigh of relief when the visitors took their leave. Maria Lucas chattered on for some time about the elegance of Miss Darcy, but Elizabeth was scarcely listening; her thoughts had returned to Mr. Darcy's pointed description of her family and her connections, and she could find little consolation for her shaken spirits.

THE FOLLOWING MORNING ELIZABETH DRESSED for church slowly but with unusual care; her desire to avoid the occasion completely was great, but she knew that her absence would be noted and that she could not plead a headache forever. *Surely we can meet for the brief time needed at church as indifferent acquaintances,* she thought, but her anxiety would not be quieted.

She was still far from certain of what she thought of Mr. Darcy. His letter, she was in a fair way of knowing by heart. She had studied every sentence, and her feelings towards its writer were at times widely different. When she remembered the style of his address, she was still full of indignation; but, when she considered how unjustly she had condemned and upbraided him, her anger was turned against herself, and his disappointed feelings became the object of compassion. His attachment excited gratitude, his general character respect; but she could not approve him; nor could she for a moment repent her refusal or feel the slightest inclination to continue the acquaintance. In her own past behaviour, there was a constant source of vexation and regret and, in the unhappy defects of her family, a subject of yet heavier chagrin. They were hopeless of remedy. Her father, contented with laughing at them, would never exert himself to restrain the wild giddiness of his youngest daughters; and her mother, with manners so far from right herself, was entirely insensible of the evil. Elizabeth had frequently united with Jane in an endeavour to check the imprudence of Catherine and Lydia; but, while they were supported by their mother's indulgence, what chance could there be of improvement? Catherine, weak-spirited, irritable, and completely under Lydia's guidance, had been always affronted by their advice; and Lydia, self-willed and careless, would scarcely give them a hearing. They were ignorant, idle, and vain. While there was an officer in Meryton, they would flirt with him; and, while Meryton was within a walk of Longbourn, they would be going there for ever.

She was no less severe on her own defects. She was mortified by having been taken in by Wickham's amiable manners. For the first time, she was grateful to have no fortune of her own—if she had, she should have been in extreme danger from Mr. Wickham and likely would have found herself married to him before discovering him to be a dishonest wastrel. She could not bear the humiliating notion that Darcy knew this of her—he might forgive the fault in his sister, who was only fifteen, but she had no such excuse of tender age for her folly.

Anxiety on Jane's behalf was another prevailing concern, and Mr. Darcy's explanation, by restoring Bingley to all her former good opinion, heightened the sense of what Jane had lost. His affection was proved to have been sincere, and his conduct cleared of all blame, unless any could attach to the implicitness of his confidence in his friend. How grievous then was the thought that, of a situation so desirable in every respect, so replete with advantage, so promising for happiness, Jane had been deprived by the folly and indecorum of her own family!

When to these recollections was added the development of Wickham's character, it may be easily believed that the happy spirits which had seldom been depressed before, were now so much affected as to make it almost impossible for her to appear tolerably cheerful.

She was mortified at the prospect of having to see Darcy—he who knew just how much of a gullible fool she had been. She had thought so highly of her own perspicacity, and now she knew herself to be quite lacking in that regard. Not only had she been wholly taken in by Wickham and predisposed to find reasons to dislike Darcy, she had also completely failed to observe any sign of his increasing attachment to her in time to circumvent the disaster of his proposal. When she looked back, those signs were obvious—his asking her to dance at the Netherfield ball when he danced with no other lady from Hertfordshire; his frequent, seemingly accidental, meetings with her, joining with her on walks when he easily could have excused himself; their very frank and slightly improper discussion of the nature of the Collins's marriage, which had to her represented nothing more than her very strong sentiments on the subject, but the very intimacy of which could easily have been interpreted as a sign of her regard for him. Of course, it was true that she did have a certain regard for his incisive intelligence, otherwise she would never have entered on the subject. Oh, how had she missed it? Even Charlotte had noticed, and tried to warn her of it, but she had been blind, so blind…

"Cousin Elizabeth!" came the voice of Mr. Collins. "We shall be late! Make haste, make haste!"

With a sigh, Elizabeth went downstairs and practiced on Mr. and Mrs. Collins the bright smile she was intending to wear in church. Charlotte gave her a sharp glance, but interpreted her artificial behaviour as a response to the scurrying of Mr. Collins.

"Cousin Elizabeth," Mr. Collins scolded. "Lady Catherine is quite firm on the subject of the desirability of promptness. Any tardiness on our part would be looked on with *great* disapproval and hardly show respect for the condescension she has demonstrated toward you!"

Fleetingly, Elizabeth wondered how Lady Catherine would have responded to Elizabeth being presented to her as her future niece. She could not think, without a smile, of what her ladyship's indignation would have been, but the smile engendered by this idea was rapidly smothered by the recollection of Darcy's words on the degradation his attachment to her represented. She felt ill as she thought on the folly and indecorum of her own family and how it reflected on her, and how materially it had affected both her and Jane.

She reminded herself firmly that Darcy's behaviour was as ill-bred as that of anyone in her family, though excessive pride could not be interpreted to be as humiliating a fault as the ignorance and complete lack of decorum of Lydia and Kitty or the stupidity of Mr. Collins. But the style of his address during his proposal, and indeed throughout their acquaintance, deserved censure. No, that was not quite true either, her sense of fairness forced her to admit. He had been insulting and excessively proud on some occasions, but in most of their meetings she had nothing worse to accuse him of than being overly quiet. *Yet another failure on my part*, she thought.

Mr. Collins was voluble in his relief when they discovered that the Rosings party had not yet arrived at the church, and he hurried off to prepare himself for the service, leaving Charlotte to fend for herself in greeting the parishioners. Elizabeth, equally relieved although for quite a different reason, found her heart pounding each time she heard a carriage pull up outside.

She had not long to wait; soon Lady Catherine swept in, her party following in her wake. She was prompt in demanding her share of the conversation, introducing the ladies to Lord and Lady Derby—"Mrs. Collins, and Miss Bennet and Miss Lucas, visiting from Hertfordshire," she said in a dismissive voice.

Elizabeth politely expressed her pleasure in making the acquaintance. When it came time for her to greet the rest of the party, she found that she could not bring herself to look directly at Darcy; she made her curtsey with her eyes firmly fixed on his cravat, and she knew that her cheeks must be flushed. She managed to keep her polite smile on her face, however, and was able to greet Colonel Fitzwilliam and Miss Darcy with tolerable composure.

There were several minutes before the service was to begin, and Elizabeth was for the first time grateful for Lady Catherine's propensity to dominate the conversation, as it relieved her of the burden of finding something to say. As she attended to her ladyship, though, she began to despise herself for her cowardice. She forced her eyes up to Darcy's face, only to meet his implacably cold gaze.

That she had expected scorn and anger did not lessen the distress Elizabeth felt on seeing it on his face. She held his gaze only briefly before taking the excuse of Lady Catherine's ongoing discourse to look away. She thought of how he had said that his good opinion, once lost, was lost forever. *How he must be congratulating himself for his near escape from a woman of so little perception and judgment!* she thought, humbled by her fall from grace and surprised that the thought of his disapproval troubled her.

When she chanced to raise her eyes to his face again, unable to resist the painful impulse of curiosity, she found him looking on no object but the ground. It was with the greatest of relief that she heard Lady Catherine pronounce that it was time for the service to begin.

Elizabeth was grateful that she was seated behind Mr. Darcy, where she need not fear his incisive gaze. *You must allow me to tell you how ardently I admire and love you.* How he must regret those words, those sentiments which had led to his harsh and unfair castigation at her hands! In addition to blindness and prejudice, she was also obliged to claim cruelty and short-temperedness among her many faults.

Her eyes drifted to him—the tousled dark curls against the brilliant white of his cravat as he sat proudly upright in the pew. She could not deny that he was handsome; she had acknowledged that even at the Meryton assembly when she first saw him. It was only his insulting behaviour and forbidding countenance on that occasion that had led her to disregard the appeal of his appearance. But good looks and a good fortune could not by themselves determine a good husband. *In vain have I struggled. It will not do.* Although she wished she had dealt differently with his proposal, when she thought of his humiliating references to how greatly he had striven to rid himself of his feelings for her, she could not bring herself to regret her decision. An image came to her of his intent gaze as it had so often rested on her, and unaccountably she shivered, wondering at his thoughts on seeing her again.

The object of her thoughts was at that moment brooding on the question of whether his life could possibly become any worse. He could not help being viscerally aware of Elizabeth's presence any more than he ever had been, only now it was like an ache in his breast rather than the guilty pleasure it had so often been in the past. If that were not enough, he had to suffer through the sycophantic ramblings that her idiot of a cousin considered a sermon—a reminder of just how low he had sunk in offering her marriage. And then there was *his* family…but he was not even going to think about that now.

He had spent the last two days struggling to convince himself that the Elizabeth Bennet he had loved was a figment of his imagination; he had never known the real Elizabeth Bennet at all, she of the cruel and spiteful words and the misjudgments. She was as misguided and capricious as all the other women he had known. He had taken her fine eyes and wit and spun them into a fantasy of a woman of real sense and feeling who would understand him, and now he knew that no such woman had ever existed. He was mortified for himself and furious with her, and the worst of it was that the instant he had laid eyes on her again, standing in front of the church, he had wanted her every bit as much as he ever had. He hated her for her power over him and despised himself for a weak fool.

As attuned to her presence as he was, he could not fail to notice that she was lacking her usual sparkle that morning. He hoped that this meant that she had realized what a dreadful mistake she had made, and that she was going to pay for the rest of her life for listening to George Wickham's lies and then spewing her venom all over Fitzwilliam Darcy. She would end up a poor spinster, dependent on the charity of her family, or married to some ignorant pig of a tradesman, she who could have been mistress of Pemberley. *If she is suffering now, it is no more than she deserves,* he thought with vindictive fury, and then closed his eyes in pain, knowing that all he had wanted when he had seen those dark circles beneath her eyes was to take her soft body into his arms and kiss those tempting lips, and to tell her that she need not worry, that he would take care of everything…

But fantasies would not provide him any answers, he told himself grimly.

And if his uncle said to him one more time, "It would be different if you were married and settled, but with a bachelor lifestyle, it simply will not do," he would not be responsible for his actions. He could ignore Lady Catherine's repeated demands that he marry Anne immediately; he had a lifetime of practice at that, but to face the accusation that it was *his* fault that he was not married just at this bitter juncture was more than a man should have to bear. He realized that his fists were clenched, and that he had not heard a word that Elizabeth's embarrassment of a kinsman had servilely uttered—not that it was any loss.

He could see that Georgiana was looking at him strangely. He took a deep breath to calm himself and forced a pleasant smile to his face, at which point she resumed the sullen expression that she had worn ever since her arrival, a reminder of her obvious disappointment with him for his inability to make all her problems disappear. What had happened to the sweet, docile girl she had been? Sometimes he could still see that girl, but more often these days she seemed angry with him about one thing or another. Colonel Fitzwilliam thought it was but a matter of her being at a trying age, but Darcy could not help suspecting that the whole George Wickham affair had something to do with it. Georgiana could not know, of course, how harshly he continued to castigate himself for his error in choosing Mrs. Younge as her companion. The thought brought back the all too familiar refrain of reproaches: *Why did I not question her references further? Why did I allow myself to believe that her amiable manner implied impeccable morals? Why did I send Georgiana off with her so quickly, instead of keeping her under my observation for a longer period of time? Why did I give in and agree to let Georgiana have her own establishment in the first place when she was still so young? The entire situation was wholly my fault.* No, on the whole, Darcy did not think that his life could be substantially worse.

He was forced to reconsider this a few minutes later when he heard his aunt issue an invitation to Mr. Collins and his party to come to Rosings that evening. He ought to have expected as much; she had done so the previous two Sundays as well, but he had thought that with so much of her family around her, her interest in having her pet clergyman fawn over her would be diminished. Apparently he was to have no such reprieve, and he was beginning to think of the excuses he could make when he saw Elizabeth turn her head away in an attempt to hide her distress at the idea, and he knew that he would not be able to stay away. He damned himself for his susceptibility to her. *Remember, she thinks you devoid of every proper feeling and completely lacking in honour,* he reminded himself. *She is nothing but a silly girl who would throw away an opportunity most women spend their lives dreaming of because she was offended by your honest scruples.* With a stab of pain, he heard her voice again saying, *"You are mistaken, Mr. Darcy, if you suppose that the mode of your declaration affected me in any other way, than as it spared me the concern which I might have felt in refusing you, had you behaved in a more gentleman-like manner."*

What spiteful fate had determined that the woman he loved should be the one woman in the world who wanted nothing to do with him? He wondered whether such a turn of events constituted a tragedy or a farce. He managed the semblance of a civil nod to Elizabeth and the rest of her party before forcing his feet to carry him away from the woman who had so bewitched him.

ELIZABETH FELT QUITE UNEQUAL TO company following the painful excursion to church, and knowing that she would be required to face an even more excruciating version of the same torture that evening, resolved to take some time to herself for reflection in her favourite manner. She therefore excused herself for a solitary walk after luncheon, brushing aside Charlotte's protests regarding her pallor and recent headaches. Sooner or later, she knew, she would have to face her friend's growing suspicions that all was not well with her, but she could not begin to face that task at present.

Her feet led her without conscious thought to her favourite grove. On recognizing where she was, she felt a moment of panic, knowing now that it was where Darcy had often sought her out in the past. She realized, though, that she was quite safe, as there would be no place that he would more fervently avoid at present. He had, after all, made the state of his current regard for her more than clear, that his feelings were cause for shame and could not be forgotten too soon. His cold look in church demonstrated that he had lost no time in putting those tender feelings behind him. She could not blame him; she certainly deserved no special notice after she had abused him so abominably.

Her sense of shame over her behaviour led directly to thoughts of the unhappy defects of her family, the subject of yet heavier chagrin. She burst into tears as she thought of it, and from actual weakness leaned against a tree as she wept. She had always avoided acknowledging the extent to which the lack of fortune of the Bennet girls, combined with their mother's improprieties, materially affected their prospects for marriage; it was easy enough to say that she should not marry where she did not love, but Mr. Darcy's words were forcing her to face the truth that even the beautiful, gentle Jane had only had the one suitor when she was sixteen before Mr. Bingley, and Elizabeth's assets were certainly no greater than her sister's.

She was sufficiently deep in her own distress as to be unaware of approaching footsteps. Darcy stopped short at the sight of her across the grove, immediately thinking to leave before he was observed. At the realization that she was weeping, however, he was torn by uncertainty. He could not be sure of the cause of her distress, but it could be assumed to relate to his disastrous proposal. A part of him longed to go to her and comfort her, while at the same time it felt only proper that she ought to suffer as he did. Nor could he expect her to welcome his attempts to relieve her distress— she had made it perfectly clear what she thought of him, and he would be the last man she would wish to offer her solace. With an unfamiliar sensation of helplessness, he realized there was nothing he could offer her for her present distress. The question in his mind, however, was as to *why* she was upset. *He* was the rejected suitor; *he* was the one misjudged and falsely accused. The answer was not long in coming; with a bitter taste in his mouth, he realized that her tears had nothing to do with him at all but must represent the pain of her disillusionment over Wickham. Her feelings for him must have been more tender than Darcy had ever considered, and a surge of hatred rose in him. Was it not enough that Wickham had injured his beloved sister, without taking away the woman he loved as well?

"Do you think that any consideration would tempt me to accept the man, who has been the means of ruining, perhaps forever, the happiness of a most beloved sister?" Could it be possible that Elizabeth despised him as he did Wickham for the hurt wilfully done a beloved sister? The thought that his actions could be seen in such a light was acutely disturbing, the more so because he could not even defend himself against the charge. Whatever his motives, concern for the feelings of Jane Bennet had never entered his head, only the advantages he perceived for Bingley and for himself in their separation.

His heart aching, he turned and retreated as quietly as possible to reflect upon his painful realizations—his Elizabeth, so deeply involved with Wickham as to be devastated by his revelations about her favourite, and her right to despise him as being no better than Wickham himself. How was he ever to face her? How was he to live with the knowledge that she would never be his?

ELIZABETH KNEW IT WAS HOPELESS to think she could appear even tolerably cheerful at Rosings that night, and had settled it with herself that merely maintaining her composure would be enough of a goal. That she was quieter than usual was not immediately a problem; Lady Catherine was perfectly capable of handling the conversation without input from anyone, and it appeared that this was a tendency Lord Derby shared with his sister.

Darcy gave no visible reaction to her arrival, though she noticed that he quickly abandoned his seat opposite her to walk behind her where she could not see him. She could feel, however, the pressure of his gaze on the back of her neck, and she remained acutely conscious of his presence, all the more so after Lady Catherine said irritably, "Darcy, *will* you stop that pacing? You are making me quite dizzy!"

Darcy obeyed his aunt's command somewhat ungraciously, feeling that pacing was a substantial improvement over the other possibilities that came to his mind, both of which involved taking bodily hold of Elizabeth Bennet, though whether to shake her or kiss her he was not quite clear. He ignored her further directives to sit down immediately by Anne.

Darcy being insufficiently responsive to her demands, Lady Catherine's vexation grew, and as her eye fell on Elizabeth, she turned to this new target. "Miss Elizabeth Bennet, you are very quiet tonight!" exclaimed her Ladyship. "No more of your decided opinions for you?"

Aware of the gentleman behind her and the wrong she had done him, Elizabeth seized the opportunity to make a sort of apology. In as composed a manner as she could manage, she replied, "Your ladyship has brought to my attention that there is a danger in owning decided opinions. I have realized that there is the risk that one might hold them on the basis of false information, which could lead to regrettable circumstances."

Lady Catherine was undecided as to whether this response qualified as impertinence or appropriate humility but decided it must represent the latter. "I am glad to know my advice did not go unheeded, Miss Bennet, and to hear that you are not above taking the counsel of your betters in these matters."

Darcy, who had been frozen in place by Elizabeth's unexpected admission, winced at his aunt's ill-bred words. Was that how *he* sounded to Elizabeth?

Lady Catherine's attention now shifted to Miss Darcy. "Georgiana, your brother has given me excellent reports on your progress at the piano-forte. I should be pleased to hear you play now."

Georgiana paled. "Please excuse me, Lady Catherine. I could not possibly play before all these people."

Her aunt frowned at this disobedience. "Nonsense, Georgiana. You play quite acceptably, though perhaps not quite so well as my Anne would have had she had the chance to learn. I must insist that you play for us."

"I beg you to excuse me," the girl said in a voice barely above a whisper.

"I will not have this, Georgiana! You are my niece, and I refuse to believe you unable to perform before a small family party!" Lady Catherine's annoyance with her niece's stubbornness was clearly growing rapidly.

Elizabeth had never seen Lady Catherine in a mood quite as vindictive as tonight, and her heart went out to Miss Darcy, who was clearly petrified. She could not even bring herself to answer, and tears were beginning to gather in her eyes. Elizabeth was relieved to see Darcy move to stand beside his sister's chair, his hand resting comfortingly on her shoulder. "If Georgiana does not wish to play," he said deliberately, "I see no reason why she should have to do so."

"Now, see here, Darcy," rumbled Lord Derby. "You are mollycoddling her again. That is no way to help her!"

Darcy's jaw was set in clear lines of anger. Elizabeth could not understand the precise nature of the problem at hand, but she could see that Miss Darcy was on the verge of losing her composure completely.

With sudden resolve, Elizabeth fixed her eyes firmly on Darcy, willing him to look her way. As if drawn by a magnet, his gaze turned to her. She gestured slightly with her head toward the piano-forte. He watched her unreadably for a moment, and then said, as if unwillingly, "In fact, I had been looking forward to hearing Miss Bennet play tonight."

"As have I," added Colonel Fitzwilliam quickly.

Elizabeth stood before any objection could be raised. "It would be my pleasure. Miss Darcy, might I impose upon you to turn the pages for me?"

Miss Darcy agreed to this idea with embarrassing alacrity, escaping in Elizabeth's shadow to the piano-forte. As they sat down to the instrument, Elizabeth began paging through the sheet music. "Thank you," said Georgiana softly.

Elizabeth turned to her with a smile. "You are quite welcome. I hope that you do not pay overmuch attention to what was said," she said quietly.

"What do you mean, Miss Bennet?" she asked shyly.

Placing her fingers on the keyboard, Elizabeth said mischievously, "I daresay that you will hear criticisms of my playing tonight, but I would have to play a great deal worse than I do in order to be as ashamed of my playing as I would of being so ill-mannered."

Colonel Fitzwilliam drew a chair near them, putting an end to their conversation, but the interchange had not gone unnoticed by Darcy. Although unable to make out their words, he could see Georgiana's look of surprise and admiration, and he wondered what Elizabeth had said to her. Before her playing could begin to cast its usual spell on him, he looked straight at her to remind himself of the accusations she had made, and the familiar rush of anger at her wilful misunderstanding of his nature filled him once again.

Lady Catherine, misinterpreting the look of distaste on his face and quite prepared to criticize anything about her nephew, said, "Miss Bennet plays none too ill for one who has not had the advantage of a London master. One could hardly expect her to meet the standards to which you are accustomed, Darcy, nor to have taste equal to Anne's or Georgiana's. If she would only practice more, I believe that she would be a pleasant performer."

Elizabeth inclined her head toward Miss Darcy. "It begins already, you see," she whispered, amusement in her voice. "Now, I urge you to ask yourself, which of us has cause to be embarrassed."

Georgiana giggled, her admiration of Elizabeth nearing adulation as she continued to receive Lady Catherine's remarks with forbearance, but not without quiet commentary of her own. Elizabeth was pleased to see the girl's spirits rising, but wondered how her brother would feel about her attempts to encourage his sister to assert her independence. She was grateful, however, to Lady Catherine for offering her the distraction of worrying about Miss Darcy's feelings; it was far more tolerable than her own concerns. With these thoughts, she continued to play till it was time for her party to return home.

Colonel Fitzwilliam and Miss Darcy called again at the parsonage the following day. Georgiana was anxious to spend time with her new idol. Although under ordinary circumstances Elizabeth would have enjoyed her company, Georgiana continued to be an unpleasant reminder of her brother. The suspicion that Darcy would not approve a friendship between his impressionable sister and the woman he wished to forget, and that he would not wish Georgiana to be tainted by Elizabeth's low connections, could not but enter her thoughts. With her mind so occupied, it was difficult for Elizabeth to retain her concentration. Reflection must be reserved for solitary hours; whenever she was alone, she gave way to it as the greatest relief; and not a day went by without a solitary walk in which she might indulge in all the delight of unpleasant recollections. But despite Elizabeth's distraction, Miss Darcy pressed on her an invitation to visit with her at Rosings the next day, an invitation she dearly wished to decline, but she could come up with no excuse.

Thus it came to pass that the morrow found Elizabeth slowly making her way to Rosings, hoping against hope for the absence of Mr. Darcy. On her arrival, she was shown to a mercifully empty parlour while a servant went to locate Miss Darcy. To calm her nerves, she picked up a book lying on a table. Finding it to be a volume of poetry she had an interest in reading, she took it over to the window for better light and began to leaf through it.

Unaware of her presence in the room, Darcy entered, and was immediately captivated by the picture she made, her dark curls framed by the sunlight pouring in the window. Her lips were moving as she read, clearly tasting the metre and the rhythm of the poetry. He could not look away, all his anger with her momentarily drowned by his need to touch her face and kiss those lips.

Warned by some sense that she was no longer alone, Elizabeth looked up to discover Darcy, his dark eyes intent on her with a meaning she could not comprehend. A becoming flush stole up her cheeks at what he must think of her presence there. "Pardon me, sir; I did not mean to intrude; I am waiting for Miss Darcy," she said with a certain agitation.

Say something, damn it! he told himself. "My apologies for disturbing you, Miss Bennet. I was merely looking for my book."

Elizabeth looked down at the book in her hands with a sinking feeling. She closed it quickly and held it out in his direction. "This must be yours, then, sir," she said, feeling as if she should apologize for trespassing on his property by having read it even for a moment.

"If you are enjoying it, Miss Bennet, please continue; there are many other books I can read... Are you fond of Wordsworth?" he asked desperately, not completely sure why he was pursuing this conversation. She had once again undercut his equanimity, and it was hard to recall why he had been so angry with her when she was before him.

"I have enjoyed what I have read of it," she replied automatically. "When I was in London there was a discussion one evening at my uncle's house about Mr. Wordsworth and Mr. Coleridge, and how they have been transforming the art of poetry. Mr. Monkhouse, whose cousin is married to Mr. Wordsworth, was saying that his personal vision of nature contrasts with the formal meanings that were common to Cowper and Gray, and I was curious to see for myself what might appear in this edition..." She felt as if she were talking to no purpose but to fill the empty space in the room.

"You have not read this collection before, then?" He was beginning to recover himself from the shock of seeing her so unexpectedly, and his voice grew more formal and distant.

She heard the surprise and the chill in his voice. "No, sir, I have not had that privilege," she said shortly, loath to admit a deficiency in her education to him. Since he had made no move to take the book from her, she set it down on the neutral territory of a small table.

"You are welcome to read it, Miss Bennet. You might enjoy Lyrical Ballads by Coleridge and Wordsworth as well—that was their first published work."

The turn of his countenance was making her quite uncomfortable, as did his condescension in pointing out the obvious regarding poetry. "I have read many poems from it already; it indeed heralded a new age in poetry. I am interested to see where Mr. Wordsworth goes with his current work in progress." She looked at him challengingly.

"The Prelude? What do you think of it?"

Displeased to find that she could not better him on the subject, Elizabeth said shortly, "I have seen only brief excerpts from it."

"I hope that you will have the opportunity to discover it for yourself in its entirety soon, then, or at least such parts as have been published," Darcy said lamely, aware that he had somehow displeased her.

Elizabeth heard his discomfort and misinterpreted it. "Thank you, Mr. Darcy, but we must be realistic, must we not?" she said with a bite in her voice. "I must consider my restricted opportunities; after all, my father has an excellent library for a man of his means, but that does not extend to the newest books; those of us with *inferior* connections cannot hope to have such amenities."

Darcy grew pale. "Miss Bennet," he replied, his uneasiness causing him to take on an unintentionally haughty air, "I did not mean to imply anything of the sort."

Finding his manner infuriating, she discovered that once opened, the wound would not close. "My uncle may have entertained Mr. Wordsworth himself, but of course, he is merely in *trade* and could not be expected to have such sensibilities. Is it not a *degradation* for you, Mr. Darcy, to even discuss this with me? What would your family think?" She caught her breath, horrified that she had uncontrollably poured out to him her injured feelings in such a manner. "Pray excuse me, Mr. Darcy!" Blindly, she moved past him, thinking only of escape.

Darcy, stunned by this unexpected attack, put out a hand to stop her flight. It had never occurred to him that she might feel wounded by what he saw as his factual recitation of the gulf between them. "Miss Bennet," he said, his voice pained, "It was never my intention to grieve you in any way."

She looked up at his pale face. "Then you have gone about it in a most unusual way!" She was mortified to realize that her eyes were swimming with tears. "If you would be so kind as to release me, sir."

He removed his hand from her arm instantly. "I shall trouble you no further, madam," he said formally, cut to the quick by her sudden fury. *You fool!* he raged to himself. *Did you learn nothing from that horrible night? She wants nothing to do with you; how much clearer can she be?* The conclusion was as intolerable as ever.

"Miss Bennet!" came Georgiana's light tones from the doorway, causing both Elizabeth and Darcy to immediately attempt to assume poses of exemplary propriety. Even Georgiana could not be blind to the tension in the room as Darcy bowed silently and exited. However, as she could think of no possible source of disagreement between her brother and her new friend, she quickly dismissed the incident from her mind.

Elizabeth could not forget it so easily—her sense of humiliation could not have been any greater than it was after her outburst at Darcy. It was dreadful enough that he thought those things of her; to have him know how much his scorn for her family disturbed her was worse. She was furious with herself for displaying her vulnerability to his criticism and could not begin to imagine what he must be thinking of her now. No sooner had she left Rosings after her visit with Miss Darcy than she resolved that under no circumstances would she ever set foot there again. If she had to lay abed pleading illness until her departure for London, she would do so.

Chapter 2

The following day Colonel Fitzwilliam paid a call to the parsonage and, finding Elizabeth at home alone, persuaded her to walk out with him. Elizabeth, whose spirits had been troubled by memories of her humiliating quarrel with Mr. Darcy, was pleased to accept the distraction.

"Will your family be staying long at Rosings?" Elizabeth had wondered more than once about the reason for the Derbys' sudden descent on Rosings.

"That is not clear; I believe they had only intended to stay a few days, but we are still no closer to a resolution than when they arrived," he replied.

"A resolution?"

"Yes, about Georgiana," he said. At her puzzled look, he added, "I apologize; I assumed you had heard the tale, either from Georgiana or Darcy, if not Mr. Collins."

"No one has mentioned anything to me," she said cautiously, unsure if she wished to be drawn any further into the issues of the Fitzwilliam family.

"Well, there is no harm in your knowing, I suppose. My parents have come to the conclusion that a single young man cannot provide the kind of home a girl Georgiana's age needs, and they have offered—well, perhaps it would be more accurate to say that they have demanded—to bring her out themselves. Of course, that is tantamount to taking her away from Darcy forever—he would have little say in her future or in choosing her future husband. However, Darcy is absolutely determined that she should remain in his care, and Georgiana has no interest in this new plan either. He is extremely devoted to her, you know. Of course, Lady Catherine's solution is that Darcy should marry Anne immediately to provide a stable home for his sister. Darcy has spent years ignoring her hints and demands about Anne, but for some reason he decided this time to tell her that he was *not* going to marry Anne, now or ever."

This explanation for Lady Catherine's displeasure with Darcy had never occurred to her. "But is this not a matter for you and Mr. Darcy to decide as her guardians?"

He sighed. "Legally, yes, but we do feel some sort of obligation to listen to the family. Darcy takes family loyalty very seriously—you may be certain that he would not choose to visit Rosings each year if he did not! I hope it will be resolved soon, for his sake, if nothing else. This has troubled him even more than I would have anticipated."

Suspecting with a certain discomfort that the question at hand was not the sole cause of Darcy's distress, Elizabeth limited herself to saying, "That is unfortunate."

"It was unfortunately done," he responded with a frown. "Darcy has always done everything possible for his sister, and now my father is suggesting that his care for her was inadequate—it is no wonder he is perturbed."

Elizabeth's curiosity was raised. "And what of you, sir? Are you in agreement with Lord Derby?"

"No, as I said, Darcy is a very devoted brother and guardian. It is only that, well, an incident involving Georgiana came to my parents' attention, and the truth is that there was nothing Darcy or anyone else could have done to prevent it, but my father simply refuses to believe that," he said with a sigh.

She felt a surprising moment of sympathy for Darcy—if the incident was, as she suspected, the intended elopement with Wickham, he would find it bitter indeed to be blamed for failing to prevent it completely. She saw an image of his white face after her outburst the previous day, and she could not help thinking that the timing could not have been worse for him, coming just after her refusal and accusations of cruelty to Wickham. Despite the tenor of his proposal, one could only assume that he would be feeling disappointment, and he was certainly entitled to injured feelings from her unjust accusations. *And then yesterday, I had to attack him again, when he was attempting to be civil under impossible circumstances,* she thought, not without pain. *He must think me most unfeeling, and he would without doubt be within his rights!* An unhappy sense of shame filled her.

"Miss Bennet? Are you well?" asked a worried Colonel Fitzwilliam, concerned by her long silence and troubled look.

Elizabeth returned abruptly to the present. "I am quite well, thank you, sir; I was just thinking how difficult this must be for Mr. Darcy. She is all that remains of his family, is she not?" She hoped fervently that this explanation for her reaction would satisfy him.

"Yes, she is." Colonel Fitzwilliam paused, then added with a worried look, "I could wish that my father would be a bit more thoughtful of him. I do not believe that I have ever seen Darcy quite as unhappy as he has been these last few days."

She winced, knowing that Lord Derby was not the only one who should have been more careful of Darcy's feelings. *By the time this visit is ended, I wonder whether there will be any part of my character that I find acceptable,* she thought bleakly.

The colonel continued, "It would be far simpler if he were to marry, but *that* is a subject in which he apparently has no interest."

"Indeed," murmured Elizabeth, aware that her cheeks were staining with a slight blush. *At least this suggests that he is unaware of Mr. Darcy's proposal,* she thought. With an air of mischief, she added, "I believe he is much pursued, though, by marriageable young ladies."

Colonel Fitzwilliam rolled his eyes. "It is quite embarrassing to see, Miss Bennet, how many women throw themselves in his way, saying nothing but what they believe he wishes to hear and flattering him shamelessly!"

"Yet he remains unwed." Now that she felt secure in her secret, she could indulge her curiosity.

"Sometimes I despair of Darcy ever finding a wife who would satisfy his exacting standards! Had I his opportunities, I should not be so difficult to please." He said this with a sidelong glance at Elizabeth, who coloured becomingly.

This is a complication that I certainly do not need, she thought. Firmly returning the conversation to Darcy, she said, "His standards must be exacting indeed!"

"Very much so, I fear," said the colonel ruefully. "It is frustrating to know that he can have any woman he pleases, yet will choose none."

Unable to resist, Elizabeth replied, "Assuming, of course, that the lady in question accepts him."

He gave her a look of amused disbelief. "Why would any woman refuse him? Quite apart from his wealth and lineage, he is of good character, honest, generous, loyal to a fault, well-educated and intelligent. What more could a woman desire?"

"Civility and good manners?" Elizabeth said with an arch look, remembering that even Mr. Wickham had given Darcy credit for a similar set of virtues, but only among those he found his equals in consequence.

He laughed heartily. "It is true, Miss Bennet, Darcy will never be at ease among a crowd, and he will forever appear haughty and disdainful when he is feeling most painfully anxious. It is a fault, to be sure, but hardly a fatal one. But it was not my intention, Miss Bennet, to cloud such a lovely day with my family's difficulties; let us find more pleasant matters to discuss than these." He found Elizabeth as eager for a change of subject as he, and the rest of the walk passed in a happier manner, although the previous topic of discussion continued to roil Elizabeth's spirits.

WHEN MR. COLLINS RETURNED FROM his daily visit to Rosings, he bore the news that, to Elizabeth's chagrin, Lady Catherine had invited them all to dinner the following evening, and had expressly mentioned her desire to see Miss Bennet there prior to her upcoming departure. Elizabeth spent a brief time wondering whether she could manage to avoid the occasion by using the excuse of illness once more, but concluded grimly that Mr. Collins and Charlotte would bear the burden of Lady Catherine's displeasure if she were to defy her will so far as to dare to be sick when she was specifically commanded to be at Rosings. Therefore, to Rosings she would go; and, through the remainder of the day, her mind rarely drifted from the question of how she should behave when faced once again with Mr. Darcy. These same meditations at length closed her eyes that night; and, by the following day, she was no nearer resolution than when she had begun, but even more apprehensive.

She could not recall the last time she had been in low spirits for such a time as this. Her thoughts travelled from the unfeeling mode of his declaration to the pained look on his face when she had confronted him, together with Colonel Fitzwilliam's more sympathetic portrayal of him. No matter how she tried to justify her behaviour, she could find no way to exculpate herself for causing him significant pain and distress, something she would have earlier found it hard to imagine him to be capable of feeling. She had always known that she was not so tender-hearted as Jane, but to find herself so insensitive as to have completely neglected the effects of her refusal on Mr. Darcy was unpleasant. It rankled that his proud behaviour had led so directly to her humbling realization of her own failings, and there were moments when she could almost feel glad that he was suffering along with her. But her native sense of justice and fairness would not allow that sentiment to persist for long, and she kept returning to the knowledge of how greatly her perception had failed her in this instance. At length she resolved to do her best to meet him with civility and kindness as she would any other person she knew to be suffering, though she remained uncertain of her true ability in this regard.

She would have been startled to discover Darcy was facing a similar struggle. Her words from their more recent meeting had joined those of their ill-fated encounter in the parsonage in echoing constantly in his ears. He kept seeing her face, bereft of its usual laughter, with her fine eyes filling with tears—tears *he* had caused. Until that moment, the thought that she might have been wounded rather than complimented by his addresses had never crossed his mind. He had realized with mortification that he could not recall any instance where he *had* been concerned for her sensibilities—it had never even occurred to him that she might be distressed over her sister's abandonment by Bingley. He could not understand when he had become so unfeeling; he had always thought of himself as one who put a concern for others before his own, but strict self-examination was showing him that he applied this rule only to those people who were closest to him. Had his disregard grown with each experience of a woman who made it clear that marriage to him would be her greatest achievement? Had he in fact come to believe that he was so much the centre of the universe as to honour anyone by the bestowal of his regard, no matter how insultingly given?

With these realizations came the painful knowledge that he was not invulnerable to Elizabeth's distress; her injury injured him as well. Although he could not admit complete dissatisfaction with the fact that, her words that night notwithstanding, she at least thought enough of his opinion to be affected by it, the vision of her tear-filled eyes left him with a pain in his chest and the beginnings of a self-loathing for the behaviour that had caused it. Yet, at other moments his anger with her would once again overtake him, and he would remind himself that he had said nothing to her that was not true.

To these feelings was added yet one more kind—those generated by his knowledge that she would be leaving Kent in a few days, and that this dinner might well be the last time he was ever to lay eyes upon her. For every part of him that applauded the chance to flee the humiliation of her refusal and the pain of seeing her while knowing she would never be his, there were other parts which fought desperately against allowing her to slip completely out of his world. The thought of never seeing her again—her laughter, her liveliness, her natural grace and vivacity—left him with a profound feeling of emptiness.

The moment he had alternately been dreading and longing for finally came with the arrival of the Hunsford party. It was immediately obvious to him that Elizabeth was quite subdued; this was the first time he had seen her in company when she was not at least making an effort toward displaying her usual vivacity. He caught her stealing a glance at him—was there a trace of warmth in that look, or was it only his wishes speaking? He felt a surprising wave of tenderness as she dropped her eyes again, allowing himself the pleasure of it for a moment before berating himself for falling into her wiles once again.

He took his old accustomed seat slightly away from her, from which he could see her clearly; he had avoided it since that night at Hunsford. Colonel Fitzwilliam as usual sat beside her, attempting to engage her in conversation. Darcy was too far away to hear her quiet responses, but was not displeased to see that she did not enter into the exchange in the animated manner she typically used with his cousin. He did not think he could bear to see her smiling at another man at the moment, and Colonel Fitzwilliam's open admiration of her had always been something of a thorn in his side. As if able to hear his thoughts, she glanced up at him again, looking away almost immediately.

Lady Catherine observed after dinner that Miss Bennet seemed out of spirits, and immediately accounting for it herself by supposing that she did not like to go home again so soon, she added, "But if that is the case, you must write to your mother to beg that you may stay a little longer. Mrs. Collins will be very glad of your company, I am sure."

"I am much obliged to your ladyship for your kind invitation," replied Elizabeth, thinking that staying any longer was beyond question the last thing she would desire, "but it is not in my power to accept it. I must be in town next Saturday."

"Why, at that rate, you will have been here only six weeks. I expected you to stay two months. I told Mrs. Collins so before you came. There can be no occasion for your going so soon. Mrs. Bennet could certainly spare you for another fortnight."

"But my father cannot.—He wrote last week to hurry my return."

"Oh! your father of course may spare you if your mother can.—Daughters are never of so much consequence to a father. And if you will stay another month complete, it will be in my power to take you as far as London, for I am going there early in June, for a week; and as Dawson does not object to the Barouche box, there will be very good room for you."

"Oh, please do stay a little longer, Miss Bennet!" exclaimed Miss Darcy. "I would so enjoy your company."

"As would we all," seconded Colonel Fitzwilliam warmly. "Surely you could stay another fortnight, could you not?"

"You are all kindness; but I believe we must abide by our original plan." *There is at least one person in the room who will not object to my departure,* she thought wryly.

"Why not stay, Miss Bennet? It would mean a great deal to Georgiana. I am sure that we could arrange your transportation." Elizabeth looked up in shock at the dark eyes of the speaker. He met her gaze with a level, serious look.

"I am expected in town on Saturday," she repeated her earlier assertion, her voice less strong in her confusion than she would have wished. *What could be his purpose?* she thought frantically.

"Surely another week could not make so great a difference," he insisted, his tone neutral.

She was bewildered by his words. His expression did not speak of any desire for her company, and certainly he could hardly wish for her presence after all that had passed between them. Perhaps it was for his sister's benefit, that she could have an escape from her aunt in Elizabeth's company. Yes, that must be the explanation, she thought.

His steady gaze disconcerted her. She tried to find the words to form an objection, and found herself uncomfortably close to tears. In a moment of sheer cowardice, in fear that further discourse would cause her to lose her composure completely, she said quietly, "Very well, then, if Mrs. Collins will have me, I will stay another week."

She could not look at Mr. Darcy as she spoke, and fortunately Georgiana's exclamations of delight covered what could otherwise have been a difficult moment. Elizabeth gratefully seized the distraction.

Darcy's gaze rested on her flushed cheeks as he wondered what mad impulse had caused him to encourage her to remain in Kent. Was he such a glutton for punishment that he needed further reminders of her scorn and dislike for him? Tonight had been the first time that he had not felt pain and hostility radiating from her—was he so desperate as to take *that* as a positive sign? *Good God! What am I thinking? She has shown herself to be everything I could have feared; prejudiced, lacking in basic courtesy, self-control, and decorum—I will not regret her, I will not!* An image came to him of Elizabeth sitting with Georgiana at the piano-forte, cajoling a smile out of her despite her own apparent lack of spirits, and he closed his eyes in pain for a moment. When he opened them, it was to find Lady Derby's quizzical gaze upon him, and he rolled his eyes in frustration at his brief loss of equanimity.

He wondered what Elizabeth was thinking, what she had made of his request, and above all why she had acquiesced to it when she had refused all the others. Her expression provided no clue; although warm colour continued to reign in her cheeks, she appeared to be purposefully avoiding his gaze, turning her attention only to Georgiana and as required to Lady Catherine.

Georgiana, delighted to have succeeded in her venture to obtain the continued presence of Elizabeth in Kent, was nonetheless determined to avoid a repetition of her humiliation on the occasion of the previous visit of the Hunsford party. She asked of Lady Catherine her permission to retire early, pleading a great fatigue. She thought to cast a reassuring glance at her brother, knowing his often irritating tendency to fret over her every move, but she found him gazing absently across the room, her request clearly not even entering his awareness. She felt a twinge of annoyance at his apparent disinterest.

Lady Catherine allowed her to excuse herself, although not before a stern lecture on the dangers of overexerting herself during the day, with a quelling glare at Darcy as if he were somehow responsible for his sister's fatigue. Shortly after Georgiana's departure, Colonel Fitzwilliam, in desperation for a diversion more pleasurable than the constant demands of his father and aunt, not to mention Darcy's inexplicable dark silence, begged the pleasure of Miss Bennet's appearance at the piano-forte once again.

Darcy observed her smiling acquiescence. Suddenly it seemed intolerable to be forced to watch her once again laughing at Colonel Fitzwilliam's charm as they sat together at the instrument, and without forethought he found himself moving in that direction, taking the seat usually occupied by his cousin on these occasions.

"Mr. Darcy," Elizabeth murmured in surprise at his appearance, and hesitated a moment before seating herself at his side. She was troubled by his actions—he could easily have avoided this unnecessary closeness, and from the expression on his face, he was by no means delighted to find himself in this position. *If his intent is to cause me unease, he is certainly succeeding!* she thought dryly.

She made an effort to focus her attention on selecting from the sheet music available, as if she had not already inspected it sufficiently frequently so as to know it from memory. Recalling with an effort her resolve to treat him with civil kindness despite her own feelings, she took several deep breaths before summoning her courage sufficiently to turn to him with a smile. "Well, sir, what shall it be? Haydn or Mozart?"

Darcy had not seen her turn such a look on him since that horrible night at the parsonage, and he found himself captivated by her lovely eyes. *How would she react if I told her that I cared not what music she played, so long as she continued to smile at me?* he wondered abstractly, knowing that he had no right—nor would he ever have the right—to say anything of the sort. Recognizing with a start that he had been silent too long, he hastened to express a preference for Mozart.

The scent of rosewater drifted past him, and he felt a wave of desire for her. It was truly unfair, he thought, that he should still find her so bewitching despite her behaviour towards him. His eyes lingered on her profile as she played, tracing along the lines of her tempting lips. He admired the slender, tapering fingers dancing across the keyboard and imagined them touching his face, stroking his arm, bringing him to one pleasure after another.

She glanced over at him when she neared the end of the page and found a serious look on his face. Brought back to the moment, he reached past her to turn the page. The painful exhilaration of her closeness could not be denied, and he ached for the relief only she could bring him, all the while knowing that his desires were never to be fulfilled. Unable to control himself, he allowed his arm to brush against hers, seemingly by accident, as he resumed his seat.

Elizabeth was finding it nearly impossible to focus on her performance, and grew more anxious with each mistake she made. She was certain that Darcy was noting her errors and her discomposure, and redoubled her efforts to keep his presence from her mind, but with little success. The shock of sensation she felt when his sleeve touched her skin caused her to stumble in her playing, but she resisted the urge to glance in his direction to see if he had noted her confusion. By the time she came to the end of the piece, her cheeks were quite flushed. Without looking up, she sought out the simplest of the scores for her next effort.

Her rescue came from an unexpected source. Mr. Collins announced, "Cousin Elizabeth, although I applaud your musical talents as ever, it is time for us to depart this pleasant company."

She looked up at Mr. Collins in surprise; usually they stayed much later. She noticed that he appeared flustered, and she quickly gathered up the music into a neat pile before joining him. She glanced at Darcy from under her lashes, but his expression was unreadable.

They had no sooner arrived at the parsonage after a cold adieu from Lady Catherine when Charlotte drew her aside from the others. "Lizzy," she whispered. "I must caution you that her ladyship was quite displeased by Mr. Darcy's attentions to you tonight. I beg you to be careful; her wrath could quite easily move from you to Mr. Collins."

"Mr. Darcy's attentions to me? We barely spoke all evening!" Elizabeth said defensively.

"Yet his attention was focused on you all evening. Lizzy, I cannot claim to understand what is happening between the two of you, but I am not blind and, unfortunately, neither is her ladyship! I know he does not call here anymore, and I am no doubt happier not knowing if you are meeting clandestinely elsewhere, but you are playing a dangerous game, doing this under the eyes of his entire family. You must know they would not approve his interest in you."

Elizabeth could not help smiling at Charlotte's misinterpretation of Darcy's recent absence from Hunsford. "Charlotte, I assure you, you mistake my interest in this completely. Mr. Darcy does not call here anymore because he and I quarrelled, and I assure you that I am the last person whose company he would seek out. If you are sensing something between us, it is hostility, not affection." Her final words left a bitter taste in her mouth.

"Lizzy," Charlotte said patiently, "I must believe the evidence of my own eyes. I know that you have never wished to acknowledge his interest, and I must respect that; but, for your own sake, I feel obliged to recommend that you take this courtship far away from his family, or you may risk being disappointed."

Slowly and clearly, Elizabeth said with an edge to her voice, "There is no courtship, Charlotte."

Her friend looked at her, baffled. "Well, Lizzy, I know that there is no moving you when you have made up your mind; but, should you ever wish to speak of this, I hope you know that you may rely on my discretion."

Impulsively Elizabeth leaned over to kiss her cheek. "Dearest Charlotte, I know that you are only looking out for my best interests, and I assure you that if there ever is anything to tell, I will tell you."

Charlotte was apparently correct concerning Lady Catherine's view of the matter; for, despite her earlier insistence on Elizabeth's remaining in Kent, there was a decided lack of invitations to Rosings in the following days. Elizabeth greeted every day of this reprieve with a guilty relief; she was bewildered not only by Darcy's behaviour at their last meeting, but by her own reaction to it as well. She steadfastly refused Miss Darcy's invitations to call and encouraged her instead to come to the parsonage.

One fine day when Miss Darcy called, Elizabeth suggested walking out. Charlotte claimed that she could not be spared from her work, and Maria was not in the habit of walking, so the remaining two set off together. They followed the pathways into Rosings Park, Elizabeth making an effort to appear more in spirits than perhaps she felt.

They had not long been out when they spotted a gentleman at a distance. Miss Darcy, immediately recognizing the form of her brother, insisted on going to meet him over Elizabeth's objections that he might not wish to be disturbed. A disturbance of a different sort was taking place inside her at the idea of encountering him, and she struggled for equanimity despite the fluttering of her pulses as they approached him.

He seemed surprised to see them, but agreed after only a brief hesitation to Georgiana's suggestion that he join them. Elizabeth looked away as he took his place between them. He inquired civilly after the Collinses and, after receiving her none too articulate response, asked after her own plans, noting that it had been some time since he had seen her.

"I plan to depart for town on Saturday, and I will be staying with my aunt and uncle for a week before returning home," she replied, wondering if he were now eager to have her gone. She noted with amusement that he seemed no more at ease than she; when he spoke, his accent had none of its usual sedateness.

"Your aunt and uncle live in London, then?" asked Georgiana, hoping for details which might permit her to continue her acquaintance with Elizabeth.

"Yes, they live in Gracechurch Street, in Cheapside," said Elizabeth, with a particular emphasis on the final word. She stole a sly glance at Darcy, to see how he bore it; he sustained it however with fortitude. Her teasing spirit could not help but to try him a little further. "They are very great favourites of mine; my sister Jane and I usually spend at least a month with them each year. My aunt is originally from Derbyshire, in fact, not far from Pemberley." *But very, very far from it in rank,* she thought with amusement. *He has no idea how very low my connections can go.*

"Really!" exclaimed Georgiana. "Where is she from?"

Elizabeth could hardly help laughing at so convenient a question; she could almost think that Georgiana was assisting her in tormenting her brother, but it was obvious that her interest was genuine. "I believe it to be quite near Pemberley, in fact; she was born in the town of Lambton. Her father was a tailor there." *You shall see, sir, that I am not ashamed of such a relation!* she thought.

She saw Georgiana glance up at Darcy in embarrassment as if seeking assistance in finding a way to reply to such a startling assertion, but he did not seem to be attending to her, but rather was looking off into space with a somewhat preoccupied air. Feeling an odd disappointment at his lack of response, Elizabeth began to wonder if he had in fact begun to put his affection for her to rest.

"It must have been quite a change for her to move to London," ventured Georgiana at last.

"I believe it was a pleasant one; my aunt is a lady of great energy and has educated herself well beyond her means, and in London she has had far more opportunity to exercise her mind and spirit. She and my uncle are a very good match in that way."

"This, then, must be the uncle who entertains Mr. Wordsworth and his friends," said Darcy, re-entering the conversation at last with what could only be described as mild amusement.

Elizabeth looked over at him, meeting his gaze squarely. "Yes," she said with a defiant air. "My uncle is fond of society, and he and my aunt have many interesting friends; for me, one delight of visiting them is always the calibre of conversation one finds there."

If she thought that he would back down from her challenge, she was quite mistaken. "It sounds like quite a stimulating environment; I can imagine that it would be appealing to you, Miss Bennet. I find the idea of your participating in a discussion of Wordsworth a particularly intriguing one, since it strikes me that your minds are of a remarkably similar bent. I imagine the two of you more on the banks of the Wye than in a London parlour, though."

Elizabeth's eyes widened at the startling familiarity of his address. Did he truly think of her while reading poetry? "I cannot speak to that, sir, though I believe it to be lovely country," she said, surprised to find herself slightly breathless, despite the sedate pace of their walk. "I am fortunate in that I shall have the opportunity to travel to the Lakes this summer with my aunt and uncle, and to see it for myself."

"I can easily picture you in Wordsworth's country," he said, feeling a pang at the idea of Elizabeth having plans which did not involve him. It should be *his* place to take her to the Lakes, *his* should be the figure to stand beside her on the banks of the Wye. He somehow forced himself to continue. "I find in him a great believer in the inspiring force of Nature. As

36

he says, 'For nature then…to me was all in all.'" He paused for a moment as she took this in, then quoted,

> *…And I have felt*
> *A presence that disturbs me with the joy*
> *Of elevated thoughts; a sense sublime*
> *Of something far more deeply interfused,*
> *Whose dwelling is the light of setting suns,*
> *And the round ocean and the living air,*
> *And the blue sky, and in the mind of man;*
> *A motion and a spirit, that impels*
> *All thinking things, all objects of all thought,*
> *And rolls through all things. Therefore am I still*
> *A lover of the meadows and the woods,*
> *And mountains; and of all that we behold*
> *From this green earth; of all the mighty world*
> *Of eye, and ear,—both what they half create,*
> *And what perceive; well pleased to recognize*
> *In nature and the language of the sense,*
> *The anchor of my purest thoughts, the nurse,*
> *The guide, the guardian of my heart, and soul*
> *Of all my moral being.*

He stared off into space as he spoke simply but powerfully, but Elizabeth knew his words were addressed directly to her. She could not help but be moved by the vision of this proud man thinking of her as he read, and by the image he had shared. She bit her lip, realizing how much of him she did not know, and how greatly she had misinterpreted him.

Georgiana, catching some of the intimacy of the moment, looked first at her brother, then at Elizabeth, whose eyes were directed towards the ground, an abstracted look upon her face. Had she only heard their words, and been unable to see them, she would have thought it a romantic moment, but with both looking so distant and solemn, it did not seem to be such at all. She was completely baffled by his behaviour, and by the way in which Elizabeth, who called the indomitable Lady Catherine to account, seemed to be deferring to Darcy over some matter beyond her understanding.

Elizabeth felt ill-equipped to handle the feelings arising in her at that moment. She hardly knew what to say; yet, with each passing moment, the silence became heavier. Grasping at straws, she said, "His view of nature is an intensely personal one."

"Yes, very personal," said Darcy slowly. "To me it seems that he sees it as a source of inspiration, and also of grounding in a world made complex by human interactions."

Her cheeks lively with colour, Elizabeth struggled with the recognition that his words carried more meanings than one. It was such that she almost wondered whether he was attempting to court her, using his sister's presence to mask his intent. *And if he is*, her heart whispered, *how will you accept it?*

Darcy was himself even less certain of his own motivation for revealing so much of himself. It was not so much a conscious decision as a need to unburden himself of the thoughts and feelings that had haunted him for months and confess them to the only person who could offer him absolution. He was unsure whether it was an attempt to cause her to think better of him or, by airing his feelings in public, to bring them to a sort of closure. He gave her a sidelong glance; it was apparent that she felt uncomfortable, but she did not appear distressed. *It is rather more than you deserve,* he told himself sternly.

Elizabeth turned to Georgiana. "Are you fond of poetry as well, Miss Darcy?"

"Not so much as Fitzwilliam, no; he has an interest in everything, while I am more devoted to music to the exclusion of everything else." The sharp look she gave her brother indicated that this was a long-standing issue between the two, and indeed her tone seemed to indicate some scorn of his omnivorous taste.

Elizabeth stole a sly look at Darcy, who seemed to bear his sister's implied criticism well, even with a slight smile on his face, but she thought she detected that he was a bit offended. "Well, we need Renaissance men as well as fine musicians," she said equably. "I cannot claim to have a well-rounded mind; there are many subjects of which I know nothing, but I have yet to discover any learning which I regret having."

She observed a warming of his smile at her words, which caused her pulses to flutter. Embarrassed, she glanced away. Had she been able to encounter his eye, she might have seen a certain awareness on his face that would have brought a blush to her cheeks; but, though she could not look, she could listen. He said, "No one who has met you could find anything lacking in your knowledge of the world, Miss Bennet."

"I am relieved to know that I have managed to mislead you sufficiently as to the extent of my true ignorance, Mr. Darcy," she said lightly, thinking that he knew all too well the extent of her ignorance and prejudice.

He heard the apology inherent in her words, and realized with a touch of surprise that he had already forgiven her for her harsh words and accusations. "You worry yourself unnecessarily," he said gently, silently thanking Georgiana for her presence which was allowing them to have this conversation without active discord. "None of us is without faults which we would prefer to hide from the rest of the world."

She risked a glance at him, but he seemed quite sincere; she wished that she knew precisely which faults he felt that he need apologize for. She felt tears pricking at the corners of her eyes, and realized she was glad it seemed that they were to be able to establish peace between themselves before saying their goodbyes.

Georgiana's face was beginning to take on a sullen cast. She could tell that the others were talking around her and becoming increasingly oblivious to her presence, and she did not appreciate it; not only was she becoming increasingly intolerant of her brother's unconsciously patronizing manner with her, she also had come to consider Elizabeth to be her special friend, and she resented Darcy's appropriation of her attention. "Well," she said abruptly, deciding that she would rather do without Elizabeth's companionship than to suffer this, "We are almost to Rosings, and I find that I am becoming fatigued. Fitzwilliam, perhaps we should return to the house."

"Of course, Miss Darcy," said Elizabeth kindly, recalling herself to reality. "I will bid you adieu, then; it is past time for me to return to the parsonage." *And to spare myself the strain of continuing this conversation!* she thought, but not without a slight regret.

Darcy looked from Georgiana to Elizabeth in painful indecision. In any other circumstance, he would have stopped everything to attend to his sister, but he was exceedingly loath to leave Elizabeth when she seemed inclined to hear him out, with so much only partially resolved. Yet could they continue their conversation without Georgiana's presence providing the safety of propriety to them both? He recalled that Elizabeth would be leaving Kent in only a few days, and found that he had already taken his decision. "Let us all return to the house, then, and perhaps I may have the honour of escorting you back to the parsonage, Miss Bennet?" he said.

Once Georgiana was safely, if somewhat irritably, ensconced at Rosings, they walked on in complete silence, a strained silence rather than one of companionability. Elizabeth thought several times to initiate a conversation to diffuse the tension, but fear over what Darcy might say if they were to speak held her back. Darcy was far too unsure of his wishes to feel prepared to communicate, or perhaps it would have been more accurate to say that those desires of which he was certain were those which he knew to be the least acceptable. He wanted her to smile at him, to tease him once again as she had earlier in Georgiana's presence, and if he did not know what to *say*, he knew without a doubt what he wished to *do*, and it involved those tempting lips of hers. He could imagine the warmth of them against his… *Instead,* he told himself sternly, *you should remind yourself of your own responsibility in taking the smile from her face in the first place!*

The longer the silence persisted, the greater the sense of discomfort Elizabeth felt. She began to run her hands through the leaves of the bushes beside the path to distract herself, but that immediately brought to mind his earlier comments about nature. She scolded herself for her nerves and forced herself to pause as she usually did under the branches of a late-blooming wild cherry. Leaning her head over a low hanging bough, she closed her eyes and calmed herself with the sweet scent.

She was completely unaware of the enchanting picture she presented, framed by snowy blossoms, a slight smile of pleasure touching her lips. The sight of her held Darcy rapt, and he involuntarily took a step toward her. Opening her eyes, she found his gaze upon her in a manner which caused her pulses to flutter. She had never looked so closely into his dark eyes, and she discovered that their depths had the power to trap her. In an effort to break the spell of the moment, she said the first thing that came to her mind. "The cherry blooms for such a brief moment each year that I can never deny myself the chance to enjoy it."

His eyes seemed to grow even darker, and her breath caught in her throat. "Elizabeth," he said unsteadily.

She knew that she should rebuke his familiarity, but she seemed frozen in place by the sound of his voice intimately shaping the syllables of her name. Without knowing what she did, Elizabeth closed her eyes against the sight of him, and a moment later she felt his warm breath against her cheek, followed by the gentle pressure of his lips upon hers. A shock of exquisite sensation ran through her. She had never before experienced such a delectable feeling, and was astonished by the pleasure that the caresses of his lips brought to her. There was no past or future in that moment, no remembrance of their contentious history, just awareness of the heat of desire flaring between them.

Darcy, already scarcely able to believe that he was in fact finally claiming her lips, felt any remaining judgment disappear at the evidence of her response. The pleasure he found in her kiss was even more intense than he had ever imagined, and he had certainly imagined it often enough. Driven by a need beyond his control, he began to express more of the urgency he felt in his kisses, feeling her hesitancy move into acquiescence as the pleasure he brought her drew her onward.

Elizabeth felt lost in a whirl of pure sensation. She was discovering a need she had never known that she possessed, and it seemed that only he could meet it. She gasped as his fingers touched the tender skin of her neck, leaving a trail of fire as they moved to cradle the back of her head. She could not say how her hands had found their way to his shoulders, but the sense of his strength beneath them made her long for his embrace, and the intimate sensation of his other hand on her waist only intensified her yearning.

It was her increasing desire that brought to her attention the complete impropriety—nay, the insanity—of her behaviour. Her eyes flew open, but even upon this realization she could not immediately tear herself away from the intoxicating sensation of his lips upon hers, not when his kisses and caresses were sending rushes of a pleasure completely new to her through her body. It was only a sudden sense of shame that gave her the strength of will to push herself away from him. What folly could possibly be inducing her to permit such advances from any man, much less Mr. Darcy? She was aghast at the discovery of her own pleasure in it, and her voice shook as she said indignantly, "Mr. Darcy!"

As soon as Darcy first felt her stiffen beneath his hands, a sinking feeling of despair pervaded him. The look of horror on her face told him everything he needed to know. He knew that her rebuke was fully merited, but to have felt that brief moment of hope, that these last two weeks had been a nightmare from which he was now awakening in the arms of his beloved, and then to have it snatched away so abruptly…he could not bear it. His mouth set in grim lines, and the apology that he knew he should make seemed caught in his throat.

Elizabeth saw the coldness descend on his face, and knew not whether she was more injured or angered by it. "If you will excuse me, sir," she said bitingly, suddenly in desperate need to be away from him.

He watched as she turned and walked away rapidly, finally breaking into a run just before she disappeared around the bend. "Idiot!" he castigated himself harshly, running his hand through his hair. What had possessed him to kiss her, to ruin the brief moment of amicability they had shared earlier? *Do you need it engraved upon you? She wants nothing to do with you!* He had been a fool to think her response signified anything beyond being taken by surprise, but the taste of her pleasure had been so sweet… A depth of pain and desolation which he had not felt since the night of her refusal came over him, and bitterly he forced himself to turn back towards Rosings.

Elizabeth ran until she could go no further, finally collapsing against a tree to catch her breath. Her flight had taken her away from him, but unfortunately she could not leave her feelings behind so easily. She leaned her head back, wondering what on earth had come over her to allow him to kiss her, to *want* his kisses. She had never felt such wanton desires before, and could not comprehend how Mr. Darcy, who had angered and injured her so deeply, could possibly be the recipient of them. She told herself firmly that it was only the moment that had led to her unacceptable behaviour, but her honesty forced her to admit that it was he, more than the moment, that drew her.

She began to walk again in the direction of the parsonage. How could she have travelled from a place of such fervent dislike to feeling an incomprehensible attraction for him? She had known him for many months without feeling he had any particular appeal; why should it change now? Her steps slowed as she came to the startling realization that she had never been honest with herself about him—that the very degree of offence that she had taken at his insulting words at the Meryton assembly had been an indication of her sense of his magnetism, and she realized that in taking such a pronounced dislike to him, she had in essence been protecting herself from developing feelings for an unattainable man whom she found attractive and who challenged her in a way few others did.

As she realized the implications of her self-deception, her sense of distress grew. Had she not taken so strong a dislike to him, she would have questioned Wickham's unlikely story. She would not have blinded herself to the growing evidence of his attraction to her—evidence that even Charlotte was able to see. An unwilling smile began to tug at the corners of her mouth as she recognized that Darcy himself had paid an enormous price for his discourteous comment. On the other hand, it had cost her a great deal as well.

She raised her hands to her flushed cheeks. It seemed to be her fate to wander these lanes wondering how she could ever bring herself to face Mr. Darcy again. She was utterly ashamed of her own behaviour, and could not begin to imagine what he would think of her for permitting his advances. It would certainly confirm his expectations of her as a member of the Bennet family.

She wondered what had caused him to kiss her. It certainly must have been a triumph for him that she permitted it—was that the motivation, to demonstrate that he could cause her to accept that which she had rebuffed? It was beyond comprehension to think that he could have forgiven her acrimonious refusal, but what was she to make of his behaviour? For each time he seemed to seek her out, there was another when he avoided her in obvious angry contempt.

If he had kissed her out of a continuing devotion, it could only be worse for her. He would have every right to certain expectations of her after she permitted—participated in—his kisses, expectations which she needed to counter as quickly as possible. *If he understood it as a confirmation of my feelings for him, then I will indeed be in difficulties,* she thought, frantically trying to devise a way to communicate to him that it had been a mistake on her part, rather than an attempt to invite his addresses. She wanted more than anything to flee Kent forever, and to throw herself into Jane's understanding embrace, but the taste of his kiss was still upon her lips, and there was no escape from the feelings it had caused.

Chapter 3

D arcy was unable to comprehend how he had been fool enough to lower his guard to Elizabeth Bennet once again. *It is not as if she had not been clear and definite in her position the first time, but no, you had to hope for a softening in her regard!* he condemned himself harshly. It did not help to remind himself of how ill-judged her words and actions had been; all he could think of was his own foolishness. *Well, at least you need have no doubt now—she wants nothing to do with you, now or ever.* The bitterest part by far, though, was the realization he had come to when he kissed her, that regardless of what she felt for him or what faults she might have, he was still as violently in love with her as ever, and there was nothing to be done for it.

The pain of it did not leave him night or day; even Georgiana, who had seemed determined to annoy him in every possible instance, had begun to tread carefully in face of his unexplained dark mood. Colonel Fitzwilliam, thinking that their prolonged stay at Rosings accounted for it, clapped him on the back and reminded him they would be leaving soon enough. Then, at odd moments, the memory of how it felt to claim her lips, to feel her response and her hands upon him would overtake him, and the sweetness of it would be almost more than he could bear. Sometimes he even felt a moment of hope before the memory of her outraged look came to him and he tumbled once more into the depths of anger and despair.

He knew that as a gentleman he should make his apologies to her for his behaviour, and her accusations of his ungentlemanlike manner resounded bitterly in his head when he thought of it. She had the right of it in this case, he knew, for he was also aware that he would not be calling on her to do so, not because he had no regrets but because he could not trust himself in her presence. His feelings had already taken him too far beyond the confines of society's rules, and he could envision only too easily that he could be reduced to begging her to reconsider. He could imagine nothing more humiliating.

On the second day after his ill-fated encounter with Elizabeth, his uncle discovered him in the dark corner of the library to which he had retreated in an effort to avoid his cousin's genial invitations to call at the parsonage. "There you are, Darcy," Lord Derby declared. "What a young man like you is doing hiding indoors on such a fine day is beyond me. When I was your age, I would have been out and about the countryside, but all the young men these days seem to prefer only indoor amusements. Well, enough of that; I want to have a word with you."

"Yes, uncle," responded Darcy, his voice unwelcoming. It was perfectly true that he was hiding; if he went out, there was not only the possibility that he might accidentally encounter Elizabeth, but also the risk that he would not be able to stop his feet from leading him to the parsonage. It was far better to bury himself in the library.

"You know that Lord and Lady Temple are coming for dinner this evening. They are old friends of ours, connections of the Stowes of Warwickshire, and Lady Catherine tells me that their daughter Sophia has grown up to be quite a pretty young lady. Now, I understand why you might take the notion into your head that you do not wish to marry Anne; not sure I'd want to myself, truth to tell, but I want to see you make an effort with Miss Temple. She would be a good match—she has a fortune of £40,000, and I know that you have not forgotten that you must make up the loss of Georgiana's fortune if your estate is not to diminish. Now, I know, there is more than money to making a match, and I am not asking you to marry her, but I expect to see you talking to her—none of your sitting silently in the corner, now. Do you take my meaning?"

Darcy rolled his eyes. "I understand your wishes quite clearly, sir," he said, his voice cool. *As if any woman but Elizabeth could hold my interest for a minute!*

This apparently was enough of an agreement to satisfy Lord Derby, who confined himself to torturing his nephew by repeating his message no more than two or three more times before leaving Darcy in merciful silence. Darcy was far from pleased with the notion of spending an evening conversing with any young lady at the moment, but it was a small enough concession to make in the ongoing conflict over Georgiana's future. If it would placate his uncle to have him charm this girl, whoever she was, then charm her he would.

He was relieved to discover that evening that the young lady in question was at least a tolerable conversationalist, if somewhat overly deferential; he had feared he had condemned himself to being polite to yet another predatory and obsequious husband-hunter. As it was, he forced himself to smile when she gazed up through lowered lashes at him, and firmly returned the conversation to the events of the Season in town, and what might have seemed an evening of torture was reduced to a marginally tolerable situation. He only hoped that she would not take his attentions seriously; he had no desire to cause her any distress, just to be left alone from his family's demands.

He felt that the worst was over when the ladies withdrew. The presence of Lord Temple protected him from the kind of minute analysis of his every flawed behaviour during the evening which he knew would eventually be forthcoming from his uncle, and he could down his port in silence next to his more voluble cousin. He was regretful when it was time to rejoin the ladies, but hoped to be spared the need for extensive conversation by his aunt's demand for cards. His uncle, of course, insisted that he be seated with Miss Temple over the irritated demands of Lady Catherine that he join Anne's table at once. Darcy felt deep gratitude that he would be unlikely to encounter any of their guests after leaving Kent given the embarrassing display his family was insisting on putting on.

He would have been far more profoundly disturbed had he realized that his aunt had invited the Collins party to join them to make numbers enough for the games she had in mind, but Lady Catherine, still suspicious of the possible predations of Miss Elizabeth Bennet upon her nephew, had made a point of keeping this information to herself. He was therefore taken quite by surprise when their arrival was announced, and felt his heart in his throat as he rose to greet them. He had dreaded this first meeting with

Elizabeth and the distaste he expected to see in her face, and carefully looked just past her as he acknowledged their arrival.

Unlike Darcy, Elizabeth had enjoyed the dubious privilege of worrying about this meeting for the entire day. As if her own concerns and distress over it were not sufficient, she was forced to suffer through several lectures from Mr. Collins on the imperative need for her to display all possible modesty on this occasion and to avoid calling any attention to herself. Elizabeth longed to tell him that she had no intention of going near Mr. Darcy if she had any choice in the matter whatsoever. After long consideration, she still felt no clearer in her own mind as to Mr. Darcy's possible reaction to their encounter, but, as she approached Rosings that evening with the rest of the party, she could not help recall the devastating feeling of his lips upon hers.

Half afraid that her thoughts would show in her face, she kept her eyes downcast during the greetings and introductions. When she was finally forced to look up by the need to move to her table, it was to see Mr. Darcy turning an attentive smile on an attractive young lady seated next to him, who seemed far from averse to such attention. She felt an unanticipated stab of pain at his defection; she had been prepared for a reaction of distaste from him, but not to find herself so rapidly displaced in his mind. Blindly she turned to Colonel Fitzwilliam, who had seated himself next to her, and deliberately gave him the brightest smile she could manage.

She was seated at a table across the room from Mr. Darcy; she was unable to follow the progress of his conversation, but she heard his laugh ring out on more than one occasion, and the murmur of his voice. Clearly Wickham had been telling the truth in one small item—Darcy was indeed able to be pleasing among those he thought to be his equals in consequence, a group to which she did not, and never would, belong.

Her pride would not allow her to let slip any hint that Darcy's desertion troubled her. She engaged Colonel Fitzwilliam in a lively manner which soon drew a pleased response from that gentleman, who remained quite taken with the lovely Miss Bennet and had rather felt her withdrawal from him after his confession of his need to find a well-dowered bride. Her smiles were brilliant, and she teased him with many a sideward glance which might in other circumstances have led him astray, and by the end of the evening he was willing to declare it the pleasantest evening he had spent at Rosings since his arrival.

It was a conclusion that would not have been shared by his conversational partner, who felt her attention painfully drawn to the opposite side of the room. She could not justify her dislike of the situation; after all, she had refused him and had no interest in furthering a relationship with him, so why should she feel any distress to see him moving on? She finally reached the painful conclusion that it was because Miss Temple was everything she was not; wealthy, dressed in silks and jewels, and fashionably pale and languid in the manner of the *ton*. She would, Elizabeth was forced to conclude, make a much more suitable bride for Mr. Darcy, but she could not deny the pain this thought caused her.

Darcy's displeasure at seeing Elizabeth turn her sparkling eyes upon his cousin reached the level of near-torture as the evening progressed. She was facing away from him, but all too frequently he could see her dark curls brushing near Colonel Fitzwilliam's arm, and the obvious pleasure that gentleman took in her attentions. *So her subdued air lasted only so long as she thought I might be watching her,* he thought bitterly. *No sooner does she see my attention turned elsewhere than she is laughing with him once again!*

He was gripped by the desire to take Elizabeth away, forcibly if necessary, from his cousin. Better yet, to take her away from all of these people and their superficial ways, and to demand that she accept him. His mind began to travel down a familiar route as he imagined how he would convince her, a scenario in which his bedroom and her swollen lips and passion-filled eyes played leading roles. The crystal sound of her laughter reached his ears, breaking into his fantasy and bringing him closer to thoughts of murder than he ever cared to be.

"Mr. Darcy?" Miss Temple's languid tones pierced his distraction, and he turned to her half in irritation before recollecting himself. No, he would conquer this, he told himself with angry determination. Elizabeth would never be his, and it was time to move on with his life. She would be some other man's wife, and their paths would never cross again, leaving him only with the memory of one kiss among the blossoms and a book of poetry that would forever remind him of her. Finding himself unable to tolerate this torment any longer, he excused himself abruptly to Miss Temple and strode from the room.

He did not stop until he was out in the chill of the night. Finding a bench in the gardens, he dropped himself down and rested his head in his hands, allowing the aching pain inside him free rein. Why had it happened this way? Why could she not have cared for him? He allowed himself—nay, he could not stop himself from seeking solace in fancy, imagining Elizabeth as he had so many times, coming toward him with that teasing smile which had so bewitched him and her hand held out to him. Beneath the teasing there would be a warm and gentle look in her eyes just for him, and he would take her into his arms, tasting the passion that lay just beneath the surface, waiting for him to awaken it.

He had dreamt too often of her in his bed to stop there; he could almost feel the warmth of her curves beneath his hands, and see the discoveries he would make as he slid her dress off her shoulders. She would give herself to him, as generous in love as she was in laughter, and he would make her his forever, bound to him by ties as strong as blood.

Dear God, how am I to live without her? he demanded of the night sky. A sense of hopelessness filled him, as if life itself had lost its meaning when he lost her. *She was never yours to begin with!* No, he would not give in to despair; he would prove that he could conquer this need for her.

Pull yourself together, man! he told himself firmly. *You are Fitzwilliam Darcy, the Master of Pemberley, and the woman does not live who can bring you to your knees! It is time, past time, to go back in there and play the role you have always been meant to play.* With a sigh, he stood and brushed off his trousers.

He returned to make his apologies to Miss Temple. He did not glance in Elizabeth's direction again until it came time for the party from the Parsonage to depart. Only then did he allow himself to rest his eyes on her in a long, serious look, taking in her form and her visage and committing them to memory. They would not meet again; this represented the end of an era for him, and the beginning of a life which would be ornamented only by emptiness. As quickly as he could do so tactfully, he retired to his rooms, his mouth tasting of bile. He removed his coat and cravat and threw them carelessly on a chair. His valet looked at him reproachfully; Mr. Darcy usually paid more attention to these matters, but tonight he was blind to everything but the pain in his heart.

He came abruptly to a decision. He could stay no longer and risk seeing her again. "We leave for London at first light, Sawyer. Please see to it that my belongings are packed and shipped on as soon as may be."

"Yes, sir," the valet murmured in surprise, knowing better than to question his master when he was in such a mood.

ELIZABETH WAS LATE TO BREAKFAST the following morning after sleeping poorly. No sooner had she taken her seat than a bright-eyed Maria Lucas said, "Have you heard, Lizzy? Mr. Darcy left for town early this morning on urgent business, and her ladyship is beside herself with anger!"

"Maria!" exclaimed Mr. Collins, his mouth still working on a large bite of muffin. "I will not have any disrespect for Lady Catherine in this house! I find it hard to believe that after the gracious condescension she has shown you that you would repay her kindness by speaking in such a way! And if she is angered with Mr. Darcy, I am certain beyond the shadow of a doubt that he richly deserves it!"

Maria subsided, a look of shame upon her face which would have amused Elizabeth on another day. Today, though, her mind was ajumble with thoughts—*He did not even trouble himself to make his farewells to me,* she thought with an odd pain.

As soon as she could, she escaped the parsonage for a brisk walk with the intent of recovering her spirits, a challenge which proved to be beyond her capabilities. On her return, she was met en route by a man she recognized vaguely as a servant from Rosings. "Miss Bennet!" he called to her.

"Yes?" she responded.

"Madam, I was charged to return this book to you," he said to her with a bow, handing her a leather-bound volume.

She looked at it in puzzlement. Turning it over, she recognized it as the book of poetry she had been reading that day at Rosings. "I am afraid that there has been some mistake," she said politely. "This is not mine."

The servant paused, puzzled. "But Mr. Darcy specifically instructed me to return it to you, that you had lent it to him. Perhaps he was mistaken, and it was from someone else?"

She opened the book to the flyleaf where she found her name printed in a firm handwriting that had become familiar to her from her many perusals of his letter. She looked at it in confusion for several moments before realizing how neatly Darcy had trapped her. There was no way for her to refuse the book without drawing attention to the fact that he was giving it to her, with all the dangerous implications that carried. Finally she said slowly, "No, it was my mistake; I had confused it with another. Yes, this is mine."

The servant, used to the baffling ways of the gentry, thought no more of the matter, but the same could not be said of Elizabeth. She returned slowly to the parsonage, and managed to escape to her room without encountering any of the inhabitants. There she sat and held the book in her hand, caressing the letters imprinted in gold on its spine, and speculated what had motivated Darcy to give it to her. Was it in lieu of a farewell, or an apology of sorts, or an effort to rid himself of anything which might remind him of her? She could not reach any sort of conclusion, and knew that it would stand as an unanswered question forever, since it hardly seemed likely that she would encounter him again. She sighed over her widely differing impressions of him, and wondered at the part of her that regretted him.

She noticed a small silken book marker within it, and opened it to find it marking 'Lines Composed a Few Miles Above Tintern Abbey.' Wondering whether it could be a silent message to her or merely an oversight, she began slowly reading. It was the poem he had quoted to her during their walk, she discovered with a twinge, and read on in the lengthy verse to discover the undertones in Wordsworth's simple yet powerful paean to the inspiring power of Nature. It was not until she reached the end, though, that her sensibilities were truly engaged.

> *...Therefore let the moon*
> *Shine on thee in thy solitary walk;*
> *And let the misty mountain-winds be free*
> *To blow against thee: and, in after years,*
> *When these wild ecstasies shall be matured*
> *Into a sober pleasure; when thy mind*
> *Shall be a mansion for all lovely forms,*
> *Thy memory be as a dwelling-place*
> *For all sweet sounds and harmonies; oh! then,*
> *If solitude, or fear, or pain, or grief,*
> *Should be thy portion, with what healing thoughts*
> *Of tender joy wilt thou remember me,*

And these my exhortations! Nor, perchance—
If I should be where I no more can hear
Thy voice, nor catch from thy wild eyes these gleams
Of past existence—wilt thou then forget
That on the banks of this delightful stream
We stood together, and that I, so long
A worshipper of Nature, hither came
Unwearied in that service: rather say
With warmer love—oh! with far deeper zeal
Of holier love. Nor wilt thou then forget,
That after many wanderings, many years
Of absence, these steep woods and lofty cliffs,
And this green pastoral landscape, were to me
More dear, both for themselves and for thy sake!

A tear came to her eye as she read the passage once and then again. If this was indeed a message for her, she could not help but be moved by it—yet the previous night he had ignored her in favour of another woman, treating Miss Temple with a warmth and charm that he had never directed at her. *If he still cares for me, why did he make his attentions to the fashionable Miss Temple? If he no longer cares, why mark the verse? Teasing, teasing man! I will think no more about him,* she thought firmly.

Her resolution was for a short time voluntarily kept as she went downstairs to meet Charlotte's inquiries and plans for the day. However, her thoughts could not be kept at bay when her friend looked at her shrewdly and said, "You seemed quite taken by surprise by the news of Mr. Darcy's departure, Lizzy."

"I had heard nothing of it last night," Elizabeth prevaricated, "so it was something of a surprise, yes."

"Oh, Lizzy," Charlotte said, her voice filled with sympathy. "I am sorry you had to witness that scene last night. I would truly have thought Mr. Darcy above indulging in that sort of behaviour in front of you; I had thought better of him. Perhaps you are fortunate that matters went no further between you than they did."

Wearily Elizabeth thought how simple the world must look from Charlotte's perspective. Would that she could be so uncomplicated!

"Charlotte, I recognize that you are quite wedded to this notion of yours that Mr. Darcy was enamoured of me, but I assure you that there was never an understanding of any sort between us."

Her friend's look of silent compassion almost proved too much for Elizabeth as she came to the quiet realization that it was not a coincidence that this time she had not denied having feelings of her own towards him. She knew that she would never forget him—he had made an indelible impression, both in his own right and by shaking her self-concept beyond what she had ever considered possible. The memory of his kiss would not fade either, and still brought a blush to her cheeks. But she had no choice but to put her memories behind her, and with a deep, calming breath, she determinedly changed the subject to safer matters.

THE FOLLOWING DAY ELIZABETH DECIDED to take advantage of Darcy's absence to call on Miss Darcy at Rosings—she was several visits in her debt, having attempted to avoid meeting her brother at all costs. Now that he had left, her worst worry was that she might appear out of spirits . She found Miss Darcy sitting with Lady Derby, and seeming delighted to receive her. After exchanging greetings, Lady Derby suggested a game of Commerce, to which the others agreed.

This was Elizabeth's first contact with Lady Derby away from the dominating presence of her husband, and she was interested to discover that she was not quite the pale shadow that she sometimes seemed in larger company. Instead she was perfectly amiable, asking Elizabeth questions regarding her home and family, and her view of Kent. Despite Elizabeth's intent to avoid the subject, it did not take her inquisitor long to elicit the intelligence of Elizabeth's previous acquaintance with Darcy, something which proved to be news to Miss Darcy as well, who did not look pleased to discover it.

"I cannot think why my brother never mentioned it to me," she said with an air of irritation.

Elizabeth raised an eyebrow. "Our acquaintance was really quite trifling," she said placatingly. "It no doubt slipped his mind." *It is an odd turn of events that I should be defending Mr. Darcy to his family!* she thought with amusement.

"He never tells me anything," Georgiana complained. "I wish he would have more confidence in me. Sometimes I think he believes that I am still no more than eleven years old."

"You are very hard on him sometimes," Lady Derby said. "He has always done his duty by you, and I might say that he has done better than your parents did by him, and I think that deserving of respect. He cannot take the part of a parent for you, though, Georgiana, no matter how hard he tries."

Georgiana sat up straight with an indignant look on her face. "I do not know what you mean to say about my parents. They were wonderful; my brother has often told me stories about them."

Lady Derby sighed. "You say that you are old enough to hear the truth, Georgiana, so perhaps it is time that you learned that your parents were not the saints your brother makes them out to be. Your mother was a true Fitzwilliam: lovely, but proud and heedless of the feelings of others. She had little time for her children except as little pictures of her own perfections. She had no feelings beyond those of duty for your father, and after she had produced an heir, she had as little to do with him as possible for two people living in the same house. Your father had a great capacity for devotion, much as his son does now, but very early on he developed a highly unsuitable attachment, and I believe that he always regretted her. It was not an ideal home for a sensitive boy like your brother, and I believe that it was a relief when he went off to school. I have always hoped that when he comes to choose a bride, he will marry for affection and respect as well as practical considerations; I confess to some relief on his behalf that he refused to marry Anne."

This was by far the longest speech Elizabeth had ever heard from the often withdrawn Lady Derby, and she could not help but wonder at it, especially given the impropriety of sharing such intimate family views with a relative stranger such as herself. Her bitterness as she described Darcy's mother as a true Fitzwilliam led Elizabeth to suspect that she had paid a considerable price in her own marriage, and she felt a surprising moment of sympathy for her.

Georgiana fiddled with her cards uncomfortably. "My brother has always spoken quite affectionately about our parents, though," she said quietly, but with a hint of defiance.

Lady Derby's eye showed a glint of steel which came as a surprise to

Elizabeth. "Yes, he was very attached to them, and was able to blind himself to their faults, a tendency he continues to demonstrate on occasion."

"What of the other woman, the one you say my father cared for?" asked Georgiana.

Lady Derby shrugged as if it were of little importance. "She married someone else, I believe, one of the men of the estate. Her family had been servants at Pemberley, so she truly was quite unsuitable. I was under the impression that she and your father remained friends of a sort, although there was never any hint of impropriety."

Noting how shattered the girl looked by her aunt's revelations, Elizabeth said calmingly, "It is unfortunate that it is the way of the world that so few can marry where they please—it takes a certain strength to accept that one's duty may not lie where one's heart does."

She was surprised to see Lady Derby turning a penetrating look on her. "It can be a bitter thing, though, to marry where there is no affection, and bitterer yet if there is affection one has left behind. I fear that my nephew is all too conscious of his duty, and that he will pay the same price his father did in the end, but I for one shall be sorry for it."

Elizabeth coloured as she realized that Lady Derby had somehow drawn the same conclusions as Charlotte—that Mr. Darcy had earned her affections and then determined that she was beneath him—and that her comments on the Darcy family had been made with the intent of providing some comfort to herself. She turned her eyes back to her cards, cursing the ill-fortune that had kept her in Kent to expose so much more of herself than she would have wished. After a moment, though, she recalled Lady Derby's earlier description of the Fitzwilliams—*proud, and heedless of the feelings of others*—and gained a new understanding of what this discussion must have cost her. Elizabeth looked up with a confidence she did not feel, and said, "I shall hope for his sake that your fears prove groundless, Lady Derby, and since I know of no man with more eligible women courting his favour than Mr. Darcy, I cannot think that he would not be capable of finding a wife of good understanding among them. Do you not think so, Miss Darcy?"

"*He* will never marry for love, that much is certain," said Georgiana in an unkind tone. "He will choose some very appropriate young lady of good fortune with no regard whatsoever to his feelings, and he will expect me to do the same! Love means nothing to him."

Elizabeth looked at her in shock at the intensity of her statement, especially given her own knowledge that it was far from the truth. She could not imagine what would inspire Georgiana to such beliefs.

"Georgiana, my dear, you will learn with time that a young lady with a fortune can expect many young men to woo her and claim to love her while their true interest is mercenary," said Lady Derby with the tone of someone repeating an oft-spoken obvious truth.

"Who is to say that a man of little fortune may not truly love a woman of fortune?" Georgiana demanded.

Can it be that she resents her brother for the role he played in separating her from Wickham? Elizabeth wondered. *Surely she cannot believe he loved her!* Deliberately she said, "There is, as you say, Miss Darcy, no reason why a poor man may not love a woman of wealth, but it is all too common to find charming fortune hunters working their wiles upon unsuspecting women. Why, just recently in my home in Hertfordshire, there was an officer of the regiment who was most attentive to me, but when another girl in whom he had never shown any interest came into an inheritance of 10,000 pounds, he immediately forgot me and proceeded to pay suit to her. To her ill-luck, she accepted him, having failed to see the truth of his interest in her, and in truth I pity her; Lieutenant Wickham will not make so good a husband as he did a suitor, and I fear that Miss King will be quite unhappy." She looked up from her cards in time to see Georgiana flinch when she revealed Wickham's name.

Lady Derby looked at her levelly. "It sounds as if you had a narrow escape there, Miss Bennet," she said.

"In a way, I suppose so, but he had never been serious in his intentions towards me, and I already had reason to suspect that he was not the man he seemed to be," said Elizabeth, thinking that if this was not wholly true, it was certainly the case that there had been ample reason to suspect Wickham; she had merely ignored the evidence before her. "He had, I fear, misrepresented himself to me with a number of falsehoods, including some, I am sorry to say, which concerned your family, Miss Darcy, to whom he once had a connection. Once I discovered what sort of man he was, I regretted ever listening to him for a moment."

Georgiana grew pale. "He had a connection to my family?" she asked in a strained voice.

Elizabeth furrowed her brow seriously. "Yes, I believe that his father served yours in some capacity; I cannot recall exactly what it might be."

"What manner of...falsehoods did he tell you?"

A blush came to Elizabeth's cheeks, though perhaps not for the reason her audience suspected. "My apologies, I fear that I have been quite tactless to have even raised the subject. I would not feel at all comfortable repeating his words; suffice to say that they were quite unkind towards your brother, Miss Darcy, and to a lesser extent toward yourself and other members of your family."

Abruptly Georgiana stood. "Excuse me," she said, her voice shaky, before quickly departing the room.

There was silence following her sudden disappearance. After a moment, Lady Derby played a card. "Mr. Darcy owes you a debt of gratitude, Miss Bennet. It was generous of you, under the circumstances."

Elizabeth was finding it increasingly difficult to bear being thought to have been disappointed by Mr. Darcy, but since she was without any acceptable way to explain the truth, she had no choice but to tolerate it. "It was nothing more than the truth, and I have no desire to see Miss Darcy harmed by being under a misapprehension, nor to see any member of her family come to harm." *I can but hope that this will be enough to prevent further commiseration with my imagined position,* she thought. "But I must be returning to the parsonage; Mrs. Collins will be expecting me."

Thankfully, Lady Derby did not question her obvious excuses, and merely wished her a good day, leaving Elizabeth a long walk back to the parsonage to contemplate her discomfiture at having Mr. Darcy's interest in her guessed at by so many.

ELIZABETH WAS RELIEVED WHEN THE day finally came for her to make her departure from Kent. Although Miss Darcy clearly retained an interest in Elizabeth's friendship, their relations had been somewhat strained since her revelations about Wickham. Charlotte's suspicions of the reasons for her mood were becoming trying as well. She could hardly bear to wait any longer to see Jane and to observe her spirits for herself, as well as to receive her comfort. At length the chaise arrived, the trunks were fastened on, the parcels placed within, and it was pronounced to be ready. After an affectionate parting from Charlotte, Elizabeth was attended to the carriage by

Mr. Collins; and, as they walked down the garden, he was commissioning her with his best respects to all her family, not forgetting his thanks for the kindness he had received at Longbourn in the winter and his compliments to Mr. and Mrs. Gardiner, though unknown. He then handed her in, Maria followed, and the door was on the point of being closed, when he suddenly reminded them, with some consternation, that they had hitherto forgotten to leave any message for the ladies at Rosings.

"But," he added, "you will of course wish to have your humble respects delivered to them, with your grateful thanks for their kindness to you while you have been here."

Elizabeth made no objection;—the door was then allowed to be shut, and the carriage drove off.

"Good gracious!" cried Maria, after a few minutes silence, "it seems but a day or two since we first came!—and yet how many things have happened!"

"A great many indeed," said her companion with a sigh.

"We have dined nine times at Rosings, besides drinking tea there twice!— How much I shall have to tell!"

Elizabeth privately added, "And how much I shall have to conceal."

Their journey was performed without much conversation, or any alarm; and within four hours of their leaving Hunsford, they reached Mr. Gardiner's house, where they were to remain a few days.

Jane looked well, and Elizabeth had little opportunity of studying her spirits, amidst the various engagements which the kindness of her aunt had reserved for them. But Jane was to go home with her, and at Longbourn there would be leisure enough for observation.

It was not without an effort, meanwhile, that she could wait even for Longbourn, before she told her sister of Mr. Darcy's proposals. To know that she had the power of revealing what would so exceedingly astonish Jane, and must, at the same time, so highly gratify whatever of her own vanity she had not yet been able to reason away, was such a temptation to openness as nothing could have conquered but the state of indecision in which she remained as to the extent of what she should communicate; and her fear, if she once entered on the subject, of being hurried into repeating something of Bingley which might only grieve her sister farther.

One morning shortly before they were to leave for Hertfordshire,

Elizabeth and Jane were working their embroidery in the sitting room in the pleasant company of their aunt while Elizabeth recounted with amusement tales of Lady Catherine and Rosings Park. She had managed to avoid reference to Mr. Darcy—though Jane already knew of his presence there through Maria Lucas, Elizabeth was for her own self not yet ready to speak of him. Her tale was interrupted, however, by the appearance of the Gardiners' maid at the door. "There are two gentlemen outside, to see Miss Bennet and Miss Elizabeth Bennet," she said to Mrs. Gardiner, handing her two calling cards.

Elizabeth and Jane looked at one another at this unexpected announcement, wondering who in London might call on them as opposed to their aunt and uncle. Mrs. Gardiner's face exhibited well-bred surprise as she examined the cards, and she looked up at her nieces with an expression of concern. "Mr. Bingley and Mr. Darcy," she said.

Elizabeth could not have been more surprised if the caller had been the Prince Regent. Her heart seemed to stop for a moment at the thought of seeing Mr. Darcy once more. Her astonishment at his coming and voluntarily seeking her again was great. Her mind then flew to the fact of Mr. Bingley's presence—she could not account for it in any way but that Mr. Darcy had taken her criticisms to heart, and she did not know if she was more pleased or frightened by this conceit.

Jane looked a little paler than usual, but more sedate than Elizabeth had expected. On the gentlemen's appearing, her colour increased; yet she received them with tolerable ease, and with a propriety of behaviour equally free from any symptom of resentment, or any unnecessary complaisance. Elizabeth only hoped that she looked as composed as her sister; she felt an inner disturbance quite different from that which she wished to project.

Jane made the introductions to Mrs. Gardiner, who was pleased in particular to have the opportunity to meet the gentleman who had so captured Jane's heart. The usually loquacious Bingley seemed to have forgotten the power of speech as he gazed at Jane, however, and Mr. Darcy drew more of Mrs. Gardiner's attention when he spoke with her civilly.

To no one's surprise, Bingley took the place by Jane that had so often been his in Hertfordshire. Elizabeth waited with a flutter of anxiety for Mr. Darcy to approach her, but he instead sat opposite her, responding only briefly to her polite enquiries about his stay in London. Mrs. Gardiner, feeling the discomfort of the situation, employed her not insubstantial skills in engaging Mr. Darcy in conversation. Initially he was as succinct and stilted in his replies as Elizabeth would have expected him to be when dealing with his social inferiors, and for a moment she regretted having told him of her aunt's origins, as he might otherwise have taken her for a woman of fashion. She reminded herself, however, of her own pride in her aunt, and listened most attentively as Mrs. Gardiner finally succeeded in beginning a conversation with him about Derbyshire.

Mr. Darcy's eyes turned not infrequently to Elizabeth, causing her to apply herself to her work with a diligence it did not often command. Bingley's behaviour to Jane was such as showed an admiration of her, which, though more guarded than formerly, persuaded Elizabeth, that if left wholly to himself, Jane's happiness, and his own, would be speedily secured. Though she dared not depend upon the consequence, Elizabeth yet received pleasure from observing his behaviour. She was less certain as to her feelings about their other caller.

The gentlemen had not long been there when new visitors were announced, and Mr. and Mrs. Monkhouse made their entrance. Once introductions had been effected, Darcy glanced at Bingley and suggested it was time for them to make their departure. Mrs. Gardiner, with a glance at the stricken look on Jane's face, urged them to stay.

"There is often quite a crowd of callers here at this time of day," Mr. Monkhouse said very civilly. "Our hosts are most congenial, and many of us take sad advantage of that fact!"

Darcy, once again looking quite uncomfortable, replied only briefly, but condescended to agree to remain for a brief period. His eyes once again turned to Elizabeth.

With a certain slyness, Elizabeth said, "Mr. Monkhouse, Mr. Darcy is an admirer of your cousin, Mr. Wordsworth, sir."

Darcy shot her an enigmatic look before responding in the affirmative.

"Excellent!" said Monkhouse energetically. "I am always pleased to hear it. Myself, I am currently reading the new works of Lord Byron—his approach to poetry is quite a revelation."

"Indeed he has such powers of expression and real individual feeling as must make the older poets seem lame," said Mrs. Gardiner.

"More individual, or more indulgent?" queried Elizabeth. "I must say that I prefer the greater simplicity evidenced in the work of Coleridge and Wordsworth."

"Do you feel, then, Miss Bennet, that the exaltation of the individual has gone too far?" asked Monkhouse.

Elizabeth considered the question for a moment. "To me, there is something lost when the ideal of individual self-awareness is translated to a position of passivity, where the poet hopes to experience as much as possible while doing nothing." From the corner of her eye, she saw Darcy looking at her with some surprise, whether at her idea or merely that she should hold such ideas she could not tell.

"I would agree with Miss Bennet," Darcy said. "If we are to take the assumption that the divine element of man is self-consciousness, is it not more valuable to explore the possibilities of the self than to look to the effect of the world upon the self? In the works of Wordsworth, unlike Byron, the awakened consciousness leads to the awakened moral sense, and thus to the experience of the divine."

It was Elizabeth's turn to raise an eyebrow as Mr. Monkhouse engaged Darcy and Mrs. Gardiner in a lively debate on the Romantic ideal. She was sufficiently caught by the surprising sight of Mr. Darcy contending on an equal basis with those self-same people he scorned in his proposal to her that she paid less attention to the conversation itself than she might have otherwise. Matters continued in this vein, with Bingley conversing softly with Jane, oblivious to the animated discussion surrounding him, until the arrival of Mr. Gardiner, accompanied by another caller familiar to Elizabeth, a passionate-looking young man by the name of Mr. Brewer. On their entrance, Monkhouse declared cheerfully, "And now, Mr. Darcy, you will find that our debate on poetry is at an end, since our friend Brewer will indubitably discover a way to turn the conversation to abolitionism within a matter of minutes!"

Mr. Brewer laughed as he took his seat next to Elizabeth, favouring her with a warm smile. His admiration of the younger Miss Bennet was well-known to both her and the Gardiners, as was the inevitability that his political involvement would never allow him the substance to make a serious offer to a woman without independent means. Elizabeth tolerated his attentions with her usual good humour, but with awareness of the dark looks he was earning from the gentleman across the room. As Mr. Brewer launched into an enthusiastic report on his most recent activities in the abolitionist cause, she could not help but recall Darcy's attentions to Miss Temple, and the initial feelings of satisfaction she felt on observing his jealousy turned to a sort of anger that he felt that he might admire wherever he liked, but that she was off limits to all other men. She raised her eyes to him, watching until his gaze returned to her, and met it with a long and serious look.

Darcy felt a sudden lurch of uncertainty when he caught her gaze. He had become surprisingly comfortable during the previous discussion, which had been sufficiently stimulating to distract him from the combination of pain and pleasure induced by being in Elizabeth's presence. He was under no illusions that she had forgiven him for his behaviour, but she had at least seemed neutral, even a bit teasing, toward him until now. Was she perhaps communicating that the weedy stripling beside her meant something more to her than he did? He gritted his teeth in an effort to control himself.

Mrs. Gardiner interrupted Mr. Brewer's impassioned speech. "I admire your position regarding the abolition of slavery, but I must once again question the basis of your position, which would free all slaves while leaving the majority of them as the *de facto* property of the minority," she said in a dulcet tone which belied the steel underneath.

Elizabeth looked away from Darcy to observe how Mr. Brewer would handle this challenge. She was not disappointed; his colour rose as he said, "My dear Mrs. Gardiner, the basis for abolitionism is the recognition of the evil of holding rational beings as slaves, and the question of the status of women is still open at present. I would personally agree that the present company supports the argument that the educability of women is safe, but I have seen no evidence that this is the rule rather than the exception."

"I am grateful, sir, that you would acknowledge that I am a rational creature," said Elizabeth with an amused smile. "I must wonder, though, whence comes any argument that women cannot be educated; it seems we have a number of instances to prove that women may be educated safely, and no cases at all of women who have been driven mad by learning!" She cast a sly glance at Darcy to see how he bore her radical statement.

"To which I might add," said Mrs. Monkhouse, "that there is a certain danger in entrusting the rearing of children to beings whom you consider both ineducable and irrational! Natural affection cannot coexist with a state of complete dependence."

Mr. Gardiner entered the fray. "Can we, in fact, expect virtue from those who are wholly dependent on the whims of others, be they slaves, women, or children? I would posit that just as our society encourages men to live for their wealth, it encourages vanity, cunning, and manipulation on the part of women who must live by their personal charms, which are now a higher goal than virtue itself."

"I agree that it is unfortunate that women often must rely on their beauty and allures to attract a man, rather than on their moral stature," argued Mr. Brewer fervently. "This is one of the unnatural distinctions of our society, where wealth, beauty, and rank are of greater importance than virtue. However, many men believe their wives' deference to them to be a virtue and a symbol of respect, and in what way is the independence of women a greater virtue than that?"

Elizabeth winced; it did not trouble her to shock Mr. Darcy with radical thought and arguments, but she feared an entrance into the subject of the evils of wealth which would cause a most unpleasant situation. He once again surprised her not only by ignoring the potentially offensive implication but also by entering into the debate.

"I cannot agree that all men would wish for a spaniel-like fawning on the part of their wives. The current expectation is for women to be submissive," he replied thoughtfully, "but I would question the strength of mind of the man who requires a companion he can command at all times, rather than one who may stimulate his mind. I personally do not care for holding conversations with a mirror but rather with another *rational* soul. The very submissiveness of so many women in fact speaks for rather than against their educability, as it is clear that society encourages and reinforces that behaviour in every manner." He was acutely aware of Elizabeth's surprised gaze upon him; he wondered at her reaction, as she of all people should have no doubt as to his inclinations on the matter.

"Well spoken, Mr. Darcy!" cried Mr. Monkhouse. "I also would not wish for a wife who must be treated as a child! "

"And it is very good for you that you do not!" his wife said with good humour, "else you should be sadly disappointed."

"And I shall be sadly disappointed if we cannot continue this fine discussion! Gentlemen, Mrs. Monkhouse, would you do us the honour of joining us for dinner?" Mr. Gardiner said heartily.

Elizabeth drew in a sharp breath and closed her eyes, not wishing to see the look that would cross Darcy's face at the very idea of dining in such company. She opened them to look only at the floor as she heard his demurral, stating that they could not possibly impose on such short notice.

"Well, we shall not press you to stay if you must be away," said Mrs. Gardiner civilly, "but there would be no imposition; unexpected guests are a common enough occurrence here that our cook has the sense to anticipate the likelihood."

With a silent prayer that her aunt would not unknowingly humiliate her further with another invitation which must be abhorrent to a man of such pride, Elizabeth looked to Jane, whose happy smile almost made up for her own discomfort.

"Bingley, what do you say? Bingley!" said Darcy, raising his voice slightly when unable to initially attract his friend's attention.

"Yes?" responded Bingley, tearing his eyes from Jane with a clear effort.

"Mrs. Gardiner has invited us to stay to dinner." Darcy's tone was neutral.

Bingley's face lit up with a radiant smile. "I should be delighted to join you, Mrs. Gardiner, unless Darcy is engaged elsewhere."

"No, I have no fixed engagements," said Darcy. Elizabeth looked up at him in surprise, and he gave her a slight smile of apology. It was obvious that she would prefer him not stay; indeed, he knew that he should have made his excuses, but when pressed he could not convince himself to leave her presence. *God knows when I shall see her again—not until Bingley's wedding, no doubt, if that event should come to pass,* he thought. He did not know whether to hope for or dread such an occurrence; if Bingley turned his eyes elsewhere than Miss Bennet, Darcy could hardly expect to see Elizabeth again, but to be thrown into her company on occasion because of the connection to Bingley would carry not only the exquisitely painful pleasure of seeing her, but the eventual torture of watching her someday fall in love and marry another man—no, that was not an outcome he could desire. At least it appeared that he need not worry about the stripling beside her, judging by her spirited response to his assertions. He did not think he could bear to discover that she was favouring another man just yet.

He was pleasantly surprised to discover that he enjoyed the company at dinner. Being seated between Elizabeth and Mrs. Gardiner was no doubt responsible for a good deal of his pleasure, especially as the former seemed to be in good spirits and ready to tease, even if she did avoid his eyes on occasion. It was enough to be near her, to hear her voice, to catch a whiff of her fragrance drifting past him. He knew that he would never have more than that, and was willing to brave the dreams that were sure to haunt him once again in order to be allowed to pretend for a brief while that all was as it had been between them. It helped that the conversation was stimulating; he could see why Elizabeth enjoyed visiting her aunt and uncle so much, and helped explain her surprising lack of provinciality that he had noted in Hertfordshire. He could find it in himself to regret that the Gardiners and Monkhouses were not of a social stratum to permit continued intercourse.

Elizabeth had abandoned any effort to determine what Mr. Darcy was thinking after his startling acceptance of the invitation to dine at her uncle's house. *There is simply no accounting for it*, she thought. *Although I might like to believe that he has put his pride aside, it is obvious from his attitude on his arrival that this is not the case. He is clearly more than a little whimsical in his feelings about me.* She looked over to see the sheen of joy in Jane's eyes, and with a sudden rush of gratitude, favoured Darcy with a bright smile. She almost immediately regretted the impulse; looking up into his dark eyes brought back memories of his kiss which she was trying to suppress, and an ache deep within her. *If anyone here knew what had passed between us, there would be no answering for the consequences!* she thought, glancing at her uncle, whose views on the need for absolute propriety she knew well, and she bit her lip as a slight blush rose in her cheeks.

The ladies withdrew shortly thereafter, to the relief of Darcy, who had been experiencing desires of a most improper—and no doubt unwelcome—nature since receiving Elizabeth's dazzling smile. He did not know what had prompted it, nor what made her so obviously regret it only a moment later, but it was so much the stuff of his dreams that it was impossible not to carry them further in his mind, to imagine taking her into his arms and feeling her softness against him, to see her face lit with that smile when her hair and clothing were dishevelled from his lovemaking.

It was a welcome distraction therefore when the discussion among the gentlemen turned to a rather heated debate on politics. It seemed to catch Bingley, who had missed much of the earlier conversations, by surprise, and he became stumblingly defensive when Brewer, apparently still in ignorance of the financial worth of Darcy and Bingley, began to espouse extremist positions on the unnatural distinctions of hereditary wealth and privilege. Darcy could sit back and take a more amused position, being both less perturbable and having grown accustomed to this sort of thing during his Cambridge days. When Mr. Gardiner, in his capacity as host, began to attempt to stem the flow of the discourse, Darcy said, "Mr. Brewer, you state that wealth breeds idleness, causing its possessors to neglect the duties incumbent on them, but to this I say that this is as faulty a generalization as that of females being ineducable. Were I to suggest that you, by no further criteria than your class, were an envious sycophant seeking only to earn those same riches, you would by rights call this unfair, yet you are unprepared to admit that there may be those among the more prosperous who do attend to their responsibilities and act in a way driven by virtue. Are there not benevolent legislators and landowners? And by what right do you paint them with the same brush as the indolent and self-indulgent among them?"

"By that same right, Mr. Darcy, that those classes view those beneath them as unworthy and undeserving, and deny the possibility of value and virtue independent of wealth!"

"You think all the upper classes as close-minded as that?" asked Darcy, an eyebrow raised.

"Yes, otherwise why do we find such rigid distinctions between the classes? Why are the merchants of London not invited to the events of the *ton*?"

Recalling with discomfort his words to Elizabeth about the objectionable position of her family and the degradation of his making such a connection, he was forced to admit he had indeed scorned the gentry of Hertfordshire as not being worthy of him for no further reason than their lack of social status, and he could not recall the last time he had been among such mixed company as this—*most likely not since Cambridge, when I would have been ashamed of being able to make such a statement!* he thought. It was painful recognition, especially when he had just experienced a more stimulating evening of discourse among people against whom his pride would have revolted than he had known in years among the *ton*. "I do not claim such understanding for all," he said steadily, "only that it not be discounted of existing." He felt a sudden longing for Elizabeth to be by his side.

Having gained general agreement to the existence of exceptions to the rule, Mr. Gardiner, having observed the changes in Darcy's countenance, turned the discussion to the Peninsular campaign, a subject in which Bingley was more able to hold his own. Darcy retreated into his thoughts, wondering bleakly what had become of the ideals of his younger days.

By the time they rejoined the ladies, Darcy had brought himself to the point of feeling quite unworthy of Elizabeth. Thinking back to some of the misguided things he had said to her on that night in Hunsford, he decided that she had been quite right to refuse him—she deserved far better than him. He did not look at her as they entered, and took a seat as distant from the others as civility allowed, desirous only to be gone as soon as possible.

During this interval Elizabeth's thoughts had been much with him as well, although outwardly she was as happily intent on discussing the meaning of Mr. Bingley's return as the other ladies. She still could make no sense of his behaviour, but recalling how much she had misunderstood him in the past, she was determined not to allow herself to make quick judgments on him again. And she had seen much to admire in him that day, from the appearance of Bingley, which must be credited to his account, to the sentiments he had expressed in the discussions. If he had held himself back initially in his haughty manner, he had also let down some of his guard and treated the others with respect as time went on. With these thoughts, she had allowed herself to anticipate his entrance, unable to deny that her indifference toward him was slipping, only to discover him avoiding her eyes and her company. She could settle it in no way that gave her pleasure.

She resolved not to allow herself to be made unhappy over his vagaries, though, and engaged the others in conversation until Darcy made his excuses to Mrs. Gardiner and collected Bingley. Both Mr. Gardiner and Mr. Monkhouse expressed their pleasure in making their acquaintance, and a hope of seeing them both again in the future.

Elizabeth, pursuant to her aunt's direction, silently joined Jane to see the gentlemen to their carriage. If Darcy wished to be withdrawn and quiet, she resolved, she would not challenge it. Their silence provided a vivid contrast to Bingley, who was brushing the edges of propriety in his closeness to Jane and the intimacy of his tone to her. It was not until they were outside the door that Elizabeth bade Darcy good night in the manner she would employ for a casual acquaintance.

The sight of Jane and Bingley gazing into one another's eyes was more than Darcy's spirits could bear after his recent revelations. "I hope I have not troubled you with my presence, Miss Bennet," he said with the bitter taste of defeat in his mouth. "It had been my intention on leaving Rosings to bring Bingley here before your arrival, but unfortunately, he did not return to town until yesterday. I do not imagine that he will have any difficulty in returning on his own."

So he had, in fact, wished to avoid her altogether. *That should hardly come as a surprise,* she reprimanded herself on feeling a stab of pain at the idea, reminding herself that she had no reason to desire his good opinion, nor he any reason to give it. She lifted her chin and forced herself to look him in the eye while Bingley was exchanging some soft, intense words with Jane. "You have not troubled me in the slightest, sir, and I have not yet had the opportunity to thank you for the book," she said.

Darcy looked uncomfortable. When she looked up at him like that, it was impossible for him to forget the sensation of her lips beneath his. "If you enjoy it, Miss Bennet, that is the only thanks I could desire."

"I do enjoy it," she said quietly. "It was generous of you."

He closed his eyes for a moment as if in pain. The cover of darkness combined with the frankness of the earlier discussions seemed to give him a certain permission to be more direct than he might have been in other circumstances. "Miss Bennet, it was not *generous* of me. I wanted to give you all that is mine, but to my misfortune, I discovered that I only possessed two things which you wanted: another chance for Mr. Bingley and your sister, and a book." He paused for a deep breath, and took her hand for the last time. "I hope you enjoy them in good health, and that you someday find all the happiness which you deserve. Goodbye, Miss Bennet." His voice carried finality as he raised her hand to his lips and kissed it lightly, trying to store the sensation in his memory. He turned and strode to the carriage without looking back, with Bingley following closely at his heels.

"Goodbye," said a stricken Elizabeth softly to the empty air before her, wondering more than ever if she had known what she was about when she refused him.

As soon as the carriage drove away, Jane caught Elizabeth's arm with excitement. "Oh, Lizzy, he asked if he could call tomorrow! He said that he had never known I was in London until Mr. Darcy had told him. And when I told him we were returning to Longbourn soon, he said that he was considering a return to Netherfield. Lizzy, it cannot be true, can it?"

Elizabeth forced a smile to her lips. "I am certain it *is* true!," she said. "My dearest Jane, I think you are in very great danger of making him as much in love with you as ever." *And I am in grave danger of regretting that which I might have had, if only I had been wiser in my discernments,* she thought remorsefully, before taking her sister's arm affectionately with every intent of portraying good cheer for Jane's sake despite the loss she was feeling in her heart.

Chapter 4

Bingley was as good as his word, and indeed called at the Gardiners' house again the following day, and appeared more enamoured of Jane than ever. Elizabeth had no doubt that matters would be speedily resolved between them, now that Darcy had apparently given his blessing to the union. What this meant for *her* was more questionable; although she was longing to acquaint Jane with the events at Rosings and to receive her comfort, she no longer felt that she could justify it. The relief that she would feel at sharing her story with Jane could not be balanced by the sense of violating Darcy's confidence; to all appearances he would not be a former acquaintance but rather the best friend of her husband. Nor did she wish to place Jane in an uncomfortable position when the eventuality would arise of Darcy and herself being together in her company, as was certain to happen at some point or other if the match proceeded. With regret she came to the conclusion that prudence forbade the disclosure.

It was only a few days later that the young ladies set out together from Gracechurch-street for the town of _____ in Hertfordshire; and, as they drew near the appointed inn where Mr. Bennet's carriage was to meet them, they quickly perceived, in token of the coachman's punctuality, both Kitty and Lydia looking out of a dining room upstairs. These two girls had been above an hour in the place, happily employed in visiting an opposite milliner, watching the sentinel on guard, and dressing a salad and cucumber.

After welcoming their sisters, they triumphantly displayed a table set out with such cold meat as an inn larder usually affords, exclaiming, "Is not this nice? is not this an agreeable surprise?"

"And we mean to treat you all," added Lydia; "but you must lend us the money, for we have just spent ours at the shop out there." Then showing her purchase, she said, "Look here, I have bought this bonnet. I do not think it is very pretty; but I thought I might as well buy it as not. I shall pull it to pieces as soon as I get home, and see if I can make it up any better."

And when her sisters abused it as ugly, she added, with perfect uncon-cern, "Oh! but there were two or three much uglier in the shop; and when I have bought some prettier coloured satin to trim it with fresh, I think it will be very tolerable."

Elizabeth could not help thinking of the company she had left, both in Gracechurch Street and at Rosings Park, and how favourably it compared to that of her younger sisters. Their manner of speech and insensibility grated on her ears now even more than it had in the past, reminding her once again of Darcy's letter and his cutting description of the defects of her family. How had she ever tolerated it?

Lydia continued, "Besides, it will not much signify what one wears this summer after the _____shire have left Meryton, and they are going in a fortnight."

"Are they indeed?" cried Elizabeth, with the greatest satisfaction.

"They are going to be encamped near Brighton; and I do so want papa to take us all there for the summer! It would be such a delicious scheme, and I dare say would hardly cost any thing at all. Mamma would like to go too, of all things! Only think what a miserable summer else we shall have!"

Yes, thought Elizabeth, that would be a delightful scheme, indeed, and completely do for us at once. Good Heaven! Brighton, and a whole camp-ful of soldiers, to us, who have been overset already by one poor regiment of militia, and the monthly balls of Meryton.

"Now I have got some news for you," said Lydia, as they sat down to table. "What do you think? It is excellent news, capital news, and about a certain person that we all like."

Jane and Elizabeth looked at each other, and the waiter was told that he need not stay. Lydia laughed, and said, "Aye, that is just like your formal-ity and discretion. You thought the waiter must not hear, as if he cared! I dare say he often hears worse things said than I am going to say. But he is an ugly fellow! I am glad he is gone. I never saw such a long chin in my life. Well, but now for my news: it is about dear Wickham; too good for the waiter, is not it? There is no danger of Wickham's marrying Mary King. There's for you! She is gone down to her uncle at Liverpool; gone to stay. Wickham is safe."

"And Mary King is safe!" added Elizabeth; then, considering the need for discretion, she added, "Safe from a connection imprudent as to fortune."

"She is a great fool for going away, if she liked him."

"But I hope there is no strong attachment on either side," said Jane.

"I am sure there is not on his. I will answer for it he never cared three straws about her. Who could about such a nasty little freckled thing?"

Elizabeth was shocked to think that, however incapable of such coarseness of *expression* herself, the coarseness of the *sentiment* was little other than her own breast had formerly harboured and fancied liberal! To think that the habits of her family had affected her, and her all unknowing! Her colour rose as she realized how ill-bred her thoughts had been.

How pleasant it had been to be away from the ill manners and indecorum of her family, to be among people of sense and intelligence! With a strangely painful sensation, she was forced to acknowledge that she had been the one to reject the opportunity to spend her life with such a person, and for her foolishness in that she was now condemned to return to the follies of her family. She could not help but to rail at herself once again for the thoughtless misjudgment and prejudice against Mr. Darcy that had blinded her to his finer qualities until it was too late. An image of the look on his face when she had last seen him, saying his final goodbye in Gracechurch Street, came to her with a pang which startled her by its intensity.

As soon as all had ate, and the elder ones paid, the carriage was ordered; and, after some contrivance, the whole party, with all their boxes, workbags, and parcels, and the unwelcome addition of Kitty's and Lydia's purchases, were seated in it. Lydia, assisted by Kitty, gave foolish histories of their parties and good jokes, all of which embarrassed Elizabeth deeply, in an endeavour to amuse her companions all the way to Longbourn. Elizabeth listened as little as she could, but there was no escaping the frequent mention of Wickham's name, which could bring her only more pain on behalf of her behaviour toward Mr. Darcy.

Their reception at home was most kind. Mrs. Bennet rejoiced to see

Jane in undiminished beauty; and more than once during dinner did Mr. Bennet say voluntarily to Elizabeth, "I am glad you are come back, Lizzy."

She took advantage of their return to Longbourn to acquaint Jane that night with what she had learned of Wickham, disguising only the circumstances in which she received her knowledge. It was some comfort to her, but what a stroke was this for poor Jane, who would willingly have gone through the world without believing that so much wickedness existed in the whole race of mankind, as was here collected in one individual. Nor was Darcy's vindication, though grateful to her feelings, capable of consoling her for such discovery. Most earnestly did she labour to prove the probability of error, and seek to clear one, without involving the other.

'This will not do," said Elizabeth. "You never will be able to make both of them good for any thing. Take your choice, but you must be satisfied with only one. There is but such a quantity of merit between them; just enough to make one good sort of man; and of late it has been shifting about pretty much. For my part, I am inclined to believe it all Mr. Darcy's, but you shall do as you choose."

It was some time, however, before a smile could be extorted from Jane.

The tumult of Elizabeth's mind continued despite ridding herself of this secret, and she found herself often considering just how much merit she wished to attribute to Mr. Darcy. As lamentations over the impending departure of the regiment began resounding through Longbourn-house, she felt anew the justice of Mr. Darcy's objections; and never had she before been so much disposed to pardon his interference in the views of his friend. Lydia's insistence on travelling to Brighton in the company of Mrs. Forster and her father's refusal to heed her secret advice against letting her go only confirmed these feelings in her.

She considered as well all that she had learned of Darcy in the two weeks following his ill-fated proposal, coming to greater respect for his understanding and talents, and his ability to challenge her as an equal. At this distance from him, less confused by his frequent shifts of behaviour, she discovered that she could acknowledge the full depth of his affection for her, and compared it with his admirable loyalty to those he cared for. She was not blinded to his faults, to his continuing haughty manners and changes in temper, but after seeing him at the Gardiners' house, she no longer considered his manners to be irremediable, and recognized that some of his incomprehensible changes of spirits were a response to the distress of his feelings for her.

She frequently perused his letter, dwelling more on the understanding shown in it, and most particularly feeling the charity in the adieu, so like his final words to her in Gracechurch Street. More and more often she found herself returning to the memory of his kiss, and the feelings it evoked were no longer strangers to her. She longed to experience it again, and then doubted she ever should; and felt shame for her immoral longings.

She had felt the finality of his goodbye to her and wondered to what extent he might even at that moment be dismissing her from his memory. Certainly she had given him no reason to cherish tender sentiments toward her, a matter of increasing regret for her as time went on. What a triumph for him, she often thought, could he know that the proposals which she had proudly spurned only a few weeks previously might be received very differently now! He was as generous, she doubted not, as the most generous of his sex. But while he was mortal, there must be a triumph.

She passed many an hour wondering what might come to pass when they met again, and whether she would have the power to bring about the renewal of his addresses, or whether he would regard her with the coldness and distance she knew that she deserved for her treatment of him. That they would meet again seemed a matter of little doubt now, as Bingley had, as promised, returned to Netherfield but two weeks after their own return, unaccompanied this time by either sisters or friend. It was a matter of great delight, if no surprise, when Jane came to her professing herself to be the happiest creature in the world.

"'Tis too much!" she added, "by far too much. I do not deserve it. Oh! why is not every body as happy?"

Elizabeth's congratulations were given with a sincerity, a warmth, a delight, which words could but poorly express. Every sentence of kindness was a fresh source of happiness to Jane. But she would not allow herself to stay with her sister, or say half that remained to be said for the present.

"I must go instantly to my mother;" she cried. "I would not on any account trifle with her affectionate solicitude; or allow her to hear it from any one but myself. He is gone to my father already. Oh! Lizzy, to know that what I have to relate will give such pleasure to all my dear family! how shall I bear so much happiness!" She then hastened away to her mother, who was sitting upstairs with Kitty.

Elizabeth, who was left by herself, now smiled at the rapidity and ease with which an affair was finally settled, that had given them so many previous months of suspense and vexation. "And this," said she, "is the end of all his friend's anxious circumspection! of all his sister's falsehood and contrivance! the happiest, wisest, most reasonable end!" Even in her delight for Jane, she could not help wondering whether there could ever be any such end for her and Mr. Darcy, or if their ending had already been played out.

In a few minutes she was joined by Bingley, whose conference with her father had been short and to the purpose.

"Where is your sister?" said he hastily, as he opened the door.

"With my mother up stairs. She will be down in a moment, I dare say."

He then shut the door, and, coming up to her, claimed the good wishes and affection of a sister. Elizabeth honestly and heartily expressed her delight in the prospect of their relationship. They shook hands with great cordiality; and then, till her sister came down, she had to listen to all he had to say of his own happiness, and of Jane's perfections; and in spite of his being a lover, Elizabeth really believed all his expectations of felicity to be rationally founded, because they had for basis the excellent understanding, and super-excellent disposition of Jane, and a general similarity of feeling and taste between her and himself.

Elizabeth was now left more than ever to her thoughts, as she had now but little time for conversation with her sister; for while he was present, Jane had no attention to bestow on any one else; but she found herself considerably useful to both of them in those hours of separation that must sometimes occur. In the absence of Jane, he always attached himself to Elizabeth, for the pleasure of talking of her; and when Bingley was gone, Jane constantly sought the same means of relief.

When her thoughts came to be too much for her, she found an escape in anticipating her tour to the Lakes. It was now the object of her happiest thoughts; it was her best consolation for all the uncomfortable hours which the absence of Jane, the discontentedness of Kitty, and her memories of Darcy made inevitable. The time fixed for the beginning of their Northern tour was now fast approaching; and a fortnight only was wanting of it, when a letter arrived from Mrs. Gardiner, which at once delayed its commencement and curtailed its extent. Mr. Gardiner would be prevented by business from setting out till a fortnight later in July, and must be in

London again within a month; and as that left too short a period for them to go so far, and see so much as they had proposed, or at least to see it with the leisure and comfort they had built on, they were obliged to give up the Lakes, and substitute a more contracted tour; and, according to the present plan, were to go no farther northward than Derbyshire. In that county, there was enough to be seen to occupy the chief of their three weeks; and to Mrs. Gardiner it had a peculiarly strong attraction. The town where she had formerly passed some years of her life, and where they were now to spend a few days, was probably as great an object of her curiosity, as all the celebrated beauties of Derby, Chatsworth, Dovedale, or the Peak.

Elizabeth was excessively disappointed; she had set her heart on seeing the Lakes; and still thought there might have been time enough. With the mention of Derbyshire, there were many ideas connected. It was impossible for her to see the word without thinking of Pemberley and its owner. "But surely," said she, "I may enter his county with impunity, and rob it of a few petrified spars without his perceiving me."

The period of expectation was now doubled. Four weeks were to pass away before her uncle and aunt's arrival, and Elizabeth set herself to enjoying them as best she could. There was much planning to be done already for Jane's wedding, although the date was more than two months off, and this activity employed many of her idle hours. It was but a week until the beginning of her tour that Bingley mentioned to her in passing that he was anticipating a visit from Darcy.

This intelligence set her pulses aflutter both with excitement and trepidation, and it was with frustration that she eventually elicited from Bingley that his arrival was scheduled for the very day of her departure. The coincidence was such that she was forced to wonder if he had known of her trip when he made his plans to visit Netherfield, but she could think of no way to ask Bingley if he had mentioned her itinerary to his friend. After many hours of agonizing over this question, she finally admitted to herself that she would have no means to answer it until her return—if he departed Netherfield again prior to that, she could have no further doubt that he was avoiding her. The pain that this prospect gave her was considerable, and her pleasure in anticipating her tour was much diminished by these circumstances.

On the day before the Gardiners were due to reach Longbourn, the time of Bingley's usual arrival for his daily visit came and went. Elizabeth was needed in attending to Jane's anxiety for this unusual circumstance, while Kitty and Mary, after listening to Jane's concerns over the accidents which might have befallen him for the third time, decided to seek their felicity elsewhere; Kitty with a visit to Maria Lucas, and Mary with a book in her room. Elizabeth was hardly concerned, given the number of matters which might have delayed him, but obediently went to the window regularly to check if he was coming into sight. It was with no little anxiety that she saw on finally discovering his approach that he was accompanied by Mr. Darcy.

The colour which had been driven from her face, returned for half a minute with an additional glow, and a smile of delight added lustre to her eyes, as she thought for that space of time, that his affection and wishes might still be unshaken. But she would not be secure.

"Let me first see how he behaves," said she; "it will then be early enough for expectation."

She sat intently at work, striving to be composed, and without daring to lift up her eyes. On the gentlemen's appearing, her colour increased, and she ventured only one glance at Darcy. He looked serious as usual, but his gaze rested on her before being received by Mrs. Bennet with cold and ceremonious politeness. Elizabeth blushed again for her mother's lack of graces, knowing it would only confirm his view of her family.

Darcy, after enquiring of her how Mr. and Mrs. Gardiner did, said scarcely anything. He was not seated by her; perhaps that was the reason of his silence. Several minutes elapsed without bringing the sound of his voice; but when occasionally, unable to resist the impulse of curiosity, she raised her eyes to his face, she found him looking at her thoughtfully. She could not begin to guess what was in his mind; his face betrayed no sign of either anger or tender feelings.

Resolved not to be passive, she made an enquiry after his sister. "Georgiana is quite well, thank you," he responded civilly. "She greatly enjoyed your company in Kent, Miss Bennet, and regretted the interruption of the acquaintance."

"As did I," said Elizabeth gravely. "Pray give her my best regards, when next you see her." She could not look at him without remembering the intimacy of his kiss, and colour rose in her cheeks at the thought.

"Thank you, Miss Bennet; I shall do so," he replied, then lapsed into silence again.

Elizabeth was now left in an agony of uncertainty. She knew not what to make of his behaviour, and she feared her desire to see partiality on his part might lead her to suppose more than actually existed. She bit her lip, unaware of the effect of that small action on the gentleman opposite her. If only she could give him some indication of her changed position—but that would violate all the rules of propriety, which dictated that the approach must always come from the gentleman. *He proposed to me, kissed me, told me that he wanted to give me everything he had—what sort of expression do I think is required to feel certain of his interest?* she demanded of herself. *If he can do that, surely it is not forbidden to smile at him!*

Feeling all the anxiety of her position, she looked up again and waited until she had caught his eye. Her heart pounding at her audacity, she smiled at him in what she hoped to be an affectionate manner. She could see his indrawn breath from across the room, and boldly held his gaze as a new warmth lit his eyes. It was too much; she had to look away before she was caught in his look, but her eyes were drawn back to him as though by magnetism. A slight smile touched his mouth, and a shiver went through her. *How can it feel so much like he is kissing me when all he is doing is looking at me?*

"Lizzy!" Jane's voice shattered her reverie. She looked away, startled.

"Forgive me, Jane; I was woolgathering," she said apologetically.

"So it would seem," said Jane with a smile. "Mr. Bingley and I are going to take a turn around the garden."

Elizabeth longed to join them—anything to break the building tension, but she could hardly leave her mother alone with Mr. Darcy, and the idea of asking him to come with this between them frankly frightened her. She smiled apologetically at Jane and bade her enjoy the sunshine.

"Well, Mr. Darcy," said Mrs. Bennet sharply as soon as the engaged couple had left the room, "they certainly do make a lovely pair, do they not?" Her voice dared him to disagree.

"Indeed, Mrs. Bennet," he said very civilly. "I have rarely seen Bingley so happy. They are very well matched."

Elizabeth, a bit surprised by his calm response to her mother's barb, joined in. "It is a comfort to us all that she will be no further than Netherfield, as we will miss Jane sorely."

Darcy gave her a questioning glance, but said nothing, and Mrs. Bennet, after several minutes of silence in the company of her least favourite daughter and a man she had always despised, excused herself on the pretext of needing to speak to the cook.

Elizabeth could not credit that her mother had left her alone with Mr. Darcy. *At least I have the assurance that it is not with any matchmaking intent on her part!* she thought with amused anxiety. This was even more worrisome than a turn around the garden. She did not know what to say; she was afraid to even look at him. Blindly she reached for a new embroidery thread, but in the clumsiness of trepidation she instead knocked the small basket of threads to the floor.

He will indeed be impressed to find you turned into a quivering idiot the moment you are left alone! she scolded herself. Her colour high, she bent to collect the threads, but Darcy was there before her, kneeling to gather them neatly into the basket. A frisson went through her at his nearness. "My thanks, Mr. Darcy," she said as he handed it to her. For a moment as she took it her hand covered his, and the touch was a burning sensation which seemed to draw her inexorably closer to him even as it increased her apprehension. Almost involuntarily, she looked up to meet his eyes, which were gazing at her with a dark intensity. She knew that her face was unable to hide her feelings or her desire for his touch, and the increasing heat of his gaze only added to her sensibility.

He stroked her cheek lightly with his thumb, igniting a fire within her. "Elizabeth," he whispered, "do not look at me so unless you mean it; I do not think I could bear it if you changed your mind." He drew his finger lightly across her lips and down her neck before bringing his hand to rest at the nape, the softness of her curls caressing his fingers.

She struggled to find the words to tell him that her feelings were not so inconstant as that, but she seemed to have been stricken dumb by the power of his touch, and instead somehow found herself raising her lips towards his in an invitation which he accepted without hesitation. She was flooded by sensation as his lips touched hers, first gently and then with an increasing urgency as all the tightly contained need of the last three months rose to the surface. The basket dropped to the floor unheeded as he gathered her into his arms.

She fit against him even more perfectly than he had imagined, and as her arms went around his neck, his only rational thought was that his life would never be fuller than it was at this moment. A fierce desire rose in him in powerful waves, and he struggled to hold himself back lest he frighten her. Tearing his lips from hers, he covered her face with kisses. Reaching her ear, he murmured fervently, "Dearest, dearest Elizabeth, I have waited so long for this!"

Elizabeth, feeling as if she too had been yearning for this moment for an eternity, gave in to the urge to press herself even closer against him. The exquisite sensation of his body against hers created a need she could never have imagined; and, as his mouth trailed a line of fire beneath her ear and down her neck, she felt as if she were melting into him. She could not be close enough to him, she thought, an inexplicable ache beginning to grow deep inside her. How had she ever denied that this was what she needed and wanted?

Her response excited him almost beyond the boundaries of his control. He recaptured her mouth, drinking deeply of the intoxicating taste and feel of her, knowing that he could never get enough of her, when the sound of approaching footsteps somehow penetrated his desire-fogged mind.

He pulled away sharply and strode rapidly to the window, turning his back to the door to give himself an extra moment to regain his composure. The passion racing through him was difficult enough to quell, but there was no suppressing the exultant feeling of success he felt at the discovery that Elizabeth—well, he was not exactly certain whether Elizabeth's behaviour constituted an acknowledgment of acceptance, of caring, or of love, but any of these would be quite acceptable to him.

Elizabeth felt suddenly bereft when he released her, unable to understand the reason for his behaviour until Mary entered the room a moment later. She was flustered both by what had just taken place and by her sister's appearance, as if she would be able to ascertain immediately what had taken place between them. To cover her discomposure, she leaned down to pick up the basket and made a show of looking through it for the right thread.

Mary greeted them both curtly before sitting down with her book. It was evident from her attitude that she had been sent by Mrs. Bennet to serve as a chaperone for Elizabeth, and also that she felt there could be no couple in all England less in need of chaperonage than the one before her. Elizabeth hid a smile at the thought of the shock that her family would receive when they learned the truth of her feelings for Mr. Darcy. She looked up through her lashes at him as he stood looking out the window as he had so often during the course of their acquaintance, but on this occasion he seemed to feel her gaze upon him and turned to her, a new warmth lighting his eyes. She coloured as he regarded her, guessing on what his thoughts turned.

Her own feelings were in such disorder as to render her temporarily incapable of coherent speech. That he should still be in love with her after all her cruel and thoughtless words, her refusal, and all that had passed between them! It was not just gratitude she felt, but the relief of knowing her own growing affection for him to be reciprocated, and that it was not too late for them to begin again. And that he should arouse such feelings of abandon in her—had she not already been blushing fiercely, she should have begun again at the embarrassment of acknowledging her wanton behaviour, and the pleasure he had apparently taken in it. It was clear from his affect that he regretted not a moment of it.

Darcy recovered himself sooner than she, and crossed to sit beside her. "Miss Bennet, I understand that you will be undertaking some travel soon," he said, his tones caressing her.

"Yes, my aunt and uncle are kind enough to be taking me on a tour of Derbyshire," she replied, her eyes playful as she announced their destination.

He smiled, more of a real smile than she had ever seen from him before. "I hope you will be pleased by Derbyshire. It has many beauties."

"It has much to recommend it, sir; I have no doubt that I shall like it quite well," she said demurely, enjoying the game of double meanings.

"I understand you will be travelling to Lambton? That is quite near Pemberley."

"So I understand, sir."

"I regret that I will not be there to receive you, but perhaps we will have another opportunity for that some day." His eyes spoke a further message.

"I should enjoy that very much, Mr. Darcy," she replied, meeting his gaze with her own. His smile grew slightly warmer, and seemed to communicate that were they alone, he would be doing something far more intimate than just smiling at her.

"You honour me, Miss Bennet."

Mary glanced up from her book suspiciously, having observed that the conversation was far more civil than she would expect between Mr. Darcy and Lizzy, but as nothing seemed amiss, she returned to her reading.

Not wishing to raise further suspicions, Elizabeth took care to make her voice more neutral. "My aunt and uncle will arrive here tomorrow, and then we depart early the following morning." She looked to see his reaction to this intelligence.

"So I understand. I believe you will be much missed here." *Very much missed*, he thought, still unable to credit the unexpected change in her sentiments. When he had decided to come to Netherfield earlier than his initial plan, he had been giving in against his better judgment to his helpless longing to be in her presence. He thanked heaven for what he had perceived as his weakness in being unable to stay away from her. He experienced a sudden powerful need to hold her again, and had to force himself not to steal her away contrary to all propriety. Or perhaps he could even speak to her father before she left—but no, he wanted to make his addresses to her properly this time, to make up for the previous disaster. It would have to wait until he had a suitable opportunity to speak to her privately, if he could manage to keep his hands off her lovely body long enough to say his piece.

She wondered at the flash of humour in his eyes, but the reappearance of Bingley and Jane forestalled any opportunity to explore it.

They had no further opportunity for private conversation that day; even though Darcy was invited to dinner, he was almost as far from her as the table could divide them. Darcy's gaze when he looked at her spoke promises, though, and kept feelings of deprivation away. It was not until the carriage had been called for the Netherfield gentlemen that they had the occasion to speak to one another again, although even that was under the eyes of Mrs. Bennet.

"I enjoyed our conversation this afternoon very much, Miss Bennet. I hope we will have the opportunity to continue it on your return," said Darcy, his voice full of meaning.

"Thank you, sir," she replied with a curtsey. He debated the wisdom of kissing her hand, but regretfully decided that it would not be appropriate with her family around her. He limited himself to a correct bow, but with a look in his eyes that promised much more.

Elizabeth looked after him wistfully, thinking how long the oft-anticipated coming weeks would seem now. What a shock it would be for her family when she returned and Mr. Darcy revealed his intentions! Even Jane had no suspicion of her feelings, she was sure. Anticipating missing him already, she knew rather than felt herself to be happy, but it was such a relief from her many weeks of wondering whether there was, in fact, a future in which they could provide an example of connubial bliss that her spirits felt quite light.

Darcy's spirits were jubilant as he rode away from Longbourn. He did not understand what had happened to cause the change in Elizabeth, but the mere fact of having won her affection was all he needed. To think that he had almost not come to Longbourn at all! His original itinerary had been planned to arrive at Netherfield after Elizabeth's departure, and to leave prior to her return, thus avoiding scenes painful to them both. But as the time grew near, his desire to see her became overwhelming, even if only to hear her voice and experience her liveliness. He had no hopes of anything further; he had given those up that night watching her laugh with Colonel Fitzwilliam after she had fled from him. He had known, though, that she would never stop haunting his dreams and that he would never find a woman who could stimulate and challenge him the way Elizabeth could. God knows he had tried; he had never realized before meeting her how deeply alone he had felt all his life. He had a cadre of loyal friends, but many of them, like Bingley, depended more on him than the other way around, and those with whom he shared his feelings were very few. Elizabeth was the first person—the only person—whom he had ever felt could meet him on equal grounds and accept him for who he was, and her refusal of his proposal only ended up confirming this for him.

Having had his attention drawn to this gap in his life and recognizing the value a steady woman could provide for Georgiana, he had duly attended balls and soirees, making efforts to meet appropriate young ladies. He had mingled, chatted, danced and played cards with one woman after another. Most could not even begin to catch his interest; a few seemed intelligent enough, but constantly submitted their views to him for his approval. One was even playful, though not particularly clever. But none of them could capture his heart as Elizabeth had done so easily, and finally he had given up.

In fact, he had given up on more than the ladies of the *ton*, he had lost any interest in the entire society. After his evening at the Gardiners', he had received several invitations to similar gatherings, first by Mr. Monkhouse, and then as his interest became more generally known, others of that circle as well as the few well-born intellectuals in London began to include him as well. He went at first out of curiosity, then made the discovery that he far preferred to be valued for his contribution to the discussion than for his wealth or lands. It gave him something he had lacked for years, at least since he had left university and perhaps even longer, a sense of who Fitzwilliam Darcy was as separate from the Master of Pemberley. And he recognized that this was part of what he valued in Elizabeth as well—that she would never give him deference for his social standing; he had to earn his place with her.

That thought led him full circle to where he had begun—how *had* he earned her favour? They had parted on terms that were hardly cordial, yet now she was inviting his advances—what could have changed? And, even more importantly, could it change again if he made a misstep?

Chapter 5

The following day Mr. and Mrs. Gardiner, with their four children, appeared at Longbourn. They were to stay there only one night, and set off the next morning. The children, two girls of six and eight years old, and two younger boys, were to be left under the care of their cousins; although Jane was the general favourite, whose steady sense and sweetness of temper exactly adapted her for attending to them in every way, her impending nuptials forbade her from being in primary care of them.

If her thoughts were more at Netherfield than Longbourn, it did not affect Elizabeth's ability to enjoy playing with her young cousins. It gave her pleasure to see their delight in the country air as they ran about, urging her to join in their games. She relearned the skill of her younger days at graces at least sufficiently to provide a challenge to the eldest girl, then turned the sticks over to the younger of them, watching them play until the elder Master Gardiner, already autocratic at the advanced age of four, demanded a game of hide and seek in the shrubbery behind the house. Elizabeth volunteered to take the first stint at seeking, and had closed her eyes and begun to count when she heard a deep voice murmur from behind her, "Good afternoon, Elizabeth."

She felt a light kiss on her neck which tingled throughout her body. It was as if his presence had awoken her; suddenly her every sense was more active and alert. "You are quite bold today, Mr. Darcy," she responded, colouring becomingly.

"Not so bold as I should like to be," he replied daringly, "but I suspect that your cousins have sharp eyes." He moved to stand immediately behind her, so close that their bodies touched lightly.

How could his mere touch affect me so? she wondered, exhilarated by the sensations running through her. She opened her eyes and glanced over her shoulder at him with a smile. "I had not expected the pleasure of your company today, sir."

He succeeded at looking both embarrassed and self-satisfied at the same moment. "I should not have come, I know, to interrupt such a family gathering, but I fear that I could not stay away. I manufactured the excuse of a message for Bingley which I could deliver on my way to town."

A shiver went through her as she felt his breath against her cheek, and, looking even more smug than before, he placed a hand on her waist. Elizabeth raised an eyebrow to cover any further evidence of her susceptibility to his advances. "Sir, I believe that I have a task before me to which I must attend," she said playfully.

He gave her a half-smile as she walked about the garden, passing directly before the hiding place of a giggling child three times before coming to discover him to his delight. The others were found with alacrity, and another round begun. "Cousin Lizzy, *you* must hide now," said the eldest in a tone of patience appropriate for dealing with the vagaries of adults.

"Very well." Turning to Darcy, Elizabeth said with a mischievous glint in her eyes, "Come, sir, were you not attending? We must hide!"

His eyes widened slightly. "I must as well?" He was not accustomed to the games of children; this was a foreign country to him.

"I insist, sir!" she exclaimed. Taking him boldly by the hand, she led him with an infectious smile to a recessed nook behind a line of hedge.

Darcy, now quite able to perceive the advantages of this game, gathered her into his arms and began to taste the delights of her lips like a man starved for drink in the desert. Already stirred by his previous caresses, Elizabeth was ready to find her pleasure in his kisses, and slid her arms around his neck. Her playfulness, which had always attracted his desire, had only made him want her more, and he became increasingly insistent, asking and receiving a response which could only arouse him further. She was breathless by the time he released her lips, only to continue his caresses along the lines of her neck and shoulder.

Elizabeth found it difficult to credit how agreeable she was finding this activity which she knew would bring a blush of shame to her cheeks all too soon. She reassured herself by considering that Mr. Darcy was clearly far from troubled by her behaviour, and in fact seemed quite prepared to take advantage of it to the fullest. She gasped at the exhilarating sensation as he delicately trailed his lips down her neck, his hands at her back encouraging her to arch against him. How had she failed to notice his magnetism all these months?

"How long can we expect before they find us?" Darcy growled against her ear. His fingers drifted to explore the curve of her breast, creating a delirious melting sensation inside her.

Elizabeth's breath caught as exquisite feelings of pleasure rushed through her at his intimate touch. The experience was intoxicating, but she retained enough sense of self to reluctantly realize that she might have unleashed more than she could manage. "Not long, I fear," she said, hoping that her voice sounded steadier than she felt with his hand caressing her ever more intimately. The depth of reaction he seemed able to elicit from her with such ease, as well as the behaviour that reaction caused her to permit, was beginning to alarm her—she was beginning to understand all too well how women could be susceptible to seduction.

Darcy discovered he had entered into a dilemma—he desperately wanted to keep touching Elizabeth and to feel her hands upon him, but it was obvious that she was becoming uncomfortable with his attentions—*though she clearly enjoys them!* he thought exuberantly. He decided he had best slow his demands before he was told to stop, and reluctantly drew her head onto his shoulder. "My loveliest Elizabeth," he whispered.

She heard the sound of laughing voices coming in their direction, but the happiness she felt as he held her close to him was such that it was some moments before she could bring herself to pull away. Fortunately she was still in time to avoid being caught in a compromising position by the children, and she gave Darcy a laughing look which went some way toward reassuring him that he had not unduly disturbed her with his advances.

"I suppose that I should pay my respects to your aunt and uncle," Darcy said to her as they emerged from behind the hedge, reluctant to leave her company. "Will you go with me?"

She agreed, although somewhat anxious about the proposition of exposing him to her massed family. She could have no complaints at his response to them, though; he was perfectly civil even to Mrs. Philips, who could not keep herself from several tactless comments. Elizabeth's astonishment was extreme; and continually was she repeating, *Why is he so altered? From what can it proceed? It cannot be for me, it cannot be for my sake that his manners are thus softened. My reproofs at Hunsford could not work such a change as this.* Darcy further greeted Mr. and Mrs. Gardiner with every evidence of genuine pleasure, and Elizabeth was startled during the course of their conversation to discover that he had apparently been in company with them on some occasion since his visit to Gracechurch Street. She was exceedingly curious about this revelation, but no explanation seemed forthcoming, and she saw nothing to justify an inquiry on her part. Darcy's final departure, with a look that caressed her as much as his hands had done earlier, left her blushing, and her aunt and uncle with an idea in their minds as to a certain gentleman's apparent admiration of their niece.

It is not the function of this work to give a description of Derbyshire, nor of any of the remarkable places through which their route thither lay; Oxford, Blenheim, Warwick, Kenelworth, Birmingham, &c. are sufficiently known. Their travelling provided a time of reflection for Elizabeth, especially as they came to the little town of Lambton, the scene of Mrs. Gardiner's former residence. She could not help recalling that she was but a few miles from the place which she anticipated calling home, and she eagerly sought out each change in the landscape as a signpost to her future. In Lambton she considered that she would likely see the town many times in the future, and it was only with the greatest of efforts that she kept from confiding her hopes to her aunt. Her hesitation came not only from a sense of propriety that she should not discuss the matter until her father's consent was obtained, but also from the slightest of fears that she had difficulty even admitting to herself, which sprung from her realization that during their meetings at Longbourn, he had expressed admiration and desire, but not a word of love or marriage. She had faith in his sense of honour, and did not truly believe that he would toy with her, but the thought, once having entered her head, was not to be shaken. It was a thought, however, exactly calculated to make her understand her own wishes.

She delighted in slyly inquiring of the townspeople she met as to the character of the master of Pemberley. They had nothing to accuse him of but pride; pride he probably had, and if not, it would certainly be imputed by the inhabitants of a small market-town, where the family did not visit. It was acknowledged, however, that he was a liberal man, and did much good among the poor.

One morning Mrs. Gardiner, whose curiosity regarding the relationship between Mr. Darcy and her niece had not been satisfied, decided to test the waters by raising the subject of that gentleman herself. "It is a great pity, Lizzy," she said, "that we may not visit Pemberley. Should not you like to see a place of which we have heard so much? If it were merely a fine house richly furnished, I should not care about it myself; but the grounds are delightful. They have some of the finest woods in the country. Were we not acquainted with Mr. Darcy, we could see it as we have seen the other great houses. But perhaps you, as a friend of Miss Darcy, might someday be invited there."

"My acquaintance with her is really quite trifling," said Elizabeth carefully. "But all reports that I have heard do indeed suggest that Pemberley is lovely." She longed to ask her aunt regarding her further contact with Mr. Darcy, but felt the danger of appearing to take too great an interest in his concerns. Fortunately, this temptation abated as the maid entered with the post, bearing two letters for Elizabeth.

Elizabeth had been a good deal disappointed in not finding a letter from Jane on their first arrival at Lambton; and this disappointment had been renewed on each of the mornings that had now been spent there; but on the third, her repining was over, and her sister justified, by the receipt of two letters from her at once, on one of which was marked that it had been missent elsewhere. Elizabeth was not surprised at it, as Jane had written the direction remarkably ill.

They had just been preparing to walk as the letters came in; and her uncle and aunt, leaving her to enjoy them in quiet, set off by themselves. The one missent must be first attended to; it had been written five days ago. The beginning contained an account of all their little parties and engagements, with such news as the country afforded; but the latter half, which was dated a day later, and written in evident agitation, gave more important intelligence. Elizabeth read it with increasing shock, then, without allowing herself time for consideration, and scarcely knowing what she felt, Elizabeth instantly seized the other, and opened it with the utmost impatience. It had been written a day later than the conclusion of the first, and, together with it, completed the recitation of the shocking intelligence that Lydia had eloped with none other than Mr. Wickham.

"Oh! where, where is my uncle?" cried Elizabeth, darting from her seat as she finished the letter, in eagerness to follow him to acquaint him with the news without losing a moment of the time so precious. She hurried out of the room and through the streets toward the church, just short of which she discovered Mr. and Mrs. Gardiner.

She was wild to be at home—to hear, to see, to be upon the spot, to share with Jane in the cares that must now fall wholly upon her, in a family so deranged; a father absent, a mother incapable of exertion and requiring constant attendance; and though almost persuaded that nothing could be done for Lydia, her uncle's interference seemed of the utmost importance, and until she discovered him just short of the church, the misery of her impatience was severe.

Mr. and Mrs. Gardiner looked at her in alarm, fearing from her tearful affect that she was ill, but satisfying them instantly on that head, she eagerly communicated the cause of their summons by asking her uncle to read Jane's letters. Though Lydia had never been a favourite with them, Mr. and Mrs. Gardiner could not but be deeply affected. Not Lydia only, but all were concerned in it; and after the first exclamations of surprise and horror, Mr. Gardiner readily promised every assistance in his power. Elizabeth, though expecting no less, thanked him with tears of gratitude; and all three being actuated by one spirit, every thing relating to their journey was speedily settled. They were to be off as soon as possible.

But wishes were vain; or at best could serve only to amuse her in the hurry and confusion of the following hour. Had Elizabeth been at leisure to be idle, she would have remained certain that all employment was impossible to one so wretched as herself; but she had her share of business as well as her aunt, and amongst the rest there were notes to be written to all their friends in Lambton, with false excuses for their sudden departure. An hour, however, saw the whole completed; and Mr. Gardiner meanwhile having settled his account at the inn, nothing remained to be done but to go; and Elizabeth, after all the misery of the morning, found herself, in a shorter space of time than she could have supposed, seated in the carriage, and on the road to Longbourn.

"I HAVE BEEN THINKING IT over again, Elizabeth," said her uncle as they drove from the town; "and really, upon serious consideration, I am much more inclined than I was to judge as your eldest sister does of the matter. It appears to me so very unlikely that any young man should form such a design against a girl who is by no means unprotected or friendless, and who was actually staying in his colonel's family, that I am strongly inclined to hope the best. Could he expect that her friends would not step forward? Could he expect to be noticed again by the regiment, after such an affront to Colonel Forster? His temptation is not adequate to the risk."

"Do you really think so?" cried Elizabeth, brightening up for a moment.

"Upon my word," said Mrs. Gardiner, "I begin to be of your uncle's opinion. It is really too great a violation of decency, honour, and interest, for him to be guilty of it. I cannot think so very ill of Wickham, although I must admit that his reports of Mr. Darcy's pride and disagreeability have certainly not proven to be true in my experience. Can you, yourself, Lizzy, so wholly give him up as to believe him capable of it?"

"Not perhaps of neglecting his own interest. But of every other neglect I can believe him capable," said Elizabeth with bitter regret for her failure to apprise her family of what she had learned of Mr. Wickham. "He is not what he seems; I have known for some time of his true history, and it is one of deception and dishonour. He is not a man to be trusted."

"Lizzy, if you are aware of anything which we are not, I would urge you to share it," her uncle said.

Without revealing her source, Elizabeth briefly related the principal of what she had learned of him from Mr. Darcy's letter, neglecting only the intelligence regarding Miss Darcy. Her audience was shocked, but after her immediate distress subsided, Mrs. Gardiner could not help but wonder as to the source of her niece's information, which only added to her previous suspicions.

It may be easily believed that, however little of novelty could be added to their fears, hopes, and conjectures, on this interesting subject by its repeated discussion, no other could detain them from it long, during the whole of the journey. From Elizabeth's thoughts it was never absent. Fixed there by the keenest of all anguish, self-reproach, she could find no interval of ease or forgetfulness.

Her fears for Lydia were compounded by an anxiety for her own sake of how Mr. Darcy would accept this evidence of familial weakness. His words of scorn for her family at Hunsford returned to haunt her, and she dreaded facing him knowing that he had proven to be correct. She could not believe that his opinion of her would not suffer, and regretted her past behaviour with him which would only serve as confirmation of her own lack of decorum. It was a poor way to begin an engagement, and the connection with Mr. Wickham could only worsen matters. The thought that she would soon see Mr. Darcy again provided some consolation for her, though—his calm, assured presence, she knew, would help assuage her own worries and pain, however little he could do to ameliorate the actual situation.

They travelled as expeditiously as possible; and, sleeping one night on the road, reached Longbourn by dinner-time the next day. It was a comfort to Elizabeth to consider that Jane could not have been wearied by long expectations.

The little Gardiners, attracted by the sight of a chaise, were standing on the steps of the house as they entered the paddock; and when the carriage drove up to the door, the joyful surprise that lighted up their faces, and displayed itself over their whole bodies in a variety of capers and frisks, was the first pleasing earnest of their welcome.

Elizabeth jumped out; and, after giving each of them a hasty kiss, hurried into the vestibule, where Jane, who came running down stairs from her mother's apartment, immediately met her. As she affectionately embraced her, whilst tears filled the eyes of both, Elizabeth lost not a moment in asking whether anything had been heard of the fugitives.

"Not yet," replied Jane. "But now that my dear uncle is come, I hope every thing will be well." She hastened to inform Elizabeth of all that was known of Lydia's situation, of their father's presence in London, and of their mother's greatly shaken spirits. On showing her the note which Lydia had written to Colonel Foster's wife, Jane's tumult became visible.

"Oh! thoughtless, thoughtless Lydia!" cried Elizabeth when she had finished it. "What a letter is this, to be written at such a moment. But at least it shows that she was serious in the object of her journey. Whatever he might afterwards persuade her to, it was not on her side a scheme of infamy. My poor father! how he must have felt it!"

"I never saw any one so shocked. He could not speak a word for full ten minutes. My mother was taken ill immediately, and the whole house in such confusion!"

"Oh! Jane!" cried Elizabeth, "was there a servant belonging to it, who did not know the whole story before the end of the day?" *And everyone else in Meryton—and at Netherfield—by the following morning,* she added to herself despairingly.

"I do not know.—I hope there was.—But to be guarded at such a time, is very difficult. My mother was in hysterics, and though I endeavoured to give her every assistance in my power, I am afraid I did not do so much as I might have done! But the horror of what might possibly happen, almost took from me my faculties."

"Your attendance upon her has been too much for you. You do not look well. Oh! that I had been with you, you have had every care and anxiety upon yourself alone."

"Mary and Kitty have been very kind, and would have shared in every fatigue, I am sure, but I did not think it right for either of them. Kitty is slight and delicate, and Mary studies so much, that her hours of repose should not be broken in on. My aunt Philips came to Longbourn on Tuesday, after my father went away; and was so good as to stay till Thursday with me. She was of great use and comfort to us all, and Lady Lucas has been very kind; she walked here on Wednesday morning to condole with us, and offered her services, or any of her daughters, if they could be of use to us."

"She had better have stayed at home," cried Elizabeth; "perhaps she meant well, but under such a misfortune as this, one cannot see too little of one's neighbours. Assistance is impossible; condolence, insufferable. Let them triumph over us at a distance, and be satisfied."

It had been too much to be hoped for, she thought, that the news should not have spread throughout the neighbourhood. She wished dearly that she could enquire of Jane as to Mr. Darcy's response to it, but her past secrecy now forbade it. Her anxiety grew as Bingley continued to pay his daily visits with no word of Darcy. Elizabeth could well understand that under the circumstances he would not be comfortable calling at Longbourn, but knew not how to manage a meeting with him otherwise. Finally after two days with no word she took the desperate measure of inquiring of Bingley how his friend was amusing himself at Netherfield.

"He is not amusing himself there at all," Bingley said. "He returned to London on urgent business a week ago."

Until this moment Elizabeth had not dared to allow herself to entertain the suspicion that in this situation Mr. Darcy might no longer choose to honour his unspoken commitment to her. A shaft of fear went through her, and she had to force herself to inquire further as to whether he planned to return to Hertfordshire soon.

"From the letter I just received, I do not believe that he plans to return this season at all, although I hope to persuade him to attend the wedding," replied Bingley. "He spoke of returning to Pemberley once his business in London was concluded."

It was difficult for Elizabeth to believe that pain as acute as hers at that moment, was not evident for all to see. The message could not be clearer; he was renouncing any connection with her, and in truth she could not even blame him. Even if he were willing to weather the scandal for himself, he could not expose his sister either to the possible damage to her reputation nor to any risk of contact with Wickham. She was very close to tears when she finally managed to escape to her room where she sat in silent anguish, clutching the book he had given her.

She passed the next few days in a daze, alternating between agony and numbness. She replayed in her mind every moment she had ever spent with him, reconsidering opportunities missed as well as chances taken. The memory of his tenderness and kisses had the power to bring tears to her eyes, and she was thankful that she had an acceptable excuse in Lydia's situation to be severely out of spirits.

She began to feel that she was behaving like the heroine in one of Kitty's romances—pining to death over her love. Her situation and her helplessness were nigh intolerable to her, and she vowed that she would never again give any man the power to hurt her like this. It was in many ways a promise with no grounds—she could not imagine that she would ever marry or love another man. As to what her future would be, she found it best not to think—the natural choice would be to live with Jane following her father's death, but how could she live with the Bingleys with the knowledge that *he* might appear at any point?

Neither the return of her father, nor even the news contained in a letter from Mr. Gardiner reporting that Lydia had been found and that she and Wickham were to be married could provide much balm to Elizabeth's spirits. Poor Lydia's situation must, at best, be bad enough; but that it was no worse, she had need to be thankful. She felt it so; and though, in looking forward, neither rational happiness nor worldly prosperity could be justly expected for her sister, in looking back to what they had feared, only two hours ago, she felt all the advantages of what they had gained, yet for herself she knew that there would be no solution of this sort.

She could barely stand to hear her mother's raptures over Lydia's new status, sharing the mortifying news freely as if it were a subject for pride. And these were the surroundings in which she was condemned to pass her life, listening to endless conversations between Mrs. Bennet, Mrs. Philips, Lady Lucas, and all the other women of the neighbourhood—she, who might have been Mistress of Pemberley! It pained her even to think of it. But she could not avoid the commotion over the news of Lydia's engagement; she received her congratulations amongst the rest, and then, sick of this folly, took refuge in her own room, that she might think with freedom.

She knew that there was no one to whom she could turn with her sorrow; she had learnt early not to rely on either of her parents for support in times of pain—her father would tease rather than sympathize, and her mother would fly into fits of nerves when troubled by her least favourite daughter. And were she to know any of Elizabeth's history with Mr. Darcy, the punishment of being forced to hear her bemoan the loss of his ten thousand pounds a year would be equalled only by the blame she would heap on Elizabeth for failing to secure him. At such times she found it hard to argue with Mr. Darcy's early estimate of her family. As for the soon-to-be Mrs. Bingley, it would do her no favour to place her in the position of awareness that her husband's closest friend had jilted her dearest sister.

Eventually Elizabeth began to reach a resigned equanimity of a sort; she began to immerse herself into her everyday activities, and tried to teach herself not to think of Darcy, as those thoughts only brought her pain. It was not to last, though. Mr. Gardiner had written again to his brother, the principal purport of which letter was to inform them that Mr. Wickham had resolved on quitting the militia, and contained in which was a request by Lydia to be admitted into her family again before she set off for the north.

This request was received at first with an absolute negative from Mr. Bennet, a decision which Elizabeth silently but heartily endorsed. Although she could wish for Lydia's sake that she should be noticed on her marriage by her parents, Elizabeth knew that she herself would have difficulty remaining civil to her, knowing that Lydia's impulsive behaviour had directly cost her the opportunity for her own felicity. It came as an unpleasant surprise when she discovered that her father, under the influence of Jane's gentleness as well as his wife's persistence, had sent his permission for them to come; and it was already settled that, as soon as the ceremony was over, they should proceed to Longbourn.

Elizabeth's lack of spirits became so apparent by this point as to penetrate even to Mr. Bennet, who after some days of deliberating, called his favourite daughter to the library. "Lizzy," he said, eyeing her over his glasses, "Even a foolish old man like myself can hardly avoid noticing that you have not been yourself of late. What is it that is troubling you so, my dear?"

In none too articulate a manner, she gave him to understand that the circumstances of her sister's wedding still troubled her, and that she dreaded the arrival of Lydia and Wickham at Longbourn. Mr. Bennet, whose first transports of rage and guilt had long since passed to be replaced by his normal indolence, disliked this reminder of his own failures; he wished to think of it no more than to acknowledge the welcome surprise that the match had been made with such trifling exertion on his side. "Come, Lizzy, what is done is done; the worst has been averted, and I must confess that I am quite looking forward to seeing how brazen Mr. Wickham shall be when faced by our massed family, and you in particular, my love."

Elizabeth looked heavenward; the last thing she could wish for was to be reminded of her former favouritism for Wickham, for which misjudgment she had already paid dearly. Her sense of humour could not in this case extend so far as her father's. She made one last attempt to justify her position, despite an awareness that it was unlikely to be convincing without a confession of the entire reason for her reluctance. "It is easier to laugh at it, sir, when you are not one of those who have been placed at great disadvantage by Lydia's actions. Jane has the good fortune to already be engaged, but I do not delude myself that my own chances of matrimony, as well as that of my other sisters, have not been substantially altered by these events. I fear that it is beyond me, sir, to play the gracious hostess to those who have for their own pleasure injured me and those I love to this extent; do not ask it of me, I pray you, for I shall not pretend to spirits which I do not have."

"Lizzy," said her father cajolingly, seeing that her whole heart was in the subject, "Do not make yourself uneasy about the future. Wherever you are known, you must be respected and valued. Any man squeamish enough to be frightened away by a little absurdity in the family is not worth the having."

Elizabeth knew better than to expect commiseration from her father, but it was several moments before she could recover sufficient composure to respond to this remark which cut far too close for her comfort. "Sir, you asked what is troubling me; I have told you, and if there is anything further, I am at your disposal."

This was as near to insolence as Mr. Bennet had ever heard from his Lizzy, and it did not please him. He curtly dismissed her, and Elizabeth, vexation now adding to her other distresses, did not hesitate to take herself off on a long walk, despite weather which was unseasonably damp and chilly.

She did not return until dinnertime, and had little to contribute to the conversation at that meal, which was primarily concerned with the raptures of Mrs. Bennet over the pleasant notion of having two daughters married. Just before her father escaped again to his library, he said, "It occurs to me, Lizzy, that you were deprived of part of your tour with your aunt and uncle by this unhappy business. Perhaps you would like to join them in London for a time—if you go to them just after Lydia returns here, I am certain that they will be happy to be reminded that they have some sensible nieces left."

Elizabeth was pleasantly startled by this suggestion, having thought the matter closed. On further thought, she realized with some cynicism that her father was looking to his own comfort—he would no doubt be relieved by her absence; her resentful presence during Lydia's visit would be a painful reminder of his own shirked responsibility. But to go to London would run the risk of happening upon Mr. Darcy himself, which would be even worse—but no, Bingley had said that he would be returning to Pemberley once his business was concluded, and surely it could not last so very long. And London was a large place. Jane had, after all, been in London for the entire winter without catching a sight of Mr. Bingley. It would require a great coincidence for them to meet by chance, even if he should still be in town. She resolved that the slight risk was well worth the chance to be away from Longbourn, and indicated to her father that the plan met with her approval. It was determined that she should go to town on the very day after Lydia's return home.

When her sister's wedding day finally came, Elizabeth dreaded the arrival of the newlyweds. The family was assembled in the breakfast room to receive them. Smiles decked the face of Mrs. Bennet, as the carriage drove up to the door; her husband looked impenetrably grave; her daughters, alarmed, anxious, uneasy.

Lydia's voice was heard in the vestibule; the door was thrown open, and she ran into the room. Her mother stepped forwards, embraced her, and welcomed her with rapture; and gave her hand with an affectionate smile to Wickham, who followed his lady. Mrs. Bennet wished them both joy, with an alacrity which showed no doubt of their happiness.

Their reception from Mr. Bennet, to whom they then turned, was not quite so cordial. The easy assurance of the young couple, indeed, was enough to provoke even him. Lydia was Lydia still; untamed, unabashed, wild, noisy, and fearless. She turned from sister to sister, demanding their congratulations. Wickham was not at all more distressed than herself, but his manners were always so pleasing, that had his character and his marriage been exactly what they ought, his smiles and his easy address, while he claimed their relationship, would have delighted them all. Elizabeth had not before believed him quite equal to such assurance, and she resolved within herself to draw no limits in future to the impudence of an impudent man.

Wickham's gallant greeting of his new mother was enough to make Elizabeth blush for both their sakes, but when he turned to her to claim a brother's right with a look bold enough to show hints of his old admiration for her, the warmth of her embarrassment turned to the heat of anger. As she looked into the face that had spelled the death of all her hopes, she could not comprehend how she had ever failed to detect the evidence of affectation in him, and she saw with revulsion all the depth of his self-involvement and dissolution.

The distasteful sight of his slyly admiring countenance was suddenly overtaken in her mind by a vivid memory of dark eyes gazing at her intently, as if with the purpose of laying claim to her very soul. She felt it almost as a physical blow, knocking the breath from her body. She wished, oh, how she wished, for one last opportunity to tell him how she felt, to see the light of forgiveness and affection in his face once again, but she knew it was too late; and she knew as well that his suffering must be as great as her own, if not greater, owing to the long history of injury perpetrated upon him by Mr. Wickham.

Fortunately, there was no want of discourse from the others to cover her silence. The bride and her mother could neither of them talk fast enough. Wickham, who happened to sit near Elizabeth, began inquiring after his acquaintance in that neighbourhood with a good humoured ease which she felt very unable to equal in her replies. He seemed to have the happiest memories in the world, and she could not help but contrast his demeanour with her knowledge of the pain he had caused, and was continuing to cause, to the man who held her heart. Recalling the look of pain she had seen on Darcy's face at Rosings, her feelings of need for him blossomed into an aching wound. At that moment, faced with a man not worthy to speak his name, she knew that she would never be able to forget him, and that there was a part of herself which she had given to him which would always be his, even if they never met again.

Wickham, sensing her distraction, and perhaps misinterpreting it, favoured her with a winning smile. "I hear you are for London tomorrow. I am sorry for it; I had hoped for the opportunity to renew our acquaintance. *We* were always good friends, and now we are better," he said, watching her reaction closely.

His open flirtation could only serve to disgust her further, and she knew not what reply she made. *If he knew the truth of my feelings, both for himself and for Mr. Darcy, what would he say then?* she wondered in angry confusion. With an icy sensation, she realized that had Wickham known of Darcy's interest in her, he would not have been above using that connection against him, and she saw once more the bitter truth of why Darcy had no choice but to leave her.

Lydia's piercing voice broke into her reverie. "Only think of it being three months," she cried, "since I went away. It seems but a fortnight I declare; and yet there have been things enough happened in the time. Good gracious! When I went away, I am sure I had no more idea of being married till I came back again! Though I thought it would be very good fun if I was."

Elizabeth could bear it no longer. She got up, and ran out of the room. But even hiding herself away in her room, a sense of Darcy's presence continued to haunt her, and she wept once again for what she had lost. But it was a pain too acute to allow free rein for long; and when at last she calmed herself, she resolved that these would be the last tears she would shed for what was past, and she set her mind firmly on the matter of the morning's journey to London.

Chapter 6

Elizabeth reached London the following afternoon, after bidding a far from heartbroken farewell to Lydia and her husband. It was a relief to be in town; she was thankful to be away from the reminders of her woe at Longbourn. There were certainly more distractions to be had at the Gardiners' home, and Elizabeth could put aside her own cares to play with her young cousins. She no longer had to observe Jane's happiness on a daily basis when it contrasted so starkly with her own state, nor help prepare for a wedding such as she herself would never have. She was grateful for the frequent callers and the lively conversation at the Gardiners' which sometimes succeeded at diverting her attention for a few hours.

It was more difficult when she was alone with her aunt and uncle; being more perceptive than her parents, it was more apparent to them that she was out of spirits, however much she tried to disguise it. Their gentle concern almost broke her reserve, but she dared not reveal to them any of what had occurred given their own occasional connection with Mr. Darcy, and she shuddered to think of what her uncle, an upholder of the strictest propriety, would say if he knew how she had behaved.

The Gardiners did their best to offer her diversion, taking her to concerts and plays as well as to gatherings of their friends. She enjoyed these cultural delights until the night she spotted Mr. Darcy in a box at the theatre. She had dreaded the possibility that their paths might cross, but London was a large city, and she had thought it likely that he had already departed for Derbyshire. The agonizing feelings of loss that flooded her at the sight of him took her breath away; she could hardly bear the pain. He was seated with two other gentlemen and a fashionably dressed young lady; with a stab of pain, she saw that he occasionally leaned towards his fair companion, apparently to point out some item of interest. She could not keep herself from stealing glances at him even though it caused her heart to ache, until on one look she found that he had discovered her presence as well. Their eyes met for a moment across the theatre, then Elizabeth deliberately looked away. She could not imagine that he would seek her out, but she kept to the background in the interval, and managed to survive the evening with no other contact. It had the effect however of spoiling the enjoyment she was beginning to take in the pleasures of town, bringing the raw feelings of rejection back to the surface.

One day her aunt informed her that they would be attending a small party that afternoon to meet Mr. Edwards, a painter who was beginning to make his mark in London. Although Elizabeth knew but little about painting, she had no objection to the activity. They hired a carriage for the occasion, since it was apparently at some distance, and it was not until they were well into the fashionable neighbourhood near Grosvenor Square that Elizabeth asked with a sudden suspicion who was to be their host. Her aunt and uncle exchanged a brief glance; Mrs. Gardiner had deliberately avoided revealing this information, having developed a sense that her niece might be suffering from a disappointment in love.

"Why, it is at Mr. Darcy's home, Lizzy; I thought you knew. Mr. Edwards is from Derby, and Mr. Darcy is one of his patrons," said Mr. Gardiner jovially. On seeing Elizabeth's sudden pallor, he enquired, "Is anything wrong, my dear?"

Elizabeth hastened to reassure him despite the waves of anxiety racing through her. She would see him—the face that haunted her dreams, the arms that had held her and would never do so again—how was she to tolerate it? And what would Mr. Darcy think of her appearance on his doorstep? Would he think that she was deliberately putting herself in his way? The humiliation would be more than she could bear; she would have to be certain to avoid any manifestation of interest in him. "I feel rather that I will be intruding," she explained weakly.

Mrs. Gardiner, observing Elizabeth's distress, was convinced of the truth of her suspicions. She could not but think that there must be some misunderstanding; she had an excellent sense of Mr. Darcy's feelings toward her niece. It had, in fact, been quite a surprise to discover that he did not come to call after Elizabeth's arrival in London, and to find that Elizabeth was pretending to no connection whatsoever. "Do you not think that your friend Miss Darcy will be pleased to see you?" she suggested gently, not wishing to press her.

Elizabeth's fears would not be soothed, though, and in fact grew as they arrived at the door and were shown in by the butler. Elizabeth was relieved to see that it was a largish assembly; it included several persons she recognized from their visits to the Gardiners, offering her at least the protection of numbers. It pained her that, despite her embarrassment and apprehension, part of her was longing desperately to see him.

Their host rose to meet them. Darcy's heart was pounding; she had come after all. He had hoped for it, he had prayed for it, but he had not expected that she would actually agree to cross his threshold. The mere sight of her was sufficient to fill his heart, but his hopes sank when he saw that she did not meet his eyes. His fears must be true, then; she could not forgive him for the role he had played in her sister's disgrace. The voice of Mr. Gardiner echoed in his mind from their very first meeting regarding Lydia's situation—*I do not know that Lizzy will ever forgive herself for knowing what Wickham was and failing to expose him.* And if she could not absolve herself for keeping the secrecy that he himself had requested of her in his letter, what chance had *he* to ever earn her forgiveness, he who had put his pride before all else and allowed Wickham to be free to work his wiles on unsuspecting girls like Lydia? Well, he would not force himself on her, but he would show her by every civility where his heart lay, in hope that she might someday see her way to pardoning him.

He made enquiries after her family in terms of perfect civility, if not of perfect composure, receiving brief answers that demonstrated her confusion. She immediately asked after his sister, and he directed her to where Georgiana sat. The alacrity with which she left his company to join his sister could not but pain him, but he was determined to let none of it show. If she could take the step of entering his house, it was enough for now. He watched her smile at Georgiana, seeing how Elizabeth remained subdued even with her. Perhaps, he hoped, she missed him at least a little.

Georgiana was pleased to see her friend once again and abandoned the petulant attitude she had been displaying for the benefit of her brother's friends. It was a matter of particular satisfaction that Elizabeth had chosen *her* company over that of her brother. She was still irritated with him for his attempts to monopolize her at Rosings. Today, however, Elizabeth seemed focused on her to the exclusion of all else.

Her concentrated attention was, in fact, an intentional ploy on the part of Elizabeth to keep herself from looking at Mr. Darcy. She was overpowered with shame and vexation. Her coming there was the most unfortunate, the most ill-judged thing in the world! It must seem to a man of such pride that she was pursuing him. He had looked so ill at ease when they spoke, and she felt almost desperate to know what he thought of her appearance in his house.

The occasion passed with agonizing slowness for Elizabeth. The subject was one which, while appealing, was not one in which she could claim any expertise, so while she listened with as much interest as she could muster under the circumstances, she had but little to contribute to the discussion. Darcy posed some insightful questions, which at least provided her a natural opportunity to look at him without being obvious about her longing to do so. She would look away as soon as the discussion turned, for she felt more than saw the weight of his gaze returning to her again and again. She knew not what to think, nor what she herself felt.

Sometimes, when she turned her eyes to him, she felt a sharp sense of loss, and the wish that matters could be otherwise; at other times, when she felt his gaze on her, she possessed some of the anger of the woman spurned, no matter how well she understood the spurning. She felt most acutely the unfairness of it; that *his* sister should have come so close to making the same error which Lydia had, yet should now be untouched by it; and that he, in order to protect his sister, would forswear Elizabeth, who by any account should be held blameless.

When the guests finally began to take their leave, she felt a sense of relief coloured slightly with regret. In a way she was glad that this first meeting was over, with no worse result than a fresher grief in her heart. She knew that once Jane married Bingley, it would be inevitable that they would meet from time to time, and overall, she had to count the occasion a success, albeit a painful one, since neither had embarrassed themselves or the other, nor given rise to any speculation. *It had the potential to be much worse,* she thought philosophically as she moved to join her aunt and uncle, who were conversing happily with Mr. Edwards. They seemed in no hurry to depart, while she was almost in a fever to be gone before Mr. Darcy's attention could move to her with the attendant risk to her spirits as well as her composure. When the last of the other guests had gone, though, she was surprised to discover Mr. Darcy once again inviting them to sit. Her aunt, noting her look of concern, whispered to her, "Mr. Darcy has invited us to dinner—did you not know, Lizzy?"

Elizabeth could hardly speak to form an answer. Her first thought was a panic of how she was to face him—it was easy enough to avoid him in a crowd, but not at an intimate dinner. And how was she to look at him, to converse with him, knowing that all she desired was the impossibility of being in his arms? No sooner had she finished this thought than she began to wonder *why* he had invited them to stay—why would he put himself directly in her way like that? She could not believe that even he would do that for the sake of his sister; it made no sense. Or was it an attempt to prove how completely he had put her behind him?

Although Elizabeth usually owned a healthy appetite, that night she picked at her dinner as daintily as any lady of the *ton*. All of her energy was focused into appearing composed and at peace. She could no longer hope to avoid his eyes nor his conversation, and she resolved that she would meet them as she would for any casual acquaintance. No matter how deeply pain cut her, she was determined to show no part of her loss, through no fault of her own, of the only man she ever expected to love.

On the other side of the table, Darcy was contemplating a painful truth—that he desired her now even more than he had when last they met. Seeing her in the setting of his house, at his dinner table, and yet knowing that she was not willing to take her proper place there as his wife only reinforced the emptiness he had felt since leaving Netherfield. Now more than ever he wished that he had found the time to talk to her instead of just kissing her—how he wanted to know now what had warmed her to him then, so that he could bring it to play again! These last weeks had been as close to hell as he ever hoped to come—to have had that brief moment of brilliant happiness of seeing his love returned, only to have his past sins come back to haunt him and to tear it all away. *Why,* he asked himself, as he had so often already, *why of all the woman in England did Wickham's eye have to light on her sister?* His only remaining hope was that she had forgiven him once; was it not possible that she could do so again? He stared at her intently as if the answer might be somewhere hidden in her countenance.

He had, for a time, clung to the hope that he might have overestimated her resentment toward him for failing to expose Wickham earlier; but, when she had looked away from him so pointedly that night at the theatre, he knew that it was not to be so. Even so, he had not been able to take his eyes off her. He had missed her abominably when she had left on her tour, but it was nothing to how he had felt when he realized that he had lost her completely. Since her arrival in London, his thoughts had constantly been on that place where she might be found. Despite his early resolution not to open himself to her rejection once again by seeking her out, he knew that if she had not come tonight, he would have begun hounding poor Tom Monkhouse for invitations, simply because he lived on the next street from the Gardiners, and Darcy knew that they were frequent guests at his house. He had no plan for what he would do when he saw her; he only knew that he could not bear to stay away, knowing that she was in London. There were even those midnight moments of brutal loneliness and need when he had contemplated going to her uncle's house and making a public offer for her, knowing that he could not be refused; if he did not feel she would never forgive him for such a course of action, he was not certain he would have been able to stop himself. *How am I to survive without her?* he wondered. *Could I have imagined a more bitter punishment for my failure to lay my actions before the world?*

Elizabeth made the error of raising her eyes for a moment. Once she had encountered his steady gaze, she felt helpless to do anything but to return it, and she felt as if her heart were breaking once again. She wanted so desperately to see the old warmth in his eyes, and she knew that her ability to hide her feelings was failing. It was time for her to acknowledge defeat; she could not keep her resolve to maintain a neutral appearance with him. And what did it matter if he knew that she had suffered from his abandonment? *Let him have that satisfaction, if satisfaction it is,* she thought. She acknowledged him silently with a tilt of her head, then turned to speak once more to Georgiana.

She had a brief respite when the ladies withdrew, but it was only a short time until the gentlemen rejoined them. Darcy seated himself next to her, but she felt too embattled by the evening's emotions to feel any great sensibility beyond the pain of loss and rejection.

"What did you think of Mr. Edwards' work, Miss Bennet?" he asked, watching her closely, and determined to take this final opportunity for a civil conversation with her. He wished he understood what had been passing through her mind earlier when she looked at him; it was clearly not a happy thought, but had it been anger, sadness, or something else entirely? He found himself in the unusual position of hoping that the woman whom he loved to watch laughing should be sad and suffering regrets.

"In truth, sir, I know nothing of the art of painting," Elizabeth responded, no longer able to care if Mr. Darcy exposed the gaps in her education. "I find his work to be attractive and intelligible, but beyond that I cannot in all honesty go."

"I cannot say that I take a traditionalist approach to painting myself," he said carefully, "but I do have a fondness for the fine use of line and curve in a naturalistic style."

"I must take your word for it, since I do not pretend to understand your meaning," she responded somewhat flatly. Their eyes met and held, with sparks of friction rather than of affection, as he realized her effort to separate herself from him. *Oh, that this evening would only end, and free me from this hopelessness!* she thought, but she could not deny the attraction that made her long to look at him and be by his side.

He would not be cowed quite so easily, though. "Perhaps, Miss Bennet, you would permit me to show you what I mean," he said, accepting her gauntlet. "Mrs. Gardiner, Mr. Gardiner, would you have an interest in viewing our small gallery here?"

As her aunt and uncle expressed their desire to do so, Elizabeth considered for a moment refusing the opportunity, but realized that such behaviour would make more of the matter than seemed necessary. She joined him as he led them down a hallway. As they walked, she noted that the furnishings were neither gaudy nor fine; with less of splendour, and more real elegance, than the furniture of Rosings—his taste was one more part of him she might admire.

Elizabeth, wishing for the sake of her own pride for Mr. Darcy to know that she had not expected to encounter him that evening, began by observing as they went that she had been unaware of the location of the day's gathering until they were nearly there, and added an apology for intruding upon an invitation clearly meant for her aunt and uncle.

Darcy's disappointment in her words was so great that he was at a loss for a moment. So she had not meant to indicate any form of forgiveness by her presence—it had been too much to hope for, in any case. After a moment he began to feel for her position, however, and said, "Miss Bennet, you need never apologize to me; you are very welcome here." *So welcome that I would happily keep you here when your aunt and uncle take their leave!* he thought wryly.

Elizabeth coloured at his words, but was spared the need to respond by arriving at the gallery. Mr. Darcy now called her to look at a picture. She took her place beside him, not without feeling that magnetism which called to her so strongly, and she wondered, as they viewed the painting, whether he was feeling any of the same, and what regrets he might have for how matters had turned out. "This, Miss Bennet, is by Georges de la Tour, and it is one of my particular favourites in the collection here. You see how he portrays the Virgin as a near-hypnotic figure, yet still with intense naturalism. And here in these lines we can see his characteristic simplification of forms, yet still with great attention to detail." He reached around her to indicate a portion of the painting. Elizabeth was far more conscious of how this movement brought him closer to her than she was of the subject he was pointing out.

She groped for coherent words for her reply. "The figures appear almost luminous." She heard the Gardiners in the background, commenting on another picture to Georgiana.

"Yes, I find that quite striking," he said quietly, in a voice that left her unsure as to his actual meaning. "And over here is another of my favourites—it is an etching, a self-portrait by Rembrandt. Notice how the light from the window illuminates him and the drawing table while the rest of the room is in darkness—his use of chiaroscuro seems to add depth and drama to the scene."

Under the guise of examining the picture more closely, she drew away from him slightly. His presence was too disturbing to her, and his tone unsettling—it was almost intimate, and it fluttered her pulses far more than she would care to admit. She bit her lip, wondering what his intent was—

why should he be trying to charm her now, when he had been the one to walk away from their understanding? True, he had probably not wished to do so, but the choice was his; he had made his choice, and he should not toy with her now. She raised her chin slightly as hopelessness began to shift to anger; the anger she had been trying so valiantly to repress for these past weeks. "Very nice, Mr. Darcy. Is the lesson completed now?"

He had the gall to look injured. "My apologies, Miss Bennet; it was not my intention to impose upon you."

She forced herself to look at him steadily; although there was in her a tolerably powerful feeling towards him, she would not have him know it. Without a word she turned and rejoined the Gardiners.

Miss Darcy, picking up on the tension between the two, could not resist needling her brother. "What, Fitzwilliam, you have shown her the de la Tour and the Rembrandt but not the book!" she exclaimed, in a manner that bespoke criticism. "Those are his treasures," she said to the Gardiners, "and he adores sharing them."

Darcy thought darkly that Georgiana had a lesson coming to her on proper respect and how to behave in front of company; he would have a word with Mrs. Annesley in the morning. "I believe that Miss Bennet's interest might not extend that far, Georgiana," he said levelly. "Would you show our guests back to the drawing room, and I shall follow in a moment." *I shall need more than a moment,* he thought bitterly, *to prepare myself to meet the massed hostility of Elizabeth and Georgiana!* Georgiana gave him a mutinous glance, but complied with his request.

Elizabeth's attention had been caught by their pointed interaction, and her eyes were drawn again to his face, where it was impossible for one so attuned to him as she to miss the pain and sense of exhaustion. It took only one look for her to realize that she had been less than truthful with herself; she knew that he would never toy with her, that such deceit would be foreign to him. Her anger grew not from his actions, but from her own fear, a fear of allowing herself to care for him again, a fear of her own vulnerability to him. With an impulse she did not care to examine too closely, she said boldly, "If you have another favourite work, sir, I should like to see it if you are willing." No sooner were the words out of her mouth than in her confusion she wished them unsaid, but the lifting of the pain in his eyes gave her a combination of pleasure and relief. She felt her resentment towards him slipping away as he met her gaze with his old, warm look, and she had to firmly instruct her treacherous body to remember that he was no longer hers.

"It would be entirely my pleasure, Miss Bennet," he said formally, not trusting himself with words any closer to his heart, for fear of what more he might say. "Would you like to see more paintings?—or, if you prefer, I have an interesting Book of Hours, to which my sister alluded."

"I will follow your recommendation, sir," she said, attempting without success to still her heart. *Anger is far safer for me than is sympathy!* she thought ruefully.

He gestured to her to follow him across the hall into a well-lit room which evidently served as his study. From a glass-covered bookcase he removed a large book and carefully slipped it out of its wrappings before setting it on the desk. He pulled out the chair for her, and she seated herself, shivering a bit at the intimate notion of sitting in *his* chair at *his* desk.

"This is the Great Book of St. Helen's Abbey," he said as he gently opened the tome. "You may find the illuminations of interest, although the text is in Latin and unremarkable."

If Elizabeth was lacking in knowledge regarding artwork, the same could not be said of history. Her father had inspired an interest in the subject in her, and her reading had been both broad and deep. As she carefully examined the book, turning the pages slowly and carefully with respect for their age, she asked him several questions about its provenance and history, grateful for the distraction from her feelings it provided.

He stood back and watched her as she examined each page, her slender fingers resting lightly on the desk next to the book. He traced the lines of her hand with his eyes, imagining for a moment how it would feel to have her touch him again. The sensation in memory of her hands upon his shoulders overtook him with a power which surprised him. In the headiness of being alone with her, he could barely bring himself to recall any reason why she would refuse him. He took a deep breath to calm himself, and paused to point out a particular characteristic of the page she was reading. She looked up at him with a brief smile, but her attention was clearly on the book.

His eyes travelled along the exposed skin of her shoulders and neck, remembering how soft it had felt beneath his lips, its rich, warm scent of roses and fresh air, and how she had arched herself against him at his touch… *Stop it!* he admonished himself harshly. *You are doing nothing but torturing yourself!* His imagination, however, was not to be directed away. His eyes fastened on the tiny curls of dark hair escaping their confinement to lie against the nape of her neck, and he felt an urgent desire to reach out to stroke them and to caress the sensitive skin beneath them—he could almost imagine how she would gasp with pleasure at his touch. *She would do nothing of the sort; you would be fortunate if she did not berate you soundly for your presumption!* he reminded himself, but it was of no use.

In a vain attempt to bring an end to his dangerous musings, he tried to return to a discussion of the book. "The calendar illustrations…" His speech halted briefly as, when he leaned in to point out a section, her well-remembered fragrance wafted past him. "The calendar illustrations are particularly fine; June and August are favourites of mine."

A certain tension in his voice alerted Elizabeth, whose attention had been drawn by the Book of Hours, to his proximity. From the corner of her eye she could see him gazing at her intently, and her breathing quickened imperceptibly. She wished she could think of a rejoinder to relieve the tension, but her wit seemed to have deserted her. Unconsciously her fingers caressed the elaborate binding of the book. "The binding is well preserved, and very beautiful," she said, her voice betraying some of the strain she felt.

Darcy could bear it no longer it. She was so close to him—how could she fail to see that she belonged in his arms, and nowhere else? His senses already spinning from her nearness, he saw her bite her lower lip as if in indecision, and the sight of it moved him beyond his accustomed caution against allowing himself any vulnerability. His hand moved as though of its own accord to rest on her shoulder.

A spark lanced through Elizabeth like lightning at his touch. Their eyes met as she turned her head to look at him, and his dark eyes spoke eloquently to her of his need. She knew that she should tell him to desist, but she hesitated a moment, and in that moment she was lost.

The look in her eyes told him that there was still hope, and he was desperate. "I beg of you, do not push me away, Elizabeth," he entreated in a hoarse whisper as he began to move towards her, his eyes fixed on the curves of her lips.

She could no more have denied him than she could have kept the tide from rising, and she trembled as he met her longings with a kiss which bespoke the depth of his passion. The now familiar sense of desire raced through her, and even the exquisite sensation of his lips upon hers could not quite outweigh her feelings of pure relief and gladness at discovering that he was still no more indifferent to her than she was to him. His lips met hers time and again, as if fearful to demand more, until her need grew so great that she turned to find her fulfilment in his embrace. His arms tightened around her convulsively as he whispered her name.

It was more than Darcy could take in—that she was truly in his arms again, that she was responding to him with as great a need as he himself felt, and, for the first time, apparently without reservation. He deepened their kiss, exploring the routes of passion with a possessive urgency, as if he feared that she would disappear at any moment. He could sense her surrender building, and wanted to demand that she admit that she was his, that she would never leave him, but in fear of what she might say, he instead used his lips and his hands to insist on more, to exact from her every ounce of passion and caring she would give. In complete disregard for their situation, he worked his fingers into the softness of her hair, caressing its silkiness even as he held her to him—not that she was making any attempt to escape, but he was desperate for her.

Her legs were becoming weak as his passion wreaked havoc with her sensibilities. She could no longer deny her own need for him, or her terrifying desire for him to touch her ever more intimately. Recklessly, she clung to him even more closely with no wish to deny him, entranced by the comfort and the excitement of his strong body against her own. The feeling of his hand so intimately entwined with her hair, and brushing against the sensitive skin of her scalp, seemed to tap into a deep desire to abandon all propriety for the sake of the sensations only he could induce in her. Her ability to recall anything in the world outside of him was beginning to fade when her heedless abandon was punctured by an unexpected and unwelcome sound.

"Mr. Darcy!" Mr. Gardiner's voice was sharp and icy.

Elizabeth froze at the sound of her uncle's voice. The sudden shock of shifting from the heat of passion and the almost frightening fervency of Darcy's lovemaking to the reality of the compromising position in which she had just been caught was wrenching. She slowly and numbly stepped away from Darcy, feeling quite faint. Mr. Gardiner's strict standards had been impressed on her over the years; she knew all too well how seriously she had violated them and that the consequences would not be light.

"Mr. Darcy," repeated Mr. Gardiner, his tone cutting, "I am aware that many people are under the impression that liberal political attitudes are necessarily accompanied by loose morals, but I can assure you that this is not the case."

There was a glacial silence as Darcy tried to regain his composure, torn between concern over Elizabeth's pallor and the need to deal with Mr. Gardiner. "Sir, I am under no such impression," he said finally. "If I have allowed temptation to get the better of me, it is not because I do not have the highest opinion of Miss Bennet's morals. I hold her in the most tender regard and hope to have the honour someday of calling her my wife."

Elizabeth closed her eyes at the words which she had only a few minutes earlier longed to hear. Then they might have filled her with happiness, but to know that he was saying them when in honour he had no other choice, made the taste of them bitter. "Uncle..." she began hesitantly.

"Lizzy, I will speak to you later!" he interrupted sharply. "Mr. Darcy, I will not deny that I am gravely disturbed by this behaviour toward a guest under your own roof, and I must insist on knowing if you intend to stand by your words."

Darcy drew a deep breath in anger at this slight, but his answer was forestalled by Elizabeth, who found herself experiencing a quite unexpected protective impulse towards him. "Uncle, you need have no doubts of him," she said softly. "He has already made me the offer of his hand." As unpleasant as the situation might be, she could not in conscience allow Darcy to take the blame for her errors in judgment.

"Is this true?" Mr. Gardiner demanded of Darcy.

Although tempted for a moment to take the excuse offered by Elizabeth, Darcy could not bring himself to take such a step so shortly after his honour had been directly questioned. "Miss Bennet is very kind to me," he said levelly, looking at her. "While it is true, the occasion she speaks of was some months ago, and she declined to accept." He met Mr. Gardiner's fierce gaze directly.

The almost palpable tension between the two men grew as Mr. Gardiner said, "And does your offer still hold then, sir?"

"I have already said that it does," Darcy said sharply. Turning to Elizabeth, he added in a gentler tone, "Miss Bennet, will you do me the great honour of becoming my wife?" The trepidation he felt in making this public offer after his previous reception and in these strained circumstances made his words seem rather cooler than he intended, and he could only hope she would understand his intent.

Elizabeth looked away. She no longer had any doubt that he still cared for her, and cared passionately, but she could not bear to see him forced into a marriage that would bring him in close relationship with the man he detested above all others and a family mired in disgrace. "Uncle," she said, her voice low, "there are circumstances of which you are not aware."

"I have seen all the *circumstances* I need, and I must say that I am surprised at you, Lizzy," Mr. Gardiner replied. "I am awaiting your answer."

"Please, let me speak with you privately," she pleaded.

"Elizabeth!" Mr. Gardiner said with a sharpness that would not be gainsaid.

Elizabeth gazed at the floor for a moment, and then resignedly she looked up at Darcy and essayed a small smile. "I thank you, Mr. Darcy, I would be honoured to be your wife."

Darcy drew in a sharp breath in silent triumph. No matter how unfortunate the circumstance, he had her consent now, and he knew that she was not indifferent to him. He could take the time he needed to prove to her that he could be trusted in the future without fear of her fleeing him. If her reluctance disappointed him, it did not come as a surprise.

Mr. Gardiner appeared to relax slightly with this resolution, and a little more of his customary good cheer began to appear as he said, "Well, then, that is settled, and I wish you both all the best fortune. Lizzy, I will write to your father tonight, and tell him that I have acted in his stead and given my consent. Mr. Darcy, do you have a preference as to when and how this is announced?"

"If you do not object, sir, I will write to Mr. Bennet as well to ask his consent in any case," Darcy said. "As for announcing the engagement, I will want to tell my sister first; but, apart from that, I see no reason to wait, unless Miss Ben…Elizabeth feels otherwise." Darcy now appeared as comfortable with the situation as if he dealt with it every day, seeming surprised only by the notion of having the right to speak of her by name in a public manner.

Somewhat stunned by the swiftness with which her future was being determined, Elizabeth shook her head.

"Well, then, let us discuss the details, Mr. Darcy," said Mr. Gardiner. Turning to Elizabeth, he added, "Lizzy, I believe some attention to your appearance is in order."

She glanced at Darcy briefly before obeying, and was relieved to see his countenance did not suggest displeasure. She wished that she could remain for this discussion for his sake, but knew it was fruitless to question her uncle. Quietly she made her way out of the study towards the dressing rooms.

As soon as she was alone, feelings and thoughts began to flood through her. Engaged to Mr. Darcy after all that had occurred! It seemed beyond belief, after these last weeks of despair and loneliness. And that he *did* still care—Elizabeth was astonished at the enormity of the relief she felt at this; although she had assumed it to be likely, even if he no longer considered her marriageable, it was not the same as knowing. She leaned back against the door of the dressing room, closing her eyes, enjoying a deep sense of contentment.

It was not long, though, before the thought of her uncle returned to pierce her satisfaction. She knew that he was gravely disappointed in her, and it pained her to consider what he must be thinking of her. All these years she had been trying to prove that she was more sensible and respectable than her nervous mother and flighty sisters, and now the truth came forward that she could be led astray as easily as any of them. She did not imagine Mr. Gardiner would forget quickly what he had seen.

It is too late to worry about what is already done, she thought, her usual good spirits beginning to make themselves known for almost the first time since receiving the news of Lydia's flight. She quickly tended to her hair, touching her cheeks as if to cool them. She was struck by her desire to be in Darcy's company once more.

As she returned to the study, she could hear Darcy and Mr. Gardiner conversing in more normal tones. Feeling all the embarrassment of facing them after her earlier improprieties, she paused for a moment before forcing herself to enter.

Darcy looked over to her with a quick smile which somehow seemed to have the power to draw her to his side, even as she blushed for the recollection of his kisses. She could not quite meet his eyes, though—on seeing him, she could not help but recall that, despite whatever feelings he might have for her, he had left Netherfield expressly to avoid that situation in which he now found himself.

Darcy's awareness of her was such that he noticed her discomfort immediately. He felt a natural concern as to her response to their engagement; he had, after all, taken advantage of the situation and forced her, albeit unintentionally, into an engagement she did not wish for. "May I have a moment to speak with Elizabeth privately?" Darcy addressed his request to Mr. Gardiner..

Mr. Gardiner eyed him steadily for a moment. "You may *speak* to her privately if you wish, Mr. Darcy," he said, his voice carrying an unstated warning.

Darcy inclined his head in agreement. Mr. Gardiner departed the room, making a point of leaving the door open. Darcy turned to look at Elizabeth, whose cheeks were still tinged by a delicate blush, and damned the fact that he had just effectively promised to keep his hands off her; she looked so amazingly tempting, and knowing that she was to be his after all seemed only to increase his desire to make that eventuality occur as soon as possible. He was uncertain how to read her look, and her attempts to avoid accepting his proposal came to his mind. "Elizabeth," he said, "I hope that you will be able to forgive me for causing this to occur in such a manner, and that you are not unduly disturbed by the outcome. Please believe me that I will do everything in my power to make you happy."

Her expression softened slightly. "I am sorry that my uncle was quite so harsh to you as he was," she said.

Darcy shook his head and smiled infinitesimally. "There is no need to worry. I was already well acquainted with your uncle's beliefs in this regard, and I believe that I fared rather better than I might have expected." He was glad to see this comment earned a real smile from her, and his countenance warmed in response.

His look relieved her somewhat, though she was still torn between the pleasure of discovering that he still cared for her and the fear that he had been forced into this engagement against his better judgment. *He seems determined to put the best face on this,* she thought, *or perhaps he is even pleased to have the decision taken from his hands.* For a brief moment she contemplated how difficult it must have been for him to leave Netherfield and to end their connection, to bow to society's dictates when he had finally achieved all he had hoped for with her. Her expression softened, and she said lightly, "Yes, my uncle is very strict and could have been much worse. I have no doubt that *I* shall hear a good deal more from him on the subject!"

He favoured her with one of his rare open smiles, causing her to feel quite weak. "Perhaps I should take the excuse to stay by your side constantly, prepared to defend you, but unfortunately for me I have little doubt that you can defend yourself quite adequately with no assistance from me," he teased.

"Yes, you are not without experience in that regard!" exclaimed Elizabeth with an air of light-hearted chagrin, desiring to continue the current cheer in their conversation. "However, sir, I might still welcome your presence beside me, with or without an excuse." She looked up at him through her lashes, wondering how he would accept this blatant flirtation.

He took an involuntary step towards her, then stopped. "Elizabeth, my heart, I could find it in me to be quite irritated with Mr. Gardiner," he said, his voice betraying a certain exasperation with both their situation and himself. He could not stop his eyes from straying to her lips; the effort it took not to kiss her was nearly immeasurable.

She gave him an impish look, perfectly able to discern his meaning, and indeed sharing a certain amount of the sentiment. The burning look in his eyes was by itself sufficient to make her skin tingle and her body long for his touch, and she found her breathing becoming more shallow. *If he can do this to me simply by looking at me, how dangerous will it be when he can touch me whenever he pleases?* she wondered abstractly, and the thought of that future created a heat inside her which made her dizzy.

Darcy, observing the blush rising in her cheeks and the darkening of her eyes, found himself in an even more intense struggle; he thought that it would take almost nothing at that moment for him to not only kiss her, but to carry her off to his bed, where he could uncover her mysteries and taste all the delights of her body; to touch her as she had never been touched before and to be the one to discover what would occur when that passion which had always been so evident in her was at last unleashed. Would she have that same look in her eyes when he finally took possession of her, thrusting himself into her depths?

The dark intensity of his gaze finally became too much for Elizabeth, and she looked away. He chuckled softly at her reaction, and she looked back at him with a self-conscious but amused smile. "We had best return to the others," Darcy said reluctantly, knowing that his self-control was definitely in danger.

"As you wish, sir," she said with a mischievous look, unaware of how potently her playfulness affected his already strained equilibrium. He expelled a sharp breath, then took her hand and put it firmly in his arm.

"Come, then," he said, struggling to keep his voice even when so slight a touch as this wrought havoc with what little remained of his restraint. But temptation could not be completely ignored, and he said softly in her ear, "Or else I shall not be able to resist kissing you until you no longer care what your uncle or anyone else thinks, my dearest, loveliest Elizabeth."

A fiery blush lit her cheeks at his forwardness as they left the study, unable to trust herself to words after making the mortifying discovery that his suggestion had great appeal for her as well. *Where have these wanton desires come from?* she chided herself, all too conscious of the warmth of his body at her side, and how little it would take to move into his arms. It was a relief to finally reach the parlour with the others, although she could see her uncle looking askance at her high colour and Georgiana's frown as she perceived the clear currents running between her brother and her friend.

Elizabeth attempted to collect her dignity as she took her seat. Her aunt gave her an inquisitive look which she did not know how to return, and she found her own embarrassment to be such that she felt her guilt to be obvious to all. Disinclined to meet the eyes of anyone in the party, and with much to think on, she fixed her gaze on the floor in front of her, reviewing in her mind everything that had changed in the last hour. A small, warm smile of contentment crept across her face at the thought of her future with Darcy. She gave in to the urge to glance up at him, and found he was watching her with apparent satisfaction. Their eyes met with a look of mutual understanding until her attention was drawn away once again by the demands of the conversation.

Chapter 7

There was an uncomfortable silence in the Gardiner's carriage upon their departure from the Darcy townhouse. There had been no opportunity to inform Mrs. Gardiner of the new developments, but it had been quite apparent that there had been a change; Darcy had been most attentive to Elizabeth following their return from examining his artwork, sitting by her and prone to gazing at her with a warmth which was almost embarrassing for the remainder of the party. On their departure, he had lingered over the quite unnecessary act of kissing her hand with no objection from Mr. Gardiner and asked her permission to call on her in the morning, so in short, there was sufficient evidence to raise a curiosity in Mrs. Gardiner that she was now longing to satisfy.

"Well, Lizzy," her uncle said to break the silence, "this has certainly been an eventful evening."

Feeling quite discomfited by having to explain all that had come to pass, Elizabeth said, "Yes, it has; perhaps you would like to tell my aunt about it."

Mr. Gardiner eyed her for a moment, then conceded silently and turned to his wife who was looking to him with interest. "My dear, Lizzy has become engaged to Mr. Darcy," he said.

"Engaged!" exclaimed Mrs. Gardiner with great pleasure but without great surprise. "What delightful news! I am so happy for both of you; I know how much he admires you, Lizzy, although you have both been quite sly about it!"

Elizabeth looked to her uncle. She had no intention of admitting to being forced into the engagement; she knew that he would tell her once they were alone, but she had no desire to embarrass herself further at the moment—she would rather have the opportunity to dwell a little longer in the feelings that Darcy's attention had inspired in her.

Misinterpreting her silence, her uncle said gently, "Lizzy, I admit that I do not understand what your objections might be to the match, as Mr. Darcy seems to be a fine and intelligent man towards whom you are apparently not indifferent; but, my dear, do you not realize that in any event, given how much your family owes to him, if he wants you as his wife, you have an obligation to honour his wishes?"

"An obligation! My family owes him nothing!" exclaimed Elizabeth, taken aback by this notion. "In truth, none of them even like him, and I do not doubt that my father will not be best pleased by this turn of events!"

Mr. and Mrs. Gardiner looked at one another in consternation. They appeared to have a silent conversation, then, apparently reaching some form of resolution, Mrs. Gardiner turned to Elizabeth. "Do you then consider all that he did for poor Lydia as nothing?" she asked in a voice more kindly than her words would suggest.

"What he did for Lydia, or what she did to him?" cried Elizabeth with more feeling than judgment, knowing just how much misery Lydia's behaviour had caused both Darcy and herself.

"Lizzy," her aunt said, her voice carrying a gentle warning, "are you unaware that he was the one to discover Lydia's location, and that he paid off Wickham's debts and purchased his commission in exchange for his agreement to marry Lydia?"

Elizabeth paled with astonishment, scarcely able to believe her ears. Suddenly it all made sense—Darcy's hurried departure from Netherfield, the impossible sums her uncle had been thought to put forth, the Gardiners' apparently close acquaintance with Darcy. But while the logic of it was evident, the rationale was less so.

It cannot be! she thought. *He could not endure the mortification attendant on meeting with the man whom he always most wished to avoid, and whose very name it was punishment to pronounce! And to not only do so, but also to persuade him and finally to bribe him to marry a girl whom he could neither regard nor esteem! He could not even bear to see me when I had such a connection!*

Her thoughts were made more painful by the immediate realization that her aunt would never have said such a thing had there been the slightest doubt in the matter. And the thought that he would do so much when his only motivation could be affection for herself, even though he was at the same time forswearing her? It taught her yet again of his value, and tears rose unbidden to her eyes.

"You did not know, then," Mr. Gardiner said, seeing his niece's amazement, and he again exchanged glances with his wife. "I am astonished to hear it; nothing but the belief of your being a party concerned allowed me to act as I did. This is most disturbing."

"Hush, Edward," said his wife. "It has clearly turned out as it should in the end. If he had not already reached an understanding with Lizzy then, it was clearly his intent to do so."

Elizabeth could not bring herself to correct her aunt's misapprehension by indicating just how much Lydia's elopement had affected Darcy's intentions towards her, but her curiosity would not be stilled. She turned to her uncle, and said, "Please, I must know the rest of the story. Will you not tell me what happened?"

"As I understand it, he came to London after hearing of Lydia's elopement with the intent of discovering them, which he was able to do by means of a woman who had previously been in his employ and a known associate of Wickham. I believe he then met with Lydia once, and Wickham many times. His first object with Lydia had been to persuade her to quit her present disgraceful situation and to return to her friends as soon as they could be prevailed upon to receive her, offering his assistance, as far as it would go. But he found Lydia absolutely resolved on remaining where she was. She cared for none of her friends, she wanted no help of his, she would not hear of leaving Wickham. She was sure they should be married some time or other, and it did not much signify when," said Mr. Gardiner, disgust with Lydia's behaviour apparent in his voice.

He continued, "It remained to him only to expedite a marriage between them. Wickham of course wanted more than he could get, but at length was reduced to be reasonable. Mr. Darcy's next step was to acquaint me of the proceedings, which he did immediately following your father's return to Longbourn. By that time, the papers had been drawn up, the license obtained, and Lydia prepared—under duress from Wickham, I might add, as a condition of the agreement—to return to our home. I must tell you, Lizzy, that Mr. Darcy refused to allow me to help in any way in this endeavour, saying that it was owing to him, to his reserve, and want of proper consideration, that Wickham's character had been so misunderstood. He imputed the whole thing to his mistaken pride, and begged that we keep his role in it a secret. It did not sit well with me, but after all he had done, it seemed that we must grant him the one thing he asked. But we always assumed that *you* were aware of the entire situation!"

She hardly knew what to make of this intelligence. What sense was there to be found, when he had undertaken such trouble and mortification as she could hardly imagine! Her heart did whisper that he had done it for her. She was ashamed to think how much he had done.

She was aware that her aunt and uncle were observing her closely, but she felt unequal to meet their inspection and averted her eyes. Nor could she show the pleasure they no doubt expected for discovering such generosity and liberality on the part of her new fiancé; it was painful, too painful, to feel under such an obligation to him, and to know that she was under even further and perhaps greater obligation for his decision to preserve her own reputation when she had been foolish enough to allow herself to be caught in a compromising position.

Why, oh why did I permit him to kiss me? It was beyond foolish! Why must it be that I have so little resistance to him? Imprudent, thoughtless behaviour— no better than Lydia! she thought reflexively, but she recognized as well that Darcy's feelings were equally strong, and that given the behaviour he had initiated, she knew he would have felt honour bound to offer marriage even had they not been interrupted.

Yet when she remembered the pleasure she received from looking into his eyes and from the warmth of his gaze on her, she could not bring herself to regret it completely; even if she regretted the circumstance, she could not be sorry for the outcome that would allow them to be as one.

DARCY WATCHED THE CARRIAGE BEARING Elizabeth and the Gardiners as it pulled away from his doorstep, following it with his eyes until it turned the corner onto Park Lane. Only then did he allow the sense of triumph he had been feeling since kissing Elizabeth to show itself in a victorious smile. Who would have thought, when the evening began so inauspiciously, that it would end in such a satisfying manner? And the irony of it—that through quite unacceptable and frankly irresponsible behaviour, he had won what he most desired. Now it remained only to convince Elizabeth to be as pleased with the outcome as was he. But she is far from indifferent, he reminded himself, savouring the memory of her response to his kisses and the satisfaction of the moment she had moved of her own accord into his arms.

He turned back into the house, his step light, thinking of the best way to inform Georgiana of the developments. He had no doubt that she would be pleased; after all, she was fond of Elizabeth and would be delighted to have her as a sister. It would also put an end to the continuing pressure from Lord Derby about her future. Not for the first time, he wished he could just remind his uncle that if his father had thought him suitable to be Georgiana's guardian, he would no doubt have named him as such rather than to leave her to the care of a brother of only two-and-twenty!

He found Georgiana in the music room. He took a seat by the piano-forte until she had finished the piece she was practising, admiring her fine touch on the keyboard. She turned to look at him with a cool air. He wondered briefly what she had found to be irritated with him about this time; at least he had the means to change the subject.

"Georgiana," he began, "there is something I wished to speak with you about."

"Clearly," she said, her tone noncommittal.

He was taken aback for a moment at her attitude but continued on nonetheless. "I have some good news; tonight I asked Miss Bennet to be my wife, and she has agreed to do me that honour." He watched her face expectantly.

Georgiana could scarcely believe her ears. His obvious attentions to Miss Bennet that evening had vexed her, but she had believed them not to be serious; she had known that he would never consider marriage to a woman so much beneath him. She had been angered to think that he might be toying with her friend's affections, but any relief she presently felt that Elizabeth would not be hurt by his behaviour was far overwhelmed by the feelings of resentment and jealousy that he was so ready to have another woman, one whom he hardly knew, take *her* place in the household. And to choose such a woman after all he had said to *her* about the necessity of a proper marriage!

"I cannot believe it," she said finally, her tone coming perilously near incivility.

"It is quite true, I assure you. We will make the announcement as soon as I have her father's consent." Darcy could see no reason to make her aware of the irregular circumstances. "Shall you not like to have her as a sister?"

To his surprise, a look of resentment came to her face. "You refused to allow me to marry George Wickham because he was not good enough for me, and now you are choosing a woman of scarcely higher status and no fortune to be *your* wife?" she cried.

The irritation that Darcy had been trying to suppress at his sister's pattern of insolence could not longer be quieted. "How dare you compare the two?" he said icily. "Wickham's lack of fortune was the least of my concerns! He is a man with no morals or respectability. You should be thankful you were saved from him—he would have made your life a misery."

"And what if I am *not* thankful?" The words Georgiana had been longing to say for so many months poured from her mouth, regardless for the moment of the painful knowledge she had gained of Wickham from Elizabeth. Elizabeth! Why could he not let her have a friend of her own, but must step in and take her away from her as well? Or was it the other way around— had Elizabeth cultivated her friendship to become closer to her brother, as had many a fortune-hunter before her?

Taking a deep breath to calm himself, Darcy said, "You are young, Georgiana, but you are not a fool. Wickham was trying to take advantage of you for your fortune."

"And I suppose that you believe Miss Bennet is indifferent to your wealth? I have seen no great affection toward you on her side!"

Darcy's countenance showed no evidence that her remark had cut him. "Georgiana, you know nothing whereof you speak. Miss Bennet would not enter into a marriage solely for pecuniary advantage; it is not in her character." *As I know all too well!* he thought, but he was not about to present Georgiana with the humiliating evidence of Hunsford.

"Of course she would not have you believe as much! Shall I repeat the arguments you made to me last summer when you were trying to persuade me to give up Mr. Wickham for no better reason than his poverty?" she said scornfully.

Darcy's complexion became pale with anger. "Georgiana, would you like to know what your precious Mr. Wickham is doing now?"

Georgiana flinched, but did not give in. "Yes, I would, in fact."

"He is on his way north with a commission that *I* purchased for him after he fled his old regiment owing to his excessive gambling debts. Unfortunately, to cover his departure, he convinced Miss Bennet's youngest sister to elope with him, but his intentions with her went no farther than seduction—he still hoped to effect his fortune by marrying well on the Continent. I found them living together without the benefit of marriage in one of the worst sections of London. It cost me over ten thousand pounds, between the settlement of his debts, the commission, and moneys I settled on Miss Lydia Bennet to convince him to marry her. And *this* is the man you would have had me allow you to marry?" Darcy's voice was chillingly level.

"I do not believe you!" cried Georgiana, her eyes wide, the disturbance of her mind visible in every feature.

His temper snapped. "That is quite enough, Georgiana! If you would care to see the documents proving it, I will be happy to take you to my solicitor's office tomorrow. Otherwise, I will hear no more of this. Miss Bennet *will* be my wife, and you *will* treat her with proper respect!"

She glowered fiercely at him for a moment, tears rising in her eyes, then stalked out of the room. Darcy allowed his head to slump back. Whatever had happened to the shy, sweet girl who had adored him above all others? She had begun to vanish even before that fateful day at Ramsgate; he would never have imagined that she would even consider such wild and shameful behaviour as an elopement, regardless of how much in love she might fancy herself to be. Was it the pernicious influence of Mrs. Younge who had fooled him so successfully? Or was it something innate to her? In company she was often as quiet as ever; but, as soon as they were alone, the barbs would start to fly.

He knew that he should not have said what he had about Wickham—he had always tried to protect her by keeping her from the knowledge of just what a scoundrel the man she had thought she loved was. But perhaps it was for the best—she would have to know about his connection to the Bennet family eventually.

He experienced a sudden wish for Elizabeth's presence. He could imagine her sitting by his side, taking his hand in hers with a concerned expression on her lovely face. The thought brought him some small measure of comfort. If only he did not have to wait for her...

"WHAT IS TROUBLING YOU, MY love?" asked Mrs. Gardiner of her husband when they retired that night. "And do not bother to say that it is nothing; I know you far too well."

Mr. Gardiner sighed deeply. "I know I cannot deceive you. This engagement—something is not right about it, but I cannot tell what."

"It is true that Lizzy seems not as pleased with it as I should hope, but perhaps it is only embarrassment for her situation," she replied.

"I have to admit, Madeleine, that it was quite the shock of my life when I discovered those two! By all appearances, it did not seem that *marriage* was what was in the gentleman's mind; and given Elizabeth's rather surprising compliance—well, the truth is that it raised certain suspicions in my mind about what Mr. Darcy believed he had purchased with his financial outlay for Lydia. I was frankly relieved to discover that she knew nothing of his actions—at least that suggested that she had not made a pact with the devil in order to rescue her sister."

His wife turned to him in surprise. "Did you truly think that Lizzy would do such a thing?"

He shrugged. "If she saw it as the only way to save her entire family from ruin and disgrace—yes, possibly, I could see Lizzy making an impulsive decision to sacrifice herself. Fortunately, that does not seem to be the case, I *think*."

"You sound dubious, my love," his wife said, her manner puzzled.

"It simply makes no sense!" he said with some agitation. "Lizzy clearly did not wish to see him, and avoided him assiduously the entire evening, then suddenly decided to accept—and apparently return—his advances. Yet then she was reluctant to accept his proposal. Something is not right, and it disturbs me—what does she know about him that makes her want to refuse such a brilliant match? And then I come around once more to whether his intent was honourable; after all, I cannot believe that his family will readily accept a girl like Lizzy as his bride!"

"*He* certainly seems enamoured of her," said Mrs. Gardiner thoughtfully. "But you are correct; she does seem oddly reluctant to think well of him."

"I do not like it—I do not like having to write to her father with this news when I am so unclear, and I do not like having to force Lizzy to accept Mr. Darcy, and I most especially do not like recalling her behaviour!" He shook his head in disapproval.

"Well, my love, we can do nothing for it tonight," his wife said practically. "I shall observe Lizzy tomorrow with him, and perhaps I will find some new insight; but I must confess, Mr. Darcy does not seem to me to be a man capable of such dishonour and deceit."

Mr. Gardiner sighed once more. "Perhaps you are right, my dear. I would not have thought so before tonight myself. But I confess that I would appreciate it if you would test the waters with Lizzy, if only for my own peace of mind."

She smiled at him and held out her hand. "Of course, my love."

THE FOLLOWING MORNING FOUND ELIZABETH eagerly awaiting the promised visit from Mr. Darcy. She had awoken in a new state of happiness, feeling the dark clouds of the past weeks disappearing and a sense of hope for the future. When she thought of Darcy, it was with anticipation of the relief and pleasure she would feel when she saw that look in his dark eyes that he seemed to reserve only for her. His affectionate behaviour towards her at the end of the previous evening boded well for their future, she thought. While she did not forget the reservations which he must have regarding their marriage, she also knew that he would be too honourable to dwell on them, and would behave in every way as if this engagement was what he had most wished for. If only she could wipe the knowledge of it from her own mind! But it was not in her power to disregard such a matter; it was all she could do to resolve to give him as few regrets as possible in her own behaviour towards him, and to hope that someday his affection for her would outweigh the negative consequences to him of their marriage.

Certain of her less proper feelings for him created greater confusion. Any regrets she might have had for her reckless behaviour in accepting his kisses seemed to have no impact whatsoever on the desire she felt for his touch, even in his absence. Her mind kept replaying the sensation of being in his arms, with his lips upon hers, and she could not deny in her innermost being how greatly she longed to feel his body against hers again. Well aware of the impropriety and shamefulness of these feelings, she struggled against them, but half-heartedly, knowing her cause to be hopeless. She could not feel happy about herself, though, not only for her own failure, but for disappointing her aunt and uncle; after an extensive chastisement for her behaviour by Mr. Gardiner, followed by a lecture from her aunt on the dangers of loss of reputation, she was even less inclined to forgive herself.

She had attempted to write a letter to her father the previous night, endeavouring to the best of her ability to explain her change in sentiment toward Mr. Darcy but, after discarding several drafts, decided that it would be best to wait until she could speak to him directly. She knew that Mr. Bennet would be mystified and worried, and that it should be through her means, that she, his favourite child, should be distressing him by her choice, should be filling him with fears and regrets in disposing of her, was a wretched reflection.

She brushed aside these thoughts when she heard a knock on the front door. Colour rose in her cheeks as the maid announced Mr. Darcy. As Elizabeth rose to greet him, she saw his eyes envelop her possessively before he turned to greet Mrs. Gardiner. She felt a surge of warmth inside her at his presence. As he seated himself beside her, she considered with some embarrassment that it might take some time to accustom herself to accepting his open interest in her after so many months of attempting to disguise any connection between them. He made civil inquiries after Mr. Gardiner and the children, and Mrs. Gardiner thanked him again for his hospitality the previous day, reiterating how much she had enjoyed meeting Mr. Edwards. After this, however, the conversation seemed to languish. Elizabeth glanced at Darcy anxiously, but his countenance was difficult to read. She was able to fill the silence by beginning a discussion of a play she had seen with the Gardiners, but could not help worrying what might be troubling him given the degree of difference from his openness of manner and warmth of the previous evening. She attempted to draw him out with some teasing and was reassured to see his positive response.

It was not long, however, before the strain of carrying the burden of the conversation began to tell on Elizabeth. She knew that Darcy might be comfortable sitting in silence, but she was not, especially while under the scrutiny of her aunt. Finally she suggested walking out; and, after receiving Darcy's agreement, the two set forth up the hill to Bishopsgate towards Moorfields.

She thought that Darcy seemed somewhat more at ease once they were on their own, but his countenance still bespoke preoccupation. Elizabeth was beginning to feel with a degree of hurt as if this were a duty visit for him rather than a pleasure, and she wished that she knew better how to take a sense of him. *It is unfortunate that so many of our encounters have been either conflictual or improper, and sometimes both,* she thought with a philosophical humour. *It does not leave us with much experience of how to conduct an everyday conversation.*

They had walked some time in silence, Elizabeth acutely aware of the warmth of his arm under her hand, while she formed a desperate resolution. "I am a very direct soul, sir; and, if there is a reason that you are discontented with me, I would prefer to be told of it than to be left to conjecture," she said.

He looked down at her in surprise. "Not in the slightest, Miss Bennet— Elizabeth," he said, his voice softening as he spoke her name. "I apologize if my behaviour has led you to think otherwise."

She felt a rush of relief, and turned a lively smile on him. "I am glad to know it was my misapprehension, then."

The brightness of her eyes had a distinct effect upon Darcy, and he drew her slightly closer as the only satisfaction he could obtain at the moment. The limitations placed on his contact with her were frustrating in the extreme; his desire to take possession of her lips had haunted him all day. He was not displeased to notice her colour rising as she interpreted his intent. Turning his eyes forward to reduce temptation, he said, "I assure you, Elizabeth, there is nothing about you that displeases me in the slightest."

The manner in which he spoke made her feel a rush of happiness. She had little doubt as to where his thoughts tended, and in an effort to reduce her own awareness of his proximity, said, "Your sister seemed well last night; I was sorry not to have the opportunity to hear her play. Has she continued to make good progress in her music?"

Darcy frowned at the mention of Georgiana. "Yes, she has," he said shortly.

Elizabeth was puzzled by the rapid change in his demeanour. *Did my words disturb him somehow?* she wondered, baffled as to any way to misinterpret her polite enquiry. She felt stirrings of discontent with his seemingly mercurial changes in mood and his reticence, realizing how little she in truth knew of him.

He sensed her withdrawal, and guessing at its cause, unbent slightly. "While my sister does quite well with her music, I must admit that I am not completely pleased with her behaviour in other regards."

"Ah," she said, recollecting Georgiana's hostile manner towards him the previous night. "She is at a rather trying age; certainly I have seen difficulties enough with my sisters: too old to be a child, too young to be a woman." Her thoughts were driven back to Lydia, whose behaviour at that age was to have such lasting consequences for her, and if she might judge from his complexion, his mind was not very differently engaged. She could not think on it without recalling his part in the matter and the obligation she felt toward him on behalf of her family. She flushed, feeling the discomfort of being so much in his debt that it could never be repaid, and knowing that he was taking on as well the additional burden of being so allied to her family despite the disgraceful connection.

She knew that the issue must be addressed at some point; and, not one to avoid what must be faced, she resolved to speak on it immediately. She fixed her eyes ahead of her, not wishing to see his expression as she spoke. "You are not the only one with a sister at a difficult age, and I must thank you, sir, for your unexampled kindness to *my* poor sister. Were it known to the rest of my family, I should not have merely my own gratitude to express."

Darcy frowned; he had not wished her to feel under an obligation to him that would cause him to question her reasons for accepting him. "I am sorry, exceedingly sorry," he replied in a tone of surprise and emotion, "that you have ever been informed of what may, in a mistaken light, have given you uneasiness."

"My uncle told me last night of your generosity; he seemed under the impression that I was already aware of it. But let me thank you again and again, in the name of all my family, for that generous compassion which induced you to take so much trouble, and bear so many mortifications, for the sake of discovering them."

He could sense her discomfort with the situation, but was unsure how best to address it, finally resolving upon directness as his best solution. He stopped, causing her to turn to face him, and said gently, "If you *will* thank me, let it be for yourself alone. That the wish of giving happiness to you might add force to the other inducements which led me on, I shall not attempt to deny. But your *family* owe me nothing. Much as I respect them, I believe I thought only of *you*."

She hardly knew what to say; these were the first words of tenderness he had addressed directly to her since that night in the Hunsford parsonage, and the tone of these, far less hurried and with a completely different sort of earnestness, moved her more than she would have expected. Her eyes met his to discover a depth of emotion that bespoke the travail he had passed through on his journey to this point, and she could not help but feel somehow inadequate to the moment. She tightened her hand on his arm lightly and said, "Then *I* thank you, sir." She knew as she spoke the words that her gratitude was not simply for his rescue of her sister, but also for having loved her well enough to forgive her all the bitterness of her refusal at Hunsford.

He dropped his voice, although none of the families or strollers enjoying the pleasant day were attending to the couple stopped in the pathway. "You need not be so formal when you speak to me, Elizabeth," he said, and his tone, inviting intimacy, sent shivers through her.

She strove to lighten the moment with a teasing smile. "Very well, Fitzwilliam," she said, tasting the sound of his name on her tongue.

His eyes darkened, and she felt dizzy as she looked into them. The tension grew for a moment, and then he said, "Is there no place for us to steal a moment to ourselves?"

Elizabeth was certain that she knew quite well what such privacy would involve, and was momentarily thankful that the difficulty of achieving it precluded the necessity to determine whether she was capable of resisting the temptation. "I am sorry to say that I know of none. My uncle, I fear, does not trust us," she said with rueful humour, "not without reason, I might add."

"Damn your uncle," he swore, failing to find any amusement in the situation at the moment. "Will he prevent us from ever being alone, do you think?"

Elizabeth's smile betrayed her sympathy. "I fear he will. There are certain lapses which he will not forgive, as, I expect, might be true for you as well were you to find yourself in a similar position."

"Your point is well taken, but I am *not* in a similar position," he said, lowering his voice to a whisper. "I am in the position of a man desperate to taste your kisses again, Elizabeth."

Her eyes widened in shock at his frankness on such a forbidden subject, her body stirred against her will by his daring. For a moment she wanted nothing more than to have him meet her needs, and her eyes betrayed her to him. In an effort to distract herself from her own response, she said lightly, "Sir, you are very forward."

"By heaven you are certainly a temptation, Elizabeth," he said with unmistakable depth of feeling. "Have you an idea yet of when you will be returning to Longbourn?" His voice clearly suggested that he saw more opportunity for them there.

Elizabeth had considered this question at length the previous night, though not in this particular context; she had intended to stay in London another month altogether, but felt that the current circumstances called for an earlier return. However, in a realization somewhat galling to her independent spirit, she had acknowledged that the decision was not hers to make. "My plans are not fixed; I am at your convenience, sir."

Darcy had never heard such deferential words from Elizabeth, and something in her tone alerted him. "I fail to follow your meaning," he said.

She sighed, feeling all the difficulties inherent in her situation of moving from the sometimes erratic authority of her father to that of a man accustomed to ready obedience. Without meeting his eye, she said, "You had spoken yesterday of planning to announce our engagement immediately. I realize that it is likely to cause a stir in certain circles; it struck me that you might have preferences regarding my availability to meet the social demands that are certain to follow."

"And do *you* have a preference in the matter?" he asked with discomfort and dissatisfaction, feeling the distance between them returning after the intimacy of their earlier moments.

"I would prefer to return home, and to allow the furore in London to pass," she admitted somewhat hesitantly. "But I recognize that it may not be practicable."

"Elizabeth," he said, his voice edged with frustration, "you are going to be my *wife*, not my chattel!"

Elizabeth felt a lightening in her spirits at his words; perhaps he did intend their union to be different from some of the unequal friendships of his she had observed—she did not think that she could ever be as obliging as Bingley, even if she were to bring herself to try. She looked up at him playfully through her lashes. "I am relieved to hear it, Fitzwilliam," she said, claiming the familiarity that had eluded her earlier. "I fear that I would make a poor chattel!"

"I have noticed," he said dryly.

THE NEXT DAY SAW ELIZABETH making her way to the Darcy townhouse to call on Miss Darcy. On her arrival in Brook Street, the butler led her to an empty sitting room and requested that she wait within. When the door opened again a few minutes later, she was surprised to discover that it revealed not Georgiana, but Mr. Darcy.

"Mr. Darcy!" Elizabeth exclaimed, feeling a flush of pleasure at his presence.

"Miss Bennet," he replied with a bow, his formal behaviour doing little to disguise the look in his eyes. He closed the door behind him.

She coloured as she recognized his intent. "Sir, it is a pleasant surprise to see you today. I had called to see your sister; I imagine that one of the servants is fetching her now."

Darcy smiled slightly, his eyes darkening as he gazed at her. "I fear that is not the case; I am afraid that my butler had his instructions on what to do should you call, and it will be some time before he recalls the need to inform my sister of your presence."

Elizabeth's pulses began to flutter. "Sir, I begin to suspect a conspiracy on your part!" she essayed mischievously, hoping to lighten the atmosphere somewhat.

"You suspect quite correctly, my heart," he said, stepping closer to her. "I must seize my opportunities when I find them."

He really was quite irresistible when he smiled, she thought abstractedly. The impulses his look produced in her were far from proper, and she found herself aching for his touch.

He reached up and trailed a finger lightly down her cheek. "If you object, Miss Bennet, you need only say so."

His finger seemed to leave behind a trail of fire. Elizabeth knew she should tell him to open the door, but the pressure building inside of her when she saw his eyes fixed on her lips would not allow it. Touching her tongue lightly to her dry lips, she made one last attempt to bring humour to bear on the situation. "Sir, are you suggesting that you are not to be trusted?" she asked playfully.

He leaned towards her until she could feel his warm breath by her ear. "Elizabeth," he whispered caressingly, "I believe you already know the answer to that question." He could wait no longer; he had been imagining this embrace ever since their engagement, and imagination alone was not enough for him any longer. He caught her lips with his own in a kiss neither gentle nor testing, but full of fire and demanding as much of her as it gave of himself. Elizabeth's lips parted as the sudden heat of desire overcame her, permitting him to deepen the kiss to an intimacy beyond that which she had experienced before. It evoked a degree of response which left her clinging to his shoulders, luxuriating in the warm haven of his arms, and tasting the sweetness of his passion.

Darcy had never before desired a woman with such intensity that it seemed as if his soul depended on her, and that same force of desire could never allow him to rest on his laurels; no matter how much she gave him, it only made him hungrier for more of her. His hands moved to caress the curves of her hips possessively, urging her ever closer to him, and the excitement that the touch of her body against his produced was intoxicating. Pouring his passion into his kisses, he continued to enjoy her lips until she was breathless with desire.

When he at length with reluctance raised his head, his mind, in one of those odd transports of time, took him back to the very first time he had kissed her among the cherry blossoms at Rosings. Recalling the sweetness of her innocent response, and then the crushing blow of her withdrawal, he experienced a powerful possessive urge. He held her against him, thanking his good fortune that she was at last promised to him. He wanted nothing more than to somehow mark her as his own, to make certain that no other man would ever so much as look at her except to acknowledge that she was his and his alone. He could not resist claiming her lips again, and her immediate response gave him all the reassurance he required.

As if of their own volition, Elizabeth's hand crept up into his unruly curls, the intimacy of this touch causing her to hold him even closer. It caught Darcy off guard, but her hesitant exploration served only to increase his desire for further intimacies. His kisses grew more heated, and in an effort to regain control of himself, he tore himself away from the temptation of her lips to press kisses along the line of her jaw, bringing his lips to rest just below her ear. She gasped at the sensation, hardly noticing as Darcy's hand began to slip upwards. As it reached her shoulder, he began to lightly draw his fingers along the neckline of her gown, and her shiver of desire could not be suppressed. He could not resist the overwhelming temptation to slip his fingertips just under the edge of the fabric, even knowing the risk he was running of finding himself without the will to stop.

The strength of the feeling his touch produced in Elizabeth both shocked and stimulated her. His caresses made her body long for more, but even as she arched against him, her better sense began to assert itself. "Mr. Darcy," she said in a voice which spoke as much of desire as of resistance.

He did not mistake her meaning, however. Reluctantly he drew back slightly, though not without allowing himself a few more brief seconds of the pleasure of exploring her hidden curves. Her look of amused reproach provoked no more than a smile in which guilt and satisfaction played equal parts; and, while he permitted her to draw away, it was only within the circle of his arms.

She could not help but acknowledge the attraction of his rakish look. She knew from her own continuing response to him that she needed to provide a distraction for them both, and quickly. "I really must insist on being allowed to see your sister, or my reputation shall be quite destroyed," she said with amusement.

She could see the acceptance in his eyes of her limit, but he was not quite ready to release her. "Kiss me again first," he said insistently, and with a smile she drew his head down, meeting him halfway with a kiss of teasing deliberation. With an unexpected sense of playful abandon, she brushed her body against his, provoking an obvious response in him. When he finally raised his lips from hers, he said in a voice dark with passion, "Oh, yes, it pleases me when you are bold, my heart."

She flushed becomingly, bringing a look of satisfaction to his face. Gazing at her searchingly, he drew her towards the chair and then settled her in his lap. The shock of this new intimacy momentarily froze Elizabeth into immobility, and he took advantage of her lack of resistance to begin scattering kisses along her neck, so temptingly placed in this position for his delectation. The startling sensations this induced in her soon overcame her ability to consider a protest. When he judged her pleasure from his efforts to provide a sufficient distraction, he paused for a brief moment to ask, "So, what was this about wanting to see Georgiana?"

"Mr. Darcy, I cannot speak of anything while you are doing *that!*" she exclaimed as his lips continued their exploration into the hollows of her shoulder.

He smiled wickedly, not ceasing his attentions. "Call me by my name, Elizabeth."

She gasped as he discovered a particularly sensitive area below her collarbone. "Fitzwilliam," she said, halfway between a whisper and a plea. A wave of desire rushed through her as she felt the touch of his lips echo through her entire body. She wished for nothing so much as to be able to surrender to the sensations he was creating in her, to allow him to continue to give her this matchless pleasure. It did not even occur to her to object as his hand came up to cup her breast, creating powerful sensations of need and fulfilment which caused her to press herself against him.

"Oh, my loveliest Elizabeth," he breathed. The evidence of her response only made him want more, and he permitted his lips to wander downwards until they explored the tender flesh exposed by the neckline of her dress.

Elizabeth could not keep a moan of pleasure from escaping her at his alarmingly pleasurable activities. She knew that she must stop him, but at each moment when she almost gathered the strength, the shivers of desire rushing through her would convince her that one more minute would not matter. The potent aching need for him deep within her was growing. The touch of his lips to the sensitive skin of her breasts produced shocks of sensation so powerful that she did not realize for several moments that his other hand was dexterously undoing the fastenings of her gown.

Are you out of your mind, man? Darcy demanded of himself incredulously as his hands seemed to develop a life of their own. *You cannot do this, not now, not here!* But his desperate need to feel the bare skin of her back would not be gainsaid, and he slipped his hand inside the opening and slid it boldly under the corset. *Her skin is so soft,* he thought, *like a rose petal—and she is mine!*

His actions were enough to tip the balance between helpless desire and fear for Elizabeth. She knew that she could not allow him to continue, and somehow found the will to resist the pleasure he was creating so freely in her. She placed her fingers lightly over his lips. "Fitzwilliam, we must stop," she said breathlessly.

He raised his head and looked at her ruefully. "Very well," he said in a voice which expressed no contrition whatsoever. "I shall endeavour to behave, my heart."

The expression on his face made her laugh lightly. "Sir, your hand," she reminded him, her voice trembling slightly.

"As you wish," he said. He removed his hand, but not before tracing a light line up her spine which sent a shiver through her. He smiled with satisfaction as he addressed himself to rebuttoning the top of her gown. "It is difficult with such a temptation before me."

She could see that it would be an ongoing struggle keeping him in hand, and gave him an amused smile as she said lightly, "No, I shall not permit you to lay the blame on me, sir, by claiming that I tempt you to it!" She attempted to rise, but he forestalled her with a hand around her waist.

"You shall not escape so easily, dearest Elizabeth," he said softly in her ear. "I will behave, but I would enjoy a bit more of your company, and I have been deprived of the pleasure of touching you for far too long."

She looked at him in amused calculation for a moment before deciding that the better part of wisdom lay in accepting the situation gracefully and working to control the danger of her own susceptibility to him. "Very well," she said lightly, allowing him to gather her closer to him. She could not deny that it was a pleasant situation, she thought absently, realizing that she could still feel the ghost of his intimate touch long after he had desisted. How strange it was to have reached this juncture after all the vicissitudes of their relationship!

The company which he desired of her seemed to be no more than her presence, as he seemed perfectly content simply to hold her close with her head resting against his shoulder. With a rush of affection for him, Elizabeth abandoned herself to the feelings of warmth and safety she found in his arms.

How long they might have sat there was to remain a mystery, as a knock sounded at the door presently. Elizabeth jumped from his lap as if she had been burnt, looking at him in shock and distress at their situation.

He did not appear to share her concern; he stood, gazing at her tenderly, and touched her cheek lightly. "How I adore you, sweetest Elizabeth," he whispered in her ear. He motioned her to a chair as he went to open the door.

Elizabeth was not surprised to find that the new arrival was Miss Darcy, and she only hoped that her blushes would not reveal too much of what had been occurring only a few minutes before. She greeted her in what she hoped was a calm manner, and accepted her congratulations and best wishes on her engagement. Darcy seemed to be observing Georgiana closely, but after an interval of pleasant conversation, he excused himself to allow the ladies some time to themselves.

Although Georgiana was perfectly polite, she exhibited less anxiety to please than she had in the past, leaving Elizabeth wondering as to her true reaction to the intelligence of her brother's engagement. She could certainly understand if Miss Darcy, accustomed to having Darcy completely to herself, might be feeling somewhat jealous of an interloper. She was determined, however, to make this visit a success, and she turned her not inconsiderable social skills to being an amusing companion to Georgiana.

The conversation turned to Elizabeth's plans. "I am afraid that we have given no consideration to a wedding date, or anything else for that matter," she admitted. "We are still awaiting my father's formal consent, and that will be soon enough to plan. And I shall be returning home in a few days, so I will no doubt discover then if my mother has particular plans." She felt a sudden qualm at the idea of being separated from Darcy.

"I hope you will return to London at some point," said Georgiana, restlessly rising from her chair and going to look out the window in a manner amusingly reminiscent of her brother.

"As I said, we have not discussed it at all. Do you spend your time primarily in London, or at Pemberley?—I do not believe that I have ever heard."

"I usually spend my summers at Pemberley, and the rest in town. It would be pleasant to have you and my brother here—I might see a little more of him then."

"He does not spend much time in London, then?" asked Elizabeth, curious as to what she might expect for her own future.

Georgiana seemed quite taken with some sight in the street, and it was a moment before she answered. "Oh, he is in *London* often enough, but usually he spends most of his time in Drury Lane, so I see little enough of him. But that will be different now."

Elizabeth smiled—she had not realized his interest in theatre was so great, but it seemed in character. "He is quite a patron of the theatre, then?"

She laughed shortly. "More a patron of a certain actress, I would say."

Unable to credit that Georgiana had truly meant what she had said, Elizabeth asked, "I beg your pardon?"

Georgiana turned quickly to face her, a look of fear coming over her. "Oh, nothing. He is very fond of attending the theatre, that is all."

Elizabeth felt a sinking sensation. Georgiana was clearly no more skilled at deception than her brother—though perhaps she had underrated Darcy's abilities in that regard. She refused to lose her dignity so much as to press her, though. With an outward appearance of calm, she replied, "I see."

Georgiana, who was beginning to appear rather panicky, said quickly, "No, really, Miss Bennet, that is not what I meant to say at all! I meant nothing by it!"

Thankful for the years of experience at disguising her feelings, Elizabeth said, "No, of course not. It would be ridiculous to think otherwise." She was finding breathing to be increasingly painful.

Miss Darcy looked as if she wished, rather than believed, that the harm had been undone. "I am sorry," she said in a small voice.

"Nonsense, you have done nothing to apologize for; you merely misspoke," said Elizabeth briskly. "It is nothing to think twice about. But I must be going; my aunt is expecting me back. Would you be so kind as to give my apologies to your brother?"

"Of course," she murmured, unwilling to meet Elizabeth's eyes. Ringing for a servant, she asked him to fetch a carriage for Miss Bennet.

They would have sat in complete silence for several minutes had Elizabeth not forcibly begun a discussion about the differences she had observed between Hertfordshire and Kent, asking Miss Darcy about her impressions of the different parts of the country. Both were relieved when the servant returned to inform them that the carriage was ready.

It was not until the carriage began to pull away that Elizabeth allowed her feelings free rein. The pain she felt inside was so great that she knew not how she would manage it; the shock went deeper than she cared to admit. She could not dismiss the vision of another woman in Darcy's arms, another woman whom he was kissing and touching just as he had kissed and touched her earlier. She should have known—he had known all too well just how to touch her to achieve the result he had desired; his hands were clearly experienced in the matter of the fastenings of women's clothing. She shuddered as she realized just what she had permitted; this was a shame which would not leave her. She allowed her head to fall back against the seat of the carriage and closed her eyes.

So, what is it that has changed so much? she asked herself, attempting to argue herself out of her distress. *Now you know that he has had a mistress; surely this is no surprise! We have only just become engaged, and until then he owed me nothing, and I have no right to criticize. He is a man with a man's needs, but everything will be different now that we are to be wed.* But Georgiana had not sounded as if the relationship had been in the past—did he expect that she would turn a blind eye while he kept a mistress on the side? And what did it mean that he had been turning to another woman after kissing her at Longbourn, that he had been in another woman's arms while she was agonizing over his loss? Could he not have taken at least a little time to regret her after coming so close to marrying her?

A new doubt assailed her. Had he in fact planned to marry her, or had that merely been her assumption? Certainly he had proposed at Hunsford, but he had never again mentioned marriage until Mr. Gardiner had forced the issue on his honour. Could he possibly have decided from her behaviour at Longbourn that he could have what he wanted of her without the baggage of her low connections? She felt ill at the mere thought. Surely it could not be—she might not be on a par with the Darcys, but she was by no means as unprotected as an actress on the London stage. No, that she could not believe, not given all he had done for poor Lydia.

But what was she to do now? How could she look him in the eye again? She knew that he would not have failed to notice that she had departed his house without so much as a farewell—she would have to find some explanation for that as well. She caught her balance again as the carriage jolted over the rougher streets of Cheapside, and stared blindly out the window, but found no answers there either.

Chapter 8

With a sigh, Darcy pushed aside the papers he had been attempting to read. It was no use; his mind kept turning to Elizabeth—if not to his extremely distracting memories of her kisses and the touch of her soft skin, then to the question of why she had seen fit to depart without saying goodbye to him. Had she been troubled by what had passed between them? There was no doubt that he had gone too far; he would be the first to admit it—although he would not guarantee that he would do differently in the future, faced with the same temptation. She had not seemed troubled by his advances at the time, but he knew full well that Elizabeth was perfectly capable of disguising her true feelings when she saw fit. Or perhaps she feared a repeat of those events if she were to see him again before she left—though all she would have had to do to avoid it would have been to remain in Georgiana's company.

Or could it have been something Georgiana had said? If she had said one word about considering Elizabeth a fortune-hunter, he would lock her in her room for a week! But Georgiana had, as it happened, been on unusually good behaviour all day. Perhaps he had done the right thing by telling her about Wickham after all, though clearly *she* now wished to avoid him, too—at dinner she had told him she was tired of London, and asked to travel to Derby early. But it made no sense in any case to think that Georgiana would have accused Elizabeth of veniality—Elizabeth would have laughed, not left, had that happened. And even if Georgiana had brought up her sister's disgrace, Elizabeth would still have handled it, he was sure—in fact, he could not imagine anything Georgiana might say that could be enough to send Elizabeth away. No, she must have wished to avoid *him* for whatever reason, though God alone knew what that was.

He poured himself a glass of port and sat back, taking a generous sip. Why was it that each time matters seemed to be proceeding well with Elizabeth, some trouble or other always came up? It was becoming extremely frustrating—as were certain limitations which were placed upon them, with no relief in sight in the near future. For himself, he would be perfectly happy to dispense with this courtship period entirely and marry her tomorrow. But she no doubt would want the full engagement—it was something he should discuss with her soon. Perhaps he could at least persuade her to set a relatively early date for the wedding, though whether that mother of hers could be brought to agree to it was a different question entirely.

Well, there was nothing for it—it was far too late to follow her tonight; he would have to wait until morning to call on her to see if something was indeed troubling her. But heaven help him if she was troubled by his advances—if he was to limit himself to merely looking at her until their wedding day, he had best find an excuse for a sudden trip far away, because it simply was inconceivable to think that he could see her every day and never touch her! He sighed again. All these months when his only thought had been how happy it would make him if she would only agree to be his; and now he had achieved his goal, and was nearly as frustrated as before. Well, perhaps not quite as frustrated, he thought, remembering how she had arched to meet his touch and the sweet taste of her lips on his. He took another sip of port, and allowed himself to slip into his memories, his papers forgotten.

ELIZABETH WONDERED HOW MANY NIGHTS it had been in the last months that she had lost sleep over Mr. Darcy. It seemed at the moment as if there had been a great many of them; and now, just when she would have thought them to be gone forever, she found herself again facing a morning when it seemed as if the night had never ended. She was no nearer to a resolution than she had been the previous day, except to have made the acknowledgment that no resolution of this could be satisfactory. She had no choice at this juncture but to marry Mr. Darcy. There was little she could do to protect her heart—having already given it over to his keeping—but to try to recollect that he was not wholly the man she had thought him to be. Under the current circumstances, she did not expect that it would be difficult to develop greater resistance to his advances; although what benefit there would be from this when they would be married soon in any case was uncertain.

Her best hope was that he would terminate his connection with the actress Miss Darcy had mentioned when they married. Perhaps that had always been his intention; there was no way for her to know. She had tried to give him all possible credit as to herself—she did not deny that he clearly had powerful feelings for her, and found her enticing; it was not a matter of a misinterpretation of his sentiments towards her as one of hers regarding him. She could not imagine ever being comfortable in these feelings, but she was determined to find some manner in which to live with them, since there could be no avoiding of them.

She took some particular care in her appearance that morning. She did not doubt that he would be calling, and she wished to appear, if not at her best, at least as close to her usual self as possible. When Darcy arrived as she had predicted, she was able to meet him with tolerable composure, although the lurch she felt in her heart demonstrated that she was still more vulnerable to him than she would like. With firm resolve to make the best of the situation, she greeted him pleasantly, if less warmly than she might have previously.

Although Darcy was watching her closely from the moment of his arrival, it was not immediately obvious to him whether or not anything was, in fact, troubling her. She seemed perhaps a little subdued, but not unusually so. He wished that he could ask her directly, but the chaperoning presence of her aunt forbade it; he was limited to polite conversation. His impatience would not be ignored, however, and soon he made the suggestion of walking out in hopes of private discourse; but Elizabeth, to his surprise, declined the offer, saying that she preferred to stay indoors.

His heart sank—he had never known Elizabeth to refuse the opportunity for fresh air and exercise, and this avoidance of being alone with him spoke as proof that she was, in fact, distressed with him. He tried to discover some method to raise the question subtly, but was unsuccessful and, instead merely followed Elizabeth's lead in discussing his interest in the theatre, plays he had seen, and which theatres he preferred to patronize.

A few minutes later, the maid came in to inform her mistress that one of the children had taken ill. With an apology, Mrs. Gardiner excused herself, pointedly leaving the door open on her departure.

Darcy's relief at this unexpected opportunity to speak privately was tempered by the sight of Elizabeth biting her lip in apparent dismay at this same situation. Nonetheless, he did not intend to let this chance go to waste. "Elizabeth, is there anything that is troubling you? If I have done something to offend you, I hope you will tell me," he said with some anxiety.

She glanced up at him quickly, then just as rapidly turned her eyes away. "Thank you for your concern, sir, but I have no complaints," she said lightly.

He looked at her in concern. Quietly, so that no one could overhear, he said, "If it was my behaviour yesterday which disturbed you, and certainly you have every right to be unhappy about it, please accept my apologies. I will do my best to prevent such a situation from arising again."

She shook her head, but did not raise her eyes. "Please do not trouble yourself, sir; I have a trifle of a headache, but that is all. It is no matter." She fervently hoped that he would take her hint and leave the matter be; time was what she needed more than anything else to be able to manage this new situation.

Darcy sat back and looked at her assessingly. This was a situation beyond his experience; every instinct told him that she was unhappy, but she herself denied it. He made one last effort, a trace of annoyance beginning to show in his voice. "Should there ever be any difficulty, madam, I hope that you *will* tell me; I am a poor mind-reader."

His reversion to formality vexed her for no reason which she could explain. "I will keep that in mind, Mr. Darcy," she said coolly. She felt her irritation rising, and counselled herself on the need for calm endurance.

She was not, however, in a state of mind to take the lead in the conversation; she had been unable to resist testing the sore subject of Darcy's interest in the theatre, and her feelings were still somewhat raw from hearing his discourse on that topic. She determined to wait on his pleasure; she could sit in silence as well as he.

Darcy had never had much patience for conversation which involved more disguise of his natural inclinations than was comfortable for him. Lacking a better subject, he returned to the one which had interested Elizabeth earlier. "Do you have a particular interest in theatre, Miss Bennet?"

"I cannot claim a particular involvement in it; I have not had much opportunity to attend it, having been but little in London society," said Elizabeth, an edge to her voice.

"I believe I saw you there recently, though, in the company of your aunt and uncle," he said. "Did you enjoy the performance that night?"

Elizabeth's disquiet rose. Recalling the attentive young woman with whom he had been laughing that night, she wondered how he would respond if she were to say that she had been more engaged by the performance in his box than the one on the stage. A sudden thought assailed her—could that woman have been the one of whom Georgiana spoke? No, she realized, he would not be seen in public with such a woman, at least she could not imagine that he would. Unless, of course, she were one of the leading lights of the theatre, in which case it might have been acceptable... *I shall go mad if I cannot stop thinking of this!* she thought with a stab of pain. She was sufficiently caught up in her thoughts that she failed to respond to his question.

With a cautious glance at the door, Darcy reached over and took her hand. Startled, she flinched, the images of him with another woman battling with her inevitable response to his touch. She had to school herself not to snatch her hand away. How could her body still enjoy the feeling of his so much, knowing what she knew? Was she truly that weak of will, so subject to the sin of desire?

Darcy's eyes narrowed. So his touch was suddenly distasteful to her, was it? That was quite a change from the previous morning, when she had been all too happy to accept his lovemaking. This was beginning to take the appearance of one of the traps that he had seen women spring on unsuspecting men in an attempt to increase their ardour. Such games as these were repugnant to him; he was amazed and displeased to see Elizabeth engaging in them—she had always seemed so different, so unlikely to employ the wiles of the women he knew in the *ton*. Perhaps he had misjudged her, but if so, he would make it clear that he did not intend to tolerate this from her. He released her hand abruptly. "Why is it, madam, that my company which seemed to please you yesterday is so objectionable today?" he asked challengingly. "You seemed none too displeased when I touched you yesterday!" He allowed his eyes to travel over her body in a way which left no doubt as to his meaning.

Elizabeth stared at him in shock. Had he truly meant his words in as insulting a manner as they had sounded? One look at his face told her more clearly than any words that he did. This was beyond what she could tolerate. Recklessly, she exclaimed, "I did not ask, sir, either for your company this morning, nor for your advances, nor for this engagement!"

Darcy's complexion paled at the contempt in your voice. "I am sorry to hear that is your sentiment, madam, but I certainly shall not force my company upon you in that case. Perhaps if you feel more receptive on another day, you will be so kind as to inform me; otherwise, I shall not trouble you unnecessarily." He stood and bowed, but before he quitted the room enough regret pierced his anger to cause him to turn back to her once more. "Elizabeth, I do not understand what has happened here, but I would prefer not to part from you in strife," he said, making one last attempt at appeasement.

"I am sorry it troubles you, Mr. Darcy," said Elizabeth, cut to the quick by his willingness to dismiss her completely, her good judgment overtaken by anger. "But I am certain that you will be able to find consolation elsewhere."

Darcy's eyes widened with shock at her implication. "In that case, madam, I believe there is nothing further to say at this junction. Good day, Miss Bennet." With these words he hastily quit the room, and the next moment Elizabeth heard him open the front door and leave the house.

The tumult of her mind was now painfully great. Why, oh why, had she said such things—how could she have allowed her anger to take command of her? How was she ever to explain her behaviour this day to him, and how were they to reach some form of settlement which would allow them to co-exist in some sort of peace? Her anguish quite overcame her, and from actual weakness she sat down and cried.

A few minutes later, her aunt hurried in, fetched by the maid who had observed Miss Bennet's state of distress. "Lizzy!" she cried, coming to put her arms around her sobbing niece. "What ever is the matter, my dear?"

Elizabeth shook her head, unwilling to expose her foolishness both in quarrelling with Darcy and in trusting him in the first place.

146

"You *must* tell me, my dear!" insisted Mrs. Gardiner in deep concern. "Was there a problem with Mr. Darcy's behaviour? I must know what happened!"

She knew that she needed to acquit him on the grounds her aunt suspected, but once she started to speak, the words came tumbling out. "No, he did not *do* anything—we quarrelled, and he left—but oh, aunt, what a mistake this has been! I wish we had never met again!"

Now even more greatly concerned, since she knew that Elizabeth was not prone to flights of fancy, her aunt said gently, "What is it, then, Lizzy? I could not help but notice how troubled you seemed yesterday evening. What has happened?"

Elizabeth attempted to still her sobs, but she could not bring herself to look up at her aunt as she admitted the mortifying truth. "I found out that he keeps a mistress, an actress." Saying the words seemed to cut her anew, and her tears began to fall once more.

"Oh, my dear." Mrs. Gardiner's voice was laden with sympathy. "But is it certain? How did you discover it?"

"Miss Darcy herself told me yesterday—she did not mean to; it just slipped out, I believe."

"And what did Mr. Darcy say?"

"I did not ask him—I *could* not; I only indicated that his presence was not particularly welcome to me. How am I to doubt his sister's word, after all, and what is there for him to say to me if I should ask? I cannot change the truth, but I would *not* wish to hear it from him."

Mrs. Gardiner looked concerned. "Does he not even deserve the opportunity to defend himself? Suppose that his sister is mistaken, or you somehow misunderstood what she meant?"

"There could have been no mistake!" cried Elizabeth. "And I know it is true; I know that he is…experienced." Covering her face with a handkerchief, she was soon lost to everything else.

Her aunt, recognizing that there was little point in argument, continued to hold her and to speak comfortingly to her until Elizabeth reached some sort of calmness. After her niece had excused herself to go to her room, Mrs. Gardiner still sat for some time with a thoughtful look upon her face.

THE SERVANTS OF THE DARCY household gave their master a wide berth that afternoon. Ever since he had returned home that morning, much earlier than expected, his face had held a look of wrath that none cared to cross. His pacing was heard from beyond the closed door of his study. It was highly unusual to see the master so angry.

Darcy had held his anger in check on the long ride back from Gracechurch Street, but once he was at home, he allowed himself to feel the full force of it. He could scarcely believe the insults that Elizabeth had given him—ignoring his repeated enquiries while yet rejecting him, and then that final comment! What kind of man did she think he was, that she would tell him to seek his consolation elsewhere? He carefully avoided thinking of her other statement, the one that cut like a knife—*I did not ask, sir, either for your company this morning, nor for your advances, nor for this engagement!*

What could have come over her? Her behaviour was as inexplicable as it was unacceptable. Was this a side of her he had never seen before? If so, how were they ever to find resolution? And she had rejected his offer of peace…he would have never dreamed the previous day that his relationship with Elizabeth could go so wrong so quickly. What had happened to the passionately responsive woman he had held in his arms, who had laughed with him and teased him? Was she lost forever?

He sat down heavily at his desk, dropping his head into his hands. *Elizabeth,* he thought with a wrenching pain. *Shall we never have our moments of joy together? Instead of the liveliness I have loved, will I receive only sullenness and anger?*

He had been preoccupied with these thoughts for some time when a soft knock came at the door. "Yes?" he snapped.

The butler appeared in the doorway. "Mrs. Gardiner is here to see you, sir," the butler said in a careful voice that did not show surprise at this unusual visit from a lone married woman. With Mr. Darcy in his present frame of mind, he had seriously considered telling her that the master was not at home, but without knowing Darcy's pleasure, he had elected to take the route of caution.

Darcy's eyebrows rose, but he said only, "Thank you, show her in, please." Inwardly, his surprise and anxiety were great. Given Elizabeth's anger when he departed, he could not imagine that her aunt would be bearing any positive news. Yet the very irregularity of such a call suggested some particular purpose—he could only hope it was not one which would make matters any worse. *Surely Elizabeth does not think that she can break the engagement at this point!* he thought with a moment of panic.

He was determined to betray none of his feelings. He rose and greeted his guest civilly, inviting her to sit. She looked no different from her usual pleasant self, and seemed perfectly warm in her behaviour towards him, but he did not relax his guard.

"Mr. Darcy, you are no doubt wondering at the purpose of my visit," she said.

He inclined his head. "Although it is always a pleasure to see you, I must confess that I am."

"I wanted to speak with you regarding Lizzy. I am concerned about her; she has been quite unhappy of late. I know from experience…" She paused a moment, as if to collect her thoughts. "…that Lizzy's thoughts are not always easy to determine."

Darcy looked at her carefully. Elizabeth's behaviour had already dealt him a serious blow, and he was reluctant to make himself any more vulnerable, yet Mrs. Gardiner's concern and warmth seemed genuine. "I am aware that she is upset with me," he allowed, "although I am not entirely clear as to why that might be."

"You do not know what is troubling her?"

Darcy gave her a level look. "I have some guesses, nothing more."

Mrs. Gardiner shifted in her chair. "Mr. Darcy, may I inquire as to where your sister might be?"

Startled by the question, he said, "Georgiana? She left for Derby this morning."

"Ahh." She took a deep breath, and then continued, "By your countenance, then, I take it that you are unaware that she told Elizabeth that you have an…ongoing concern with a certain lady of the theatre."

The shock of her statement propelled Darcy half-way out of his chair before he regained control of himself. Shaken, he said, "I am afraid that I find that…difficult to credit, Mrs. Gardiner." Internally, his thoughts were racing. *She could not have! She knew nothing of it…and* why *would she have said such a thing?* Suddenly he recollected Georgiana's quietness after Elizabeth's visit to her, and her abrupt decision to leave London.

"I find the tale quite as astonishing as you do, sir," said Mrs. Gardiner calmly, "and I cannot claim to know what was said in my absence, but I

149

am quite clear this is what Elizabeth understood her to say, or perhaps more accurately, to have let slip."

It made far too much sense. Darcy raked his hand through his hair, remembering Elizabeth's parting comment about seeking consolation elsewhere. No wonder she was so distressed. "And you say she believes this to be *ongoing*?" he asked, disbelief apparent in his voice.

She looked at him in some sympathy. "That seems to be Lizzy's understanding."

Darcy could sit still no longer. He walked rapidly over to the window and looked out into the street. *Why would Georgiana have said such a thing? And how could Elizabeth have believed it of me? Is her opinion of me still so poor?* He closed his eyes and took several breaths to steady himself. "I assure you, Mrs. Gardiner, it is quite untrue that I have any connection of the kind," he said in as level a voice as he could manage, hoping Mrs. Gardiner was enough of a woman of the world not to condemn the fact that he had not denied *ever* having such a relationship.

"Mr. Darcy, I was not under the impression you did, or I should not have thought to call on you today," she responded, her voice sympathetic. "It is not my habit to believe everything I hear, but I am also perhaps less…involved in this situation than is Lizzy—and perhaps I have less reason to assume a lack of *reliability* in those people for whom I otherwise have respect."

Anger that Elizabeth would possibly think he would make love to her while keeping a mistress on the side almost clouded his ability to note the emphasis Mrs. Gardiner had put on the last part of her statement. He struggled to make sense of it—did Elizabeth feel *he* was unreliable? Good God! What crime had he ever committed that the woman he loved should have such a low opinion of him?

Mrs. Gardiner noted the set of his shoulders and made a guess as to his state of mind. "Mr. Darcy, it is my impression that my niece has a deep regard for you," she said gently. "But Lizzy is not an easy woman to understand. She has an appearance of charming self-confidence which I believe is somewhat deceptive. Having known her for many years now, I can say with some assurance that what appears to be confidence is in fact more an unusually independent sort of self-reliance. I do not know how familiar you are with her family, and I hope you will understand if I say that, despite being affectionate, her parents have not always been people Lizzy could *depend* upon in times of need. Lizzy has learned as a result to keep a great deal to herself, and it has been a concern of mine for some time that it might prove difficult for a man to earn her trust."

He did not know what to make of any of it. His mind kept travelling from Georgiana's betrayal of him to Elizabeth's lack of belief in him, as he struggled to integrate Mrs. Gardiner's words into his thoughts. Having seen both Mr. Bennet and Mrs. Bennet interacting with their daughters, he had no difficulty crediting that Elizabeth would not feel as if she could rely upon them, but had it become so general a habit for her? She always seemed so strong, so independent—it was difficult to conceive that this could be merely a façade, that she could fear losing him, of all things. Could it be possible that it was not her opinion of *him* that was so tenuous, but herself? To think of his outspoken, vivacious Elizabeth as being in some ways fragile was a radical thought, but he rapidly realized that it was not an unpleasant one. He knew instinctively that he could be the one to supply the support she needed, just as she, by her very presence in his life, provided the liveliness and spirit which he had always needed. With a shock, he realized that her very distress at this time could be interpreted as a sign of the depth of her regard for him. This thought gave him a sense of fulfilment that was new to him—even as it drew to his attention the fact that he had always avoided facing the question of Elizabeth's feelings for him. Why was it that he had settled for winning her and never once addressed the question of earning her affection? Why had he assumed that venture to be pointless; and, more importantly, was he prepared to change his view on it?

Decisively, he turned away from the window and went back to sit heavily in his chair. "Mrs. Gardiner, what is it you are trying to suggest to me?" he asked with an indecorous directness.

His guest did not seem to mind, however. "I think, sir, you are going to have to decide whether it is worth the patience it will take to win Lizzy's trust."

Darcy sat still, only his fingers moving as they drummed against the armrest of his chair. "And if I do decide it is worth it, what then?" he asked finally.

Mrs. Gardiner gave him a smile of approval. "Then you will need to be prepared to deal with Lizzy's fears of allowing herself to care for you, and also, if I do not guess incorrectly, some rather strong feelings of shame over other feelings she might have."

Fear of allowing herself to care—well, that was not difficult at all for him to understand, after all the months he had fought falling under her spell and surrendering his independence to his need for her. But shame— he could see nothing for her to be ashamed of, apart from having believed his sister a little too readily, and failing to speak with him about it. D-mn Georgiana, anyway! But it hardly seemed as significant as her aunt seemed to suggest. "I fail to see why she should be feeling any shame," he said with a question in his voice.

"Mr. Darcy, I have been quite frank with you today, but there are certain discussions which I am *not* prepared to have," said Mrs. Gardiner with a smile which took away the apparent harshness of her words.

Darcy flushed as he took her meaning, feeling rather like a schoolboy found raiding the larder. At the same time, he could not help but be impressed with the combination of nonjudgemental forthrightness and tact in a woman only a few years older than he—Elizabeth was fortunate to have such a woman as her aunt in her life.

"Well, sir, I fear I must be going," said Mrs. Gardiner briskly. "I have a handful of children and a very upset niece at home, and I have been gone too long as it is."

"Thank you for coming," he said with deep feeling. "You have given me a great deal to think about."

He walked her to the door where he found a hired carriage waiting. Abruptly, before he even had a chance to think through his offer, he said, "Would you do me the honour of permitting me to drive you home, madam?"

She gave him a shrewd look. "That would be delightful, thank you, Mr. Darcy."

ELIZABETH HAD SPENT THE HOURS of her aunt's absence closeted in her room. Her spirits had gone from a state of extreme troublement to a present sense of numb emptiness. Her regrets for her earlier behaviour were intense and intolerable. How could she have said such things, knowing this was the man with whom she would have to spend her life? Foolish, foolish girl! she admonished herself yet again. Matters were bad enough—did you have to provoke more trouble? Is a state of armed warfare truly what you desire?

She knew that she would have to make her apologies to Darcy, and the very idea made her cringe. She did not *want* to apologize, and doing so merely for the sake of peace went against the grain, yet she knew it must be done. How she was ever to live with her feelings about the present situation she did not know, but learn to live with it she must.

She had gone so far as to attempt to write to Darcy, but the exercise only made her cry once more. She knew that she needed a distraction, but felt unequal even to playing with the children. She was aware that her aunt would not tolerate this withdrawal for any length of time, and she would need to make an appearance soon. When the maid came to tell her that Mrs. Gardiner had returned and her presence was required below, she knew there was little point in hiding further.

It was not until she entered the sitting room that she realized her aunt was not alone. She grew pale when she saw Mr. Darcy, his eyes intently upon her, his expression unreadable. What was she to say?

Mrs. Gardiner took her arm. "Lizzy, you look unwell; please sit down," she said, guiding her to a chair. Leaning over her, she said softly in her ear, "Please talk to him, my dear. He needs you, and you could do well to believe in him." She kissed Elizabeth's cheek lightly, and then, to her niece's horror, left the two of them alone.

Elizabeth struggled to find the words she had sought earlier for an apology, and was still gathering her courage to look up when Darcy crossed the room to kneel before her. He took both her hands in his, pressing a kiss on each. She could scarcely credit what a profound relief it was to her to have him there, looking at her with undisguised caring.

Darcy suddenly discovered that he had thought no further than being in her company, as if his presence would be enough to communicate everything to her. Her apparent distress made it even more difficult to collect his thoughts. "My dearest, please forgive me for my anger this morning; I did not understand the situation; but, even so, I should have stayed to hear you out in any case," he finally managed to say. "It is not true, what Georgiana told you. The truth is that since I met you last autumn, I have barely given any other woman a second thought. I love you, Elizabeth—ardently, passionately, and beyond all reasonable measure, and you cannot rid yourself of me, because I cannot do without you."

A stab of shame went through her with the realization that he knew what had caused her distress. She wanted desperately to believe him but did not dare. "I am sorry as well for what I said earlier," she forced herself to say, her voice trembling. "But I cannot understand why Georgiana would have made up such a thing."

Darcy looked down at her hands, so tightly held in his own. "I cannot say, my heart; she was very angry at me for something I told her, and perhaps this was her way of striking back—if so, it has been remarkably effective, for I cannot imagine a way to hurt me more than by harming your trust in me." He took a deep breath, aware of the risk he was taking, but knowing anything less than full honesty at this moment could do still greater damage. "I will tell you the truth, though I am not proud of it— this was not a complete fabrication on her part. There was a woman some years ago, but I swear to you, it was over long before I met you, and I do not know how Georgiana even came to hear of it."

Tears started in Elizabeth's eyes. It was painful to conceive of another woman even in his past, though she knew that it would have been far more surprising had there not been at least one, and more likely many. His confession had the power, however, to convince her of the truth of the rest of his assertion, that she had no present reason for concern, and she felt as if a weight had dropped away from her.

Seeing the change in her expression, Darcy took her in his arms with an inarticulate sound. Holding her head to his shoulder, he whispered, "I am so sorry, my dearest, for hurting you; I would do anything to take the pain away."

She allowed herself the comfort of his embrace for only a few moments before she pulled away. At his look of dismay at her withdrawal, she took his hand and said shakily, "Thank you for your honesty. It is painful, but I would rather have the truth."

"I will never lie to you, my heart. You know that I abhor all forms of disguise, and I have always admired you for your forthrightness and honesty."

Elizabeth felt almost as if she did not know the man before her. She had never seen him like this before, with a directness and an intensity new to him. Without words, she knew that he was asking more of her than he ever had in the past. She hardly knew what to make of his behaviour and feared her own vulnerability to it and to him. Calling on her pride to protect her, she raised her chin slightly as she said, "Then if we are to be honest, let us be honest about this engagement, as well. I know it is not what you intended, not after my family's disgrace. I appreciate your readiness to protect my reputation, but let us not pretend this was not something you wished to avoid."

He gave her a look of incredulity. "Wished to avoid? What could possibly give you such an idea? I have wanted to marry you since long before Hunsford, and there has never been a time since then when I would not have proposed to you in a minute had I felt certain of your response! Had your uncle not interrupted us, I would have been begging your acceptance as soon as I could bring myself to let you go!"

The moment of trust she had felt earlier faded painfully, and she said coldly, "I appreciate your concern for my feelings, Mr. Darcy, but the truth of the matter is you left Netherfield to avoid me and then avoided me further in London. I am not blaming you—I understand why you could no longer look at me as marriageable at that point, but I cannot act as if it never happened."

"Is *this* what you have been imagining?" Though stunned by her assertion, Darcy could not help smiling at her misunderstanding, and he gently smoothed a stray lock of her hair. "My dearest Elizabeth, my love, I was staying away because I thought that *you* wanted nothing more to do with *me*—and even then, I did it badly; if you had not come to my house that night, I would have come seeking you out, because I could not stay away."

"Why would you think that I wanted nothing to do with you after…after how I had greeted you at Longbourn?" demanded Elizabeth, incredulous in her own turn, and more than a little mortified to be forced to refer to her own inappropriate behaviour.

They had reached the point he had dreaded since he first heard of her sister's elopement. Darcy closed his eyes, reluctant to voice this reminder of his sins. "Because what happened to your sister was my fault. I heard first from your uncle, and then in a letter from Bingley, that you could not forgive yourself for failing to expose Wickham for what he was; if you could not forgive *yourself* after I had asked for your secrecy, how could I think you would ever forgive me, who was so much more at fault?"

She examined him carefully, trying to assess the truth of his words, and suddenly found herself able to recognize again the man she had come to love. Her face softened at his obvious distress. "It never crossed my mind to blame you then, and I would not now." Her mind turned to that time when she had returned to Longbourn only to discover him gone, and the agonizing loss that had haunted her. Feeling on the verge of tears, she bit her lip and turned her face away in an attempt to control herself.

"What is it, my heart?" asked Darcy urgently, reading all too clearly the pain in her face. Elizabeth shook her head vehemently, unwilling to expose her vulnerability so blatantly. His voice turned soft and cajoling. "Please tell me—please *trust* me enough to tell me what troubles you."

Finding this unanswerable, she closed her eyes and said, "All I knew was that I hurried home, wanting nothing more than to be with you and to feel the comfort of your presence, and you were gone." Her voice cracked slightly on the last words.

Feeling the full weight of his own failures, Darcy bowed his head, resting his forehead on the backs of her hands. It was a moment before he was able to speak. "No wonder you did not want to accept my proposal. How you must have hated me! I am a fool, and worse than a fool. Had I known you wanted me, I would have been by your side, even if I had to crawl every inch of the way from London."

Something in his tone eased her fears. "I *never* hated you, not for a minute," she said gently. She bent to kiss his dark curls lightly, causing him to look up at her with a question in his eyes. She continued, "I did want to accept your proposal—I wanted it more than anything, but I did not want you to be forced into marrying me when it was not in your best interest."

"You were trying to protect *me*?" he asked, hardly able to credit her words. "You *wanted* to accept me?

"Yes," she said with a rueful smile. "It seems we have both been making a great many assumptions about the other."

What a comedy of errors! he thought as his eyes met hers in a look which spoke volumes. He recalled what Mrs. Gardiner had said about trust, and tried to put his feelings into words. "Apparently so, but you may be absolutely certain, my heart—I want nothing more than for you to be my wife, without a single doubt or question, and you are the only woman in the world for me."

Elizabeth found his words both reassuring and a little frightening in their strength. Her eyes roamed over his face, and then came to rest on his hands, firm, capable, and strong around her own. She heard her aunt's words again in her mind: *He needs you, and you could do well to believe in him.* A sense of hope which had felt gone forever began to blossom in her again.

Seeing the light in her eyes, Darcy wanted nothing more than to kiss her, to feel her forgiveness in the only way he could fully accept, but he knew that this was not the place, and moreover, that he had likely already made her unhappy with his physical demands of her. "Elizabeth," he said hesitantly.

"Yes, Fitzwilliam?" She looked into his eyes, trying to communicate the regard that she could not yet speak.

"Have I been troubling you with…my demands?"

He looked for a moment so much like a guilty child denied a treat that Elizabeth was half-tempted to laugh, but it was clear that this was a subject of deep gravity for him. She wondered how much he had guessed of the embarrassment she felt over her desire for him. "Sir, it is not your behaviour that troubles me, but my own," she said softly.

He lifted her hands to his lips again. "Your behaviour gives me nothing but joy."

Her cheeks flamed, and she dropped her eyes.

He continued, regretful acceptance in his voice, "But I can see it is not the same for you. I must apologize for my selfishness," he said, his thumbs tracing circles on the back of her hands. "When I have been with you, I have been thinking only of my own desires and not concerning myself enough with your feelings, and I shall not forgive myself for it easily. In my impatience, I have demanded more of you than is my right, and I fear that you have been paying the price for it. But no longer—you need not fear being alone with me; I shall not again attempt to take advantage of the situation." He tightened his hands on hers momentarily, then released them.

On impulse, before he could draw away, Elizabeth put her hand to his cheek and kissed him, briefly but with unrestrained passion, then moved away almost as quickly. Surprised by her own action, she glanced quickly toward the door, hoping they had not been observed. When she looked back, she found Darcy gazing at her with a warmth that fluttered her pulses.

"How dearly I love you," he said, his voice rich with feeling. "Never forget it, my heart."

His unaffected sincerity moved Elizabeth deeply, though it made her feel at the same moment shy. She could not yet be so direct with him, but wanted him to know of her appreciation. "Thank you for coming back; I was quite desolate after our argument. I will try to have greater faith in you in the future."

"Elizabeth!" His voice carried unrestrained emotion at her admission. The tenderness with which she was gazing at him gave him hope that her deeper affections might yet be his, and the more he thought on it, the more he desired it. He wanted to see her lovely eyes light up when he walked into the room, and to know he was the source of her joy as she was of his; to be the one she would turn to when she felt desolate or afraid, and to be assured she would welcome him when he was in pain. And her kisses—he wanted her to feel the same pleasure and freedom in his embrace that he did whenever he so much as touched her, with no sense of guilt or shame. But that part would take patience, something of which he was in short supply when it came to the subject of the lovely and tempting Miss Elizabeth Bennet. Having tasted her passion already, it would be painful to let it go for now, but let it go he must. He tore his thoughts away from the softness of her lips, and somehow forced himself to move to the relative safety of the chair next to hers, where he could enjoy the warmth of her gaze without the immediate danger of losing himself to temptation.

Chapter 9

"Madeleine," said Mr. Gardiner, the tone of his voice expressing grave displeasure. "What ever was in your mind when you left the two of them alone?"

Mrs. Gardiner sighed. Her husband's countenance had been grim ever since arriving home to find his niece alone with Darcy in the sitting room, he whispering intimately in her ear and holding her hand in his. Mrs. Gardiner approached him and slipped her arms around his waist, laying her head on his shoulder. "Would you prefer the practical reason, or the general justification, my love?"

It was very difficult, reflected Mr. Gardiner, to remain vexed with his wife when she behaved so prettily. "I would imagine that I should hear both," he said in a somewhat gentler voice.

"Practically, Edward has been ill all day and requiring my attention, and it seemed to me that it would be quite rude to suggest that Mr. Darcy could not be left alone with Lizzy for a few minutes, especially with the door open. But I must say that I think it best to allow them a certain leeway. I know that you disapprove, but their attachment is passionate, and I would rather find them holding hands or even stealing a kiss here than risk them becoming desperate enough for each other to find some way to steal off together without anyone's eye on them." She looked up at him to assess his response.

He was not to be mollified. "You have the knack for making the most unusual argument seem sensible, my dear, but I cannot and will not accept this—this is *my* house! Surely you can see that I cannot permit this—what if one of the girls should happen in? Do I explain that it is acceptable for Lizzy, because her intended has such *passionate* feelings for her, but will not be acceptable for them? I think not!"

With another sigh, she said, "I suppose not, my love—but will you please be gentle with her? I believe that she and Mr. Darcy had a very serious quarrel today, and have only just reconciled."

He looked at her with concern. "What was the cause of this quarrel, do you know?"

"I do know, but I shall not tell you—it has all been resolved, and it was based on misinformation. It would only spoil your digestion to know," she said with a smile.

With a suspicious look, he replied, "I somehow suspect that there is more here than meets the eye, but I know better than to argue when you have that look to you. Very well, keep your own counsel; I will trust you."

She kissed him lightly. "I will return to them now, so that you need worry no more about them."

"I *will* be speaking to Lizzy later," he reiterated.

"Yes, my dear, I know," she said.

WHEN SHE RETIRED THAT NIGHT Elizabeth was too exhausted for anything save sleep; but when she opened her eyes in the morning, her mind was still distracted and unsettled by all that had happened the previous day. She found much to be ashamed of in her own behaviour—Darcy was correct, she thought, to think that she should have had enough faith in him to ask him directly about his sister's accusation. There was the matter of Georgiana, as well; it was evident that she and Elizabeth were to be starting their new relationship on the very shakiest of terms. Elizabeth was willing to grant her grounds for jealousy; but, knowing the truth, she could not ignore the fact that her future sister had deliberately misled her in a manner which was both painful and destructive. She had not spoken with Darcy, but she could only assume that he would be angered by his sister's behaviour.

She felt no better about matters with her uncle. After Darcy's departure the previous day, Mr. Gardiner had taken her into his study for a tongue-lashing even more severe than the one he had delivered after discovering her with Darcy that evening at his townhouse. *In my house, under my roof,*

I expect that you will obey my rules, he had said. *If this degree of discipline is beyond your capacities, I am sorry to say that you will not be welcome here any longer.* She was stung by his icy tone, but hurt far more by the rejection he offered; the Gardiners' house had been like a second home to her, and to be so summarily dismissed for what she thought to be a minor violation was wounding. After the emotional stresses of the day, it had been almost more than she could take in.

She was longing to see Darcy; at the moment, he felt like her only ally. She knew that he could not be less troubled by those same events which had so angered Mr. Gardiner. She recalled what he had said the previous day, the look in his eyes attesting to the truth of his words: *Your behaviour gives me nothing but joy.*

Her distress with her uncle, and the anguish of self-rebuke were tempered by Darcy's different understanding of her feelings. He, she recognized, did not see them as inappropriate. This was so much the opposite of what she had always been told that a man would desire in a woman; it was difficult to credit that Darcy might not prefer her to be more passive in these matters; but, it was clear he did not.

Later that morning, as she was impatiently awaiting Mr. Darcy's daily call, her aunt joined her briefly in the sitting room. Elizabeth, cognizant of the dilemma her aunt faced in needing to chaperone her, as well as having a sick child to attend to, offered to walk out with Mr. Darcy to reduce the burden on her.

"If you wish, my dear, you certainly may; or you may stay here—I have no concerns on that regard either," said Mrs. Gardiner.

Elizabeth coloured, certain that her aunt was referring to the scolding she had received. "No, you need have no concerns," she said civilly, if not completely happily.

Her aunt paused, and looked at her sympathetically. "You know, my dear, there is nothing at all unusual in your desire to be with Mr. Darcy; in fact, I would say it speaks well of your affection for him. It is one of the mysteries of conventional society to me—how when we determine that a *behaviour* should not occur, instead of saying as much, we say instead that no one should *want* to behave in such a manner, as if the wanting and the behaviour were the same and one. You have a passionate nature, Lizzy, and it is not something of which you need be ashamed."

This all too perceptive statement embarrassed Elizabeth yet further, but at the same time was reassuring—if Mrs. Gardiner, whom she admired, saw nothing shameful in her desires, perhaps she was not quite as alone in her feelings as she had thought. "Thank you," she replied. "It has been rather…confusing."

"I can imagine," said her aunt, kissing her cheek with an understanding smile before leaving to attend to the children.

When Mr. Darcy arrived, Elizabeth greeted him with a pleasure that took his breath away. He had felt some slight concern as to how she would feel this morning after their conflict the day before, but the light in her eyes when she saw him went beyond reassuring him and into the realm of delight. He wanted nothing more than to take her in his arms and carry her off with him, but he had given the matter substantial thought, and had made the unhappy determination that for Elizabeth's sake it was necessary for him to be the perfect gentleman for the duration of their engagement. He hoped fervently that her parents would not insist on a long engagement, given the difficulty he was foreseeing in keeping his resolve, especially when she looked at him with such open affection.

Elizabeth, not wishing to discuss the episode with her uncle, followed up on her idea of walking out, which met with his agreement. *At least this way I can be by his side, and touch his arm with no shame to it,* she thought.

Darcy could not regret the greater warmth with which Elizabeth was suddenly treating him; it went a long way to meet his need for her affection. It did, however, try his resolve, especially when she would hold herself close to his arm, and he found that he needed to banish any thoughts of desire completely from his mind in order to maintain his composure.

Although the visit was a pleasant one, Elizabeth could not help but notice the absence of the passionate looks and forward conversation that had previously characterized Mr. Darcy's conduct during their walks. To her mortification, she discovered that she missed them, and the stimulating sense of connection they gave her. It was as if he had suddenly shut off that part of their bond, and while she knew intellectually that it was done deliberately and on her behalf, she could not help but regret its absence.

She bade him farewell that afternoon with regret, her disappointment the greater for knowing that she would not have the opportunity to see him the following day, as her uncle would be entertaining business associates. Darcy could not help lingering over her hand as well, giving himself the leeway in these last moments to allow some of his desire for her to show in his expression as he told her quietly that he would miss her.

Elizabeth was feeling rather wistful herself after his departure, but was soon distracted by the appearance of the maid in the doorway with a newly-arrived letter for her. Elizabeth saw that it was in an unfamiliar hand, and opened it with some curiosity. It began without salutation:

You can be at no loss to understand the reason for this letter. I have heard the report of your engagement to my nephew. I am most seriously displeased to even consider that you would act with such callous disregard for his honour and his duty to his family, as well as to his place in the world, as to entice him in with your arts and allurements! Had he retained the use of his reason, he would never have embarked upon a venture so contrary to the wishes of his mother and all of her family! Do you pay no regard to the wishes of his friends? Are you lost to every feeling of propriety and delicacy?

Your own honour, decorum, prudence, nay, interest, should forbid such a marriage! Yes, your own interest; for do not expect to be noticed by his family or friends if you wilfully act against the inclinations of all. I assure you that such a marriage will never be recognized by his family, and that you will make him an outcast among those he holds dearest. You will be censured, slighted, and despised by every one connected with him. Your alliance will be a disgrace; your name will never even be mentioned by any of us.

I will also add that to the objections I have already urged, I have still another to add. I am no stranger to the particulars of your youngest sister's infamous elopement. And is such a girl to be my nephew's sister? Is her husband, the son of his late father's steward, to be his brother? Are the shades of Pemberley to be thus polluted?

You may be certain, Miss Bennet, that I will also apply to my nephew, in certainty that he will come to his senses and realize the immense error he has made before it is too late. I am most seriously displeased.

C. De Bourgh

The discomposure of spirits into which this extraordinary missive threw Elizabeth could not be easily overcome. The shock of such an attack, when their engagement was already determined, was great. Surely Lady Catherine did not believe that her nephew would go back on his promise to her now? She had been aware that his family would not think highly of the match, but to be assailed in such an openly insulting manner was painfully unexpected.

Her first response was a forthright fury at the insults Lady Catherine had levelled at her and her family, but shortly it gave way to a dispiriting sense of unease. If it was true that his family would shun her, it would put him at odds either with them or her; and, in either case, their marriage would end up costing him dearly. She could not credit that, with his sense of honour, Darcy would reconsider his decision to marry her even if he wished to; but that he could come to regret it she did not doubt. She could think of little that would cause her more pain.

She knew not the exact degree of Mr. Darcy's affection for his aunt, or his dependence on her judgment, but it was natural to suppose that he thought much higher of her ladyship than *she* could do. It was certain, that in enumerating the miseries of a marriage with one, whose immediate connections were so unequal to his own, his aunt would address him on his weakest side. All the fears she had put aside when she had allowed herself to enjoy his courtship and his company returned in force. She did not wish him to come to any harm, but she also knew that she had come too far to be able to give him up, even for his own sake—and her uncle would not allow it even if she tried.

There was another dilemma to be faced—whether to tell Darcy about his aunt's letter. If she did, he would no doubt ask to read it, an outcome she would prefer to avoid. But should she decide to keep it a secret and he later discover it, he would certainly be angered with her as well. She could not for many hours learn to think of it less than incessantly and still could come to no resolution.

At dinner that evening, her uncle announced that he had finally received a reply to his letter from Mr. Bennet. When Elizabeth asked with some anxiety what opinions her father had expressed, Mr. Gardiner silently, but with a certain sympathy, produced a folded sheet of paper from his pocket and gave it to her. She unfolded it to find it contained only one short sentence: 'I give my consent,' over her father's familiar scrawled signature.

Her heart sank; his disapproval was more evident in his silence than it would have been had he violently upbraided her. *I could hardly have expected more,* she told herself. *After all, it does not reflect well on him to have another daughter caught in a compromising position, and he does not like Mr. Darcy in any case.* She resolved to do what she could to change his opinion on her return, but his reaction still pained her—she had hoped that she could return home on better terms with her father than when she had departed for London, but it did not seem that this would be the case.

Mrs. Gardiner noticed how troubled her niece seemed that evening, and tried to draw her out, but to no avail; Elizabeth was keeping her own counsel. She was uncertain how well she would be able to maintain her composure if she did not—she was feeling surrounded by the weight of disapproval of both his family and hers, either of herself or of her choices, and she found the position painfully intolerable. Her only wish was to see Darcy; she knew that she would find comfort in his presence, and that he would be able to reassure her that these obstacles would be overcome with time. If *he* began to have regrets, she did not know how she could tolerate it. And how little she had ever given him in return for his constancy and affection; she regretted every saucy speech and impertinence she had ever directed to him, every pain she had inflicted upon him by her misjudgments and her lack of trust, and even her ambivalence regarding his attentions. He deserved so much more, and she resolved that, in the future, he would receive it from her. She regretted too, that as a result of her own actions, he no longer felt comfortable even looking at her with passion, much less offering her the pleasure of his kisses.

Later, when she was alone, she shed tears over the letters, feeling most strongly the disappointment and disapproval of her father. The opposition of Lady Catherine, though it worried her, did not pain her so deeply; but it brought to the fore a feeling of betrayal of both herself and Darcy on the part of Georgiana. She was sensible of how greatly his sister's conduct must have pained Darcy, and how they were ever to make peace as a family she did not know. How much more his love for her had cost him than he had initially assessed it at Hunsford when he had felt it merely to be a degradation! Had he realized that he would be rejected by his entire family, would he have persisted in making his suit?

She passed a troubled night, and during one period of nocturnal wakefulness, she found her pain at the responses of their families transmuting to a bitter anger at the injustice of it—what had she done apart from fall in love with a respectable man who loved her, a brilliant match at that? Her conduct had not been impeccable, but it had been far from the complete disregard for the proprieties displayed by Lydia, and not even that much worse than the behaviour regularly exhibited in public by her younger sisters. Why, she wondered, had she objected so to Darcy's physical expression of his regard, when it had always occurred with her tacit consent? He had never failed to respect her choice to stop nor, were she to be honest with herself, done anything which had not left her wanting still more. She was provoked as well by the knowledge that she had been led to believe that she was somehow at fault for desiring his touch, deceived by some of those very people who were now disapproving so heartily of her natural expressions of that affection for the one person who had been treating her with kindness, respect, and love.

In that manner common to midnight thoughts, her pain and resentments only grew as she dwelt upon them, and in time vexation gave way to rejection, and then in turn to a sense of reckless disregard for those who had pained her. At last, in exhaustion, she resolved to herself that henceforth she would consider her future husband and his opinions first, and her family second—and if in the morning she felt the need she did at present to see him and to feel his comfort, then go to him she would, regardless of what anyone else might think of it. And if he was so inclined as to express his affections in a more physical manner, she would offer no objection.

ELIZABETH AWOKE THE NEXT MORNING from vague and disquieting dreams, and found that neither her vexation nor her resolve of the night had faded. She did not immediately go down to breakfast, as she did not wish to meet Mr. Gardiner. Although his manner the night before bespoke sympathy, it seemed unwise to take the risk that he would somehow perceive her new defiance of his authority over her. She spent her time perusing Lady Catherine's letter, no longer reading it as an insult to herself, but dwelling instead with righteous anger on Darcy's behalf at her ladyship's willingness to cast him out from the family fold merely for having the audacity to follow his heart. *Are you lost to every feeling of propriety and delicacy?*—

Elizabeth read this with a cynical smile, recalling how it had offended her the previous day. She saw it now almost as a badge of courage.

It was with greater pain that she again unfolded the note from her father—one could hardly call it a letter—and gazed at his quick scrawl. That he could be so quick to dismiss her! She felt anew his unwillingness to listen to her, both when she had counselled against allowing Lydia to travel to Brighton and again when he had refused to acknowledge the cost of Lydia's elopement to her.

It seemed that when her father wanted a witty companion, he was proud of her, but whenever she wanted him as a father, unless it amused him as it had with Mr. Collins, or whenever she showed a true independence of spirit, his attitude was quite different.

Such were the people who wished to stand between her and Darcy!—she was determined to no longer honour their plans for her, and remained resolved to act in that manner which would constitute her happiness, without reference to any of them. And if by their views her plans were both audacious and scandalous, it was no matter to her.

When she at length descended, her aunt, distracted by the various needs of the household, still found time to greet her affectionately, and asked, "Lizzy, are you quite well this morning?"

Hearing the concern in Mrs. Gardiner's voice, Elizabeth for a moment almost reconsidered her plans, wishing nothing more than to confess her hurt and anger to her aunt. She recognized however that Mrs. Gardiner, though solicitous of her, had no energy to spare for her today, with guests expected and ill children in the house.

Her aunt's distraction served her purpose, though, in making her escape that much more easy. Even so, it took what Elizabeth felt to be quite an inordinate amount of planning for her to make her way to the Darcy town-house undetected by anyone who should remain unaware that she would be alone with him. Her first step was to gather the courage to inform her aunt of her first plan to call on a young lady of her acquaintance, Miss Harris.

Mrs. Gardiner looked more relieved than concerned by this idea, asking Elizabeth only to pass on her compliments to Miss Harris and her mother. Elizabeth, despite a certain degree of guilt at deceiving her aunt in this manner, agreed readily to this, and set forth after breakfast. She walked several streets in the direction of the Harris house before turning off in the direction of a hackney stand. Heart pounding at her own audacity, she loftily ignored the driver's askance look at a young lady travelling without so much as a maid as a companion, and directed him to take her to Grosvenor Square. From there, she walked to Brook Street, and was happy to discover that she could go through the quiet backways past the stable and into the garden of the Darcy house without difficulty. It was then that she discovered that luck—or Providence—was truly with her. Darcy was not only at home, but in the sitting room, which had French doors opening to the garden. Taking a deep breath for courage, she rapped lightly on the glass to draw his attention.

To all appearances, Darcy had been reading a newspaper when he heard her knock; but in truth, his mind had been more agreeably occupied with a memory of sitting in this same chair, with Elizabeth in his lap. The delight of distracting her with kisses and the softness of her skin beneath his fingers as he had unbuttoned her dress made for a far more pleasant reverie than reading the latest news of the Peninsular War.

It was with surprise and a bit of mild embarrassment at being caught thinking such intimate thoughts of her, that he discovered his unexpected visitor. "Elizabeth!" he said, opening the doors to admit her, his pleasure in her appearance evident. "This is a delightful surprise." He struggled manfully to turn his thoughts from a desire to make love to her on the spot.

She was relieved to see that he seemed to take her unorthodox method of entry in stride, and her joy at seeing him dissolved any remaining doubts about her behaviour. She had not realized how powerful the urge to be in his arms would be the moment she saw him. With a deep breath, she smiled at him playfully and said, "It is a pleasure to see you, as well. I am glad to have found you at home."

The brightness of her eyes had its usual bewitching effect on Darcy. Before he could fall completely under her spell, he glanced into the garden, expecting to see her aunt, or at the very least, a maid. "Is Mrs. Gardiner not with you?" he asked.

Elizabeth coloured. This was the moment of truth; she suspected and almost hoped that he would guess her intention as soon as he realized what she had done in coming to him alone and secretly. "I must confess that I came here by myself; I fear that my aunt believes me to be visiting a friend."

Darcy's eyebrows shot up. The last thing he would have expected from Elizabeth was that she would go out of her way to be alone with him—and going so far as to deceive her family as to her intent! No sooner had he understood the situation than he realized in what a difficult position he was—it had been easy enough to give her his word that she would be safe from his advances when he believed their opportunities to be alone and private would be limited, but it was another matter completely when she was standing before him wearing a delightfully arch look, and no one in the house but a few servants.

He realized that caution was required if his restraint was to stand, but while his mind was making one set of plans, his heart was not so cooperative. *Why are you fighting this?* he asked himself derisively. *You know full well you are going to give in to the temptation to kiss her sooner or later; why delay solely to salvage a bit of pride in your self-control?* He could not voice even to himself the answer to his question—that once he started, there would be nothing to stop him.

None of his struggle was apparent on the surface. "To what do I owe the honour of this visit?" he asked politely.

"Do I require a reason to wish to see you?" she teased. "Is it not enough that I miss you when I know I shall not have the pleasure of your company all day?" She felt slightly at a loss; she had anticipated that as soon as he realized she was alone, he would, as he had in the past, not hesitate to take advantage of the circumstance. But he seemed determined to be circumspect, and she cast her mind about for other stratagems.

Her flirtatious tone eroded what little restraint he still possessed. He folded his hands purposefully in front of him where they could cause no trouble. "I cannot say I am sorry to hear it," he responded lightly.

She cocked her head. "Are you shocked that I came here by myself?" she asked provocatively.

"You never cease to surprise me, my heart," he said. The manner in which she was looking at him made him feel slightly dizzy. *If I did not know better, I would swear she was hoping I would kiss her! She would never have come, had she any notion what a struggle it is not to touch her.* He recollected once more the softness he had discovered as he had loosened the bindings on her dress that day... *Stop that!* he admonished himself. Casting about desperately for a neutral topic of conversation, he said, "Is your aunt well? and your cousins?"

"My aunt is quite well, but her youngest has a fever and a chill, so she is quite occupied today, between him and my uncle's guests," said Elizabeth. She was beginning to feel anxious—could she have misjudged his wishes? Could he be horrified, instead of pleased, by her unseemly behaviour? She would not allow herself to even contemplate the possibility, and with a surge of recklessness she approached to stand directly before him. Her own daring gave her a thrill of arousal, and as she looked up into his face, she could see for the first time his struggle for self-control. It was all the encouragement she needed, and with a mischievous look, she slid her arms around his neck.

It was more than a man could be expected to bear, thought Darcy desperately. Faced with her obvious invitation, he could not help himself; his lips descended to taste the sweetness of hers. He had intended to allow it only to last a moment, but the willingness he met in her stirred a passion which would not be denied. He pulled her into his arms and deepened the kiss, not permitting himself to consider the consequences.

He was able to forget himself in the pleasures of her mouth briefly, but as she pressed herself against him and audaciously let her fingers wander up into his thick hair, he dimly recognized the danger he was in. Managing somehow to tear his lips from hers, he warned, "Elizabeth, this is a dangerous game!"

She ran her hands lingeringly down his chest, looking up at him through her lashes provocatively. "I thought that you said you enjoyed it when I was bold, sir," she said playfully.

He could deny himself no longer. "I find you quite irresistible when you are bold, my heart," he said. *If only you knew just how irresistible!* He sought out her lips again in a kiss which expressed all the frustrated longing he had been feeling since his first sight of her at the window. She gasped at his urgency, but soon met it with her own, the denial of the past days only fuelling the fire of her desire. She was in his arms again, as she had needed so desperately ever since their argument, searching for the certainty and the pleasure that only he could provide her. The feeling of his strong body against hers made her breathless as his hands moved to pull her hips against him with an intimacy new to her.

He could not get enough of her. His hands roamed, claiming all of her as his. There was no doubt but that he should stop, and find a way to get her safely from his house—*perhaps a walk to Hyde Park?* he thought desperately. He knew what he must do, but each moment of touching her and feeling her delightful response was so sweet that he delayed for one more moment yet, promising himself he would find the strength to stop soon.

Elizabeth moaned as his hands reached her breasts, caressing the delicate flesh through the fabric of her dress. She had longed for this ever since their previous encounter, and every touch only deepened the need she felt for him. Closing her eyes, she arched toward him, only to freeze when a sudden shock of pleasure ran through her as his thumb began to stroke her nipple. Her eyes flew open to see the look of pleasure on Darcy's face.

"Does that please you, my heart?" he asked, continuing to tantalize her with his hands.

She nodded speechlessly, not knowing how she was to contain such sensations as he was eliciting in her. With a look of expectation, he began to roll her nipple between his fingers, and she could not help releasing a small moan, to his obvious satisfaction. He bent his head and began to press feather-light kisses along her neck, never ceasing his other attentions, until Elizabeth found herself clinging helplessly to his shoulders.

Darcy was intoxicated by the heady sensation of having aroused Elizabeth so completely that she seemed not to even consider the possibility of stopping him, yet he knew his danger was acute. He could not risk causing her to hate him for what he would do if this continued. With extreme reluctance, he murmured in her ear, "Elizabeth, we must stop this. We are quite alone here, and you must not trust me this far!" He continued to stimulate her nipples for the pleasure of hearing her small gasps, but was aware of his own hypocrisy—*That is right—tell* her *to stop, while making it as difficult as possible for her to do so!* he told himself with some disgust, but he knew he had no intention of doing otherwise.

At first she barely knew how to speak for the desires raging through her. "Must we stop?" she managed finally to say. "All I desire is for you to make me yours." Her heart pounded with trepidation as she said the words which committed her.

Darcy could scarcely believe his ears. "Elizabeth, my dearest, darling Elizabeth," he said, burying his face in her neck, his hands dropping to circle her waist. "You cannot imagine how much I would like to do just that, but I do not wish to take advantage of you, or for you to do anything that you will later regret."

Feeling the absence of his touch acutely, she said, "I will not regret it—it is why I came to you today."

He went completely still at her words. He knew what he *ought* to do, but knew as well that he would not be able to deny himself what she was offering freely and he wanted so desperately. Somehow he found the will to say, "Are you certain?"

A small, slightly mischievous smile came over her face. "For my part, I am certain—the question is as to whether it is what *you* wish."

His hands moved of their own volition to rest on her hips. "You know perfectly well, madam, just how badly I want you in my bed," he said, his voice betraying him.

She raised an eyebrow saucily. "Well, then, sir?" she asked, her heart pounding.

A feeling of elation filled him—she was going to be his at last! Darcy bent his lips to capture hers once again in a kiss that was both a promise and a demand, seductively exploring her mouth with a thoroughness that left her breathless. "Yes, my heart, I am going to make you mine," he murmured, claiming her with his eyes as he did with his words. "Come with me." Taking her hand, he led her to the door.

"What of the servants?" she said anxiously. "Might not they see us?"

He paused to give her a deep and breathtaking kiss. "Damn the servants," he said succinctly. Her cheeks were flushed with embarrassment, but she held her head high as she followed him up the stairs. His arousal was such that he could not bear the lack of her touch even for so short a time as that, and on reaching the landing, Darcy felt the need already to pull her back into his arms and repossess himself of her kisses for a few moments before proceeding.

Down the hallway they came to a large room dominated by an elaborately carved four-poster bed. Elizabeth paused a moment at the door, recognizing the step she was taking by entering the forbidden territory of a man's bedroom, then resolutely walked in. Darcy, never allowing his eyes to drift from her, closed the door behind them, then rapidly stripped himself of his cravat, coat and waistcoat.

The look of shocked fascination on her face made him pause for a moment. "Second thoughts, my dearest?" he said, his voice low, praying that her answer would be in the negative.

She shook her head mutely. The sight of him in the loose shirt which draped itself revealingly along the lines of his body took her breath away, and the fiery look in his eyes promised many more discoveries to come. He ran his finger lightly across her lips; they parted involuntarily, causing a flare of satisfaction in his eyes; then he trailed his touch along the line of her jaw and down her neck. He paused for a moment, holding her eyes with his own as his finger drifted downward, coming to rest just above the neckline of her gown between her breasts. She felt a pulse of desire rush through her as he smiled slowly, then dipped his finger lightly inside her gown. How could so small a touch fill her with such exquisite sensation? Her eyes widened in shock as the slight movements of his finger began to fill her with an urgent need.

"Oh, yes, my Elizabeth," he said softly. "I want you very badly, very badly indeed, but there is no hurry, and I intend to enjoy every inch of you—and to watch your pleasure in it." He nibbled on her earlobe as his hand left her breasts to travel to the back of her neck. She felt his hands exploring her carefully arranged coiffure, and he began to remove her hairpins, strewing them carelessly on the floor until he could fulfil his fantasy of running his hands through her long dark curls. With his fingers still tangled in her locks, he stood back for a moment to admire the picture she made, her hair dishevelled about her shoulders and her lips swollen with his kisses. "I will ask you one last time—are you certain that this is what you want?" he asked with an intense look, wondering how he would possibly bring himself to let her go if she denied him.

Her eyes were dark with passion. "Yes, I am," she said, knowing that she was beyond the point of being able to stop even if she so wished. "I want to be yours."

Darcy made an inarticulate sound deep in his throat. "In that case, my heart, you are wearing far too many clothes," he said. He moved behind her and addressed himself to the fastenings of her gown, tasting the tenderness of the back of her neck with his kisses as he did so.

The sharp arousal Elizabeth felt at the touch of his hands was accompanied by a moment of fear—she had never imagined this part, the actual disrobing. She gasped as she felt his hands sliding around her waist inside her gown—the intimate sensation of his touch through nothing but her chemise raced through her, and she leaned back against him, allowing his hands to travel downwards to her thighs. A deep, throbbing ache grew within her, and she pressed her hips against him.

How was he to be slow and gentle when she responded so urgently to his every touch? He had long dreamt of unleashing the passion he could see within her, and the reality was proving even beyond his dreams. If he could not find a way to control himself, he would not be able to stay himself any longer. Reluctantly, he withdrew his hands to her shoulders, and turned her to face him.

His breath caught in his throat as she looked up at him with eyes filled with desire. "Kiss me, Elizabeth," he breathed.

She could almost see the heat of his passion stirring. With a smile, she touched his lips just barely with her own, playfully tantalizing him until he impatiently deepened the kiss. She shivered as she felt his hands easing her unfastened dress from her shoulders, tracing their way down her arms until she was freed from the sleeves.

As the dress dropped unheeded to the floor, he hungrily returned his hands to her breasts. Now in a higher state of arousal than earlier, she responded even more fervently to his caresses, her mouth pressing urgently against his, as his fingers on her nipples sent intense shocks of pleasure through her.

He could not wait to touch her. He was intoxicated with the taste of her, the feeling of her, and most of all with the knowledge that he was going to make her his at last. It did not matter that it was too soon, or that there might be consequences—all that mattered was the woman in his arms, and the awareness that they would soon be completing each other in the oldest manner known. God, but it felt right to have her in his arms, to touch her, and to know that he was bringing her to his bed where she belonged, where she had lived in his dreams for so long.

Impatiently he untied her chemise, thrusting his hand within it until the softness of the skin of her breast met it. How he had hungered for this moment, when he could begin his possession of her lovely body! With a surge of impatience, he swept her into his arms and carried her to the bed.

Drawing the open chemise down until he could feast his eyes on her exposed breasts, he lowered his mouth to her neck, where he began to place tantalizing kisses along the sensitive hollows. When she began to move beneath him with a moan, he allowed his lips to move downwards until they could explore the sensitive skin of her breasts. He could feel her hands gripping his shoulders tightly, and he raised his head just long enough to murmur, "Oh, my sweetest, loveliest Elizabeth!" before capturing her nipple with his mouth.

Her body stiffened fleetingly in surprise, but it took only a moment until all she could think of was the extraordinary pleasure he was giving her as he suckled her. It created an urgent heat within her. She ran her hands insistently over his shoulders and back, longing for a fulfilment she could not quite understand. But as he continued to stimulate her, it was not long until thought left her entirely, leaving only a deep desire for him.

He could feel the shift in her, as the tension of newness left her body and was replaced by the writhing of a woman in the grips of passion. Satisfied that she was his to do with as he willed, he lifted his head, and rapidly stripped off his shirt. Lying down beside her, he captured her eyes with his own, and commanded softly, "Keep looking at me, Elizabeth, just like that."

As she complied, she felt his hand slide down to the edge of her chemise, now bunched around her waist. A thrill of desire ran through her as he moved his hand ever lower, now sliding it beneath the fine fabric to reach toward her most private parts. Every inch he went seemed only to stoke the fires of her need, and she closed her eyes to appreciate the wash of sensation flooding through her.

"No, my heart, *look* at me," he repeated, his voice dark with passion. "I want to see your eyes." As she opened her eyes, taking in his intimate look, he let his hand cover the last distance to reach the heart of her desire. Her natural embarrassment at the deep intimacy of his touch was quickly submerged as his finger began to move rhythmically against her, leaving her at the mercy of intense sensations such as she had never dreamed of.

He continued to hold her eyes with his, and she could see a small satisfied smile growing on his face at what he saw in hers. "Oh, yes, my beloved, just like that," he said, clearly aroused by her response, as she gasped at the building intensity within her. Without ceasing those actions which were bringing her such pleasure, he kissed her with a tender intimacy, then brought his mouth once more to her breast.

She would not have credited that the power of the fires of desire running through her could increase, but it seemed every time she thought he could arouse her no further, she was proven wrong. As his mouth and his hand continued to pleasure her, she lost all sense of time, moaning and arching against him. This was so far beyond anything she had imagined that she could do nothing but allow herself to be carried away by sensation as the need deep within her welled up to an almost intolerable pitch. Just as she reached that point, Darcy made a subtle shift in his touch, and suddenly she was completely overtaken and lost within wave after wave of pleasure and deepest satisfaction. She cried his name as shudders ran through her body. As she finally returned to herself, his fingers drawing the last spasms of pleasure from her, she looked to him in astonishment. For a moment it was as if her ability to move or to speak failed her, and a rush of embarrassment at her abandoned behaviour ran through her, only to be soothed by the look of deep pleasure and satisfaction on Darcy's face. With a moment of discomfiture, she asked, "Was that...intended to happen?"

Darcy's dark gaze lit with gratification. He had been uncertain whether he would succeed this first time in bringing her pleasure or whether that would only come with time. Feeling quite pleased with himself, he said, "Oh, yes, my dearest, that is exactly what I wanted to happen, and there is much more yet to come."

He drew away from her for a moment to dispose of his trousers. Elizabeth could not quite bring herself to look in his direction; although it was far too late for maidenly fears, a lifetime of training could not be erased so quickly. But feeling already bereft of his presence, she reached out for him, and he returned to her arms as if to his true home. He kissed her deeply, knowing that his deepest desires were about to be fulfilled.

He moved his hands caressingly down her, removing the crumpled chemise which still surrounded her, and admiring the newly exposed beauty before him. It was beauty that he had to have, and he could wait no longer to take possession of it. He lowered himself onto her, her legs instinctively parting to make room for him. He could feel her heat against his arousal, urgently calling out to him.

Almost roughly he caught her face between his hands, bringing her to look at him, wanting to see her as he took possession of her. "My heart, are you ready?" he asked, his voice hoarse with desire.

She pressed herself against him in response, astonished by the overpowering sensation of his skin touching hers in the most private of places. "I love you," she said, finally able to give him the gift in words that she had long since given him in her heart.

His eyes flared at her unexpected admission, and he could no longer hold back. He thrust himself into her depths, taking all the satisfaction of the moment, but halted to kiss her gently at her soft cry of pain. "I know, my heart—it hurts, this first time, but it will not last," he said, glorying in the knowledge that she was his at last.

Her pain was gradually replaced by a delightful sense of arousal and fulfilment. "It is…well," she whispered, holding herself close to him as he began to move rhythmically within her, producing a pleasure quite unexpected after the initial pain. She had never experienced an intimacy such as this, and she wrapped her legs around him, instinctively trying to allow him even deeper within her. Each thrust seemed to bring new waves of exquisite sensation to her. The small sounds of pleasure she made as he moved within her only drove his desire yet further. His excitement spiralled rapidly to his final moment as his need for her sent him past the edge, and with a final deep thrust he filled her with his seed.

It was some moments before Elizabeth was able to return to herself once more. *So this is what occurs in the marriage bed,* she thought, feeling some amusement at how far this experience seemed from her mother's vague warnings of general unpleasantness. She felt a remarkable contentment in Darcy's arms, their bodies still joined. It was beyond her comprehension how it could feel so natural to be with him thus, without concern for her own modesty or shock at his state. She gently caressed his face as he lay spent in her embrace until his breathing slowed and he turned to kiss her, then shifted himself so as to hold her close by his side, her head upon his shoulder.

Darcy felt a deep happiness within which it seemed no sorrow could ever touch. He had never fully understood Elizabeth's change of heart towards him after Hunsford, and because of that, had been equally unable to fully trust in it, no matter how certain he had been in his mind about the inviolability of their engagement. But this was all in the past now; he might have no further understanding of *why* she would care for him, but her words of love in combination with her gift of herself spoke a truth to him that no legal commitment ever could. The joy of feeling secure in her affections was a new one to him; it occurred to him that despite his various friends and family, he had never before felt the sense of acceptance that he did at that moment.

The only shadow clouding his bliss was a concern for Elizabeth. Although he wished that he could believe she had found the same delight in their lovemaking as he had, he knew from her responses that parts had come as a surprise to her, and that the entire event must have provoked a certain anxiety in her. He felt a sudden and powerful urge to protect her, although he had to acknowledge that there had never been any sign that she was in need of his protection. Still, only her reassurance would stem his apprehension. "My heart, are you well?" he asked, stroking her hair gently.

She smiled at him impishly. "Quite well—I hope you have no reason to think otherwise!"

Reassured to see her sense of humour intact, he kissed her lightly. "I am glad. I have heard that for some women the first time can be…difficult; I would not have wished it to be so for you."

"Perhaps it is the company I keep," she teased; then, with a moment of shyness, she asked, "And you?"

He tightened his arms around her briefly. "My heart, if you have no regrets, I have never been happier."

"None at all," she replied with a serious note, "although I am almost afraid to ask what you thought of me—were you shocked that I came to you?"

His hand stroked the curve of her spine almost absently. "Shocked? I must confess that I was, but not in the least dismayed. This was a most delightful surprise, although I cannot claim to understand what might have changed your opinion so much from two days ago when it seemed that my advances troubled you!"

Elizabeth laughed. "And then I appeared, making even greater demands upon you!"

He kissed her slowly and deeply. "Demands which I was only too happy to meet, my heart, and I shall happily meet them again as often as you like."

"You are too kind, sir," she replied with mock seriousness which turned to laughter as he nibbled her neck in a pretence of punishment for her impudence.

Her playfulness enchanted him, but so did immersing himself in the joy of her affection. "My heart, it occurs to me that you took advantage of my distraction to tell me something of great import a few minutes ago that I should like to hear again now that I can give it my full attention," he said with a roguish air, covering a certain trepidation native to him regarding the ability of those whom he loved to express a similar regard for him.

She was puzzled for a moment until she traced his reference, then she raised herself on one arm and boldly showered him with light kisses, both on his lips and across his face. "I love you," she whispered between kisses. "I love you passionately, and I adore you, and I never wish to leave your side. There, does that quite cover the subject, sir?"

Delighted, he pretended to consider the matter briefly. "I suppose it is adequate for the moment, but it bears frequent repetition."

That he could feel at all anxious on the subject of her regard after what they had shared was touching to Elizabeth. "Then I shall say it, my love, until you quite tire of the subject," she responded, nestling contentedly against him.

He held her to him, one arm holding her close, the other hand seeming to find its natural home cupping her breast. She glanced up at him in surprise at this new intimacy, and with a look that expressed his deep pleasure in having the right to touch her so, he began gently to caress her.

She was surprised to feel the first stirrings of excitement at his touch— *Is satisfaction then so brief?* she wondered. Her question found its own answer quickly as his fingers continued to stroke the tender skin of her breast, and she made the discovery that now, knowing how much more he could give her, her longing for more was greater than it had been when she had been ignorant of it. She lay still, allowing his touch to produce enjoyable tendrils of desire in her. Glancing up at him again, she saw the corners of his lips turn up, and realized with amusement that he was taking distinct pleasure in wakening her desire once more.

Darcy was indeed enjoying evoking a response from Elizabeth; however, he also had other matters on his mind, and was not averse to combining the two. "I have often wondered, my heart," he said, trailing his thumb once slowly across her nipple, "what it was that changed your mind about me, between Hunsford and when I saw you once more at Longbourn."

His touch sent a quick thrill of pleasure through her, leaving her wishing for more, but he had instead returned to caressing her skin lightly. "Let me see," she said, her voice teasing, "I believe it was when I discovered how delightful I found your kisses."

"A very pretty answer, but somehow I suspect it not to be the entire truth," he said with an amused smile. "As I recall, you ran away from me when I tried to kiss you."

She laughed. "That was only because I found it altogether too delightful for my comfort!" she said. "Very well, then—it came on gradually, as I grew better acquainted with you. I realized that I had never taken the trouble to know you, and that once I began to look, I liked what I saw."

He rolled her nipple gently between his fingers, and she closed her eyes to enjoy the sensation. "And what did you see, my heart?" he asked, his attentions once again ceasing.

Elizabeth was beginning to find his behaviour quite distracting. "I saw a gentleman of deeper understanding and sensibility than I had known, and I began to appreciate your mind…ah!" Her response was cut short by the return of his tantalizing touch, which seemed to become more effective with each interruption, and she could see by the self-satisfied expression on his face that he was perfectly aware of what he was doing to her.

"And that caused your change of heart? I must say that I could not tell the difference at the time," he said, easing her gently off his shoulder so that she rested on her back. He propped himself up beside her, where he occupied himself with gently stroking her body with the back of his hand. It was an exercise which appeared to require great concentration on his part.

"I do not doubt it," she responded tartly. "I seem to recall that the last time I saw you in Kent you were paying so much attention to Miss Temple you hardly noted my existence!"

"Hardly noted you!" he exclaimed indignantly. "You were having such a lovely time with Colonel Fitzwilliam that I spent the entire evening concocting schemes to murder him and carry you off!"

Elizabeth could not help laughing at this view of that painful evening. To think he had been doing just the same as she, pretending interest in another while thinking only of her! But his voice also carried a message for which reassurance was a more appropriate response than laughter, so she said, "I was making a great effort to appear as if your attentions to Miss Temple troubled me not at all! I believe that I would have been unable to recall a word your cousin said to me an hour later."

"Good," said Darcy succinctly, but with feeling. "I should hate to have to call him out at our wedding if you happened to smile in his direction."

"Pray do not," said Elizabeth lightly. "It would quite distract me from the ceremony, to which I am already likely to be paying little enough attention because my thoughts will all be filled with you."

Unused to extravagant compliments of this sort from Elizabeth, but finding the sensation quite agreeable, Darcy was silent for a moment. Finally he said, "I shall just have to recall, then, what it is that I have which he does not." Leaning over, he gently took her nipple into his mouth and suckled it just long enough to leave Elizabeth filled with unsatisfied desire, then he returned to her lips to explore them with concentrated thoroughness. "But you have not yet told me, my heart, what impelled you to come to me today, and I should *very* much like to hear it," he said, his eyes displaying that familiar intensity that spoke of his desire.

Having reached that point where acting on her reasons had greater appeal than speaking about them, Elizabeth decided that he deserved a small dose of his own medicine. She ran her hand down his chest in what she hoped was a tantalizing manner, then smiled at the look upon his face. "It was a combination of circumstances, actually—a comment you had made, and one of my aunt's as well, but mostly it was the realization that my loyalties lie with you. I have seen you ready to defy your family's wishes and all the expectations of society to marry me, and I wished you to know that my commitment to you is every bit as great."

"My Elizabeth!" said Darcy, unaccountably moved by her words, in his heart as well as quite profoundly in his body. "And now you *are* my wife in very truth, if not yet solemnized by the church."

She looked at him in amusement. "That may be so, Fitzwilliam, but you appear remarkably disinclined to act upon it at the moment," she teased. "Perhaps it is time for me to return to my uncle's house and leave you in peace."

Almost before the words had left her mouth, Darcy trapped her body with his arm and insinuated his leg between hers. "Do not even *think* about it, my heart! I will have more than enough difficulty letting you go when I must." He buried his face in her hair.

The strength of his response took her by surprise, but the serious undertone in his voice could not be missed. Affectionately, she reached up and caressed his cheek. "Very well, sir, you have convinced me," she said gently, realizing that she was seeing a new side of him today, a vulnerability he habitually masked with demands. In hindsight she could see that it had always been thus, at least since they had met in Kent, and she had failed to recognize it. Even his proposal in Hunsford had been so—now, knowing him better, she could look back and see the agitation and worry behind the words which on the surface demanded immediate obedience. *Had he always been so guarded?* she wondered, and to her mind came the confidences of Lady Derby—what had she said? That he had idolized his parents, but they had little interest in him? Perhaps he had never learnt another way to express his all too human need for affection. "I love you," she whispered, and a tension that she had not recognized left his body.

He seemed content for the moment just to hold her, one hand toying lightly with her soft curls. She recalled his words after their quarrel: *You cannot rid yourself of me, because I cannot do without you.* She was unaccustomed to being necessary to another person—Jane would perhaps have come closest, but even she tended to keep her own counsel and to expect Elizabeth to do the same. The idea that he might need her was more than a little frightening, but it also gave her a certain feeling of warmth and protectiveness. She suspected that it was an even more difficult admission for him than it had been for her, and heaven knew *she* had resisted coming to need *him*. Who would have thought it, when first they met, that she would come to depend on him for her happiness, and he on her? Who would have thought that she would feel a love so strong as to make her see a virtue in violating so many of the precepts taught to her? Who would have thought that doing so could feel so natural and right?

She became aware that his hand was beginning to stroke her curves once again, and she abandoned her thoughts to enjoy the pleasure of his touch. Unfortunately, his fingers travelled a bit too lightly along her ribs, causing her to start with a gasp. "Fitzwilliam, I will thank you not to tickle me!" she exclaimed with a laugh.

He raised his head to give her a devilish look. "Are you ticklish, then, my heart? I shall have to remember that—it might be to my advantage some day," he said.

"You already have quite enough *advantages* over me, thank you!" she said with rueful good humour. "I am altogether too susceptible to your form of argument."

The expression on his face changed subtly. "Is that so?" he asked softly. "Perhaps I should test out this theory." He cupped his hand around her breast and lowered his mouth to hers.

After a kiss which began gently but grew gradually to greater excitement, she said, "Altogether too many advantages!"

"I shall take advantage wherever I may," he said, reaching to lightly stroke her inner thighs. "After all, my dearest, all *you* need do is smile at me, and I cannot resist you." He watched her with pleasure as she began to move against him.

She could feel his arousal pressing against her. "Perhaps, then, I should test out *your* theory," she said with a deliberate smile of mischief.

Parting her legs with his knee, he gently insinuated his fingers into the heart of her desire. As Elizabeth gasped at the sudden intense pleasure of his touch, he said, "My theory was proven months ago, dearest, loveliest Elizabeth. It does not even take a smile—a passing look, a thought, the sight of you from across the room—and I am yours to command." The gentle movements of his finger were sending a rising tide of desire through Elizabeth, and she shivered from the building excitement within her. Darcy's eyes darkened with passion at her response, and suddenly there was no more need for words.

Chapter 10

Darcy would not hear of Elizabeth finding her own way back to Cheapside that afternoon. Although he acknowledged reluctantly that it would risk discovery if he took her as far as the Gardiners, it would do no harm, he argued, were he to drive her within several streets of their house. His motive was not only her increased comfort; in truth, he was finding it difficult to face the prospect of letting her go and was trying to delay the inevitable as long as possible.

He elected to drive her himself in order that he might at least be allowed to sit by her, rather than be forced by propriety to sit across from her, unable even to touch her. Elizabeth smiled at this obvious ploy, but found nothing on her own part to object to.

There was an issue on Darcy's mind, however, and this seemed a good time to raise it. "We have not yet considered the question of a wedding date, my heart," he said as he steered his horses towards Cheapside.

"No, we have not," replied Elizabeth with amusement, feeling perfectly certain of what he wished to say on the subject. She had no objection to giving him an opening, though, so she added, "Have you any thoughts on the matter?"

He gave her a sidelong glance. "I would prefer not to have a long engagement."

It was difficult not to tease him, but she was beginning to learn that she should not tease him about herself. She kept her face solemn with an effort and said, "I thought perhaps not." The effort proved too great; her mirth would not be completely suppressed, and she smiled despite herself.

"You find the subject amusing?" he asked, with a slight frown, his attention focused on navigating the busy streets.

She laid her hand daringly on his arm for a moment and gave him an affectionate look. "Not the subject, sir, but perhaps how formally we are discussing a matter on which, if I am not mistaken, you have already reached a conclusion," she said

With a sardonic look, he replied, "Very well, madam, since you find me so easy to read, what are *your* preferences?"

As it happened, Elizabeth shared his preferences more than he could know, since the prospect of more time in either her uncle's house or her father's did not at present appeal to her at all. In a case such as theirs, however, too much of a rush to the altar could look compromising in and of itself, and there was already enough scandal associated with her family to risk inviting more. "It would seem to me that if a shorter engagement is preferable, the simplest way to accomplish this would be to have a double wedding with Jane and Mr. Bingley next month," she said, watching for his reaction.

The same thought had occurred to Darcy more than once. "That might be the most reasonable," he said reluctantly, feeling that a month was a very long time to wait, but knowing that convincing Elizabeth of anything sooner would be unlikely. He added, "Once your father has formally given his consent, we can begin making the arrangements."

Elizabeth's smile vanished as if it had never been. "My apologies; I neglected to tell you that my uncle received a letter from my father last night, and he has given his permission," she said. She had forgotten her distress over Mr. Bennet's response while she had been with Darcy; now it came rushing back into her remembrance.

"No need to apologize, my heart," said Darcy. "It was not as if there were any doubt, and I believe you may have been somewhat...distracted." He directed a smile at her, recalling the source of her distraction. To his dismay, he saw Elizabeth biting her lip as if in distress. "Is anything the matter?" he asked in concern.

Elizabeth's first instinct was to deny any difficulty, but she stopped herself before she was able to do so. Reminding herself of her resolution to trust him, she glanced up at him, and recalling the intimacies they had shared that day, made her decision. "Although my father consented, it appears that he is not pleased," she said, feeling all the anxiety of sharing this concern with him.

Darcy frowned. "On what grounds?" he asked.

"He did not say," she replied. "I do not believe, though, that he ever saw reason to change his first impression of you. I could wish, however, that our families were pleased about our engagement."

"*I* am pleased about it, more than pleased, and if you are as well, that is all that truly matters," he said gently.

Elizabeth accepted his assurances, and the ride passed in pleasant and affectionate conversation. Leaving her was as difficult as Darcy had imagined, though; as she walked away from the curricle towards Gracechurch Street, he felt a sharp pain of loss, and he knew how empty his house and his bed would feel without her. He could not even begin to regret what had happened that day, but he knew that it would be all the more difficult to be without her because of it; that theirs was a love which, once shared, would be desired and needed all the more for it. As she reached the corner, she turned to look back at him with a wave and a smile, and his every instinct demanded that he race after her and take her back to Brook Street where she belonged. He consoled himself with the memory of how it had felt to have her body beneath his, her shyly passionate responses only adding to his pleasure. He suspected that he would be living more on these memories in the weeks to come than on food and drink.

He would have been reassured to know that Elizabeth was already missing him as well, although her mind had already begun to turn to how to prevent questions from arising in the Gardiners' minds. She had taken great care before they left his townhouse to restore her dress and her hair to as pristine a state as possible, and thought that there was nothing there to be noticed, but feared more that the change in *her* which felt so profound would somehow be visible. If her uncle were to discover what had occurred, he would be quite distressed, and no doubt indeed send her home, though not before marching her down the aisle forcibly if necessary—*perhaps not so bad an option*, she thought. She felt a rush of emotion at the idea of returning to Darcy's house as his wife, never to have to leave or be forced into subterfuge, and she could almost wish that it would come to pass, were it not for her desire to save both him and her family from scandal. But the thought gave her the courage to walk into the Gardiners' house with a confidence she had not previously possessed, and to pass without question.

It was not until that night when she was alone once again that she allowed herself to reflect on what she had done. She gazed in the mirror, wondering why there should be no difference in her appearance when she felt such a profound change from within her. She had known from an early age that some engaged couples anticipated their marriage vows in one way or another, and that society turned a blind eye to it; but she had never thought she would be among them. On the other hand, it seemed there was so very much she had never anticipated—the powerful feeling of connection and bonding that came of falling in love, the deep joy of giving happiness to one's beloved, and the intensity and the pleasure of physical contact with him which confirmed and deepened that connection, setting it apart from all the other loves of family and friends. The greatest surprise, though, had been the discovery that there was a point where Mr. Darcy had become more important to her than anything else. The change she felt in herself, she reflected, came more from this shift in priorities than the physical act that had occurred between them, powerful as it had been. She wrapped her arms around herself tightly, recalling the pleasure and comfort of his embrace, and longing for the time when they would no longer need to be parted, but could be proudly and publicly together.

Darcy arrived the following morning for his call even earlier than was his custom, bearing a gift of a pair of elegant silk gloves for Elizabeth. At his first look, she knew precisely where his thoughts tended, and from the heat of his glance, she doubted that she would have resisted him for an instant had they the opportunity of privacy. She had not anticipated just how much more strongly she would feel the urge to be in his arms now, nor that rejoining her lover would carry such impact as it did upon her sensibilities. Unfortunately, she knew that they would be lucky to have the chance for anything more than private discourse. From the way Darcy's eyes were caressing her, she did not know how either of them would maintain their distance. She wondered how it was that he could with a mere look make her feel as if he were removing her clothing and making love to her.

They managed somehow to carry on an appropriate conversation for a time in the presence of Mrs. Gardiner, although the subtext of their tête-à-tête would have read quite differently. It was a relief to them both when Mrs. Gardiner suggested that they walk out despite its being a cold day.

As soon as they had walked far enough to have even a modicum of privacy, Darcy looked at her and said, "Elizabeth!" as if the syllables of her name could carry all the desire, the longing, and the pleasure he felt in knowing that she was his.

She gave him a sweetly arch smile. "Yes, Fitzwilliam?" she said.

His eyes seemed to look through her to her very soul. "I missed you in my bed last night," he murmured intimately.

His words, as he had no doubt hoped, threw her into turmoil, and made her long to be much closer to him than was proper. She said lightly, "Only last night? I am disappointed."

Purposely misunderstanding her, he replied in her ear, "No, I also missed you there this morning. I would have far preferred to have awakened in your arms—I would have enjoyed reacquainting myself with every lovely inch of you, and discovering even more ways for your pleasure to become mine."

Elizabeth's cheeks flamed. She was too embarrassed to speak, and felt this to be just as well, since she would not have known what to say if she could. She knew only that his words awoke her desire, and that although it might be best if he were to stop this discussion, she did not truly wish for it.

"Did you think of *me* this morning, my heart?" he asked.

Elizabeth was caught off guard by his question. When she had been alone in her room she had indeed thought of him and what they had shared, recalling the closeness she had felt to him and the astonishing pleasures to which he had introduced her. Embarrassed almost beyond the ability to answer with honesty, she murmured without looking at him, "Yes, I did."

He seemed to consider her answer for a moment, and then said intimately, "I hope it was with pleasure, then." He touched her cheek lightly, encouraging her to turn to look at him.

She was immediately caught in the depth of his dark eyes. Almost breathlessly, she responded slowly, "Yes, it was."

His look of gratification at her words could not be denied, and it only added to the heat within her. "Thank you," he said softly. "I do not know what good angel brought you to me yesterday, but I shall be grateful for your gift forever."

She felt as if she were trembling inside. That they were having this conversation at all, much less on a public street, even if none could overhear, was both shocking and exciting at the same time. It was as if his words were touching her as intimately as his hands had the previous day; this very conversation was forbidden by a propriety to which she no longer felt bound. She looked at him as if entrusting him with a secret, her lips tingling as if in anticipation of kisses they were not to receive. "I am glad that you were not outraged by my actions," she said.

She would not have thought that his gaze could become more intense. "I shall never forget, Elizabeth, that you came to me of your own choice, rather than as a duty of our marriage," he said, his voice conveying the depth of his feeling. "To know that the pleasure I took in you I was able to repay in some measure brings me great happiness."

"I…" she began, finding herself lost for words as desire for him mounted within her. "I am glad you were…pleased."

His eyes moved slowly down her body, seeming to caress her and manifestly recalling with appreciation the discoveries he had made. "Pleased beyond measure," he said slowly. "My loveliest Elizabeth, you do not know what you do to me."

Feeling almost faint from the exquisite tension between them, Elizabeth could do nothing but cast her eyes down.

He seemed to read her sentiments in her countenance. "Elizabeth!" he said, as if laying claim to her name since he could do no more. "This will be a painfully long engagement, no matter how short in time it may be—until I have the right to have you in my house, in my arms, and in my bed, I know I shall not be content."

She raised her eyes tentatively to meet his. "Nor shall I, my love," she said softly, the endearment seeming to come naturally to her lips.

His eyes flared in response to her admission, but instead of responding, he placed his free hand gently over hers and accelerated their pace. She followed his lead, although her expression posed a question as to his reason.

"This would be an excellent time to raise a new topic of conversation," he said after a pause. "We are in public, my heart, and my self-control is *seriously* endangered at the moment."

Despite the surge of desire his words sent through her, Elizabeth's response was an amused look. "I shall try not to tempt you further, then," she said playfully.

He drew in a deep breath. His voice carried an earnest warning as he said, "Do you realize how very little it would take for me to bring you back to my house this minute and damn the consequences?"

Elizabeth looked aside, astonished and dismayed at the extent to which she longed to tell him to do just that. She closed her eyes a moment in an attempt to calm herself, and conjured an image of her aunt's disappointment in her were she to risk her family's disgrace by going openly with him. This was enough to break the spell upon her, and left her able to respond to him without compromising them further. "Then by all means let us choose another subject," she began. "You were telling me last week of your plans for your tenants; I have been wondering how the other gentry in the district will respond to them."

He seized upon the distraction with gratitude, and talked of it with great perseverance until both were able to feel the comfort of one another's company without the danger of their earlier feelings.

ALL TOO SOON CAME THE day of Elizabeth's departure for Hertfordshire. Although she would be pleased to be at home, and to have the opportunity to explain herself at last to her family, the idea of even a few days without Darcy's company was making her feel near-panicked with distress. When he arrived for his daily visit, she found it nearly impossible to so much as smile at him, and she wanted nothing more than to throw herself into his arms and never let him go.

Darcy himself was no happier; each day without Elizabeth in his arms seemed to last an eternity, but at least he had the consolation of her company while she was in London. There were moments when he almost felt regret for their tryst, not because he would have chosen to do anything differently, but rather because it had only increased his desire for her and his longing to have her with him all the time. He thought he had been handling his feelings rather nicely until Elizabeth asked him to delay his arrival in Hertfordshire to allow her the opportunity to convince her family of the merits of their engagement. He understood her reasoning immediately, but the idea of it was so unpalatable that he could hardly accept it. In moments when he was alone, he had on occasion even wondered if she herself was tired of his company, but the look in her eyes as she greeted him each morning provided all the reassurance he needed.

Although Darcy was concerned this particular morning that Elizabeth's spirits were obviously low, he had to admit to a certain satisfaction in perceiving that she would feel his absence just as keenly as he would hers. It was difficult to make conversation, even though they had only a brief time together. Finally, her departure was imminent. Mrs. Gardiner had given them the unexpected gift of a private moment for their farewells, although not without the near presence of a servant. As they stood by the carriage that was to take Elizabeth away, Darcy, feeling rather self-conscious, produced a small box from his pocket and handed it to her.

She looked up at him seriously. "There is no need to give me gifts," she said. "You have given me so much already."

"I shall never be able to give you as much as you have already given me, my heart," he replied. Leaning toward her, he said softly in her ear, "If I cannot make love to you, you will perforce have to at least permit me to give you presents."

Her cheeks coloured becomingly. "I fail to see the connection," she said, but with a smile that belied the seriousness of her words. She opened the box to see an exquisite strand of matched pearls. She gazed at it for a moment, then said, "You are very generous, but it is too much; we are not yet married."

He gazed at her until their eyes met, an intent look in his dark eyes. "In name only," he said quietly, relishing the opportunity to see the memory of his lovemaking in her eyes. He wondered whether he was reminding her or himself more of those moments. "They are for you, my heart; they were my mother's."

Elizabeth felt that if she said a word, she would burst into tears, and her usual sense of humour seemed to have deserted her. She could only look at him, her heart in her eyes.

He took her hand in his. "I shall miss you, Elizabeth; I will give you no more than three days to work upon your father on my behalf—I cannot bear to be away from you longer than that," he said, his gaze intent upon her.

She found the touch of his hand to be reassuring, and looked up at him. "I shall look forward to your arrival, sir."

"And when I arrive, we shall finalize the wedding plans, so that we need face no more of these partings."

His words brought a blush to Elizabeth's face, and she found herself too embarrassed by her own thoughts to say a word. Finally, with a self-mocking smile, she said formally, "Then I will bid you farewell, Mr. Darcy."

"Until we meet again, Miss Bennet," he replied, then, to her great surprise, he bent and touched his lips lightly to hers, despite the presence of the Gardiners' servant. "Dream of me—you may be certain that I shall be dreaming about you," he whispered.

Her cheeks now flaming, Elizabeth allowed him to hand her into the carriage before bestowing a teasing smile upon him. "Such forwardness, Mr. Darcy!" she exclaimed mischievously. "Certainly you cannot expect me to permit such behaviour prior to our wedding day!"

He laughed, always a pleasure for Elizabeth to hear. "Of course not, Miss Bennet. I cannot imagine what came over me," he said dryly. She gave him one last wave as the carriage pulled away, and he watched with deep regret until it disappeared from his sight.

ELIZABETH'S RETURN TO LONGBOURN COULD not have been more different from her homecoming after visiting Rosings. She was greeted immediately by her mother, who was full of voluble praise for the brilliant match she had made. Elizabeth was without question her favourite child, courtesy of ten thousand pounds a year. Mrs. Bennet could not restrain herself from giving every possible piece of advice concerning Elizabeth's wedding clothes before her daughter had even passed the vestibule. Elizabeth listened to her effusions with tolerant amusement.

By contrast, her father came out from his library only briefly to greet her in a grave manner. Despite Elizabeth's concern, the impossibility of interrupting her mother prohibited her from further conversation with him.

It was not until that night that the two elder Miss Bennets were able to be by themselves, and Jane instantly availed herself of the opportunity of making many enquiries, which Elizabeth was equally eager to satisfy.

"But Mr. Darcy! Dearest Lizzy, I could not have been more shocked when I heard! I had always thought you disliked him, although I have always had a value for him. Were it for nothing but his love of you, I must always have esteemed him; but now, as Bingley's friend and your husband, there can be only Bingley and yourself more dear to me. It is only that I had no idea at all that he was partial to you, although it does not seem to have come as a complete surprise to my dear Bingley. However did it come to pass? You must tell me all of it!" cried Jane.

"Then you shall be listening until your ears are tired, my dear Jane!" teased Elizabeth.

"Oh, be serious, Lizzy! I have been nearly unable to sleep at night for wondering how this has happened."

"Then I shall tell you it all, leaving out nothing except that which would reflect badly on anyone, of course," she answered with mock gravity. Taking Jane's hand, Elizabeth proceeded to relate her tale, from the disastrous proposal at Hunsford and her meetings with Darcy afterwards, to his role in bringing Bingley to Gracechurch Street, their coming to an understanding when he visited Netherfield, and—after swearing her to secrecy—his role in arranging Lydia's marriage. She left out only her last visit to Brook Street; not even to Jane would she trust that secret. Jane looked all amazement, and Elizabeth more seriously assured her of its truth.

"But are you pleased, Jane? Shall you like to have such a brother?" Elizabeth asked.

"Very, very much. Nothing could give either Bingley or myself more delight. But do you really love him quite well enough? Oh, Lizzy! Do anything rather than marry without affection."

Elizabeth soon satisfied Jane by her solemn assurances of attachment. All was acknowledged, and half the night spent in conversation.

IT WAS NOT UNTIL A full two days later that Elizabeth finally managed to find a private moment with Mr. Bennet, who clearly had been attempting to avoid such an occasion. His attempts at evasion had distressed her, but came as no surprise; it had never been his habit to confront problems directly when they could either be defused with wit or avoided altogether.

When she finally discovered him in the library one afternoon and resolutely began a discussion of her engagement, he removed his glasses and said, "Lizzy, I see no point in discussing this. What is done is done, and neither you nor I have any choice in the matter. I am sorry that you must marry a man you have always hated; I wish I could offer hope that he might change, but I do not believe it myself. However, there is no point in regretting it now." His tone was clearly dismissive.

How earnestly did she then wish that her former opinions had been more reasonable, her expressions more moderate! It would have spared her from explanations and professions which it was exceedingly awkward to give; but they were now necessary, and she assured him with some confusion of her attachment to Mr. Darcy.

Her father looked at her cynically. "Do not think that I do not appreciate your attempts to reassure me in this matter by trying to suggest to me that you are not unhappy with this; however, if you think that I credit for one minute that he has changed his ways, you are sadly mistaken. I have lost one daughter through my own folly to one of the most worthless young men in England and now must lose another to a man she hates; this time it is at least not my fault, but I assure you that I do not wish to dwell on it any further, Lizzy. So away with you!" He looked away from her and picked up his book once more.

Elizabeth was not prepared to surrender so easily. "Have you any other objection," she said, "than your belief of my indifference?"

Mr. Bennet shook his head in disbelief. "I have too many objections to begin to name them, and that is but one of them."

"I cannot, sir, address objections that I do not know, but I do, I do like him," she replied, with tears in her eyes. "I love him. He is perfectly amiable, and the best man of my acquaintance. You do not know what he really is; then pray do not pain me by speaking of him in such terms."

Mr. Bennet looked at her seriously. "This summer has made me quite aware of my failings as a father, Lizzy. It has not passed my notice that you would attempt to protect me from my own folly by pretending that this match was pleasing to you; and, if it comforts you to imagine it so, by all means continue to do so. But for my part, I cannot keep up the pretence."

"It *is* pleasing to me, more than pleasing!" she cried.

He sighed deeply. "I wish that I could believe you, Lizzy. There is nothing I want more than to see you happily situated. I know that you will be neither happy nor respectable unless you truly esteem your husband, unless you look up to him as a superior, and I cannot see that in Mr. Darcy. Your lively talents will place you in the greatest danger in an unequal marriage such as this. I had hoped never to have the grief of seeing *you* unable to esteem your partner in life; but, unfortunately, all I can hope is that you will find recompense in the other advantages Mr. Darcy has to offer."

Elizabeth, still more affected, said, "Indeed you are mistaken if you think I do not esteem him highly. Is there nothing I can say to convince you that he is not the man you believe?"

"Nothing at all, my child. I have trained you too well not to come to me with difficulties, and now I pay the price of knowing that you are unlikely to turn to me when you are in a predicament. It has been my doing, and I ought to feel it."

"You will not listen to me, then?" she asked in despair.

"No, my child; I will not," he said with finality.

She was forced to accept this answer, and she left him disappointed and sorry.

ELIZABETH LOOKED FORWARD TO HER reunion with Darcy on his arrival in Hertfordshire with an almost painful degree of anticipation. She could never have imagined that she could miss him so deeply as to feel that a part of herself was absent. Though it embarrassed her, she could not keep from watching out the window for the first sight of him, nor from feeling a tremendous rush of relief when he finally rode into view.

It was a challenge to school herself to sit at her work while waiting for him to be announced, but it was nothing to fighting the extraordinary urge to throw herself into his arms when he appeared. It was nearly a physical ache to be near him; when he greeted her with a warm look which encompassed her entire body before returning to her eyes, she knew he was feeling something of the same. He greeted her mother, as was proper, and was received by her with a degree of civility which made her daughter ashamed, but his frequent glances in her direction told her he was not offended.

He sat down beside her, and immediately she felt the magnetism that had so often drawn her to him. Their eyes caught and held; she had forgotten the depth of feeling he could convey to her in a glance. The intensity was too much to maintain in the presence of her family, and she had to look down at her work to distract herself, but she could nonetheless feel his happiness at being with her again.

They spoke of inconsequential matters, more for the pleasure of hearing each other's voice than for anything else, until after a very brief space of time, Mr. Bennet joined the family group. He greeted Darcy in a manner just short of incivility, then seated himself directly across from the new couple, and watched Darcy closely and coldly.

Elizabeth, ashamed of her father's ill-bred behaviour and hurt by his clear hostility to Darcy, tried to engage Mr. Bennet in conversation. When this ploy failed due to his lack of cooperation, she did her best to cover his poor manners by attempting to keep up a lively discourse with the others. This was no mean challenge with as diverse a group as Mrs. Bennet, Mary, Kitty, Darcy and herself. As her energy began to flag and her annoyance to grow, she changed her tactics and suggested walking out, knowing how her father disliked pointless rambles. Of the others, only Kitty was likely to enjoy a walk, but she seemed to have the tact to realize that perhaps Elizabeth and Darcy might prefer a little time to themselves after their separation.

Elizabeth went to fetch her spencer since the day had become quite cool. When she met Darcy in the vestibule again, he was holding a package which he gave to her. She untied it to discover an elegant shawl embroidered in the finest silk. As she thanked him, he draped it around her shoulders and said with underlying meaning, "It is purely in my own self-interest; I had the suspicion that we might be taking a number of long walks in the next few weeks, and I would not wish you to be discouraged from doing so by taking a chill."

She smiled up at him playfully, her vexation with her father set aside. She took his arm, deriving great enjoyment from touching him again, even so slightly. "You are most considerate, Mr. Darcy," she said. "Well, whither shall we wander today—into town, or through the countryside?"

"I shall leave the decision entirely to you, Miss Bennet," he said lightly. "However, I would express a preference for finding some secluded spot along the way."

She felt a warmth rising within her at his words. With a look of mock innocence, she said, "You are fond of secluded places, then, sir?"

"Elizabeth," he said significantly, "would you prefer that I kiss you before we are even out of sight of Longbourn?"

"Sir, I am all astonishment!" she said playfully.

They were just then passing the gates, and without further ado, he pulled her to one side so that the wall stood between them and the house, though they remained in plain view of anyone who might come along the road. Placing an arm on either side of her as she stood against the wall, he proceeded to carry out his threat with a passion and a thoroughness that left Elizabeth feeling quite weak, yet longing for more.

"Do you have any further questions, Elizabeth?" he murmured. The temptation of the look of desire in her eyes was too much, and he lowered his head to taste her kisses again. He was aware of how reckless his behaviour was, but he had lost the ability to care during the many days when he could not so much as touch her.

"I take your point, sir!" she exclaimed when he finally released her, feeling bereft of his touch. With a sly look, she added, "I must admire your dedication to preventing me from feeling the chill!"

"Anything for you, my dearest," he said dryly as they began to walk again. "I hope you realize the self-restraint it took not to follow you here as soon as you had left London! I never realized three days could be so long."

She glanced around them, hoping they had not been observed. Seeing no one, she said with an arch smile, "It was a very long time indeed."

Darcy gave her a sidelong glance, his lips twitching. "How far is it to this secluded place?" he said pointedly.

Elizabeth laughed. "I shall try to take mercy upon you, my dear," she said. After his earlier kisses, she found herself no less eager to be alone with him.

"I take it that these three very long days proved insufficient to reconcile your father to our marriage," he said. The change of subject was not only to distract himself from the all too fascinating subject of Elizabeth's kisses—Mr. Bennet's recent display of hostility had disturbed him.

"No, I am afraid I did not succeed in that regard," she replied with a small frown, her frustration with the situation evident in her tone. "To tell the truth, I could not even succeed in having him tell me what his objection is, apart from his insistence that I am unhappy with the idea of marrying you, which no reassurance of mine seems able to shake."

"He has not withdrawn his consent, has he?" asked Darcy with a sudden concern.

"Oh, no, nothing of the sort has been mentioned!"

"Good." Darcy was silent for a few moments, then added, "Will you reassure *me* of one thing, my heart?"

She looked up at him affectionately. "Anything you wish, Fitzwilliam."

He wondered briefly if she had any idea how profoundly she affected him when she looked at him like that. "Are you of age yet?" he asked.

She gave him a smile of amused understanding. "Yes, I am; since July, as it happens. And yes, my dearest love, I will still marry you even if he withdraws his consent; but I think it highly unlikely."

"I am glad to hear it." Darcy could not explain why he still felt he needed reassurance about her regard for him. "I have written to Georgiana and informed her of our wedding plans."

"Will she be coming here from Derby, then?"

He ventured a sidelong glance at her. "I left that to her; I thought the possibility of having her here unwillingly was worse than not having her presence at all."

Elizabeth looked at him in surprise. She had been of the opinion that Darcy made all the decisions for Georgiana, but she was pleased to discover that this did not seem to be the case. "That was wise, I think; she needs to have the freedom of making her own decisions, and would only resent having one forced upon her."

A small pleased smile appeared on Darcy's face. Before writing the letter, he had tried to consider what Elizabeth would do, since she seemed to have, on the whole, better success with Georgiana than he did. He was glad to be able to discuss these matters with her; he had faced them on his own many times; but especially now, when his sister was being so uncooperative, it helped to have Elizabeth's reassurance and support. *If only I could marry her now, it would be perfect,* he thought, allowing himself for the moment a fantasy of taking Elizabeth back to Netherfield with him, reacquainting himself with her lovely body, and demonstrating in a very direct manner just how much he had missed her.

He had long since reached the point of wanting her in his bed again quite badly, and found it a cause for endless frustration that he could discover no safe and discreet way for them to be together. Netherfield was too risky, and Longbourn completely out of the question. The late October weather prohibited anything outdoors, and that he had even thought so far was evidence of his desperation.

"Is anything troubling you, Fitzwilliam?" she asked, concerned by his sudden silence and serious look.

"Nothing that marriage will not cure," he said with a look that left little doubt as to his thoughts.

Elizabeth blushed at his forwardness. "And to think I used to consider you so proper!" she teased.

"I cannot imagine why; I would think that my behaviour towards you has been anything but proper since the beginning!" he responded, noting that they were approaching a small copse of trees. "I might add that I see no incentive to change."

Elizabeth laughed and affectionately tightened her hand momentarily on his arm. She had missed him so much in the few days they had been apart; it was such a joy to her simply to be with him, to see the smile he showed others so sparingly, to be able to lean her head upon his shoulder as they walked.

As they reached the wood, Darcy looked down at her significantly. With a look of mischievous amusement, she took his hand and led him into the field alongside it until they reached a small opening in the trees. Darcy needed no prompting to enter it.

As soon as they were deep enough into the thicket as to be invisible from the road, he turned to her and took her hands in his. Holding her eyes with his, he raised first one hand and then the other to his lips. He murmured her name, and drew her slowly into his arms as if he were savouring each moment.

Elizabeth, who had been anticipating an approach as passionate and demanding as he had made earlier, felt her knees grow weak at the look of tenderness in his eyes. She had longed for this moment, and now that it was here, she felt anew the power of their connection. Glorying in this brief time when they could set aside society's rules in favour of openness, she wanted nothing more in the world than to be with him.

Finally, as he felt the exquisite pleasure of her body against his, he claimed her lips once more, first delicately, then, as he felt her response, with a gradually increasing ardour. He was not prepared to permit himself too much latitude; to allow himself a taste of her passion was a delight like no other, but he knew that he could all too easily become intoxicated with her, and their circumstances were not favourable. Her passionate response as she pressed herself against him was all that a man could have hoped for, and it proved his undoing. His hunger for her took control from his better sense as he lost himself in the sensation of her he had lacked so long.

Elizabeth was no less affected; she clung to him as if he were her only hope, as the pleasure of his kisses washed through her, leaving her longing for more. The sensations were all still new enough to her as to seem quite uncontainable, and her desire for the intimacy of his touch was close to overwhelming.

As his first onslaught of need was sated by her urgent kisses, Darcy began to move his lips across her face, tasting the softness of her skin. He left featherlight kisses along her neck, travelling down to the hollows of her shoulder where he knew her to be particularly sensitive. As she gasped with pleasure, she leaned back to allow him to continue to delight her, a position of which he took full advantage, bringing his hand to the fore to take possession of her breast.

The feeling of his hand around her breast soothed a deep need in her, and shivers of delight began to course through her as he toyed with her nipple. It had been so long since she had felt the pleasure he gave her so generously, and it only left her longing for more of him. Reeling with sensation, she slid her hands inside his coat, feeling the warmth of his body through the fabric of his shirt, circling them around him instinctively to pull his hips into closer contact with her.

Unwillingly Darcy recognized the danger of the rapid conflagration of their ardour, and knew that she did not. He forced himself to slow his demands, releasing her breast to caress the curves of her back. "Ah, Elizabeth," he murmured against her skin. "I lived without you for eight and twenty years—how is it that I can no longer do without touching you for so short a period as a week? And how I am to wait three more until we are wed?"

"I cannot say," she confessed, feeling the same dilemma. While they were apart, she had dreamt only of being with him, but now that she was in his arms, she wanted so much more. She moved herself against him gently, appreciating the sensation of his body against hers.

The feelings she was inducing in him were bringing him to the edge of his self-control. "Elizabeth, heaven knows I want you," he said, the strain in his voice apparent. "But there is no place we can go to take this further, and if we continue it will be…difficult to stop."

With a rush of embarrassment, Elizabeth realized how completely she had been relying on him to know all the answers in this regard. She instantly disentangled herself from him, unable to bring herself to look at him. Attempting to cover her discomfort, she said, "Of course; then we shall stop now."

Darcy could see that he had hurt her. Cursing himself for his clumsiness, he touched her cheek and turned her face towards him. "You have done nothing wrong, nothing at all, my heart—except perhaps to cause me to love you quite beyond reason." He paused, desperately searching for an acceptable way to explain himself to her on a subject so far beyond the reach of proper conversation, but finally admitted defeat and elected to take the risk of honesty. "There are ways, you see, that I *could* take my pleasure in you here; but I fear, given your…inexperience in these matters, it would likely be both uncomfortable and somewhat unpleasant for you, and *that* is a price I am quite unwilling to pay. But you do tempt me so very greatly, my dearest, loveliest Elizabeth," he said tenderly. "If you can find your way to forgiving me for my tactlessness and lack of self-restraint, I would dearly love to kiss you again, just more…sedately this time, in deference to my own susceptibility."

Her relief as she entered his embrace once more was palpable, though her mind was not yet quite at rest. She buried her face in his collar, wishing she could simply set aside those feelings of shame she had been taught so well, and be able to trust fully in his respect and regard for her which had never yet failed. She felt foolish for her overreaction, then felt a sudden amusement with herself for once again sliding into the trap of self-blame, not a minute after she had just chastised herself for doing so.

Darcy was relieved to feel her body relax once more in his arms, and was all too glad just to be able to hold her close to him. "My dearest, you cannot know how much I have missed you," he murmured in her ear, seeking the comfort of her reassurance.

Elizabeth responded as he had hoped. "If it was no more than I missed you, it was still far too much!" she said in a heartfelt manner.

He leaned his face into the softness of her hair, breathing in the sweet scent of it. Almost unaware of what he was saying, he answered, "I have never before felt such a reliance on anyone; I am relieved that we need not be separated again, for the pain of your absence is more than I can tell you. With you beside me, there is nothing I cannot face; without you…" his voice trailed away.

She looked up at him to see a distant pain in his countenance, and impulsively she put her hands to his face, drawing him towards her until he looked directly at her. "I am here, my love," she said tenderly, and offered the pleasurable assurance of meeting his lips with hers once more.

Chapter 11

The pattern of the days in Hertfordshire for Elizabeth and Darcy settled rapidly. Mr. Bennet, despite repeated pleas from his daughter, did not change his attitude of unremitting hostility to his future son-in-law, and furthermore made an effort to be present at all of his visits rather than retiring to the library as was his norm during Bingley's calls. After a few days, the unpleasant atmosphere that resulted became too much for Elizabeth, and she requested Darcy to limit his visits to Longbourn to those times when they could walk out or take a drive together. While loath to allow Mr. Bennet to separate him from Elizabeth, with great reluctance Darcy agreed to this limitation and prevailed on Bingley to make frequent invitations to the Bennet ladies to Netherfield. To all intents and purposes, it meant that he was left to himself for a large part of each day, which displeased him heartily and left him more than ever counting the days until their wedding. As if in compensation, he continued to shower Elizabeth with gifts—one day some fine Brussels lace, another a piece of precious jade from China—to the extent that she began to tease him about his excessive generosity. He would not be moved, however, and continued his practice of arriving with a new present nearly every day.

One morning, about a week after Darcy had arrived, Bingley and the females of the family were sitting together in the dining room while Darcy remained at Netherfield until such a time as he could call to take Elizabeth out. The attention of the Longbourn party was suddenly drawn to the window by the sound of a carriage, and they perceived a chaise and four driving up the lawn. It was too early in the morning for visitors; and, besides, the equipage did not answer to that of any of their neighbours. The horses were post, and neither the carriage nor the livery of the servant who preceded it were familiar to them. As it was certain, however, that somebody was coming, Bingley instantly prevailed on Miss Bennet to avoid the confinement of such an intrusion and walk away with him into the shrubbery. They both set off, and the conjectures of the remaining three continued, though with little satisfaction, till the door was thrown open and their visitor entered. It was Lady Catherine de Bourgh.

They were of course all intending to be surprised, but their astonishment was beyond their expectation. Mrs. Bennet and Kitty were amazed, though she was perfectly unknown to them, but Elizabeth felt it even more strongly.

She entered the room with an air more than usually ungracious, made no other reply to Elizabeth's salutation than a slight inclination of the head, and sat down without saying a word. Elizabeth had mentioned her name to her mother on her ladyship's entrance, though no request of introduction had been made. Mrs. Bennet, all amazement, though flattered by having a guest of such high importance, received her with the utmost politeness.

After sitting for a moment in silence, Lady Catherine said very stiffly to Elizabeth, "I hope you are well, Miss Bennet. That lady, I suppose, is your mother."

Elizabeth replied very concisely that she was. After the letter Lady Catherine had sent her the previous week, she was under no illusions that this was a friendly call to welcome her to the family.

"And that I suppose is one of your sisters."

"Yes, madam," said Mrs. Bennet, delighted to speak to a Lady Catherine. "She is my youngest girl but one. My youngest of all is lately married, and my eldest is somewhere about the grounds, walking with a young man who, I believe, will soon become a part of the family."

"You have a very small park here," returned Lady Catherine after a short silence.

"It is nothing in comparison of Rosings, my lady, I dare say; but I assure you it is much larger than Sir William Lucas's."

"This must be a most inconvenient sitting room for the evening in summer; the windows are full west."

Mrs. Bennet assured her that they never sat there after dinner, and then added, "May I take the liberty of asking your ladyship whether you left Mr. and Mrs. Collins well."

"Yes, very well. I saw them the night before last."

Mrs. Bennet, with great civility, begged her ladyship to take some refreshment, but Lady Catherine, very resolutely and not very politely, declined eating anything and then, rising up, said to Elizabeth, "Miss Bennet, there seemed to be a prettyish kind of a little wilderness on one side of your lawn. I should be glad to take a turn in it if you will favour me with your company."

"Go, my dear," cried her mother, "and show her ladyship about the different walks. I think she will be pleased with the hermitage."

Elizabeth had no intention of allowing Lady Catherine to be alone with her, in hopes that an audience might stem the worst of her ladyship's disagreeable insolence. There was, however, no polite way to refuse the request, so Elizabeth sought the least uncivil response. "I am very sorry to disappoint you, Lady Catherine, but I fear a walk would be too much for me today; I must ask your indulgence to remain within doors."

Mrs. Bennet turned to stare at her daughter in shock and disapproval. "Lizzy, what are you saying? Of course, she will be happy to show you the walks, your Ladyship," she said hurriedly.

"I fear that I should not be able to do justice to them today," Elizabeth said with an effort at composure as she saw Lady Catherine's ire rising. "I would be very happy to keep your Ladyship company here."

"Insolent girl!" exclaimed Lady Catherine. "Is this your gratitude for my attentions to you last spring?"

How could I ever think her like her nephew? thought Elizabeth, as she looked in her face. She wished desperately for Jane's presence. "On the contrary, I am most grateful for your attentions, both then and now," she said coolly.

"Lizzy!" exclaimed Mrs. Bennet in deep agitation. "What has come over you? I simply cannot understand, your Ladyship, why she is behaving this way!"

Lady Catherine simply ignored her. "You can be at no loss, Miss Bennet, to understand the reason of my journey hither. Your own heart, your own conscience, must tell you why I come."

Mrs. Bennet, flustered by this unknown situation, whispered loudly to Mary, "Fetch your father immediately!" Mary, with a look bespeaking moral superiority to her ill-mannered elder sister, obeyed instantly and left.

"Miss Bennet," replied her ladyship, in an angry tone, "you ought to know, that I am not to be trifled with. But however insincere you may choose to be, you shall not find me so. My character has ever been celebrated for its sincerity and frankness; and, in a cause of such moment as this, I shall certainly not depart from it. I was most alarmed and disturbed when I received the scandalous news that you had found the presumption to enter into an engagement with my nephew!"

"I regret that you are displeased with the news, your ladyship. The engagement is official; I cannot imagine what you would hope coming to see me would accomplish."

"To insist that you show good sense and attention to the well-being of my nephew by breaking off this farce of an engagement immediately!"

Colouring with astonishment and disdain, Elizabeth responded coolly, "I am sorry to disappoint your ladyship, but I will certainly *not* indulge you in such a course!"

"Obstinate, headstrong girl! Is nothing due to me? You are to understand, Miss Bennet, that I came here with the determined resolution of carrying my purpose, nor will I be dissuaded from it. I have not been used to submit to any person's whims. I have not been in the habit of brooking disappointment."

"*That* will make your ladyship's situation at present more pitiable; bit it will have no effect on *me*," stated Elizabeth, her anger overcoming any desire to attempt to conciliate her for Mr. Darcy's sake.

Her father at that moment appeared in the doorway with a look that suggested he was anticipating unparalleled entertainment. Elizabeth, grateful for his presence, took the liberty of introducing him to Lady Catherine, though no request of introduction had been made.

"Mr. Bennet," said Lady Catherine with her most condescending air, "am I to understand that you have given your blessing to this ill-advised engagement?"

Mr. Bennet's eyes lit with amusement. "I have given my consent, if that is what you mean, although Lizzy is not of an age to require such a formality any longer. As for my blessing, that is quite a different matter," he said.

Elizabeth looked at him in shock. Clearly he must not have understood that Lady Catherine had been insulting her and attempting to force her to break the engagement.

"Let me be rightly understood. This match, to which you have the presumption to aspire, can never take place. Mr. Darcy is to marry *my daughter*. Now what have you to say?"

"Only this; that if this were true, he would never have made an offer to me!"

"My daughter and my nephew are formed for each other. They are descended on the maternal side from the same noble line and, on the father's, from respectable, honourable and ancient, though untitled, families. Their fortune on both sides is splendid. They are destined for each other by the voice of every member of their respective houses; and what is to divide them? The upstart pretensions of a young woman without family, connections or fortune. Is this to be endured! But it must not, shall not be. If you were sensible of your own good, you would not wish to quit the sphere in which you have been brought up."

Mrs. Bennet could hold herself back no longer. Her awe of Lady Catherine was overcome by the direct insult to her daughter and her family, and she cried, "Your Ladyship, we are by no means without connections, and my daughters have been brought up in every way as ladies!"

Lady Catherine turned to Mrs. Bennet with a look which quelled even that redoubtable lady and reduced Kitty, sitting by her side, to terrified tears. "I did not ask *you*, madam! I have made my inquiries as to your family, and I find nothing, *nothing* that would make me consider your daughter as even marginally acceptable as a bride for my nephew!"

Elizabeth glanced at her father, anticipating an indignant response to this series of affronts, but discovered that he looked disinclined to intervene and still even had a smile upon his face. With a sense of utter betrayal, she said, "In marrying your nephew, I do not consider myself as quitting that sphere. He is a gentleman; I am a gentleman's daughter; so far we are equal."

"True. You are a gentleman's daughter. But who is your mother? Who are your uncles and aunts? Do not imagine me ignorant of their condition.

And your sister—I know about her marriage, that it was a patched up business at the expense of your father and uncles. And is *such* a girl to be my nephew's sister? Is her husband, is the son of his late father's steward, to be his brother? Heaven and earth!—of what are you thinking? Are the shades of Pemberley to be thus polluted?"

She heard a sob from her mother, who was clearly crushed by these double slurs on her family and her favourite daughter. Elizabeth, appalled by this outrageous insult in front of Mrs. Bennet and further horrified to find it still not countered by her father, could scarcely bring herself to reply, "Whatever my connections may be, they can be nothing to you—your nephew does not object to them."

Between the affronts from Lady Catherine, her concern regarding Mr. Darcy's reaction when he heard of this contretemps, and her sense of betrayal that her father was permitting this to proceed, Elizabeth was at the end of her reserves. Her shock was such as to render her speechless; she could only try not to listen and to hope it would end soon.

"You refuse, then, to oblige me. You refuse to obey the claims of duty, honour, and gratitude. You are determined to ruin him in the opinion of all his friends and make him the contempt of the world."

They were joined at this moment by an agitated Mr. Bingley. Lady Catherine spared him one brief glance before continuing her tirade. Bingley listened for only a minute, looking towards Mr. Bennet occasionally with bewilderment before surprising all those present by interrupting. His voice trembling with indignation, he addressed Lady Catherine. "I must protest! Madam, I have not the honour of your acquaintance, but I must ask you not to speak to Miss Elizabeth in such a manner!"

Lady Catherine was all astonishment. She turned to stare condescendingly at Bingley. "And who are *you*, sir, to make such demands of *me*?"

"I am Charles Bingley, and this lady is my future sister, and I will not tolerate *anyone* speaking so to her!" By now Bingley was casting frequent and somewhat frantic glances in the direction of Mr. Bennet as if expecting him to come to his aid.

"*I* am Lady Catherine de Bourgh, and I am not finished with this conversation!" She turned back to Elizabeth. "Have you come to your senses yet, you insolent girl? Are you still determined to ruin him?"

Bingley's uncharacteristic interruption had given Elizabeth the time she needed to recover herself. Without a further glance at Mr. Bennet, she said resentfully, "You may not have done, your ladyship, but *I* have! You have insulted me in every possible way. I have nothing further to say." She turned abruptly and left.

Just outside the door she discovered Jane. Her sister lead her rapidly out into the garden and said, "Oh, Lizzy! I am so sorry! Who is that dreadful woman?"

Elizabeth bit her lip, trying without great success to hold back tears. "*That* was Lady Catherine de Bourgh, Mr. Darcy's aunt."

Jane's face took on a look of astonishment. "It cannot be!" she exclaimed, as if hoping rather than believing her sister to be somehow mistaken. "When Bingley and I heard the loud voices and the horrible things she was saying to you, we could not imagine…" Her voice trailed off as she began to take in the implication of the events. "Oh, my poor dear Lizzy!"

The tumult of Elizabeth's mind was now painfully great, and she began to cry in earnest. She was beyond words, and Jane could offer her only the comfort of her embrace. They remained thus until Bingley appeared to join them, looking rather flustered at Elizabeth's tears and shocked at his own behaviour. "Well, that is done," he said with a bravado which was not fully convincing to the ladies. "She is gone, Lizzy; you need not worry any longer."

Elizabeth, though, was beyond any hope of consolation. She was troubled less by her ladyship's insolence than by her thoughts of Darcy's distress when he heard of his aunt's virulent disapproval of their engagement, and even that worry was dwarfed by the feelings of betrayal that her father had done nothing to stop Lady Catherine's invective. The image of the slight smile on his face as she had enumerated her objections to the match would not leave her. And that it had been so shocking and remorseless as to convince Bingley—charming, self-effacing Bingley—to step in to her defence in front of her own father! It was unthinkable.

"Come into the house now, Lizzy," cajoled Jane. "Let us go to your room, and I shall ask Hill to fetch some tea for you."

She shook her head. "I cannot go back in now; forgive me, Jane, but I cannot!"

Jane, who had only heard the altercation and not seen the passive role played by Mr. Bennet, was confused. Bingley, with a better understanding of the situation, took Jane aside for a brief consultation. Finally he said with a nervous energy, "Well! We certainly cannot have you standing here in the cold, Lizzy! Shall I order my carriage, and we can all go to Netherfield?"

Elizabeth for a moment knew neither what to say nor even what she wished for; but, knowing that Darcy was still at Netherfield, she gave her consent. Bingley strode off in the direction of the stables. Jane said, "I will return immediately, Lizzy—I will just take a moment to inform my mother of our plans."

"As you like," said Elizabeth bitterly, thinking that for herself she saw no need of such a courtesy to her parents at the moment. She wandered up and down the garden to warm herself as she waited, her mind almost a blank. It was as if as soon as she knew she would be seeing Darcy, she had stopped allowing herself to think about what had occurred. She wanted nothing more than to be with him and let him share her burdens, and it could not happen soon enough to please her.

Jane reappeared shortly, carrying Elizabeth's spencer and the shawl Darcy had given her. Elizabeth, who was shivering as much from the shock as the cold, accepted them gratefully, wrapping the soft warmth around her. Her sister said hesitantly, "Dearest Lizzy, if it would help you to speak of it, I shall be happy to listen."

Elizabeth managed a brief smile. "Oh, Jane, you are a great comfort to me, but there is little to tell; Lady Catherine disapproves heartily of my engagement and wishes that I would break it off. She is a lady of remarkable...directness."

"I could scarcely believe what I was hearing! I do not believe that I have ever seen my dear Bingley so angry before!"

There was little more conversation before Bingley arrived with the carriage. He handed both the ladies in; and, though Jane held tightly to Elizabeth's hand throughout, it was a silent trip to Netherfield. Bingley was too embarrassed, Jane too concerned, and Lizzy too preoccupied with her own concerns to speak. Her fear was that Lady Catherine would have preceded her to Netherfield. Though she had no doubt of Darcy's commitment to her, she knew that his aunt's disapproval would put him in a painful position.

On their arrival, she saw that her fears were indeed justified; Lady Catherine's carriage was at the door, her waiting-woman within it. She heard Bingley mutter something under his breath, and then he said, "Allow me to fetch Darcy—I shall return in a moment."

Elizabeth was not prepared to be apart from Darcy when they were so near. "Thank you, Mr. Bingley, but I think that I will come in with you as well."

Bingley gave Jane a flustered glance but acquiesced. They were no sooner inside the door than the piercing voice of Lady Catherine could be heard from the drawing room.

Darcy knew better than to attempt to interrupt when his aunt was ranting; he also knew better than to bother paying any particular attention to her words. She would be perfectly satisfied by his sitting in silence with an appearance of interest in what she was saying, and then she would go away. He had years of experience to teach him that arguing or taking offence at her disagreeable diatribes had only a negative impact on the length of her admonishments. It was no surprise that she disapproved of his engagement to Elizabeth—only Anne was acceptable to her as Mrs. Darcy. So her complaints of Elizabeth's poverty and lack of connections had little impact; he knew that if Elizabeth had been wealthy and well-connected, it would have made no difference except to change the particulars of her complaints.

The appearance of Bingley at the door promised no relief—Lady Catherine would let nothing and no one stand in her way when she was determined to have her say. He tried to suggest to Bingley with his eyes that he would be better off elsewhere, but Bingley seemed to miss his signal and entered anyway. Darcy rolled his eyes, and then spotted Elizabeth behind Bingley. She was a different matter; he had no intention of allowing *her* to hear Lady Catherine's idiocies when they were at her expense. He rose to greet her, and only then noticed her pallor and tearstained cheeks.

At just that moment, Lady Catherine turned to Bingley. "You again!" she exclaimed disagreeably. "Well, you cannot stop me from speaking with my own nephew!"

Darcy, already across the room in his haste to reach Elizabeth, turned to Lady Catherine with a sudden misgiving. "You have already met Mr. Bingley?" he said, his voice suspicious.

"To say that I *met* him would be an overstatement," she sniffed imperiously. "He tried to interfere while I was attempting to talk some sense into Miss Bennet there, but she would have none of it. She does not care if she ruins you, Darcy! Such an alliance! Can you not see that she has trapped you?"

Now understanding Elizabeth's distraught appearance, Darcy was suddenly furious. "That is quite enough!" he said in a tone that matched hers for imperiousness but with an iciness all his own. "I will *not* have you insult my betrothed! If you cannot be civil, I must ask you to leave immediately."

"You would deny your own family for the sake of this insolent girl?" demanded Lady Catherine. "Everyone connected with you will deny you! Do you wish this upon your sister as well? Shall Georgiana be deprived of her family, because *you* choose to marry a woman who will ruin you?"

"At the moment, madam, depriving Georgiana of her family seems no great loss to me," said Darcy angrily. "I must ask you to leave at once—you are no longer welcome here; and, until such a time as you decide to treat my *wife* with respect, all relationship between us is at an end!"

Lady Catherine drew herself to her full height. "I never thought to see such ingratitude and incivility from my sister's son. If you do not see reason, however, you are no loss to *me*." With that, she haughtily swept from the room.

Darcy sighed and ran his hand through his hair. Moving past the shocked Bingley, he took Elizabeth's hands in his gently. "I am so sorry, my heart, that you had to hear that. It is of no matter to me, and I hope it is of none to you."

Elizabeth could only look at him. It seemed that their engagement was meant to cost them dearly in terms of their families. Of Lady Catherine's wrath she only worried for *his* sake, but Mr. Bennet's lack of support hurt exceedingly. With a small sound, she sought his embrace.

Bingley looked like a man cornered. He had defended Elizabeth from Lady Catherine as well as from her own father—was he now to protect her from Darcy, who seemed all too happy to hold her close to him, whispering soft words in her ears between light kisses to her forehead and hair? He cleared his throat prominently, wondering what he could possibly be expected to do now. "Darcy," he said tentatively, "I brought Lizzy here because she was upset following your aunt's call."

Darcy looked up at him levelly. "Thank you, Bingley; that was the right thing to do. Now, Bingley..." he paused until his friend met his eyes. "Please go away."

Bingley's eyes widened in shock. Surely Darcy could not expect him to leave them there alone together? A second glance at Darcy confirmed that this was in fact exactly what his friend did want. He wavered, torn between his responsibility to Jane, and thus to Elizabeth, and his long friendship with Darcy. Finally, looking at Elizabeth who was showing no sign whatsoever of protest, he turned and went to the door. With his hand on the door, he paused for a moment and said, "Darcy? Please be certain to ask Lizzy about Mr. Bennet." At Darcy's quick nod, he reluctantly turned and left, closing the door behind him, wondering how he would possibly explain this to Jane.

Elizabeth had thought herself relatively calm; but, as soon as she was enclosed in Darcy's arms, she felt an upwelling of panic. She could not have said why, when it seemed her only surety was with him, she felt so much more frightened and overwhelmed than she had only a few moments before. She barely noticed Bingley's departure as she sought to control her trembling.

"My poor sweet love," said Darcy softly. "I am so sorry that she was so hateful to you. I hope you know better than to listen to anything she says." On receiving no reply, he experienced a moment of fear. Finally he tipped her chin up to look at him and said, "Please, my heart, will you not at least talk to me?" He brushed his lips lightly against hers.

It was more than she could bear; she burst into tears, pressing her face against the fabric of his coat. Wrenching sobs shook her uncontrollably. All that had happened—her father's overt hostility towards Darcy, his unwillingness to listen to her, and now his readiness to allow her to bear Lady Catherine's insufferable insults, seemed far too much for her. It seemed not only would she be leaving behind her family in only a few weeks, but the family she had believed in had never truly existed. What would there be for her at Longbourn ever again? Jane would be at Netherfield, and as for the rest…she could not even complete the thought.

Darcy, having never seen her in such a state before, could only say something indistinctly of his concern and murmur endearments in her ear. He felt helpless to relieve her suffering, a feeling which did not sit well with him, and it made him angry both at his aunt for hurting her and at himself for failing to somehow protect her. As the minutes passed and her tears continued unabated, he led her to a chair and, after a moment of hesitation, situated her on his lap.

She wrapped her arms around his neck and buried her face in his shoulder. A thought sprang unbidden into her mind—*I must stop this! My mother always said that gentlemen despise a weeping woman!* She struggled valiantly to control herself, but it only led to another storm of sobs as she heard him whisper tender reassurances to her. Finally, after what seemed to be a lifetime, it appeared that all her tears were spent.

Darcy, feeling quite at a loss in this situation, could do nothing but take comfort in the feeling of her body so close to his. He had longed so to be alone with her; and, now that he was, his only thought was to take away her pain, little as he understood it. He was relieved as she grew calmer and her breathing became more regular. He reached for his handkerchief and placed it gently in her hand.

Feeling as if she had been quite foolish, Elizabeth wiped her eyes. Finally looking up at him with a tear-stained face, she said wretchedly, "I am sorry—I have quite soaked your coat."

"Damn the coat, my dearest! You are my only concern," he said, not particularly articulately.

"It is *I* that should be concerned for *you*!" she exclaimed contritely. "How must it be for you to have your aunt casting you off!"

He laughed softly. "Put your mind at rest, my heart. I have known for years that it would come to this as soon as I made up my mind to marry; her accusations vary only in the particulars from what I have always expected. My aunt's good opinion is not worth the price it costs." He frowned. "What I find unforgivable, though, is that she hurt *you*."

She touched his cheek lightly. "It was not as bad as all that. I did not expect her to call on me, but once she did I knew that she would be vitriolic."

He kissed her tenderly, wishing that she felt more able to confide in him. Perhaps that would only come with time. "You do not need to pretend for me—it is quite obvious she upset you badly. I know how cruel she can be."

Elizabeth looked down and fell silent for a moment. Her feelings about her father were so personal and so raw that she did not know if she could share them, yet he deserved an answer that was closer to the truth. And what did *she* deserve? She looked at him again and, to Darcy's surprise, kissed him fiercely. "It was not Lady Catherine who upset me so," she said slowly, not quite able to look him in the eye. "It was my father. He was there, and he stood by and did nothing. Nothing at all. He let her call me all sorts of despicable names, and he smiled as she did it! It was Bingley—Bingley!—who heard her from outside and rushed in to tell her she could not speak to me so! He would defend me when my own father would not!" Her voice trembled again at the last of this.

Darcy drew in a sharp breath of anger. He would certainly have some words to say to Mr. Bennet when he saw him next! He would not tolerate this, even if it meant taking Elizabeth away. He was about to tell her as much when he saw the look of pain on her face and realized with a startling new insight that she did not need his righteous anger or his defence, but rather his sympathy and affection. He gathered her closer to him. "My dearest," he said, feeling quite lost for words. "I can only imagine how hurtful that would be. It should not have happened."

Elizabeth let out a long sigh. "It should not have been so unexpected. He has been so *different* of late, and I cannot understand at all why he has taken against you so and why he has no faith in my judgment." She paused, then continued, "I was always his favourite, and that meant a great deal to me; but I can see now that it was more that I was a favoured companion rather than someone whose worth he truly valued. It is…bitter."

"Your worth is beyond precious jewels to me," he said, moved by her confidence. He was silent for a moment, nuzzling her hair. "When I was young, I idolized my parents, and lived for their praise. It was not until I was older that I realized their interest in me, and later in Georgiana, was only as deep as wishing me to be a good reflection upon them and not to cause trouble. I remember one time—I must have been perhaps fourteen or fifteen and home from school for the summer—I finally mastered some feat of horsemanship I had been struggling with for some time. I was terribly proud of myself, and raced off to tell my father—my mother cared nothing for horsemanship. I discovered him playing cards in his study, with George Wickham, as it happened, who knew how to flatter and entertain him in a way I never did. I announced my news, and he barely looked in my direction to give the very briefest of praise and a caution not to interrupt him again as it would throw him off his game. I think it was at that moment that I realized I was little more than a pawn to him, and I remember going out to the lake and sitting on the bank, resolving that I would never allow Georgiana to feel so uncared for as I felt at that moment." It was not a story he had ever told before; it made him feel both oddly safe and vulnerable at the same time. He laid his head against her chest, taking comfort in the firm sound of her heartbeat.

His confession, in addition to soothing some of her own heartache, elicited a protective instinct in Elizabeth. She had never seen him open up so, and it touched her deeply. She stroked his hair gently, realizing for the first time in her heart that he needed *her*, not just for her wit or her appearance or her kisses, but for her very self, and that she had an intrinsic value to him, quite separate from all the externals. It was an eye-opening concept, so different from how she had ever experienced love in the past; and she could see that, unlike her father, he found relief rather than a burden in sharing her pain. She did not know how to accept such a love, how to permit herself the emotional honesty he clearly desired from her; but she remembered, as far back as the library at Rosings, even when they were most at odds, that he had acknowledged and accepted her feelings. She felt a profound rush of affection for him, and found the courage somehow to say, "How I love you, my dearest!"

He stiffened slightly at her words. She had told him as much before, but he could hear the qualitative difference in her voice and in the way her body seemed to melt into his, and he heard it for the first time as a feeling, not an abstract comment or as a platitude to soothe his sensibilities. Instinctively he could feel that it had been this he had been longing for from her since the very beginning, even without knowing it. He caught her face in his hands and kissed her fervently. Laying his forehead against hers, he spoke the words that he had often thought in regard to her, "'Thou hast ravished my heart!'"[1]

She could feel his hands trembling, and the recognition of the true strength of his devotion to her broke over her in a wave which washed away the last of her resistance. She could not put words to her thoughts, but she could put those thoughts into her eyes as she gazed at him, at least until such a point as they filled with tears of mingled joy and sorrow.

"I wish there were something I could do to make it better," he said in a husky voice, holding her close to him.

"You *do* make it better," she whispered. She leaned against him, allowing herself just to be held and to bask in the warmth of his affection. She felt

---

1 Song of Solomon, 4:9

that she could stay there forever; and, indeed, they sat together for quite some time in a close silence and stillness broken only by the occasional caress or light kiss.

At last Darcy, who, in addition to his joy in her presence, was beginning to feel desires which he thought Elizabeth still too upset to be troubled with, said idly, "Will you unpin your hair, my heart?"

She gave him a knowing smile, and reached back to remove her hairpins. When her dark curls came tumbling over her shoulders, he buried his face and hands in the silky mass. "I love your hair, my Lizzy," he said, his voice slightly muffled.

Her heart seemed to skip a beat when he named her so familiarly for the first time; he had never been so informal with her before, and it seemed an almost unbearable intimacy now when he did. She pressed light kisses on his head in response, until he raised his face to claim her mouth with a kiss which expressed ardent passion without demand.

They sat there together for some time, sharing the comfort of each other's nearness, with kisses and endearments as their primary form of communication. The interlude eased Elizabeth's spirits yet further, but after a time Darcy found his mind wandering back to the challenges they would face once they emerged into the world again. Elizabeth, noting that he was becoming increasingly less relaxed, asked him gently whether anything was troubling him.

Darcy sighed heavily. "I was thinking about your father, and it reminded me that I do not know what it is I should do regarding Georgiana," he said slowly. "She has not replied to my letter."

Elizabeth had wondered about this very matter several times but, recognizing how strongly protective Darcy could be of his sister, had felt it best to leave the matter completely to him. Recognizing what a step it was for him to be turning to her with his feelings in this matter, she resolved to proceed cautiously. "What have your thoughts been on the matter?" she asked gently, nuzzling his neck.

Her actions provoked the response she had hoped for as he smiled tenderly at her for a moment before speaking. "I do not know *what* to think! She was always a very sweet child, but her behaviour in the past year or two has been steadily deteriorating. I have no doubt been more tolerant of it than I should, but it cannot continue. What she said to you…" His mouth hardened as he thought of her comment, and all the pain which had followed. "That was unforgivable, and I cannot let it go."

"She may be very well aware of that, and I imagine she would find it quite frightening," interposed Elizabeth. She herself would have a difficult enough time forgiving Georgiana, but she did understand something of the mind of a 16-year-old girl.

Darcy frowned. "She cannot, though, neglect her responsibilities. I must take some action soon; if nothing else, I must know what her plans are regarding our wedding." It was evident how painful he found the possibility that his sister might not attend.

"Will you write to her again, then?"

He looked distinctly displeased by this question, and Elizabeth, disliking seeing his discomfort, began to kiss the side of his face and his ear until his body relaxed a bit. "I know that I *ought* to ride to Derby and discuss it with her directly, but I dislike leaving you for so long, my heart, especially with what has happened today. So perhaps it would be best to write, although I know not what to say." He wound his fingers more deeply in her hair, thinking how difficult it would be to let her even return to Longbourn after what they had shared. He wanted only the intoxication of being in her presence and feeling her love, and was quite ready to damn all the proprieties in order to keep her with him.

Elizabeth thought for a moment, then said unwillingly, "Much though I would prefer it to be otherwise, I think that you should go to Derby. There is too much at stake for a letter."

Impulsively he said, "Go with me, then."

Elizabeth's eyebrows shot up with surprise, and then she smiled with amusement. "As tempting as that idea might be, I fear it is hardly prudent."

"We could go to London first and be married immediately, and then no one could complain," he said hopefully, knowing that she would never agree.

"Apart from my family and the entirety of my acquaintance, indeed there would be none to complain," she teased.

His face took on a rakish look she recognized well. "Perhaps I should try to…persuade you otherwise," he said, his hand drifting down to her breast.

"While I have no doubt that you could persuade me to *something*, I doubt it would take me as far as London," she said archly.

"*You* are a temptress," he said, scattering kisses across her face.

She nibbled lightly on his lip. "'Let him kiss me with the kisses of his mouth: for thy love is better than wine,'"[2] she said, matching his earlier quote.

He responded with a kiss that stole her breath away with its intensity, sending shivers of warmth through her. *How can he do this to me so easily?* she asked herself yet again as his hands began to make themselves free in the curves of her body. She sighed as he caressed her breast, teasingly stroking her nipple. She could feel his arousal against her, and felt a weakness inside as she recalled how he had touched her and filled her that afternoon in London.

He did not release her lips until he was satisfied by the feeling of her body in his arms that he had aroused her. "You need only ask when you desire my kisses, Lizzy," he said.

Her eyes sparkling with mischief, she replied, "Well, if this is how Bible verses affect you, my dear, I will have to reconsider the wisdom of our attending church together."

"Once we are married, you will be fortunate if you are given the opportunity to leave my side for a minute!" he retorted. He wished fervently that Bingley were not in the house, or that the servants were ones who owed loyalty to him instead of to the gossips of Meryton, or that they would all miraculously vanish and allow him to make love to her without heedlessly risking her reputation. It had been so long since London…but he reminded himself that he must not forget that she had been in tears only a few minutes earlier, and that it was his comfort, not his desire she needed. He forced himself to relax, to concentrate on her, and to remember the happiness her love brought him. Distracting himself with the conversation interrupted earlier, he said, "As far as my sister, I am frankly tempted to simply tell her that if she is so unhappy with my guardianship, she should remain in the custody of my aunt and uncle—but that I might come to regret."

It took some effort for Elizabeth to still her racing heart and to bring her thoughts back to the subject at hand after the desire he had provoked in her. "Perhaps you could instead ask her whether she thinks she might be happier with your aunt and uncle. Let *her* make the choice of with whom she wishes to live—otherwise you will only be giving her further grounds

---

2 Song of Solomon, 1:2

for resentment. She is almost a woman; perhaps it is time to give her the responsibility that comes with that status."

Darcy was silent. Finally he said, "You are right—love and respect cannot be commanded, only given. *You* have taught me that—it was a lesson that was hard indeed at first, but most advantageous. If she would be happier living with them, then I should allow it, though I would hope for a better answer." He paused and then added, "But I shall write again, instead of travelling to her—if she is to decide against me, I would want to hear it with you by my side."

She was swept with a wave of tenderness for him, for his honesty and openness, for his weaknesses as well as his strengths. "You are the best man I have ever known," she said softly.

A knock came at the door before he had time to reply, accompanied by Bingley's voice calling his name in a determined manner. "I think that we are out of time, my heart," said Darcy regretfully.

With a rueful smile, she twisted her hair into a simple knot and attempted to stand before Bingley could see them in such a compromising position, but he tightened his arms around her, preventing her escape. "I am not ashamed to let Bingley see what you are to me," he said intently.

She could see his desire for her to commit herself to him publicly once more. She said playfully, "Perhaps you are not, but I would not want to embarrass *him*!"

"Very well," said Darcy, clearly less than pleased, but he released her.

With an impish smile, she moved off his lap only to sit beside him, nestled much closer to him than could ever be considered proper. "Come in, Mr. Bingley," she called.

Darcy did not spare his friend a glance when he entered. "You, my love, are *very* wicked," he said, and kissed her lightly. His look, when he drew back, was self-satisfied.

"Darcy," said Bingley plaintively, "take pity on me, for God's sake! I am *completely* out of excuses to give Jane for why I have left you alone together; *must* you try to make matters worse?"

Elizabeth stood. "Pay no attention to him, Mr. Bingley," she said engagingly. "He enjoys causing trouble." She heard Darcy's chuckle.

"So I can see," grumbled Bingley good-naturedly.

JANE HAD BEEN REASSURED TO see Elizabeth returned to her usual spirits and, though obviously concerned about propriety, allowed herself to be convinced to stay at Netherfield until after luncheon. The two couples enjoyed a pleasant, if somewhat subdued, time together; but, as it drew towards time for the ladies to depart, Darcy asked to speak with Elizabeth privately once more. In deference to Jane's feelings, they sat together in the parlour with the door open, doing nothing more compromising than holding hands. This was just as well, Darcy reflected, given that his natural response to the closeness they had shared was a strong urge to match that emotional intimacy with physical intimacy.

The two did not so much converse as allow their eyes and hands to speak for them. The day had been full of intense emotions, and each was finding their comfort in the other's presence and the new sense of trust between them. The unpleasant prospect of parting was in both of their minds, and it was to this that Elizabeth finally spoke, wistfully expressing her wish that she could remain with him longer.

Darcy was by no means displeased to hear this, and on impulse he said, "Stay here, then. You could send a note back to Longbourn and say you are taken ill and will stay here tonight. We could ask your mother or Mary to come—it would be quite proper."

The notion was so very tempting that Elizabeth actually gave it brief consideration—not only to be away from her father and the confrontation that must inevitably come, but to be with Darcy, to feel the comfort of his presence and, no doubt, to share his bed, no matter how many chaperones were in the house. She wanted it so very badly, yet she knew the situation at Longbourn must be faced and that delay would only raise suspicions and make it worse. There was a part of her that almost hoped she would not be able to resolve matters with her father, giving her the excuse to go off with Darcy as he had suggested, but she found she was not yet prepared to give up on him entirely.

"I wish I could, my love," she said slowly, "but I must allow my father the opportunity to explain himself; I do not wish to burn my bridges."

He was disappointed and would have liked to try to persuade her, but he could hear in her voice that it would make her unhappy. With an effort, he said, "Then *I* shall take you back when you are ready; it is past time for me to have some words with your father as well. We cannot continue this foolishness of avoiding one another."

Elizabeth sighed. She could not deny him his rights there, although she felt a grave concern for what seemed likely to be an unpleasant confrontation without a happy resolution. "As you wish," she said softly.

"My wish is that I knew how to convince you to smile again," he said impulsively.

Her face softened. "My very dear," she said. "I do love you so." Looking at him, she saw in his eyes a desire which quickened her pulses, and, heedless of who might see them, she raised her lips to his. He met them in a kiss of deep tenderness which did not disguise the depth of his need for her after their emotion-laden day.

It ended too quickly, the demands of propriety once again forbidding further contact, and it was far too little for Darcy, who was still caught in the power of their new, shared vulnerability. "Elizabeth," he said, as if the words were coming from him almost unwillingly, "if I could discover a likely place, would you be able to come to me one night?"

Her breath caught in her throat. She saw more than just desire in his eyes—she could see how very difficult it was for him to be parted from her and to acknowledge that for the moment her family had a greater claim on her than he had. She could tell as well that he would accept it if she refused, but in truth the idea of being with him again, of sharing the intimacy as well as the pleasure, was a temptation she did not wish to resist.

"When you have found a place, Fitzwilliam," she said, "I will come to you."

Chapter 12

Darcy remained firm in his intention to speak to Elizabeth's father before leaving her in his company. Although he shared her concern about the outcome of such a discussion, he felt it could no longer be avoided. On their return to Longbourn, therefore, he made his way directly to the library.

"Come in!" Mr. Bennet called.

Darcy entered and shut the door firmly behind him. He had no doubt that this discussion would become heated; he was in no mood to be trifled with, and he intended that Mr. Bennet should know it. He would no longer permit her father to use Elizabeth as a battlefield between them. He walked over to Mr. Bennet's desk and leaned forward, splaying his fingertips on the top of it.

Mr. Bennet deliberately removed his glasses and set down his book. "Yes, Mr. Darcy?" he said smoothly.

"I would like to hear one reason," said Darcy with great deliberation, "why I should allow Elizabeth to return to this house tonight."

Mr. Bennet raised an eyebrow. "I fail to see how it is your place to *allow* her to do anything; you are not yet her husband; and, though it may not please you, until such a time as you are, she is under *my* authority."

"Which you have ceded today," retorted Darcy immediately. "If you are not prepared to act the part of her father, I assure you, I am perfectly prepared to act the part of her husband. If you are not willing or able to protect her, *I* am not willing to leave her in your custody. I ask you again for even one reason I should not take Elizabeth to London today and marry her immediately."

His eyes narrowed, Mr. Bennet said, "If you are referring to the behaviour of *your* aunt, I fail to see how *I* can be held accountable for that. And if it so happens that, for my own reasons, my opinion coincides with her own, I see no reason why I should try to dissuade her from making her case."

"Your opinion coincides with her own?" Darcy repeated incredulously. "In what way?"

In no temper after Elizabeth's disappearance to humour Darcy, Mr. Bennet said, "In that I think it would be in Lizzy's best interest to break her engagement to you."

Darcy could not believe what he was hearing. "You may *think* what you like, sir, but it will never happen. And I fail to see why any father would find it preferable to see his daughter ruined by the scandal such as that would cause rather than be in an honourable marriage."

"Because, Mr. Darcy, *you* will make her life a misery!"

Darcy's temper was now well and truly lost. "On what basis do you make that allegation?" he snapped.

"Lizzy has never liked you, and she has never violated the proprieties. Surely you do not think that I would believe that she would suddenly tolerate your…attentions had she a choice in the matter? And you ask me to believe that she could be *happy* with a man who has forced himself upon her? I had no choice but to consent to this marriage, but you will *never* have my blessing!" Mr. Bennet's fury, which had been building ever since he had received Mr. Gardiner's letter, was now in full force.

Darcy stared at him in incomprehension for a moment, then as he finally took the older man's meaning, his incredulity was such that he could not help but laugh. "And *this* is what you believe? Mr. Bennet, I would *pity* the poor man who tried to impose himself on your daughter if she were unwilling! However much you may dislike it, the truth is that your daughter is willing, and she is marrying me for no other reason than that it is what *she* wishes."

Of all the reactions Mr. Bennet had thought his accusation might engender, this was the most unexpected. It was impossible he was wrong. He could see no way to any other conclusion: Lizzy, caught in a compromising situation with a disagreeable man whom she was known to dislike intensely, yet to somehow make Mr. Gardiner unhappy about the brilliant match she was making…no, he could make no other sense of it. Elizabeth had told him herself that she wanted the match—but how could her opinion have changed so quickly, and for this proud, demanding man who was to take her so far from her home and family?

Mr. Bennet's silence did not improve Darcy's estimation of the situation, and his anger that such a thing should even be thought of him was rapidly escalating. "That you would even consider such a possibility only demonstrates a profound lack of understanding of both your daughter and myself. I can only suggest that you *talk* to your daughter rather than jump to such an extraordinary conclusion!" Recognizing that any continued discussion at this point was likely to lead to his becoming even more intemperate in his words, he favoured Mr. Bennet with a last hard glare, turned on his heel and strode out.

He retrieved Elizabeth from the sitting room crowded with her sisters and her mother with such a look on his face as to cause her not to question him, but only to follow. He did not say a word until they were well outside the house.

Finally he stopped and raked his hand through his hair. He let out a long breath, then looked at Elizabeth. "Your father," he said distinctly, "is an idiot."

Although concerned as to what had passed between the two men, Elizabeth smiled sympathetically at Darcy, recognizing somehow that his outburst of temper was not quite as serious as it seemed. She took his hand in hers, causing a distinct softening of his gaze.

He continued, "He seems to have the idea in his head that I was *forcing* my attentions on you."

"Oh!" said Elizabeth in surprise. "Wherever did he come upon such an idea?"

"I cannot even venture a guess. I am sorry to say that he angered me sufficiently with the accusation that I simply denied it and walked out," he said with a grimace.

"I can imagine!" she said feelingly.

He looked down at their joined hands. "Are you sure that I cannot convince you to come away with me, Lizzy?" he asked almost plaintively.

She reached up on tiptoe and brushed her lips against his. "Tempting as that sounds, I know that I would regret not attempting to see if this can be resolved," she said.

Darcy glanced over at the house as if doubting this possibility and, as he did so, noticed Mr. Bennet at the library window looking in their direction. With a certain savage pleasure he turned back to Elizabeth and kissed her again, starting gently, but gradually deepening the kiss until she slipped her arms around his neck and pressed herself against him. He did not hurry the occasion, taking the time to enjoy the pleasures of her mouth and her slender form in his arms, reminding himself that she was his, even if he did have to wait for her, even if he did have to deal with her difficult father before he could take her to Pemberley as his bride. He defied even Mr. Bennet to say that Elizabeth was unwilling after this display!

The depth of his passion was tempting Elizabeth more than he could know. She wanted desperately to leave conflict behind and to be only with him, and knowing that she only need say so was an enticement hard to resist. It was so simple to avoid the question by losing herself in the pleasure of his touch and his kisses, and she did not wish to think about self-discipline or consequences but simply to forget everything but him.

Her lack of restraint communicated itself to Darcy through the small movements of her body and her gasps as his hands explored her curves. He was intoxicated by it; and, in a need to do something more, he began to press tempting kisses across her face and down her neck. He could feel her body melting into his, and the desire not to stop was almost insurmountable when faced with her passionate responsiveness, but he knew their position to be quite untenable. It was almost a relief to his senses when she froze in his arms in a reaction of clear distress. He drew back to look at her in concern, only to see her looking with horror over his shoulder.

"Your point is taken, Mr. Darcy," said Mr. Bennet in a tight voice. "It is time for you to come into the house now, Lizzy."

Mortally embarrassed, she looked first to Darcy, who looked remarkably untroubled by the situation. He nodded, and she took his hand more for support than anything else as they silently followed a retreating Mr. Bennet into the house.

There was very little that Mr. Bennet liked less than the idea of his Lizzy moving far from him and of her transferring her allegiances to another man, but among that very little was a strong dislike of being found out to be in the wrong. It could be seen that he would not be in good spirits on an occasion such as this, and having to prove himself greater than his errors required that he be cordial to a man whom he still detested. It was no mean feat, then, that he managed a modicum of civility in the presence of his family and Mr. Darcy; but, then again, he was a man quite practiced in disguising his feelings and intentions. Elizabeth, waiting for the retribution certain to come for her untoward behaviour as well as for her disappearance that morning, kept glancing at her father nervously; and Darcy, by her side, was careful to keep on a face of complete neutrality despite some distinctly self-satisfied sentiments regarding his disproof of Mr. Bennet's earlier slights to his character.

Somehow the three managed to maintain a calm demeanour throughout dinner, the first Darcy had taken at Longbourn since his arrival. Afterwards, when Elizabeth had bid Darcy a tender adieu in the privacy of the front portico, she went with some trepidation past her father's library on her way to the sitting room. She was not surprised to hear him call her in, but she awaited his anger with a significant degree of anxiety as he sat silently for a moment looking at her, reminding herself that he was not the only one with a cause for resentment.

"Well, Lizzy," he said finally, "I withdraw my objections to your engagement."

This was so far from what she had expected to hear that for a moment she could not think. At last she managed to say, "I am glad to hear it." She found this startling reversal difficult to comprehend.

"That is all, my dear; off you go, now," he said dismissively.

She lingered a moment, and then looked at him and said, as if hoping to convince him, "He is a very good man and is perfectly amiable."

"Yes, yes; well, think whatever you like," he said dryly.

His failure to take her words with due seriousness vexed her. "He *is*," she said forcefully. "You have never allowed me to tell you of my feelings for him."

He looked as if the last thing he wished for in the world was to hear about her affection for Darcy, but with obvious reluctance he invited her to do just that. She explained the gradual change which her estimation of him had undergone, relating her absolute certainty that his affection was not the work of a day, but had stood the test of many months' suspense.

"Well, my dear," said he when she ceased speaking. "You have given me a good deal to think about. And now I *will* bid you good night."

She accepted her dismissal this time, wishing him a subdued good night before going up to her room to think on her own about all that had occurred that day.

DARCY GAVE CONSIDERABLE THOUGHT TO the matter of Mr. Bennet. He was still angered by Mr. Bennet's failure to protect Elizabeth from Lady Catherine, not to mention the direct insult that had been levelled at him regarding the nature of his relationship with Elizabeth. Under normal circumstances, this would constitute more than he could forgive, but this was Elizabeth's father, and for some reason she still retained a fondness for him. As such, he considered that he had a responsibility to make every reasonable attempt to appease the man, little as he liked the idea.

On his arrival at Longbourn the following morning he therefore asked for Mr. Bennet instead of Elizabeth—*duty before pleasure*, he thought gloomily. Mr. Bennet seemed quite surprised to see him but offered him a seat quite civilly.

"This should only take a moment," said Darcy, hoping rather grimly that this estimate was accurate. "I wished to apologize for becoming intemperate yesterday. Given the misapprehension you were under, your attitude was quite understandable. I hope that now we both have a better understanding of the situation." If Mr. Bennet did not accept this peace offering, Darcy could hardly be blamed.

"Thank you, Mr. Darcy," said Mr. Bennet in a perfectly amiable manner. "I must apologize as well for having reached an unwarranted conclusion."

They had now exchanged several civil sentences, which Darcy considered a success and more than adequate to the occasion. He therefore limited himself to acknowledging Mr. Bennet's apology and, with a bow, turned to leave.

"Just a moment, Mr. Darcy," Mr. Bennet said, his manner indecipherable. "Do I take it, then, that you do *not* intend to apologize for endangering my daughter's reputation at the bottom of my garden yesterday?"

Darcy turned and looked at him levelly for a moment. "That is correct, sir; I do not."

"You do not," repeated Mr. Bennet in a voice suggesting a certain degree of disbelief.

"No," repeated Darcy evenly. "I do not. If you wish, however, I am willing to marry her immediately in order to protect her reputation." *Willing and eager!* he thought to himself.

Mr. Bennet laughed. "Oh, no, Mr. Darcy," he said, a flash of amusement in his eyes. "I have no intention of giving my Lizzy to you a moment before I have to."

Darcy raised an eyebrow. "As long as you intend to do it then, we need have no disagreement."

"As long as there is no more behaviour like that in the garden, we do not," Mr. Bennet retorted dryly.

Clearly the rules of his relationship with Mr. Bennet had changed, and he knew a challenge when he heard one. Darcy looked him in the eye. "I have noted your opinion," he said. "Good day, Mr. Bennet."

As Darcy left, Mr. Bennet sat back in his chair, thinking that since it appeared he had to tolerate the man, it was just as well that he could provide a source of amusement.

Two nights later, Elizabeth waited until well after the household was abed to find her way out of the dark house. This was the hardest part; once she was outside, the light of the nearly full moon allowed her to see the road clearly, though the cold made her shiver. Her heart lifted as she approached the church, and she smiled when she saw Darcy's familiar shape emerge from the shadows, a frisson of desire running through her at the thought of what was to come. Although she could not see his face clearly, she could feel the pleasure radiating from him at her presence.

He kissed her hand as he greeted her. They did not speak much after their initial greetings, more out of a fullness of feeling than out of any fear of discovery. Walking hand in hand as they had never been permitted to in the light of day, Elizabeth felt a deep contentment. Finally she said quietly, as though not to disturb the silence of the night, "I have been wondering where you are planning to take me, my love."

"It is an old cottage, now unused—quite rustic, I am afraid, but warm and comfortable enough." He stopped and turned to her, taking both her hands in his, and said, "You need not feel that you are obligated to…anything; just the chance to be alone with you without interruption and to hold you will be enough, if that is what you want."

She reached up to kiss him. "*You* need not worry so much! I know quite well what I am about."

His kiss in return was rather deeper. "Well, then," he said, his voice full of warm satisfaction.

He led her along the back lanes until they reached a small cottage. When she entered, Elizabeth, who knew that it had been abandoned some years earlier, expected to find the signs of long disuse, but discovered instead that it was clean, with a low fire burning in the fireplace. A few neat, if simple, furnishings were in place. The bed, out of keeping with the rest of the room, was covered with elegant bedclothes.

She turned to Darcy with a look of amusement. "You have been busy, sir!" she said.

Darcy looked slightly uncomfortable. "It is not much; it is far less than I would wish to offer you. I had thought to give you Pemberley, yet here we are in a simple labourer's cottage."

She embraced him impulsively. "It does not matter where we are as long as I am with you; you do not need a fine estate or beautiful gifts to win my heart."

He held her close to him, moved by her statement and knowing it to be the truth: that he had won her with himself, not with his fortune or position. It was a gift more priceless than any he could give her.

"You have done remarkably well here, though, I must say," she added playfully.

"It is not completely my doing, I must confess; I have a valet who is both talented and extremely discreet—I believe he looked on this as something of a personal challenge."

She could see by the intent look in his dark eyes that his thoughts were far from their conversation. She laced her arms around his neck and kissed him. Her heart fluttered as she felt his hard body against hers, knowing what was to come, and feeling her need for him building.

While her kiss fed his rising passion, Darcy could not help but note how cold her arms were under her shawl. When they paused for breath, he said, "Come over to the fire, my heart, and warm yourself; I will not have you taking a chill," He drew up a chair for her and settled her in it; then, to her surprise, he sat on the floor by her feet, his head resting against her leg.

Unable to resist, Elizabeth ran her fingers through his thick dark hair. He caught her hand and placed a light kiss in it. She was puzzled by his behaviour; she had expected, given his anticipation of this meeting, that he would lose no time in taking her to bed, yet he seemed completely unhurried and content just to be with her.

Had she been able to read Darcy's thoughts, she would have found a different picture. His desire for her was quite undiminished, yet he had discovered that there was a delightful excitement that lay in knowing that he would soon be making her his, and he was not ready to give up this anticipatory pleasure quite yet. Enjoying the relaxing sensation of her hand stroking his hair, he began to imagine the delights of her body, and he slipped his hand under her skirts and curled it around her ankle.

Elizabeth felt a flash of desire rush through her at his unexpected action, and her hand paused for a moment in his hair. A trace of a smile crossed Darcy's face, and he began to gently stroke her leg, taking time to allow his fingers to explore. She was astonished by how much sensation such a light touch could bring, and she felt a throbbing building deep inside her. That these were such forbidden explorations only enhanced her excitement. She was starting to wonder how much more of this delicate torture she could tolerate before being reduced to quivering when he turned to unlacing her halfboots.

After tugging them off, he returned to his explorations, his hand drifting gradually up to her knee. Elizabeth could no longer prevent herself from a slight gasp as he moved slowly and tantalizingly to encircle her garter.

Darcy was experiencing a deep enjoyment in taking possession of Elizabeth's body one inch at a time. He felt her fingers clenching in his hair, and his desire rose in response to hers. Very deliberately he hooked his finger inside her garter and turned to look up at her. Her cheeks were flushed, and her eyes smoky with passion; and, despite the simplicity of dress and hairstyle which her midnight escape had required, he had never seen her look more beautiful. It occurred to him that they were totally alone in a way that he was quite unaccustomed to—there were no family, no friends, no servants anywhere to be found, just the two of them. It was never possible to be completely alone in a house such as Pemberley or Netherfield, and he had no doubt that, with four sisters, it was the same for her. Only out of doors could they be alone, and then there was no privacy.

The novelty of his current situation lent a new aspect of pleasure and freedom to their encounter. She was his, this cottage was theirs, and there was no one to answer to or be responsible for, no one for whom standards must be maintained, no rules to be followed except their own.

He felt an intense rush of desire at this realization. He met her eyes and held them as he unfastened her garter and drew her stocking down and off, allowing his fingertips to skim her warm skin as he did so. Returning for the remaining stocking, he paused to caress the tender skin of her inner thigh, watching her expression as the firelight flickered over her face. He wanted more than cooperation and desire from her—he wanted an intimacy with her in body like that in spirit he had found so fulfilling at Netherfield. The second stocking joined its partner on the floor, and he let her skirts fall to their natural position once more, only keeping his hand resting lightly on the tender skin of the top of her foot. There was something very arousing, he thought, about seeing Elizabeth unshod, a familiarity that spoke of closeness and confidence.

There was still little physical contact between them, yet their desires seemed to forge a powerful connection—it was almost as if she already felt his touch and the fiercely pleasurable sensation of having him inside her. She was almost shaking with need, and they had not yet truly begun.

Darcy put his hands up to her waist. "Come to me, then," he said. She expected he would take her to bed, but instead he brought her down to sit between his legs on the floor, her back resting against him. He did not kiss her or caress her, but merely leaned his head against hers, and with his hand began to kilt up her skirts until he could see her shapely legs. He had more than looking in mind, however, and began to brush his fingers lightly along her thighs, moving ever higher until with a moaning sigh she parted her legs to allow him the pleasure of access to her.

He slid his fingers between her legs, seeking her pleasure and finding it. As he moved his finger against her, she began to moan and to press against him. He found it arousing indeed to be touching her so intimately while they were both still clothed, when he had barely even kissed her. The trust with which she gave herself over to him, here in their own private place, was something he craved; that sense of absolute union and understanding that provided such nourishment to him. He could not resist sliding his fingers deep inside her until she gasped with the pleasure he was providing her. He stroked her delicately until she reached the pinnacle of fulfilment and then returned from it once more, trembling in his arms.

He simply held her to him for a brief interval, allowing her time to recover, but her response had driven his need, and he sought her lips with a passionate urgency. His desire to delay his gratification had fled, and his fingers rapidly dealt with the fastenings of her dress, pushing it down her shoulders as his lips followed with a hungry need to taste her skin. She arched into his hands as they reached her breasts.

He reached behind her to unbutton her dress. She slipped her arms out of her sleeves, then stepped out of the skirts until she stood before him. His eyes roved appreciatively over her, and Elizabeth began to feel the deep arousal that comes only with such intimate and honest exposure.

"Your hair. Will you let it down?" His voice had become almost hoarse.

With a bewitching smile, she unpinned her hair and shook it free over her shoulders. Emboldened by his heated look, she stepped towards him. She slid her hands under his driving coat, encouraging its removal, and then applied herself to his shirt, a matter which required a certain amount of co-operation from Darcy, who was finding great pleasure in her ministrations. She hesitated a moment before touching his trousers—even in London she had felt too much modesty to look at him directly—but found her courage to continue in his eyes. As she unfastened them and let them drop, on inspiration she took into her hands that part of him which still provoked her blushes. His clear response gave her confidence, and she watched his pleasure as she caressed him.

Before long he moved to stop her. "Come, my heart," he said, leading her to the bed and drawing back the bedclothes. She slipped in, her feet discovering with pleasure that his valet's preparations had extended to warm bricks in the foot of the bed, and held her arms out to him. Her longing to have him within her was increasing rapidly, but he would not be satisfied until his hands had the opportunity to rediscover all of her body. He was determined to know that her urgency matched his, and he delayed to suckle at her breasts.

Ripples of desire tugged through her at the touch of his mouth, and she arched against him, holding his head to her as he increased the intensity of the stimulation he was providing her. She moaned his name as her hand sought out his arousal.

He could wait no longer; he broke off and poised himself above her, his eyes claiming hers with a near desperate need. He had meant to go slowly again, lest he hurt her, but he could not hold back, and he thrust himself deep within her.

Elizabeth gasped as he connected to her in the most intimate of ways, she pressed herself against him as he began to move slowly within her. As he shifted to hard, rapid strokes which claimed her as his own, his arousal grew until he found his release and collapsed in her arms. He was not so spent, as not to hope for more, and his fingers travelled to that spot which gave her pleasure so easily and caressed it for the brief time needed for her to be overtaken by waves of pure satisfaction.

She could not say why it was she felt so very close to him at these moments, but the truth of it could not be denied. He could have asked anything of her then, and she would have given it with love; had he once again tried to persuade her to an immediate marriage, she would have agreed just to see his happiness in it. It was a fortunate thing, she reflected, that he did not know the power he had. She nestled in as close to him as she could, and was pleased to feel his arms tighten around her.

He felt all the comfort of holding her close, and thought of his good fortune in having won the love of this woman. Her generosity and freedom with him could not but amaze and delight him anew. "My heart," he whispered in her ear. He could have happily stayed in that moment forever, but eventually Elizabeth pulled away from him far enough to raise herself up on her elbow, her fingers tracing the lines of his face as she honoured him with a gaze of deep affection. He felt her absence acutely, and held out his arms to her. "Come back to me, Lizzy," he said, a certain seductiveness evident in his look.

She looked amused. "It is a tempting an idea, but if I did, I would relax too much. It is very late, and I would be all too content to be in your arms the whole night through—I doubt that I could stay awake long."

"All that is true for me, too, *and* you have pleased me enormously as well; I can think of nothing I would like better at the moment than falling asleep with you," he said engagingly. "I know that must wait—but must you leave so quickly, then? I am enjoying having you to myself, far from family and servants, nothing but you and I in the world."

She could not resist him, and settled back into his arms. "Very well, sir, but I am relying on you to keep me awake," she said teasingly.

"I am certain I can think of something should I become desperate," he said dryly, running his hand down her side suggestively. "I think that perhaps I shall build a cottage just for us at Pemberley, where I can steal you away and we can be completely alone together. Would you like that, my Lizzy?"

The thought raised associations she would rather not consider at the moment, but once they were in her head, she could not force them away. Her feelings of closeness to him began to vanish, and sadness started to pervade her. Her natural instinct was to try to put it aside and make a light response, but she checked herself, recalling that he wished her to share her concerns with him. Still, this might be a subject he would rather *not* hear her thoughts on; yet she did not want it to stand between them. Before she could reconsider further, she said slowly, "Sir John Hennessey, in Letchworth, has such a honeymoon cottage. I know girls are not supposed to know such things, but it is where he keeps his mistress." She knew from local gossip that it was far from an unusual use for such a hideaway.

Darcy kissed her forehead. "Well, fortunately, you need not worry about such a thing," he said readily. "It will be solely for you and me, my sweetest, loveliest Elizabeth." He tangled his hand in her hair comfortably, enjoying the feeling of the silken strands between his fingers. He was so deep in his own contentment that it was a few minutes before he realized she had not replied, and when he looked at her, he could see a certain unhappiness in her eyes. Concerned, he thought back over what had been said and, in a moment of realization, said with dismay, "You *do* worry about it! Dear heart, how can you think it? Why should I ever wish for another woman when I have you?" He could not imagine how she could possibly undervalue herself so; but then again, as he thought of her father's behaviour, perhaps he could.

"I am not completely naïve, Fitzwilliam," she said reluctantly. "I am aware of the realities of life, and that you will likely not always feel this way. I understand the…expectations for such a situation, and I know it is my role to accept it—but no, I would prefer that you not build such a cottage; I doubt I could enjoy it." *The price of honesty is high indeed,* she thought, her throat tight. She wished fiercely that the subject had never arisen; she wanted only the comfort of the closeness to him she had felt a few minutes earlier.

Darcy pulled away from her just enough to be able to look at her directly, the light of the dying fire casting shadows across him. He was silent for a minute, his face troubled. "Elizabeth," he began, then paused again. "I cannot deny that there have been women in the past—I doubt any gentleman could—but only within limits; I have never ruined a woman, nor have I been with a married woman, though God alone knows there has been more than enough opportunity! No, my heart, the sanctity of marriage is a boundary I would not bridge—and I cannot tell you how desperately unhappy it would make me if *you* ever did."

"Hush," said Elizabeth with embarrassment. "How can you say such a thing!"

"Just as you did, because the very idea of your even looking at another man is more than I can tolerate; and because I do know how very lightly many of the ladies of the *ton* hold their wedding vows, once they have produced the obligatory heir. So have no doubts of me; if that were the kind of marriage I desired, I could have had it anytime in the last eight years, but I did not."

His words had the unmistakable ring of authenticity, and provided some relief to Elizabeth. She could not be completely reassured so easily on a subject of this magnitude, though; he had become so important to her that the very thought of him looking elsewhere was enough to make her miserable. She asked quietly, "Why did you not? Certainly that would have been by far the easiest course for you."

He held her tightly to him, having some idea of what exposing her insecurities like this must cost someone as self-sufficient as Elizabeth. He could understand all too well how such fears could arise; he had certainly suffered enough agony over the possibility of losing her to know the feeling well. "Why did you not marry Mr. Collins, my heart? He would have been considered a good match, after all," he said gently. "No, my dearest, I know what it is to live without affection, to think that caring and concern are a paid duty of servants, and that familial love was a luxury that no one had any interest in affording. I decided long ago that I would not marry a woman whom I could not respect and care for—though I confess that I had not expected to find her where I did, so far from the society of London; though perhaps in hindsight I should have been looking there the whole time." He smiled at the conceit. "And you, dearest Lizzy? You taught me some time ago what qualities you did *not* value in a husband—but what did you *want*?

She was quiet for a moment. "I always hoped to marry for love and knew I could not marry without respect, but in truth I do not think I knew what love meant. I had to *experience* it to know its power."

His dark eyes looked deeply into hers. "And having known it, how could you doubt me?"

She could not be anything but honest with him. "Because I know you are a man of the world, and that your entire life has been lived by rules different from the little society I have known here, and that I am moving into your world without knowing what it is I do. In truth, I do not know what it is *you* want from a wife."

"You—nothing but you," he replied instantly, but his thoughts were unquiet. The moment she had spoken, it was obvious to him—how could he have failed to realize that along with the very practical benefits this marriage offered her came a difficult change? He was asking a great deal of her, while thinking only of what he offered. "I cannot say that we will not face challenges, but as long as we face them together, I have no doubt of the outcome."

"Thank you," she said softly.

He could feel her body gradually relax in his arms, but his mind was now less pleasantly occupied, as her very doubts led him to question his security in her affections. "Elizabeth?" he said abruptly.

She kissed his shoulder. "Yes, my love?"

"I…" he began, then stopped again. Damn, but he hated this vulnerability! "Lizzy, I would be happy if you were to tell me that you care."

She raised her head to look at him, finding that same distress she had felt earlier now on his face. "Oh, my very dear! I could never imagine loving anyone as I love you; you are my joy and my delight. I wish I could always be with you, and that we should never be apart," she said. As she saw his relief, her spirits turned to playfulness, and she daringly pinned him to the bed with her body. "And does my presence here tell you nothing?"

He responded as she hoped to her boldness and teasing; with a wicked smile, he reversed their positions before she could protest. Punctuating his words with kisses, he said, "It tells me many things, my heart—it tells me that you are as generous as you are lovely, that you know how passionately I adore you, and," he added significantly, "that you *are* my wife, even if I cannot persuade you to run off to London with me." He kissed her deeply, and then, abruptly serious, held her face between his hands and looked into her lovely eyes. "There is very little in life which frightens me, Elizabeth; but the possibility that I might somehow lose you—or lose your affection—is one that terrifies me."

"Oh, my love, you cannot lose me so easily!" she whispered, touched by his admission. In truth, she wanted nothing more than to be with him, and found the idea of running off with him all too appealing; yet she knew that an inability to tolerate being apart was the wrong reason to do so. She was forced to admit to herself that part of wanting to be with him always was her own fear, a fear born of a love so deep as to carry the power of hurting her just as deeply, and her own need for a constant reassurance within it. It was acutely difficult to trust, not so much *him* as the world itself, for if anything were to happen to him she did not know how she would bear it. *How intimately love is bound to pain,* she thought, *that this same love which brings such happiness when we are together carries also the ache of absence and the fear of loss!* It was a conundrum without a solution.

Darcy was idly drawing lines with his finger down her body. "It is going to become more difficult for us to have time alone," he said, "since Georgiana arrives tomorrow. I will attempt to find some way for us to spend some time together, but much will depend on how she is taking this, and that I cannot predict." He gave her a sidelong look, then added, "Of course, we could always return here."

Elizabeth laughed. "And when do you propose that we sleep, my love? You would not wish for a bride with dark circles under her eyes, I daresay."

He kissed her slowly and tantalizingly. "If it meant you were spending your nights with me, I could tolerate a great deal," he said with a smile.

Elizabeth could not help but be amused at how quickly he could melt her resistance. *What do you expect,* she asked herself, *when he is only suggesting those things that you yourself want as well?* "Well, perhaps not *every* night," she said with a smile.

"You drive a hard bargain, madam," he said. He began pressing light kisses on neck, choosing all those places in which she was most sensitive to his persuasion, and working his way gradually downwards. "I hope you understand, then, that I will not be inclined to let you go quickly."

She gasped as his lips reached her breast. "No," she said, "do not let me go."

ELIZABETH WAS ALREADY MISSING DARCY when she finally returned to Longbourn. It still lacked some hours before dawn, and longer yet until the household would arise, so she had no concerns as she entered into the house as silently as she could. She was therefore quite startled, and indeed took a step backwards, her hand over her heart, when her father appeared at the door of his library in his nightshirt and robe, a candle in his hand.

His mouth twisted with irony. "Did you have a nice walk, Lizzy?" he asked.

Caught unawares, the only thought she had was that she wished she had agreed to go off to London with Darcy. Recovering herself, she said, "Yes, I did; the night air was very refreshing."

"Refreshing, is it?" said her father cynically. "And how is Mr. Darcy?"

She would not give him the satisfaction of a confession. "When last I saw him, he was quite well. Good night, sir." She walked toward the stairs.

"Elizabeth!" he called after her. When she turned to look at him, he said, "There will be no more night-time walks."

Had it not been for the mocking tone of his voice, she would likely have accepted the restriction without argument as well within his rights. As it was, all her feelings of injury and offence came to the fore with a sudden anger, and she said defiantly, "Perhaps a trip to London would be preferable." She ran up the stairs, failing to see the look of pain on his face.

Mr. Bennet looked after her for a minute, then slowly turned and went back into his library.

ELIZABETH WOULD HAVE LIKED TO sleep in the following morning, but knew that her absence from the breakfast table would only be subject for further comments from her father, so she rose only a little later than her usual, and was downstairs on time. She had no intention of acting on her threat of the previous night, knowing that it would only hurt Jane and her mother, who were quite innocent in this regard. Mr. Bennet mercifully spared her from any further barbs, for which Elizabeth was grateful. She had enough to consider in the fact that Miss Darcy was due to arrive at Netherfield that morning, and she had not yet decided how to approach her after their last meeting when Georgiana had spread her disturbing information.

By the time she went to Netherfield to greet her that afternoon, she was no more resolved than to watch how Georgiana responded and decide how to behave from there. When she arrived, Elizabeth shared a look of longing with Darcy, and then greeted Georgiana equably, asking after her journey. The girl seemed even more withdrawn than she had when Elizabeth had first met her at Rosings, barely even looking up when Elizabeth spoke to her and replying in a voice just above a whisper. Questions about her stay at Derby and her music received monosyllabic answers.

Elizabeth looked over at Darcy with a question in her eyes, and he shrugged slightly, as if baffled by his sister's behaviour. It was evident to her that he was unhappy about the situation, but she felt at a loss to understand the circumstances and wished she could speak with him alone even for a few minutes. In order to disguise the uncomfortable silence, she initiated a conversation with him regarding the arrival of other guests for the wedding. He answered stiffly at first—*I shall have to remember that they can make one another more reserved!* thought Elizabeth—but at length he became easier, and more the man she had grown to know.

The discussion turned to Pemberley, and Elizabeth expressed her eagerness to see it at last. "Or at least I am eager to be shown it," she said with rueful amusement. "I am quite intimidated by the idea of the house itself— I fear from all I have heard that I shall become hopelessly lost in it, and you will have to bring in the hunting dogs to find me!"

The corners of Darcy's mouth turned up. "The hounds may be so delighted to have the run of the house that they will take a goodly while to find you," he teased. "I will have to have a map made and provide you with a compass, just in case."

Elizabeth laughed. "I will depend upon it!" She glanced at Georgiana to include her in the jest and, to her dismay, discovered that she was in tears.

Darcy, feeling the contentment of being in Elizabeth's company after the stress of dealing with a nearly mute sister, at first noticed nothing, as he was enjoying the pleasure of resting his eyes on the woman he loved. He could not miss the look of concern that crossed her face, though, and was horrified to see Georgiana's distress as he followed her gaze. Elizabeth quickly crossed the room to sit beside her and placed her arm gently around her shoulders.

"My dear Georgiana," she said soothingly. "Whatever is the matter?"

Georgiana made no reply. Darcy knelt at her feet and took her hand between both of his, which only made the girl cry harder.

Elizabeth made a quick decision. "Fitzwilliam, would you see if someone could bring us some tea?" At his puzzled look, she gestured to the door with her head.

"Excuse me, Georgiana. I will return in a few minutes," he said, uncertain, but willing to rely on Elizabeth's wisdom regarding his sister.

"Thank you," said Elizabeth. As he left, she turned once again to his sister. "Now, Georgiana, what is all this about?" she asked gently.

It took several minutes before Georgiana was calm enough to manage a few words. "What I said that day—I am *so* sorry—I have felt *terrible* about it—I never thought you would take me seriously; you are so strong, I thought you would just go to him and demand the truth, and he would be embarrassed—I never meant to hurt you!" she said brokenly, between sobs.

Elizabeth squeezed her hand gently. "I think we all have gained in understanding since that episode, and I hope we can put it behind us."

"I cannot understand why you are being so kind to me—why you would ever wish to see me again," said Georgiana, and as she finished she was overtaken by sobs so intense that she could scarcely breathe.

There was nothing Elizabeth could do for her until she became somewhat calmer, so she merely sat with her and chafed her hands while reassuring her of her welcome. Finally she settled, but into a state of numb dispirit rather than a true peace. "My dear Georgiana," said Elizabeth, "if there is something else troubling you, I will be happy to listen, but I have no wish to force your confidence."

Georgiana shook her head slowly, her eyes on no object other than the floor. "It is only that…I never thought it could ever be that he would not want me anymore. I know that I deserve it, I just never thought he would…but I know he has you now, and he is so much happier with you than he ever was with me, and I will be with my aunt and uncle…" Her voice trailed off.

Elizabeth looked at her in amused exasperation. "Are you attempting to suggest that you think your brother does not want you to live with him anymore?" The absolute silence which met her question was a clear indicator that this was, in fact, Georgiana's understanding. "Wherever did you get such an idea?"

For the first time, Georgiana looked up at Elizabeth. "He wrote me a letter. You must not think that I blame him; I know that he has done more than his duty for me for years, and I have been so...difficult of late," she said hopelessly.

"I believe that what he offered you was a choice," replied Elizabeth, not unkindly. "He wants you to be happy, you know; and it has seemed that you have been less than content in his care. It was a difficult offer for him to make."

"I am not happy because I am all wrong for everything, not because of him!" she cried.

"What makes you say that?" asked Elizabeth, sensing that they were approaching the heart of the matter.

"Because it is true—there is no one less suited than I to be Miss Darcy of Pemberley. I will never be able to meet my duties. I am terrified of balls and society, I do not understand fashion or the *ton*, and the idea of men seeking me for my fortune makes me feel ill. I have had nightmares about coming out ever since I was old enough to know what it meant! I will be a disgrace to my brother and my family, and some poor man will find he has a pitiable bargain in me when he discovers that I cannot manage a grand household or host a ball. Some other girl should be me, and I should be living in some quiet backwater with no demands upon me beyond everyday ones," she said in distress.

Elizabeth looked at her closely. "It sounds as if you have been very unhappy," she said. It was now apparent why the idea of eloping with George Wickham had such appeal for her; it had been her escape from her responsibilities, or so she must have thought.

"The only time I am happy is when I am at my piano-forte and I can forget all this!" said Georgiana. "Oh, but please do not tell my brother—I should not have said any of this, and I do not want him to know how badly I have disappointed his every expectation. If he will only have me back— if *you* will only have me back—I promise I will try harder, and I will do everything he says." She looked at Elizabeth beseechingly.

"I am trying very hard to convince your brother that he need *not* be in charge of everything—please do not undo all my good work!" said Elizabeth with a smile. "It does him good to be questioned from time to time."

Georgiana looked at her in disbelief for a moment before gaining an inkling that she was being teased. She could not quite smile, but her eyes brightened a little. "He does like to have matters just as he pleases," she said shyly, watching Elizabeth closely to be certain she had not offended her.

"He does indeed," said Elizabeth comfortably. "But do you think that your brother would not understand your fear of balls and society?"

"He wants me to make a good marriage," she replied sadly.

"I am sure he does; but, given that he himself is never at his best among large groups and I think would be perfectly happy never to attend another ball in his life, I imagine he might understand better than you think."

Her countenance lightened briefly at this idea and then fell again. "It would make no difference, though; even if he understands, it will not change my responsibilities."

"That, perhaps, is grounds for a different discussion, one which I am not qualified to enter into," Elizabeth said thoughtfully. "Perhaps we could take this one step at a time."

Darcy chose that moment to reappear at the door, looking quizzically at Elizabeth. She gave him a reassuring smile, but Georgiana steadfastly refused to look at him. There was an uncomfortable moment of silence, then Elizabeth, feeling that directness was called for, said, "There seems to have been a misunderstanding, Fitzwilliam. Georgiana is under the impression that you would prefer that she not live with us."

He looked disbelieving for a moment, then came to take his sister in his arms. "Of course that is not the case, sweetheart!" he said, distressed that she should ever think such a thing. "I would never wish such a thing."

"Are you sure?" she asked timorously.

"I am absolutely certain," he replied strongly, his concern for her evident.

Seeing the two in a close embrace, Elizabeth chose to make a quiet exit, but before she could do so, Darcy caught her eye with a look of gratitude. She was pleased with the resolution; it was clear that they were in for some further trials, but perhaps a base for understanding had been prepared. She would address Darcy later about Georgiana's other concerns, and surely they could find some sort of solution.

Chapter 13

M r. and Mrs. Gardiner arrived at Longbourn the day before the wedding with the intent of staying there several days after the ceremony. It was a pleasure for them to see the Bennets, despite the chaos attending the upcoming wedding, and also to visit with the two young men whom they had come to know in London. Both Bingley and Darcy, along with Miss Darcy, joined the Bennets for dinner that night to enjoy their company along with that of their brides-to-be.

It was a pleasant occasion full of lively conversation between the young couples and the Gardiners to which Mr. Bennet added the occasional dry comment; Mrs. Bennet paid no attention at all and talked only of the wedding to Mary and Kitty. After the ladies withdrew, Mr. Gardiner's amiability and wide-ranging discourse came to be useful; Darcy and Mr. Bennet were still observing their fragile truce, but it was not one such as to allow free and easy discussion. Darcy was relieved when the time came to rejoin the ladies; he considered each encounter where he and Mr. Bennet did not come to verbal blows or end in dead silence as a success and did not wish to press his luck.

Later that evening, after the guests had departed, Mr. Gardiner sat with Mr. Bennet in his library drinking brandy and making desultory conversation. Mr. Bennet finally said with a certain sheathed resentment, "You and your wife seem quite fond of Mr. Darcy."

Mr. Gardiner, as yet unaware of the history between the two, allowed this to be true and said, "He is pleasant company and has a lively intelligence."

Mr. Bennet sipped his brandy. "I had been under the impression that you had certain reservations regarding Lizzy's engagement to him."

"Less the engagement than the circumstances, although it did take me some time to be assured that Lizzy was happy with the arrangement. Although I believe him to be a very responsible young man, he has a certain lack of control where Lizzy is involved, and I am sorry to say she did not seem to be doing anything to discourage him. I confess I was rather glad to hand that problem back to you," said Mr. Gardiner. "I would like to say that I hope they have been learning some restraint, but I doubt it to be true, judging from the look on your face."

Grimacing, Mr. Bennet said, "He could hardly have been worse. He offers her every encouragement—do you know that I caught her creeping into the house in the middle of the night? I do not call *that* responsibility on his part."

"Nor would I," said Mr. Gardiner with a shocked look. "Well, at least this particular problem will resolve itself to everyone's satisfaction tomorrow. I try to console myself by remembering that he clearly adores Lizzy and would do anything for her, which has a more literal meaning in his case than in most, given his involvement with Lydia's marriage. And that was when he and Lizzy were apparently in the midst of a quarrel it seems neither expected to resolve, though I did not understand this until much later."

"*What* had Mr. Darcy to do with Lydia?" asked Mr. Bennet with grave suspicion.

Mr. Gardiner looked at him in dismayed surprise. "You mean to say that Lizzy did not tell you? Oh, dear; I have rather put my foot in it this time, then."

"I do *not* like secrets where my family is concerned—so I ask again, what had he to do with Lydia?" Mr. Bennet's expression was approaching a glower.

With a sigh, Mr. Gardiner replied, "Having let that much slip, I suppose I must tell you it all, though I confess that Darcy had requested that we keep it secret from your family. The truth is that he did it all—found her, made the match, paid off Wickham's debts and purchased his commission, and left me to take the credit for it."

Mr. Bennet stared at him in shock, then leaned forward and rested his forehead on his hands. There was little worse, he thought, than finding oneself overwhelmingly indebted to a man one heartily disliked. These last few months since Lydia's elopement had been difficult enough for him even without the problem of Darcy. This was a complication he did not need, even though it gave him a certain relief regarding his indebtedness to Mr. Gardiner. "Ah, why did it have to be *him*?"

Mr. Gardiner looked at him incisively. "You do not like him, do you?"

"*That* is an understatement, my friend."

"What do you dislike about him?"

Mr. Bennet sighed. "He is proud and disagreeable, and I do not like the way he treats Lizzy." His list of Darcy's sins was not as impressive as it had been a week earlier when he had been forced to cross off a few of them, and he was not completely happy about this.

"Proud and disagreeable?" Mr. Gardiner sipped his brandy. "Now I have never seen any evidence of that—he has always been perfectly civil and amiable with me. But perhaps the more important question is how Lizzy feels about the way he treats her. He is not perfect, though frankly it is possible that he *is* just perfect for Lizzy."

"Edward, I am not looking for ways to forgive the man!" he exclaimed angrily.

"*That* is apparent. I feel sorry for Lizzy, caught between the two of you."

"Lizzy manages well enough," said Mr. Bennet curtly.

"Well, I see there is no moving you on this one, so I shall not waste my breath," said Mr. Gardiner. "Shall we talk of more pleasant matters instead?"

THE DAY OF THE WEDDINGS dawned bright and cold.

Mr. Bennet finally caught Mr. Darcy inside the nave of the church. He had spent a less than pleasant night and was not looking forward to this conversation. It had not passed his understanding that, just as Lydia's fall was related directly to his failure to impose discipline upon his daughters, many of his recent difficulties were owing to an attempt to overcompensate by controlling the behaviour of his remaining daughters. He wanted to end this as quickly as possible and return to his native state of indolence, but first there remained this unpleasant task. "Mr. Darcy," he said.

Darcy turned to look at him. "Mr. Bennet," he responded courteously, quite preoccupied with the upcoming ceremony.

"It has come to my attention that I owe you a debt of thanks for your efforts on behalf of my youngest daughter," said Mr. Bennet.

Darcy's full attention now turned to him. "Sir, I am sorry if learning of it has caused you any discomfort; I never intended you to know of my role. You owe me nothing—I took the actions I did for my own reasons."

"Nevertheless, you have my thanks." Mr. Bennet paused, then added with an effort, "And my apologies; it seems that I have misjudged you on a number of counts."

It took a great effort for Darcy to keep himself from agreeing aloud with that statement. Instead, he thought about Elizabeth, and what he was willing to suffer on her behalf, and said with all civility, "I hope we are both learning to understand each other better. To be quite frank, though, you are telling this to the wrong person; it is your daughter who needs rather badly to hear this from you."

Mr. Bennet smiled ironically. "You may well be right. Until later, then." He walked off towards the front of the church.

Mrs. Bennet was fluttering all about Jane and Elizabeth, making last minute adjustments to their hair and their gowns while her daughters looked at one another with amused patience. Jane could not be happier, and her smiles showed it; while Elizabeth's happiness was more felt than expressed. She was both happy and relieved that this day had finally arrived, and her sadness over parting from her family and home was tempered by the glad knowledge that there would be no more separations from Darcy.

As the moment approached, Mr. Bennet joined them, preparing to give away his two eldest daughters at once. He kissed Jane's cheek, and told her that he knew she would always be happy, since Bingley would never permit anything else, and then turned to Elizabeth. "Lizzy, my love, you have all my best wishes for your health and happiness."

Though she wished no discord on her wedding day, Elizabeth could not help saying sadly, "But not your blessing."

To her surprise, he smiled at her dryly and kissed her cheek. "You have my blessing as well. Your young man will just require some growing accustomed to—he is not so placid as Jane's. Now, I believe we are required inside."

Elizabeth felt tears spring to her eyes at his words. "Thank you," she said softly, as he offered her his arm.

Afterwards, she could recall little of the actual ceremony beyond the look in Darcy's eyes when he saw her, and the intensity of his gaze as they took their vows. The wedding breakfast was slightly clearer, and was notable to her mostly for the reason that she had never seen Darcy smile and laugh as freely in public as he did that day. This expansiveness seemed to be contagious; she also saw Georgiana in earnest conference with the diffident eldest son of Lord Allington. She made a mental note to invite Lord Allington and his family to dinner when they returned to London, thinking this might be just the thing to build Georgiana's confidence.

The new Mr. and Mrs. Darcy planned to depart early; Darcy hoped to reach Blenheim by nightfall, as he had made arrangements for the use of a small house there for the night before continuing on to Pemberley. Elizabeth took her last looks at Longbourn, knowing it might be quite some time before she saw it again. She shared a tearful embrace with Jane, and many promises to write faithfully, and listened patiently to Mrs. Bennet's anxious final advice for her future.

Just before they were to leave, Mr. Bennet came up and, taking Elizabeth's hands in his, spoke to her quietly. "Well, my dear, it will be a time before I see you again, so there are a few words which I should say now. I am sorry for any distress I may have caused you these last weeks; you seem to have known what you were about better than I did. I hope that we can start again with a better understanding in the future."

Elizabeth, who dearly wanted to part from her father on good terms, said lightly, "You are forgiven; I know that it is not an easy thing to part with so many daughters at once!"

He smiled somewhat stiffly, and said, "Thank you, my dear." He indicated that the conversation had come to a close by handing her into the carriage, where she was immediately joined by her new husband. Darcy called to the coachman, and the carriage began to move away to the accompaniment of many cries of farewell and the waving of handkerchiefs.

They had barely reached the road when Darcy, noting that Elizabeth was biting her lip, moved to sit next to her and took her hand in his. "It will not trouble me to find that you are sad at leaving your home behind," he said. "It is very understandable."

She looked up at him in the dimness of the coach with a weak smile. "I feel more as if I have been leaving it in stages for some time," she replied. In a stronger voice, she added, "And I am very, very happy that we are married at last."

"As am I, my sweetest, loveliest Elizabeth," he said softly, placing an arm around her shoulders.

It began to rain. The ride had been a long one, and the rhythm of the raindrops on the top of the coach lulled Elizabeth into a restless slumber, her head against Darcy's shoulder. He had never seen her asleep before, and the sense of her vulnerability moved him deeply. He felt as if he could just hold her like this and watch her sleep forever. This theory was not tested, though, as it was not long until a brisk wind kicked up, making the carriage sway and waking her. She smiled at him sleepily, and he could not resist kissing her tenderly.

Not long after, the carriage's pace slowed to a crawl. Darcy looked out the window to assess the situation, and saw that the rain had been freezing on the road, leaving patches of ice. He did not want to worry Elizabeth, and he had the greatest of faith in his coachman and team of horses, so he said nothing until the carriage pulled to a halt in a small hamlet. "Excuse me, my heart," he said before stepping out into the cold rain to confer with the driver.

The driver was toweling down the horses, whose manes and tails sported droplets of ice. On seeing his master, he said, "Mr. Darcy, sir, to my way of thinking, we'll not make Blenheim tonight."

Darcy, who had already reached this conclusion, said, "Can we reach Oxford, do you think?" It was not quite what he had in mind, but the Mitre had excellent accommodations and food, and could certainly do.

"I'll do my best, sir, but no promises—you can see for yourself what the road is like," came the response.

Darcy returned to the carriage and explained the new plan to Elizabeth. "It sounds lovely," she said absently, brushing the droplets of rain from his coat, and wrapping the blankets back across his lap. Darcy smiled at her solicitude.

The road, unfortunately, only grew worse, and from time to time they felt the carriage skid and slip on the ice. It was growing dark, and Darcy, holding Elizabeth in his arms, began to feel some qualms about their safety.

He was not surprised when they turned into a cobblestone yard in a small village. Looking out the window, he saw a sign identifying the building as The Red Lion. He frowned—this was not what he had in mind at all, but it would have to do.

The coachman came around and conferred with him briefly, then went into the inn. He returned, accompanied by an ostler. "They have a room, sir; it won't be what you are accustomed to, but it is dry."

Darcy shrugged, then turned to Elizabeth. "I am afraid we will be stopping for the night here," he said apologetically. He was surprised when she gave him a mischievous smile along with her assent.

He stepped out of the carriage, and Elizabeth heard him say, "No, take care of the horses first, our belongings can wait." He handed her out and hurried her through the rain to the shelter of the inn.

It was a typical small country inn, Elizabeth saw, and went with gratitude to warm herself by the fire while Darcy spoke briefly with the proprietor, making arrangements to have a hot supper brought to them in their room. The man's wife showed them up a narrow staircase and opened a door, indicating their room.

Darcy thanked her, ushered Elizabeth in and closed the door behind him. The room was small but clean enough, with the beginnings of a fire warming it—they must have lit it as soon as they realized they had paying guests. Elizabeth had taken off her bonnet, and was inspecting the environs; she stirred the fire and closed the curtains. Darcy leaned back against the door, enjoying watching her domesticity. She looked up at him with a bewitching smile as she removed her wet pelisse.

"This is not quite what I hoped to offer you for our wedding night," he said ruefully. He could not help thinking how any other woman of his acquaintance would have responded at being forced to spend her wedding night under these circumstances and thanked heaven for the one who was actually with him. He hoped it was not too much of a disappointment to her and vowed to himself that he would make it up to her somehow.

She came over to him with a mischievous smile and kissed him lightly. "It has a door that locks, a bed, a fire, and you—what more could I need?"

He pulled her to him and joined his hands behind her back. "You are a woman in a thousand, Mrs. Darcy," he said, bending his head to kiss her deeply.

They were interrupted by a knock on the door. When Darcy stepped aside and opened it, a servant came in and deposited their valises beside the bed, clearly in awe of such wealthy guests. When he left, Elizabeth said, "I suspect that he will be telling this story to his family for weeks!" She opened her valise and began setting out her necessities. As she laid out her comb and brush—the silver ones he had given her with her new initials engraved on them—he settled back again to watch her.

It was a profound intimacy in a way to be seeing this part of her life— the bedroom of a lady had always been forbidden to him. Now it was his to see whenever he wished, though naturally at Pemberley such work as Elizabeth was now doing would be done by her maid. She shook out and hung her clothes on the post, and then turned to him and crossed her arms in front of her. "And what have I done, sir, to earn such a stare?" she asked with amusement. "Am I doing work unsuitable for the mistress of Pemberley? It is fortunate for you indeed that tonight you have a wife who knows how to fend for herself."

He shook his head. "I am enjoying watching you, my heart," he said.

She raised an eyebrow. "Not only can I fend for myself but also provide a source of amusement—I am glad to know that I am so useful!" With another lively smile, she turned back to smoothing wrinkles from the dress.

"I am sorry you should be having to do any work at all tonight," he said. "This night should be special."

She gave him a sharp glance. "Did we not just discuss this, my love?" she said gently. "It *is* special, because you are my husband now, and I will be with you all night long and awaken next to you in the morning. Do you truly believe that the surroundings make such a difference to me?"

"You have the right to expect something more than this for your wedding night."

She put her hands on her hips. With an amused look, she said, "You have not been listening to me, sir! I did not marry you for Pemberley, or Blenheim, or Brook Street—I married you because I love you and want to be with you always, and that is precisely what I have now, and so I am perfectly satisfied!"

He looked dubious, so she reinforced her words by kissing him tenderly. It was still difficult for him to grasp that Elizabeth saw more merit in him as a person than as master of Pemberley, and he hoped he could live up to her belief in him. Without all the trappings of his position, he felt less sure of who he was, but his one certainty was that Elizabeth was necessary to him.

She had brought such pleasure into his life, but the joy of her company until now had always been intermittent and intense; he knew only how to bask in her presence with the knowledge that it would soon be taken away, leaving him flat and lonely, and a seemingly eternal period until he could see her again. Now there was no one to take her away, no demands of family or society to be met before his needs, and he scarcely knew how to manage it. How was he to feel now that he knew she would be with him always, a constant presence bringing joy into his life? He could not imagine it.

He had never known a time when he could rely so on another, trusting in their love and affection, and the thought was almost frightening. He was accustomed to being left alone; the moment he started to think about Elizabeth being with him from now till death did them part, his mind sprang to all the ways they could be untimely parted, be it by illness, accident, or being brought to bed—not to mention his fears of the cooling of her regard, that somehow her opinion of him would change once she saw him on an everyday basis, or that she might simply lose interest in him. The anxiety of the ill weather for driving came back to him—what if his horses had not been so sure-footed, or his coachman so careful? Elizabeth could have been injured, or even killed. It was as if he had to remind himself of the inevitability of pain, just to be certain that he remain vigilant and not expect so much happiness as to be eventually disappointed by its loss.

Elizabeth looked up at him again, and seeing the sober expression on his face, went to take his hand in hers. "What is troubling you, my love?" she asked. "Are you still disappointed to be here?"

He shook his head. "No, it is only idle thoughts. I was thinking how hard it is to believe that you will not somehow disappear, and tormenting myself with possibilities."

She tilted her head back to look up at him. "Shall I have to teach you how to be happy, my dearest?" she said in a teasing manner, but with earnestness underlying it.

He pulled her into his arms and buried his face in her hair. "Yes, I think you will," he replied, his voice muffled. "I can find far too many worries."

She was silent for a moment and then said, "Life does not deal in certainties, it is true. I am leaving behind my family, travelling to a place I have never seen where I will spend my life, taking on a role in which I question my ability to succeed. You are my only constant."

"You shall never have reason to regret it," he said. "I will do everything in my power to make you happy."

"But my happiness is not within your power; it is something that can only come from me, and it can only come from accepting the joys I have," she said slowly, trying to put voice to thoughts which had been much with her of late. "Accepting them, and hoping for their continuance, but with the knowledge that there are no certainties but today's, and who knows what tomorrow will bring." She looked up at him, tenderly touching his cheek. With just a hint of amusement in her voice, she continued, "My happiness comes from my own love for you and my faith in you, not from anything you give to me or do for me or promise me. And my love and faith will not be shaken."

He was silent for some time, and Elizabeth had begun to worry that she had embarrassed herself with her amateur philosophizing when he finally spoke. "You are very wise, my Lizzy; it is nothing but my own fear speaking, my own fear in believing that I could be happy—as if the mere belief would set the stage for disappointment."

"Whereas I say that you *should* believe in it—have you not grown happier, rather than less, in our love over time?"

He smiled—a sudden, startling brightening of his countenance. "Yes, my heart; because the more deeply I know you, the more I find to love in you."

"It is the same for me," she said. Seeing there was still uncertainty in his face, she said, "I have trusted you more than I have ever trusted anyone, and you show me every day that I was right to do so. I am glad to have put my happiness in your hands, in my love for you, because I know that I can depend upon you."

He heard her words, and knew their accuracy for him, that it was not a lack of intimacy or affection which held him back, but his own fear of depending upon her and accepting the happiness she offered. Yet how he craved that happiness!

Acting on instinct, Elizabeth took on a business-like air. "Here, my love; take off that wet coat and give it to me, and those boots must come off as well." With a look of slight confusion, he did her bidding. She hung his topcoat on the post, and returned for his waistcoat. Her practical air made it seem that seduction was unlikely to be in her mind at the moment, though the thought occurred to Darcy as she was efficiently unbuttoning his waistcoat. That removal accomplished, she tugged on his hand, bringing him to the bed, where she sat and held out her arms for him to join her. Still rather mystified by her manner, he sat obediently, but no sooner had he done so than she encouraged him to lie back in the bed.

"Elizabeth…" he said in bafflement.

"Hush, my love," she said, lying by his side and taking him into her arms. "You need to be held, and that is what I am here for."

Embarrassed by her solicitousness, he said, "You need not worry; I am quite well."

"I never said otherwise," she replied, her lips grazing his cheeks. "But you can be quite well and still need to be held—or do you never need to be held?"

A very small bite in her voice at her last words was enough to make him pause and give her words due consideration; he could tell this was important to her. It was not a subject he particularly cared to think about—he could think of better uses for a bed with Elizabeth in it—but he finally replied with as much of the truth as he could muster. "It has been many years since there was anyone to hold me; I have not given it any thought."

"Well, there is now," she said in her practical manner, "and I intend to do it, so you may as well accustom yourself to it."

He raised himself on one elbow to look down at her. "Are you telling me what to do?" he asked mildly.

She met his eyes challengingly, a smile lurking at the corner of her lips. "Yes, I am. Were you planning to do something about it, Fitzwilliam?"

Her use of his given name, with all its childhood associations, reached deep inside him. He kissed her lightly. "No, I was only asking," he said. He lay back in her arms and rested his head upon her breast, hearing the steady beat of her heart. She was right, he thought; it had been far too long since anyone had simply held him for his comfort, or even dared imply that he might need comfort.

A sense of peace gradually stole over him, and with it a realization that Elizabeth was not going to vanish; that she was real and alive and warm in his arms, and that she intended to stay there. He wrapped his arms around her, feeling a deep happiness within and a sense of having come home at last, here in an unknown inn in the middle of nowhere. Her left hand rested on his chest, the ring he had placed on it that morning catching the light of the fire. They needed no more words then, just the silent stillness of the night and the warmth of the other's embrace.

Epilogue

Elizabeth leaned back against the familiar strength of her husband's body, content to be in his presence and among such natural beauty as she had heretofore only imagined. He kissed her hair absently, his arm slipping around her almost reflexively, resting on the newly rounded curve of her abdomen. She turned her head to look at him.

"You look very far away, my love," she said affectionately. "If this scene is not enough to hold your interest, then I do not know what will!"

He looked down at her with a quick smile. "There is nowhere I would rather be, my heart," he said. "I was thinking, in fact, of a time when we were both in Kent, and you told me that your aunt and uncle were to take you to the Lakes, and how jealous I was, because I wanted to be the one to bring you here—not that it seemed even a possibility at the time, of course."

"And now you have. I hope it is as satisfactory as you imagined."

"Eminently," he said, kissing her tenderly.

"Was that during the walk we took with Georgiana?"

"I prefer to think of it as the day I first kissed you," he said playfully.

Elizabeth smiled in amusement. "Yes, that was certainly a memorable event."

"Memorable? The memory of it tortured me for months!" he teased. At her sudden serious look, he added, "Do not start blaming yourself for my misery, my love; it was no one's fault but my own. I would not have been without that memory, no matter how much it pained me—and even then it had its consolations; it told me that you were not perfectly indifferent to me, and, probably equally important to me at the time, it told me that you were not in love with George Wickham."

"What?" exclaimed Elizabeth. "In love with Wickham? I should say not. I am not sure that you deserve to be forgiven for having such a thought."

He had the grace to look embarrassed. "Well, I did not know, then—there had been one day after I gave you that appalling letter when I came across you in tears in the grove. You did not know I was there, and I retreated immediately, but in my self-centeredness I assumed it must have been because I had disillusioned you about Wickham. It was a good thing that he was far away—I think I might have throttled him at that point had the opportunity presented itself."

Elizabeth could not help but laugh. "That was hardly the case, my love. I had been flattered by his preference for my company, but when his interest changed to another I realized that my heart had not been touched, or I should have cared far more. I never cried over *him*."

"I knew that later—while I was certain you did not care for me, I knew enough of your honesty to know that you could not have kissed me as you did if your heart belonged to another man. As I said, it was a consolation of sorts."

She kissed him affectionately and nestled in closer to him. "Well, I do not know what I *was* crying about, but it certainly was not him! But wait—was it that Sunday, after church?"

He nibbled her ear. "Yes, you minx, I believe it was."

"I was crying, my foolish love, because you had looked at me so coldly in church, and my entire life seemed so hopeless."

"Truly?" he asked, sounding quite surprised. "I had no idea. If I had, you may be sure that I would have been at your side trying to kiss your tears away, and we might have saved ourselves a great deal of time and discomfort. And I was only angry with you in church because after all that we had said to each other, the moment I saw you again, you still had as much power over me as ever."

"Well, I am not sure I would have been quite ready for *that*—it took me longer than that to come to my senses. I had a long way to travel to reach an understanding of you," said Elizabeth comfortably.

"And I was bewitched with you, but had not the least understanding of your heart, so perhaps it is as well it happened as it did," he said. "There is a poem of Wordsworth's, in fact, that always reminds me of that." He quoted,

She was a Phantom of delight
When first she gleamed upon my sight;
A lovely Apparition, sent
To be a moment's ornament;
Her eyes as stars of Twilight fair;
Like Twilight's, too, her dusky hair;
But all things else about her drawn
From May-time and the cheerful Dawn;
A dancing Shape, an Image gay,
To haunt, to startle, and way-lay.

I saw her upon nearer view,
A Spirit, yet a Woman too!
Her household motions light and free,
And steps of virgin-liberty;
A countenance in which did meet
Sweet records, promises as sweet;
A Creature not too bright or good
For human nature's daily food;
For transient sorrows, simple wiles,
Praise, blame, love, kisses, tears, and smiles.

And now I see with eye serene
The very pulse of the machine;
A Being breathing thoughtful breath,
A Traveller between life and death;
The reason firm, the temperate will,
Endurance, foresight, strength, and skill;
A perfect Woman, nobly planned,
To warn, to comfort, and command;
And yet a Spirit still, and bright
With something of angelic light.

Elizabeth rested her head back on his shoulder. She had grown accustomed in the past months to her husband's penchant for memorizing and quoting verse, which never failed to enchant her, especially when it showed he had been thinking of her.

"That is how I was, then—you were a mere phantom of delight; it was not until later, when we were engaged, that I saw the woman within," he said. "And now I know that you are a perfect woman—but you do bewitch me still." He cupped her chin in his hand, and caught her lips with his in a kiss of deepest passion. She was breathless by the time he released her mouth, only to trail his lips seductively down her neck. His hand began to caress her breast, a delight he had only rediscovered recently after some weeks of deprivation when her condition had made them too painful to touch.

Elizabeth moaned softly. Darcy had only grown more skilful with time at arousing her. Before he had the opportunity to cloud her mind further, she said playfully, "Do you remember when we were engaged, the day you came to Longbourn for the first time?"

Darcy, who was less interested in talking than kissing by this point, murmured between kisses, "Of course."

"Do you recall that you asked me to take you to a secluded place, and you said that there were ways we could…go farther, but that I had not the experience to tolerate them?"

Darcy discovered that the conversation held more interest for him than he had initially thought. "I recall it vividly, my heart," he said, his voice warm. "It was quite a sacrifice, but well worth it for your sake."

She kissed him tantalizingly, running her hand under his coat. "I was thinking, I am a *great* deal more experienced now."

"So you are, my dearest," he said admiringly. "So you are."

THE PEMBERLEY VARIATIONS by Abigail Reynolds is a series of novels exploring the roads not taken in *Pride & Prejudice*. The main characters and occasional lines of text are the original creations of Jane Austen.

❧ Impulse & Initiative ❧

❧ Without Reserve ❧

❧ The Last Man in the World ❧

❧ From Lambton to Longbourn ❧

❧ By Force of Instinct ❧

Made in the USA
Charleston, SC
11 January 2011